BIONIC BUG

A Mystery Novel By

NATASHA BAJEMA

NUCLEAR SPIN CYCLE
PUBLISHING

This book is a work of fiction. The characters, incidents, and dialogue are drawn from the author's imagination and are not to be construed as real. Any resemblance to actual events or persons, living or dead, is entirely coincidental.

The views expressed in this novel are those of the author and do not reflect the official policy or position of the National Defense University, the Department of Defense or the U.S. Government.

For Cheryl and Reneé

Prologue

THE FUTURE IS CLOSER than you think. In 2006, the Defense Advanced Research Projects Agency (DARPA) announced it was seeking innovative proposals to develop technology to blend insects with machines. This call led scientists to develop bionic flies, roaches, moths and beetles. The first remote-controlled beetle took flight nine years later in 2015.

ONE

Wicked Bloom

_____

October 12, 2027

NOW THAT'S where I draw the line.

A documentary about the dawn of passenger drones flashed across the lonely flat-screen television hanging on the wall. Lara Kingsley imagined what it would be like to live in the 1960s animated sitcom *The Jetsons,* and her inner control freak shuddered. In her lifetime, she'd probably be forced to fly through the sky in some autonomous contraption.

Suppressing the thought, Lara squeezed herself between two stools and leaned over the sticky wooden counter to shout her drink order to the bartender—a beer for herself and a cocktail for Maggie, who tended to run late. She avoided soiling her stretchy black dress; it was the first one she'd bought since her late twenties, and she wanted it to last just as long as the previous one.

Located in Bloomingdale, a trendy neighborhood north of Massachusetts Avenue in Washington D.C., Wicked Bloom offered a cozy urban décor of exposed brick and wood paneling, and the perfect mix of local draft beers, upscale cocktails, and homestyle cooking. Her friend and fellow private investigator, Phil "Sully" Sullivan, owned a townhouse several blocks away. The bar had quickly become their favorite hangout spot. Every week, they met, grabbed a drink, and exchanged information on their latest cases.

Waiting for the drinks, Lara glanced toward the end of the bar where a strange young man in his early twenties sat by himself and nursed a beer. There was something off about the kid. He wore black, thick-framed glasses and preppy, college-style clothing. Despite his youthful appearance, there were dark circles under his eyes and a foreboding about his presence.

Lara couldn't shake the feeling he was watching her, but when she looked at him again, he turned his pale blue eyes back to the liquor bottles on the backlit shelves lining the wall behind the bar. She made a deliberate note of his features in her head. *Probably just one of the many university students that swarmed the D.C. social scene during the academic year.*

"Who are you and what have you done with my mate?"

Lara looked up to see her friend Maggie towering over her like a supermodel, in three-inch red heels and a matching floral dress. It had taken a little work, but she'd convinced Sully to let her introduce him to Maggie at this party. Once he laid eyes on her, of course, he'd drool just like any other man.

Lara rolled her eyes and laughed.

Maggie lightly tapped Lara's shoulder. "No leather jacket today? Is the world coming to an end?" She laughed. "But, seriously, you look great. I thought we were forever caught in a cycle of leather and leggings."

For once, Lara had left her black leggings and leather riding jacket at home. With an actual purse slung over her shoulder, she felt less out of place beside Maggie, who was always decked out from head to toe in the latest trends. It didn't help that she also had a Ph.D. in Entomology. No one was supposed to be that perfect.

Lara smirked. "It wasn't easy. You're lucky I'm not wearing my Army cammies." Dressing up meant she had to do two things she hated: leave her motorcycle at home and take a driverless cab.

But she willingly made the sacrifice for her closest friend Sully. They'd first bonded over their shared orphan status while working on a group project as undergrad students at MIT. From that point onwards, they'd pledged to have each other's backs for life. They were family.

Sully had just secured the safe return of a kidnapped teenage girl. Her wealthy father had given him a large reward for his private investigation, which had clinched the case. The mayor even gave Sully a personal accolade. With his five minutes of fame, Sully wanted to celebrate. He also wanted to blow off steam. The past couple weeks had been intense. So, he'd invited his friends and several colleagues from the D.C. Metropolitan Police and the FBI Violent Crimes Division for drinks and food at Wicked Bloom.

"So, which one is Sully?" Maggie asked as she bit her lower lip and scanned the room.

Lara turned and pointed to a table in the far corner where Sully was talking to another black man. As usual, he gestured with every word, his facial expressions dedicated to whatever story he was telling. "He's the well-built, handsome black guy at the table over there."

She frowned. "I thought you said the bloke was a PI. With that starched white shirt and khakis, he looks just like a federal agent."

"Not the stocky one, the taller guy with the goatee, wearing the blue polo shirt."

Maggie's frown turned into a broad smile. "Yeew, he's cute all right. Good-looking, smart, a successful private investigator, and now a bloody local hero. I can't understand why you don't go for him now that you're single again. Are you sure you're okay setting us up?"

Lara sighed. "If we had that kind of chemistry, it would've happened already. Plus, as fellow PIs, we're practically colleagues. It's never a good idea, mixing business and pleasure."

Sully must have sensed they were staring at him. He looked, grinned, and gave a casual wave. But he remained seated, engrossed in his conversation, and didn't come over to greet them.

The bartender placed two drinks on the counter and slid them toward Lara. "Put these on Sully's tab?"

Lara nodded, grabbed the cold, wet, pint-sized glass of Blue Moon, and handed the champagne cocktail to Maggie. She glanced over at the counter. The creepy kid had disappeared. The beer sat unfinished, a thick layer of foam at the top of the glass. Lara scanned the bar, but there was no sign of him.

"Cheers," Maggie said, clinking her glass against Lara's, but she barely noticed it. "Earth to Lara?"

"Sorry." Lara turned back to her friend and smiled, taking a large sip of beer. The cold citrus-tasting liquid soothed her parched throat.

"Hey, Lara!" A familiar voice called out.

Nearly spilling her beer all over the floor, she spun around to see Vik bounding into the bar with a goofy grin on his face and excitement beaming from his dark brown eyes. His thin arms swayed back and forth as he approached. For a young Indian man, Vik was on the taller side, but the rest of his features betrayed his nationality and age.

"Do you always have to surprise me like that?" Lara groaned at the splatter of beer on the front of her dress.

Vik made an "I'm sorry face" and shrugged. "The Langstons want to sign with us for their new surveillance system." In his excitement, he couldn't conceal his natural inflection. Having spent his formative years in the U.S., Vik normally hid his Hindi accent.

"That's great news," Lara said, relieved Kingsley Investigations might finally have a new client. She'd been waiting on pins and needles for their email after sending them a quote last week. "I'm really glad you could make it. Sully desperately wants to talk to you about some computer work you can help him with. But, you should grab a drink or something to eat first."

Vik looked around the room as if he were calculating the costs based on what people were wearing. His eyes dimmed as he gave a half-smile to Lara. "I'm not really hungry."

"Sully's buying."

"Oh goodie," he said as his eyes lit back up. "I'm actually famished! What's good here?" Vik stared up at the giant chalkboard where the specials of the day were displayed.

"Uh, barbecue, brisket, steak, and burgers…" Lara read off the list on the chalkboard, gauging Vik's expressions for a positive response.

His shoulders slumped with disappointment. "I guess I'll just have the spicy collard greens then." Vik sauntered over to the bartender to place an order. Maggie followed after him, her auburn curls bouncing.

Shaking her head, Lara didn't understand how vegetarians could survive. Tofu was *not* a satisfactory replacement for meat.

Sully strode toward her, holding a pint of Guinness in his hand.

"Cheers to the man of the hour," Lara said, raising her glass.

"Thank you, and thanks for coming. I've been so wrapped up lately, we haven't had time to celebrate your last case. Does that put you in the black yet?"

Lara looked away and shuffled her feet. "Getting closer."

Sully smiled, clinked his glass against hers, and took a long, slow drink.

"Besides, tonight is supposed to be about you, and I have a certain someone here to meet you." She turned her face toward the bar.

"Is that *the* Maggie?" He beamed, pointing across the room to where Maggie and Vik were ordering food.

Lara nodded.

"Wowza! *She's* friends with *you*? How did that happen?" Sully shot her a mischievous grin and took another long drink.

Lara glared at him. "Hey, that's not funny. I met her two years ago at a Mensa event. We're different, but we clicked. She's a great person. Incredibly successful, too."

Sully frowned, itching his elbow. "Mensa? That's not the genius group thing you used to attend all the time, is it?"

Lara nodded. She'd joined the elite high-IQ group as an alternative to online dating. She was sick of dumbing herself down to get a first date. The guys always found out the truth, and then they'd go running for the hills. Lara had a penchant for learning nerdy details about everything and couldn't hide her technical knowledge.

At Mensa events, she'd hoped to find herself a match among the brightest top two percent of the population. Instead, she ended up meeting Rob. Her motorcycle had run out of gas two miles from a Mensa event. To make matters worse, she had forgotten her wallet again. Rob, the FBI special agent with a normal-ish IQ, bought her a tank of gas, won her heart, and eventually shattered it.

"Are you intimidated because she's smarter than you? Cuz if that's the case, I don't think we can be friends anymore." Lara stuck her tongue out at him.

Sully smirked. "Nah, you know I can hang with smart women. I'm not insecure like your ex-boyfriend. Plus, she's smoking hot. You said she's Australian, right?" When Lara nodded, Sully pressed his lips together. "Mmm-hmm. I can't resist a woman with an accent…"

Lara grimaced. "I sure hope you're interested in more than that."

Sully smiled and rolled his eyes. "Course I am. Those are just nice perks."

Lara shook her head in disapproval. "Anyway, speaking of my ex… why isn't he here tonight? I thought he weaseled his way into working with you on the kidnapping case."

Sully finished his beer and motioned for the bartender to give him a refill. "No weaseling, just the regular jurisdiction game."

Lara raised an eyebrow. "But he doesn't work kidnappings."

"Ricin. The kidnapper threatened to poison the girl if the ransom wasn't paid. Since it involved a threat of biological weapon use, Rob's entire unit was called in."

Lara furrowed her brow. "Ricin, again?" Bad guys seemed obsessed with the rare toxin. She and Sully had several theories, her favorite being it all started with a TV show protagonist using ricin to kill off his enemies. "Any chance you might have slipped Rob some?"

Sully gazed awkwardly at the floor.

"Just kidding. I'm okay if he's here."

Please don't be here.

Another woman had lured Rob away from her six months ago. Lara couldn't fathom why he'd dumped her for Bimbo Barbie Doll. It grated on Lara's ego that Bimbo Barbie was nothing like her, except for the blonde hair and blue eyes. Though she tried not to let the whole thing bother her, it still did, even after so much time. She'd thought she knew Rob, thought she knew what he wanted. Maybe she never knew him at all.

Sully absentmindedly scratched his neck. "He's not coming. I didn't invite him. You've worked so hard to get over him, and you're finally back on your feet. I didn't want to mess with that."

Lara snorted. "You mean you want me out working so I can pay you back…" She fidgeted with the sleeve of her dress. "You know I'm good for it, right?"

Sully shook his head. "C'mon, Lara. You know it isn't like that with us. And I just got a huge chunk of change from this case, so I'm good, okay? You pay me back when you've got the cash."

Lara nodded. She felt uncomfortable even using the take-a-penny at the gas station, and Sully had loaned her the funds to cover three months of bills. It wasn't enough, but she couldn't bring herself to ask any more of him.

The bartender took Sully's empty glass and handed him a fresh pint.

Lara gave him a curious look. "How many is that?" Sully

never threw back beers so quickly. "Is something going on with you?" Her instincts gnawed at her.

Grasping the beer glass tightly, Sully shifted back and forth on his feet. "Nah, I'm fine, Lara… just kicking back after a stressful few days." Sweat glistened on his brow.

Lara could tell he was lying. "Is it another case?" As she looked down, Lara's eyes caught a strange discoloration in his fingernails on the hand wrapped around the beer glass. "What's wrong with your nails?"

Sully switched the beer glass to his left hand and shoved his right into his pocket, hiding his nails from sight. His eyes darted around the room as he lowered his voice to a whisper. "Lara, I can't talk about it here."

She shot him a concerned look. "You'd tell me if you were in any real trouble, right?"

Sully nodded, stealing a glance across the room. "This is just not the right time or place."

Lara couldn't shake the feeling something was off, but didn't want to force the issue. At least not now. "Okay, let's meet up later this week then? I want to hear all about it."

He didn't respond.

Lara caught a glimpse of the creepy kid out of the corner of her eye as he returned to his stool at the bar. His gaze pointed straight at them. "Do you know that guy over there? Something seems weird about him."

Sully glanced, and his body went tense. "Lara, I gotta go. We'll talk later, okay?"

"But, it's your party," she said as he raced out the front door, phone in hand.

And I haven't introduced you to Maggie yet.

Lara shook her head and watched him leave. She wanted to call after him but didn't want to cause a scene. Outside the bar, something metallic caught her eye, sending a shiver up her spine.

Was that a monster bug of some sort? She inched forward and squinted to see better. A small flying object flickered for a moment directly under the street lamp and then disappeared into the darkness.

No, that was too big for a bug. My eyes must be tricking me.

Lara turned around and headed back toward the back of the bar to find Maggie. The corner spot was empty.

He's gone again. Lara swung her head around, searching for the kid. *Does Sully know him? Was that kid why he ran off? Or was it something else?*

She spent the next several minutes searching but couldn't see the kid anywhere. She sipped her drink and tried to turn her detective voice off. *It's a party, not a mystery.*

"Hey Lara, I'm going—"

Startled by Vik's voice, Lara dropped her beer glass on the ceramic tile floor. As the glass shattered and flew in multiple directions, the blood drained from her face. Lara stood frozen in place, surrounded by broken glass and beer splatter.

"Uh... Lara? I'm sorry I scared you," Vik said sheepishly, rubbing his stomach. "I'm starving. I've got to get some real food."

A server rushed about her with a broom and dustpan, cleaning up the glass and reassuring her that it was fine while Lara kept apologizing.

After the mess was cleaned, Lara turned her attention back toward Vik. "Yeah, you should get something to eat."

"You going to be okay by yourself?" Vik asked.

"I'll be fine. Maggie's here."

"No, Bug Lady left a few minutes after she noticed Sully leaving."

Lara threw him an annoyed glare. "Why can't you just call her Maggie?" He'd given her the nickname after finding out about her obsession with insects. Her friend's awe of bugs couldn't surpass Lara's dread of them. There were few things she feared more.

Vik shrugged.

Lara glanced around for Maggie, but didn't see her. "I guess I'll be calling it an early night, too. I should have driven." A terrible realization crossed her mind, and Lara dug her hand into her purse, feeling around for her keys. *Shit.* "I locked myself out of the townhouse again. Could you lend me your keys?"

Vik scrunched up his face. "You remember I'm coming to work at the office super early tomorrow morning, before class, right?"

Lara grimaced. "Ugh, I had forgotten all about that." She'd rather not have to get out of bed at zero dark thirty to let him in. "Would you mind coming with me so I don't have to call the landlord?"

Vik seemed hesitant.

"I'll pay you for your cab and even buy you a veggie pizza."

Vik laughed. "Sure, boss. Whatever you say…"

* * *

THE DRIVERLESS CAB pulled up to her Georgetown townhouse, the brakes screeching like they were overdue for maintenance. D.C. Council may have had a laundry list of reasons for approving the mandate on self-driving vehicles, but for Lara, driverless cabs had only one redeeming quality: no more tipping drivers.

The motorcycle lobby fought against a blanket requirement for autonomy advocated by the local government, arguing it would mean the end of the biking industry. Had she owned her bike at the time, she would have been at the front of the picket line.

As Lara tapped her credit card on the machine to pay the fare and waited for the transaction to go through, Vik climbed out of the back seat and hopped up the stairs to unlock the front door.

She gazed fondly at her shiny, blue Harley Davidson Street 500 parked in front of the townhouse. The only thing she loved more than her bike was her baseball glove. Until she bought the bike, she didn't realize how much she coveted freedom of the road. Sure, riding a motorcycle was incredibly convenient in a city of self-driving cars. Easy street parking and incredible fuel economy were great perks, but the liberation she felt with each roar of the engine kept her falling in love with the bike all over again with every ride.

Plus, it would never lie, cheat, or slip out in the middle of the night. Or drive away with Bimbo Barbie and later have the nerve to ask through text if she could pack its things and drop them off.

Lara bought herself the bike as a reward for hitting her first salary goal a year ago. She still had a way to go before hitting her dream salary, but she was all about baby steps. And rewards. Given her current financial circumstances, the purchase might have been premature. She flinched at the thought.

Never count your chickens before they hatch. Or better yet… before they have chicks of their own.

The credit card machine beeped, and a receipt shot out of the slot. Lara grabbed the slip and exited the cab. With her feet back on solid ground, the knot in her stomach loosened. Vik had already gone inside the townhouse and left the front door cracked open. She glanced nervously up at the third floor.

No lights, thank God.

The outside of the three-story row house was in decent shape for being built in the late 1800s, but the interior needed an update. Despite the building's three separate units, only two tenants occupied the old red brick townhouse. Her firm was located on the first floor of the building with her apartment conveniently situated on the second. Her third-floor neighbor and landlord, Jake Crawford, was an extremely quiet and overworked lawyer, who came and went mostly during the wee hours.

Jake made a killing each month renting out the other two floors to Lara. For the past two months, however, she couldn't pay the rent. He'd given her a formal notice to pay, but she asked him to cut her a break. To avoid the trouble of finding a new tenant, he agreed to stand down for a month. But his patience had just run out, and he recently filed an eviction lawsuit against her to recover past due rent and force her removal from the premises. She now had only thirty days to pay the past due rent or to move out.

Lara remained on the fence about whether to stay or move. There were more affordable locations, but for her two-year-old business, the posh location in Georgetown sent the right impression to prospective wealthy clients. If things didn't turn around fast for Kingsley Investigations in the next few weeks, she might not have a choice in business location or anything else.

Hopefully, it won't come to that.

When she walked through the door into her office on the first floor, Vik was already on the phone ordering the pizza she'd promised him. Lara put her purse down on the kitchen island and plopped down on a stool.

When she moved in two years ago, she'd converted the entire first floor apartment into her base of operations. The living area with direct access to the kitchen served as office space for herself and Vik. The bedroom in the back housed the photocopier and other office equipment. Filing cabinets took up any extra space in the room; they contained all her case records and personal files.

Vik put the phone down and shot Lara a serious look.

"What?" Lara glowered back at him.

He shoved his hands in his pockets. "I've been meaning to have a conversation with you. There's never a good time, but I suppose now is as good as any other."

Lara raised her eyebrow. "What's up?" She was too tired to have an important talk.

Vik pressed his palms to his cheeks. "Um, I've been noticing some troubling trends in the business expense account. There are large sums of money going out, but nothing coming in at the moment. I am not sure if we have enough to cover this month's expenses."

Lara shrugged her shoulders. "Oh that? I wouldn't worry. I've been paying off the back bills from the few months when… well, you know, with *Rob*." Vik opened his mouth to speak but Lara kept talking. "You know we're about to land a huge client.

I'm planning to take the Langstons to the ballgame next week. I'll close the deal before the ninth inning. The retainer should cover everything for this month."

Vik frowned. "But what if something goes wrong? Will you still be able to…" he broke eye contact and finished, "… pay me? Because Sully needs some work done and—"

"Of course. I've got you covered. Don't worry about it, okay? And I don't mind you working for Sully, but I'm going to need you here for the new job." Now Lara looked away. If she was being honest, she couldn't guarantee she could pay Vik for his time. But the thought of losing him, even to Sully, was too much. Vik wasn't just an employee; he'd been her rock through the roughest months since her return from Afghanistan two years ago.

After deploying twice to Afghanistan and returning home wounded from a drone IED attack, Lara concluded her term of service with an honorable discharge from the Army and transitioned to the National Guard. She could never have imagined the government would repay her years of service and tremendous sacrifice with betrayal.

Shortly after returning home, a Pentagon bureaucrat contacted her with some bad news. Under pressure to fill gaps in the Army's ranks, the recruiter had offered illegal incentives to entice her re-enlistment. To her disbelief, the bureaucrat explained to Lara that since these incentives were against the law, she'd have to pay them back in full with interest.

Requiring veterans to pay back bonuses when they'd no idea they were illegal fell squarely on the side of just plain wrong. Lara railed against the injustice of the system to no avail. The bureaucrat apologized for the inconvenience, claiming their hands were tied.

The law is the law, she said.

This left Lara with two choices. She could take it up with the justice system or begin repayment. She didn't have the money to hire a lawyer, and her faith in the system to deliver justice was forever tainted. She agreed to repay the debt, but had recently fallen behind on payments. The few months she'd spent wallowing in her grief over Rob's deception had made things even worse.

After several minutes of silence, Vik gave her a half-smile. "I wouldn't have brought it up... it's just that my aunt and uncle have been on my back lately about finishing school and becoming financially independent. I need a steady income to secure my U.S. citizenship. Without that, they're worried about the marriage proposal falling through. Shanaya's family comes from money, and they have high expectations for her match. I need to demonstrate 'the right way of living' before they'll agree to a wedding date. My aunt and uncle are threatening to make the trip all the way from New York City to put me back on the straight path." He pretended to shoot himself in the head.

Lara chuckled uneasily. She found it odd that the institution of arranged marriages continued to thrive in many countries. Vik and Lara often debated the virtues of an arranged marriage versus falling in love, and she wasn't about to get into it with him again.

Then again, maybe I could use the help.

After her last experience with love, she doubted she believed in marriage at all. Her parents died when she was young, she had no living relatives, and her time in the Army gave her front row seats to failed marriage after failed marriage. Lara had never seen the value of marriage, arranged or not.

The doorbell rang.

"That must be my pizza." Vik smiled eagerly.

Lara's eyebrows shot up as her stomach growled for thirty seconds straight. She and Vik both stared at her middle until it stopped.

"Geez," Vik said, grimacing. "That was... disgusting."

Lara rolled her eyes. "Here, take this and get us some food." She thrust a twenty-dollar bill into his hand.

It's official. I'm broke.

As Vik went to get the pizza, Lara's smartphone buzzed, and a text appeared on the screen from Mr. Langston.

Sorry to cancel our meeting next week
We've decided to go in a different direction

Shit. Lara's face fell. *That didn't take long. Different direction… so they're hiring a man to do the job.* She couldn't confirm her assumption, but she'd run into too many men who didn't think a woman could know her way around surveillance technology. *Their loss.*

Her stomach growled again in response to the intense aroma of melted cheese, grease, and green peppers floating through the air. Vik walked back into the kitchen and put the box on the counter. He grabbed a slice and stuffed the whole piece into his mouth. He froze at the look on her face.

"What's wrong?" Vik asked through a mouth full of food.

His uncanny ability to detect the slightest change in her mood didn't go unnoticed. Of course, he had tons of practice reading her, having been the only person capable of coaxing her off the couch after her heartbreak.

Change the mood. Lara forced a toothy smile. "Guess what?"

Vik's eyes widened expectantly. "What?"

"You get to go to the baseball game with me next week!" Lara exclaimed with a facade of white teeth. Vik had been complaining about his cricket withdrawal for months. It wasn't cricket, but baseball came close enough.

Vik screamed with delight and ran over to her, hugging her tightly. Then he pulled back, and a paranoid look came over his face. "But wait, I thought you were taking the Langstons? Did something happen?"

"They texted while you were getting the pizza. We had to reschedule our meeting." Her stomach twisted as the words came out, but she kept the plastered smile in place and changed the subject. "Did you notice that strange kid sitting at the bar tonight?"

TWO

Nationals Park

_____

OCTOBER 19, 2027

AT THE CRACK of ball against bat, Lara leaped to her feet, hotdog in hand, and cheered on the Nationals player sliding into home plate. Some relish plopped onto her shoe, but she didn't care. With the series tied 2-2, this game would determine if the Atlanta Braves or the Washington Nationals advanced to the World Series. The baseball park was filled to the brim and full of tension.

Her mouth watered at the smell of grease wafting under her nose. When she'd jumped out of her seat, she'd accidentally squished the bun a little. The hotdog, slathered with condiments, still looked delicious. As she leaned forward to take a bite, a large man standing next to her bumped her arm and knocked her off-balance. Fighting to regain her footing, she nearly tripped over her motorcycle helmet on the cement floor below. Then something wet hit her leg, and she cringed.

And that's why I wear black.

She carefully wiped the glob of ketchup from her leggings with a napkin. Glancing at her feet, she groaned. A large drop of mustard had landed on her lucky baseball glove tucked inside her shiny black Harley Davidson helmet.

"I told you not to pile on so many spices." Vik chuckled next to her.

"Condiments," Lara retorted. Suppressing a glare, she rubbed the glove clean with her sleeve before straightening up again to watch the game.

"Whatever," Vik said, grinning from ear to ear as if nothing could bother him. "Say, were you able to reschedule the meeting with the Langstons?" An uncertain look on his face replaced his grin. He must have just remembered the source of his good fortune.

Lara nodded, not making eye contact. She didn't have the heart to tell him that the Langstons had dropped her for someone else.

"That's good. I'm going to get something to eat." Vik motioned he was leaving. "For some strange reason, I have an unrelenting hankering for falafel." He grinned broadly and raced up the stairs.

Falafel? The kid was always hungry. She wasn't sure if any ballpark vendor served deep-fried balls of ground chickpeas but remained silent on the matter. She'd never met anyone so infatuated with different foods—all vegetarian of course.

Lara kept her eyes fixed on the game and finished her supper before it could cause any more damage.

At the bottom of the sixth inning, the score was now tied 3-3 with two outs, and the bases loaded for the Nationals. She clenched her teeth and kept her eyes glued on the pitcher.

Her smartphone buzzed. *What now?*

Glancing away from the game, Lara scanned the news headline flashing across the home screen of her phone:

WEALTHY COUPLE, ACCUSED OF USING GENE EDITING TOOLS
TO CREATE A DESIGNER BABY, FACES TEN YEARS IN PRISON

Lara shook her head in disbelief. Many of the technological

changes on the horizon promised enormous benefits. The drawback was all the new ways people could commit crimes and screw with society. She shoved the smartphone in her pocket. *I should be savoring the game, not worrying about the future.*

She found it strange that in the middle of dramatic technological change, some things stubbornly remained the same—like hot dogs and baseball. The familiar tastes and sounds in the ballpark comforted her, giving her the elusive feeling of home.

What's taking Vik so long?

Lara turned her head away from the game to scan the mezzanine level for him. She wanted him to have the full experience of her favorite pastime—even if it wasn't as good as cricket. She'd purchased season tickets to the Nationals to schmooze with prospective clients. That way she could write off the tickets she would probably have bought anyway—in theory, it was a win/win.

I guess I could write them off as team building if Vik ever gets back up here.

She massaged her temples. Every time she thought about the failed Langston contract, her head began to throb. There was no backup plan. Nothing else waiting in the wings to pay her bills. Lara squeezed her eyes shut and breathed deeply.

C'mon. Just relax. It'll be okay. Enjoy the game. She opened her eyes and decided to live in the moment.

Her season tickets were located on the first-base foul line and offered a great view of the entire ballpark. From this vantage point, she had a decent shot at catching a foul ball or a home run —that is, if she had her glove ready.

She looked down at her lucky charm near her feet. Bittersweet memories surfaced. Her father would've loved these seats. He'd given her the glove on her sixth birthday, taught her the right way to break it in, the right way to oil it, and the right way to catch a foul ball, or if she was really lucky, a home run.

Lara shook off the pang of her father's absence and looked once again for Vik.

He's missing the best part of the game. She sighed heavily. *For the hopeless mission of finding falafel.*

Vik never listened to sense when he had his mind set on something. This determination, or "grit" as she liked to call it, was one of the reasons she'd hired him. After a year of his help, she didn't know how she could survive without him.

Vik was a graduate student at Georgetown and took the job to help pay his way through school. Lara hesitated to hire him at first, but he won her over when she learned he'd turned down a full ride to MIT for electrical engineering and computer science to study criminal justice instead. His family never let him forget it, and for good reason. He could've made a lot of money with his tech skills. Lara had seen him do some amazing things.

Lara bit her lip as the Nats all-star hitter, Kyran Farrell, came up to bat at the bottom of the sixth inning. Farrell had already hit a home run in the first inning, and a grand slam would likely seal the win for her team.

The crowd became silent with anticipation. She sat on the edge of her seat, inhaling the crisp air and trying to calm her nerves. To stay warm, she wore her prized leather riding jacket, which fit snugly over her baseball jersey. As superstition demanded, she adjusted her baseball cap, which kept loose strands of her sandy blonde hair in place.

You've got this.

The pitch flew straight and fast. She clenched her teeth as the crack of the bat echoed around the ballpark. The crowd murmured in unison. It was too close to call. Leaping to her feet, she followed the trajectory toward center field, but lost the ball in the bright stadium lights. Her eyes anxiously scoured the air.

There it is… it's going… going… GONE.

The crowd went wild, jumping to their feet and screaming in celebration. Farrell had done it. With the grand slam, he'd likely clinched the National League Championship. Elated, Lara turned to congratulate her fellow fans and nearly jumped out of her skin. Vik was standing right next to her, beaming with a wide, goofy smile.

Sheesh, he's so sneaky.

"Where have you been? Did you see it?" Lara asked, lifting an eyebrow.

"Oh yes, that hit was nothing short of full blooded," Vik said. "I was up there in the stands watching the batsman—"

"What?" Lara wrinkled her nose. "Full blooded?"

Vik nodded, grinning. "Yep. It's a good thing. Trust me."

Lara shrugged. "Did you find your falafel?" she asked as they both sat down.

Vik shook his head vigorously and held out a bag of buttery popcorn. "No, I looked everywhere." He pointed toward the food vendors in the park. "Eventually, I asked someone, and they looked at me like I was mad or something. I mean, how can they not have falafel? It's an essential staple. You'd think those new automated food machines could manage something as simple as falafel. But no, they only do things like burgers, pizza, and hot dogs. Where's the variety? I simply don't understand this country sometimes."

If she ever made it to India someday, she'd likely say the same about his country. Lara chuckled and grabbed a handful of popcorn. "I totally get it, Batsman." Vik either ignored or didn't hear her teasing.

On the field below, the game moved by rather quickly, at least for baseball. Lara wanted it to be over before the Braves could recover from the Nats' quick surge. With the score 7-3, the loudspeakers announced the 7th inning stretch.

"Take Me Out to the Ball Game" blared over the speakers a few feet above her ears as fans began getting up out of their seats. Some people stretched out their arms and legs and moved about in the aisles. Others raced up the stairs to make a final beer run before the end of the game.

Something small appeared in the sky, high above left field. Lara squinted, trying to decipher what it could be. At first, she thought it was her imagination.

What the…?

And then another came into view… and another… and

another… and another. They kept coming. Her heart began to race.

Are those mini UAVs?

In seconds, hundreds of quadcopter drones were buzzing high above the stadium seats. In a flash, the stadium lights grew dim, and the familiar ballgame tune stopped mid-song. Bright colors filled the air—blue, green, red, and yellow beamed down from the drones. The crowd fell into a hushed silence, entranced by the show.

A few seconds later, the opening notes of Beethoven's Symphony No. 5 came over the loudspeakers at top volume. Instantly, the drones began flying in unison, changing their formation and colors to the beats of the music.

Her eyes widened. It was mesmerizing.

And terrifying.

Lara gripped her armrest as a distant memory of the Afghan desert sky coming alive with armed drones flashed through her mind. Swallowing hard, she focused on her breathing, trying her best to suppress the dark memory. Her arms came to her chest as her entire body tensed. *No Lara, this is not the same thing.* She took a deep breath and pushed it out as fast as she could, releasing tension. As the breath escaped, her muscles relaxed.

Vik glanced at her, worry in his eyes. "Are you okay?"

"I'm not a fan of drones—at least not anymore."

Vik looked back at the show. "But they're beautiful."

Lara refused to look up at them. More like incredibly agile platforms, capable of ever-greater distances, carrying heavier payloads, and effortless navigation. Capable of killing…

"I'm not sure I'd use the word beautiful, Vik."

For the first time in human history, nearly anyone could project power into the air—for good or for bad. She never understood why the U.S. Government allowed drones with significant capabilities to become mainstream. In the early years of the drone revolution, the Army underestimated the threat, and her comrades paid the price with their lives.

Until recently, the District of Columbia and most of the

surrounding areas had been a no-drone-zone. At least until Congress approved nationwide commercial drone delivery. The change relaxed the rules to allow citizens in the nation's capital to benefit from speedier delivery services, but key segments of the District, including the ballpark, remained strictly "no-drone" zones for national security reasons.

"This is the most amazing thing I have ever seen in my entire life," Vik said, his eyes wide as he gazed at the sky in complete awe. "Lara, can you imagine how much work went into programming the software that instructs them to follow certain flight paths, turn their lights on and off, and move so precisely in coordination with one another?"

Of course, he sees the code.

"Yes, I can," Lara replied, her jaw clenched tightly. What she couldn't imagine was the bureaucratic and security nightmare of getting such a stunt approved. Authorities would never permit a swarm of drones to take flight this close to the U.S. Capitol Building and the White House. *Would they?*

Squinting to see in the dim light below, she studied the behavior of the security personnel. From their frantic body language, constant radio chatter, and how they pointed their flashlights into the sky, she could tell they knew nothing about this so-called "show."

"Something's not right with this picture," Lara said, abruptly getting out of her seat.

"Lara, why must you always think there is a conspiracy behind everything?" Vik asked. "Enjoy the show for once. The ballpark management obviously arranged it as part of the seventh inning break."

Lara snorted. "It's the seventh inning stretch, and you're right. This *was* planned."

Just not by park management.

THREE

The Drone Show

A DISTANT RUMBLING of engines and rhythmic thumping of rotors filled the air. Seconds later, two helicopters from the D.C. Metropolitan Police arrived. They hovered above the stadium for a moment before flying in a circular pattern and pointing spotlights onto the baseball field.

As she scanned the crowd, something caught her eye in the field-level seating down below. A tall black man wearing a navy coat and a red baseball cap stood in the aisle facing the field and holding up some type of gadget with two thick antennas. He directed his gaze upwards and appeared to be interacting with the drones.

This show is over. If she hurried, maybe Lara could catch him and end this spectacle.

As she turned toward the aisle, the drones turned off their lights, stopped their formations, flew straight up, and disappeared out of the stadium. Down below, security personnel scrambled in all directions as the police helicopters raced after the drones, the thumping already far in the distance.

Screams for more rose from the crowd as they broke into a standing ovation. The commotion blocked her sight of the man with the gadget. The stadium lights switched to full power, and pop music blared from the speakers once more.

Lara pushed through the crowd just in time to see the man with the gadget turn toward the section exit. Lara thought he looked oddly familiar.

Is that? No, it can't be Sully.

The man stumbled up a few stairs and stopped to rub his eyes with vigor. Slamming into an empty seat, he bent down and vomited onto the floor. Several people jumped out of his way to miss the projectile. As he tried to find his balance, he looked up toward the next level.

Their eyes met for a moment. Lara gasped in dismay and spun on her heel, ready to jump into the aisle and make her way down to Sully. Before she could move, Vik placed a hand on her arm.

"What's wrong?" he asked.

"I don't know, but Sully is down there, and he doesn't look good."

"Do you need my help?"

"Not with this. I'll check on him, but I want you to go down to the field level and talk to security personnel. Give them your card and ask them if they knew about this spectacle. Then offer them our investigative services. They're going to need our help on this one."

"Okay, whatever you say, boss…" His tone revealed his hesitation.

Lara ignored Vik's narrowed eyes and pursed lips. He could be skeptical as long as he did what he was told.

She grabbed her motorcycle helmet and sprinted up the stairs. At the top of the stands, she caught her breath and then made a beeline toward the nearest stairwell. Descending two flights of stairs, she burst through the double doors into the field-level corridor and raced toward the section where she'd seen Sully.

"Ma'am, do you have a ticket for this section?" a female attendant asked sharply. Her whole body was tense, and sweat beaded on her forehead. She planted herself in Lara's way and crossed her arms, possibly trying to hide the fact that her hands were trembling slightly.

Maybe she knows the drone show was unauthorized?

Lara shook her head. "Please, my friend is in this section. He's sick and needs my help."

The attendant swallowed audibly and looked over her shoulder. She dropped her arms and bit her lower lip. Then she nodded. "Okay, ma'am, help your friend, but then come right back out. I'll radio for medical assistance, and I'm going to keep an eye on you." She gave Lara a stern look.

Lara held her hands up and nodded. "That's fine. I just need to help my friend." The attendant let her by, but the stairs were blocked by a stream of people hurrying to get whatever they needed before the next inning began. Lara jumped into an empty row of seats and stood on her tiptoes, surveying the section as best as she could. Sully was nowhere to be seen.

Maybe he made it out already?

Lara turned around and charged back into the corridor. Her heartbeat went wild as her instincts screamed at her; something was terribly wrong. She scanned the entire area, looking for any sign of Sully.

There were people everywhere, queuing for beer and food. Other fans, celebrating the Nationals' lead, filled the corridor in droves. She'd be lucky to catch him before he disappeared into the masses.

About fifty feet away, a group of people made a hole in the crowd, jumping back as a figure stumbled through them.

"Sully!" she called as his red baseball cap and navy coat came into view.

Mothers pulled their children close, teens pointed and giggled, and a few older fans shook their heads in disapproval as Lara's friend passed by. They probably thought he was drunk. She was slightly surprised security hadn't picked him up yet, but then again, they had bigger problems at the moment.

She strode forward, but a group of college-aged guys filled

the corridor and blocked her path. "Sully!" She pushed through them and caught a glimpse of Sully staggering away from her. He teetered awkwardly against the wall.

"Sully," Lara called out again, trying to get his attention. She moved toward him and shouted, "Hey, Sully!"

He didn't appear to hear her voice over the noise. Before she could reach him, he lurched down a dark hallway and out of sight. Instinctively, Lara reached for her sidearm before remembering she'd left it at home. Guns at the ballpark drew unwanted attention and required cutting through mounds of red tape, so she never bothered with it.

Lara darted quickly toward the dark hallway. A few moments later, she turned the corner to check if it was clear. The hallway dead ended. Lara pulled out her smartphone and clicked on her flashlight app. A small beam of light illuminated the hall, and that's when she saw Sully on the ground.

He lay face down, convulsing on the concrete. Foam formed at his mouth, his eyes wide and crazed. She sprinted the short distance and fell to her knees beside him. Next to him lay the large, black device he'd been using.

"Sully, what happened?" Lara shook his shoulder, but he was unresponsive. "Talk to me!"

Sully coughed, gasping for air, and then his eyes seemed to recognize her. He opened his mouth but only gurgling came out.

"Take it easy, I'll get help."

His eyes bulging from their sockets, he shook his head and reached into his pocket. The convulsions returned, his entire body in their grip.

Lara dialed 911. "Hang on, Sully!" The phone rang.

Sully opened his eyes wide again and gaped at her. "Feh has… the Buh…" Sully gurgled. "Cy—"

"What are you saying? Talk to me," Lara pleaded.

"Daarp… " He pawed at her leg, and as their eyes met, his rolled back and showed only the whites. In less than a minute, he stopped shaking and lay completely still.

"Sully!" She shook him but there was no response. Panicked, Lara felt for a pulse, but couldn't find one.

She dropped her smartphone and started chest compressions. More foam bubbled out of his mouth. Still no pulse.

"911, what's your emergency?" Lara's smartphone chirped on the cement next to her.

"Noooo!" Lara screamed. A burst of energy coursed through her body. "Sully, you're not leaving me… I'm not going to let you." She continued the chest compressions and breathed into his mouth several times. She felt for a pulse again. Nothing.

Her chest tightened, and tears welled in her eyes. She squeezed them shut, allowing a single tear to escape and roll down her cheek.

This can't be happening.

Opening her eyes again, Lara felt lightheaded. She climbed to her feet and staggered backward a few steps into the wall. She braced herself against the cold, cement wall, her body shaking.

The faint 911 operator's voice persisted through the phone's speaker, asking for a response. She bent over and picked up the phone with her shaking hands, nearly dropping it a few times as she brought it to her ear. As she answered the operator's questions, her own voice sounded distant, as though she wasn't the one speaking.

Her heart pounded in her chest as she disconnected from the call and dialed Vik's number.

"Yes, boss?"

"I need you to come here," Lara said, a slight tremor in her voice.

"But I'm still trying to make contact with security."

"Vik—"

"The guards are all in quite a tizzy about the drone show, and I haven't been able to get their attention." She tried again to cut in but Vik continued, "They keep brushing me aside like a pesky fly that—"

"Vik… Sully's dead." The words thudded like bricks in her head.

There was a pause. "What?" Vik asked. "How?"

"I don't know. I found him convulsing in a hallway. Foam was coming out of his mouth. I couldn't save him."

"Like he was poisoned?"

Lara looked at her friend's lifeless body. *Could it be poison?*

"Lara, are you still there?"

If he was poisoned, who could have done it and why? She replayed the scene in her head. He had slid his hand into his pocket.

Sully tried to tell me something. Was he also trying to show me something?

Kneeling next to Sully, she placed her smartphone on the floor and pulled his hand out of his pocket. His discolored fingernails clutched the Star Wars stormtrooper keychain she'd given him for his birthday.

She stared at the dangling keys. *Were you trying to give these to me?* Lara carefully opened his hand and pocketed them.

"Lara, I think I lost you."

Shivering, Lara glanced down at Sully's body. *Sully is gone.* The heavy numbness in her limbs and chest prevented the horrible truth from sinking in. Her mind floated above her, struggling to make sense of it.

Then she remembered his strange behavior at the bar. The creepy kid. Sully had wanted to tell her something. Now he wouldn't get the chance. Looking at his hands, she examined his purple finger nails.

This is not normal. A hint of anger rose in her chest. Her heart pounded, and her spirit filled with determination. *Someone did this to you, Sully. I'm going to find them.*

"Lara?"

She grabbed her phone and took a deep breath. "Sorry. I'm still here. Scrap the original plan. I need to go check out his townhouse, but I can't leave the scene. I need you to come to the concessions area behind section 137 and wait here with Sully's body until the police arrive."

"What's at his place?"

"I don't know, but nothing feels right about this, and I'm not waiting for the police to mess it up." Lara glanced at Sully's body again. Her chest tightened, choking out a shallow gasp.

"Are you sure you shouldn't wait for the police? To answer questions…" Vik asked. "I don't think you should interfere with the investigation… I mean—"

Lara clenched her fists to stop them from trembling. "I'll be of far more use to Sully by tracking down his killer. By the time the police figure out this was a homicide, the bastard will be long gone. There's no time to lose."

Vik heaved a sigh. "Okay, I'll be right there… uh, Lara?"

"What?"

"I'm really sorry about Sully. He was a good man."

Lara gulped, holding back tears. "Thanks, Vik. Let's just get some answers, okay?"

She climbed to her feet and rested against the cement wall in a daze while she waited for Vik to arrive. For a few minutes, she watched numbly as baseball fans walked by the hallway entrance with arms full of craft beers and fatty foods, oblivious to the dead body lying on the ground in the dark corridor, mere feet from them.

Inside the ballpark, the crowd shouted with fury. She briefly hoped her team hadn't lost their lead already, but as she looked back at Sully, she quickly dismissed the thought.

It isn't important.

Staring down at him, her arms and legs felt paralyzed. Out of nowhere, a high-pitched ringing pierced her ears. For a moment, it felt as if she were back there roasting in her gear under the desert sun, recovering from the explosion and searching in desperation for her unit. The sudden ringing made no sense. Back then, there had been a bomb. Now, silent foam trickled from Sully's mouth, shockingly white against his dark skin.

C'mon Lara, this is no time to freeze up. Shaking the tension out, she battled the urge to recoil and regretted stuffing the hot dog down her throat earlier. As a military officer in the National Guard Army Special Forces, Lara prepared herself for grizzly situations. But she'd never prepared herself for this.

Somehow this shocked her even more than losing her entire unit to Afghan insurgents. Experiencing death on the battlefield was expected. She would never forget the smell of burning flesh —the foul stench was permanently seared into her memory. Her unit died while she'd survived with only a minor injury. And now Sully was dead, and again she was left alive.

Snap out of it, Lara. Sully needs you now.

Feeling a renewed sense of determination, she began searching the scene for clues and snapped a few pictures with her smartphone. She picked up the gadget Sully had been using in the park, and her hand dipped from its weight. In all her years of experience with electronics, she'd not seen anything quite like it.

The gadget had two thick antennae and a rugged construction, both which suggested it was military grade. With the previous display in the park, her gut told her it was a remote-control device for maneuvering drones, but she would need to take it apart to know its real purpose.

Sully, what were you doing with this? Were you running the drone show?

Lara rummaged through his pockets, searching for some evidence of his activities in the ballpark, but they were empty except for a game ticket. Reaching into the chest pocket of his coat, she found his wallet and dug through it. She pulled out a personnel ID hidden inside an interior pocket. Sully's picture and name were on it, but upon closer inspection, the slightly uneven edge of the photograph suggested it was a forged ID for the Defense Advanced Research Projects Agency (DARPA). At the very least, Sully committed a felony simply by being in possession of a fake federal ID.

You must have had a good reason to risk getting caught. What could've been so important there? She rubbed her thumb over the hard plastic. The ID was in pristine condition, definitely new. *You must have used this recently.*

"Hey boss," Vik said, coming around the corner.

Lara nearly jumped out of her skin. Without turning, she

shoved the ID in her pocket, hoping Vik hadn't noticed. *What he doesn't know can't hurt him when the cops arrive.*

"Where have you been?" Lara winced at the harshness of her own words.

Vik shrank back slightly. "I'm sorry. You were hard to find. There are a lot of dark hallways back here."

Lara took a breath to calm herself. "Well, I'm glad you're here now. I'm going to check out Sully's townhouse. Tell the cops I couldn't stay, but I'll follow up with them later." She handed Vik the wallet. "Also, keep an eye on that remote. I have a feeling about it, and I don't want the cops losing it in the bottom of their evidence locker."

"I've got it from here, Lara," Vik said reassuringly.

Lara nodded. She glanced one more time at Sully, her eyes lingering on his face for a few moments, unable to leave him until she caught the familiar squawk of a police radio approaching. She tore her eyes away, whispered a last goodbye to one of the best friends she'd ever had, and forced her legs to move. She had a murder to solve.

FOUR

The Townhouse

HER MOTORCYCLE WAITED for her on the side street next to the ballpark. Lara took off her baseball cap and packed it along with her glove in the seat compartment, shoved her helmet on, and climbed onto the bike. Revving the engine for a few minutes, she plugged the location of Sully's townhouse into the GPS on her dashboard and inched away from the curb.

Giving the bike throttle, she raced down South Capitol Southwest at high speed, which usually sent a thrill up her spine. This time, a hardened sense of determination came over her. She'd never been involved with a criminal investigation before, but she was not about to let the bastard responsible for killing her friend get away with it.

Fifteen minutes later, she pulled her bike into the narrow alley behind Sully's townhouse in the NoMa neighborhood. Recently painted and renovated, it looked so inviting. He'd purchased the fixer-upper before the area became some of the hottest real estate in town, and it was now worth upwards of $900K. Guilt pricked at Lara for having been jealous of his good fortune.

What good is all that now?

She hoped the keys she took from Sully would open the back

door. Neighbors might notice her coming through the front, and the last thing she needed was some old, nosy lady calling the cops.

Lara dismounted her bike in a nook behind Sully's fenced yard and hung her black helmet on the handlebar. The alley was dark, quiet, and empty. In the distance, the rhythmic wail of a police siren echoed through the night air.

As she walked toward the gate, Lara wrinkled her nose at the sharp odor of rotting garbage mixed with a hint of motor oil. Pairs of green garbage cans and blue recycling bins lined the alley, set out in time for pick-up the next day. Sully's were notably absent.

He must have forgotten to put them out.

As Lara unlatched the gate, her foot accidentally kicked a hard object lying on the brick-paved surface of the alley. She grimaced as a glass beer bottle tumbled down the slope, making loud rattling sounds as it went.

So much for stealth.

She ducked into the backyard and closed the gate quietly, hoping no one heard the racket. Inside the fence, Sully's refuse containers lay sideways on the overgrown grass, and garbage was strewn about the backyard.

Someone was here, looking through Sully's trash. But what were they looking for? As she searched through several sticky items on the ground, a crinkling sound came from the green bin at the far end of the yard. When it quivered, Lara jumped.

She instinctively reached for her gun before remembering again that it remained locked away in her safe at home. On high alert, she inched closer to the bin. Just before she reached the can, an orange-striped cat bolted from behind the trash. Lara's body tensed. The cat made a beeline for the mulberry tree next to the balcony and scampered into the leaf cover above. Lara let out a shaky breath. *Scaredy-cat.*

Her heart pounding, Lara stepped lightly around the garbage remnants to avoid getting anything on her shoes.

Sully's expansive brick townhouse had three floors plus a

basement. The new light-gray paint matched the charcoal cast iron railings of the first and second-floor balconies. Lara strode up the stairs to the first-floor entrance, keys in hand. The door was opened a crack.

This is a bad idea.

She pushed the door with the tip of her shoe, wishing she had her pistol.

Well, it's not exactly breaking and entering if the door is unlocked. Right?

She wasn't above bending the rules. Sometimes there was a difference between right and wrong and what was legal or illegal. She'd learned the hard way that the two didn't always mesh. When it came to breaking the law, she relied on her own moral compass to guide her in making the right decision.

As she stepped inside, Lara gasped. The townhouse was in shambles, everything overturned. Whoever broke into Sully's house had searched everywhere and left nothing untouched. Food covered the floor. Cupboards stood wide open, and dishes were spread all over the counter. Lara wondered if the intruder had found whatever they were looking for.

But did they find Sully's safe room?

Sully's specialty as a private investigator involved helping the D.C. police and the FBI hunt and catch the worst of the worst. After a case in which he'd helped the FBI apprehend a jihadist cell planning a bomb attack on the D.C. subway, he'd received several death threats from the organization's leadership, making him understandably paranoid.

When Sully renovated the townhouse a few years ago, he made sure to install a fortified safe room, complete with its own weapons cache, office space, bathroom, and sleeping area. Sully hired Lara to install the surveillance electronics, and Vik to hardwire the room for high-speed Internet access and to program the system. From the monitors in his safe room, Sully could monitor his entire townhouse and its exterior perimeter. Whenever he felt off about a job, Sully would use the space as his main office.

Lara walked into the library, a large room with oak hardwood floors and antique trim at the back of the townhouse, just off of the kitchen. Lined with wall-to-wall bookshelves, Sully's library contained everything from the classics of American literature to computer programming instruction manuals and even a few self-help books.

There were books scattered near the entrance of the library, but the intruder hadn't spent too much time there. Most of the books were left untouched.

Lara breathed a sigh of relief. They must not have known about the safe room. *Maybe I can find a few clues to figure out what Sully got himself into… what got him killed.*

Facing the center bookshelves on the back wall, she scanned the shelves, meticulously alphabetized, for the book *I, Robot*, a collection of short stories by Isaac Asimov. She knew the general location but still had to search several rows.

There it is.

If someone knew about Sully's penchant for order, the book would look oddly out of place stuck in the middle of Asimov's *Foundation* science fiction series. Tilting the book spine toward the ceiling, she felt underneath for the hidden button. When her fingers found it, she pressed hard. The button clicked and two bookshelves creaked as they swung outward, exposing a steel door with an electronic combination keypad.

Hopefully, Sully hadn't changed the combo since the last time she had upgraded the surveillance equipment.

Lara entered the code from memory and to her relief, the door lock released. Once she entered the safe room, she pulled the steel door shut and pressed the lock button on the wall. From inside the safe room, she could hear the faint sound of the bookshelves creak once more as they hid the door.

She scanned the safe room quickly. Constructed of reinforced concrete and lined with corrugated steel walls, the interior of the safe room was rather austere. Sully designed it to ensure safety and survival rather than comfort. There were three rooms— Sully's office and command center, a small bathroom, and a storage space, which contained a bunk bed for sleeping, supplies, and a weapons cache.

Lara could tell Sully had left the safe room in a hurry. On the desk next to his computer, there was an unfinished cup of coffee, a half-eaten bologna sandwich, and an empty plastic container.

A bank of high-res monitors lined the wall behind his computer. From here, she could see and hear every room in Sully's townhouse, including the front and back porches. Lara sat in the leather office chair and brushed her fingers across the touchscreen to wake the computer.

The login screen appeared, and a red light shone on the desktop in front of her, revealing a holographic keyboard. Lara typed in the username and password she'd used to set up Sully's system.

After a few seconds, the screen display appeared and showed a strange web browser. It read "Tor" in the upper left-hand corner with an onion icon in place of the letter "o." Across the top of the website, she read "This browser is configured to use Tor." Lara moved the cursor over the search bar.

Tor. She'd heard that name before. *Maybe Vik?* She needed to know more.

His phone rang three times before he picked up. "Hey, boss. Cops are still here, but not much has changed."

"Still have eyes on that remote?"

"Don't worry, I've got it handled. Did you find anything?" Vik asked.

"Maybe… could you tell me what Tor is again?"

"The browser for the Dark Web," Vik said. "I told you about that several months ago."

"You know I wasn't paying attention, Vik." She could hear him take a deep breath. "Can you tell me again? Please?"

"Okay. You need to picture a giant iceberg floating in the ocean. What you see above the surface of the water is the worldwide web, which is visible to everyone and indexed by search engines. This portion is only a tiny fragment of the entire network. The Deep Web—"

"I thought you called it the Dark Web before…"

Vik sighed audibly. "No, first I'm talking about the Deep Web to help you understand how everything is connected. It's what makes up the majority of the Internet and lies beneath the ocean's surface. The Deep Web refers to any encrypted website with restricted access."

Lara wrinkled her brow and squinted, trying to understand. "But I don't have Tor, and I access my banking site all the time."

Vik responded to her question with a sigh. "Most of the sites on the Deep Web are accessible using a web browser, including your bank account, health records, and anything password protected," he said. "Buried within the Deep Web is the Dark Web. It is a collection of websites that are *not* indexed by conventional search engines but accessible through Tor onion routing."

"Onion routing?" Lara scratched her forehead.

"Messages sent using Tor have several layers of encryption, like the layers of an onion. The encrypted message is transmitted through a series of nodes in the network called onion routers."

"Kind of like Internet servers?" Lara asked.

"Yes. When users sign up for Tor, their computers can become part of the Dark Web network as volunteer nodes for data transmission. Tor traffic bounces around the network of computers owned by its users to disguise the physical location and identity of the real user. When a message is sent, each of the routers peel away a layer of the encryption until the message is decrypted at its final destination. The sender remains anonymous because each node only knows the locations of the nodes immediately preceding and following itself. A large share of the websites on the Dark Web are shady and sell drugs, guns, hacking services, or other illegal wares."

"What would Sully want with shady websites?" Lara asked, frowning.

"I don't know, boss, but a cop is waving at me. I have to go."

The phone went silent.

What were you doing on the Dark Web, Sully?

Lara stared aimlessly at the monitors. As a private detective, she avoided engaging with the deep, dark underworld. Most of the time, she didn't have to go there. Whereas Sully thrived in hunting down dangerous criminals, Lara preferred to work straightforward surveillance jobs for wealthy clients, which included everything from locating and removing unwanted forms of electronic surveillance to installing covert eavesdropping devices for law enforcement agencies. Everything was legal—or at least legal*ish*—but many of her clients had big names and would pay even bigger money for discretion.

She tried to find Sully's browsing history but couldn't uncover anything beyond the search bar. She guessed Tor didn't have a browsing history. After all, that would defeat the whole point of anonymity.

Right?

She'd have to ask Vik about it later. Only Sully would be able to tell her what he had searched for, and he wasn't talking anymore. Lara sat for a few minutes, trying to figure out what to do next.

Duh. I should check the video surveillance tapes.

Lara smacked her forehead, irritated that she didn't think about it immediately. If she searched the video footage, she could see what Sully had been up to before he died.

Clicking on the control room app on Sully's desktop, Lara loaded up the video archive and selected the most recent video file for the library. After a few seconds, the file opened to reveal only static gray and black dots with white noise in the background.

That's odd.

Lara pressed reverse and watched the timer race backwards. Several days went by without any images—more static. *Someone must have tampered with the video system.* Just as she slowed the video to a stop, an image of Sully appeared on the screen. Lara reduced the speed of the rewind to go back a few more frames and then pressed play.

Sully exited his safe room carrying a small cardboard box. He walked back and forth in his library as if looking for a hiding spot. He appeared disoriented and unsteady. Then he looked up into the surveillance camera as if remembering he was being recorded. His bloodshot eyes were filled with dread.

Was he drunk? Sick? What is going on?

Lara watched as he stumbled from the living room into the front hall. Determined to know where Sully had gone with the box, she searched the video archives for footage from the other cameras. But all the footage turned up static, not one clear image from the timeframe she needed to see.

Drumming her fingers on the keyboard, Lara stared at the nearly empty desk and thought of the many occasions she'd seen stacks of Sully's active case files next to his computer.

His desk is too tidy.

She looked down at the computer touchscreen. A tiny piece of white paper peeking out from underneath its base caught her attention. It had been well camouflaged against the shiny, white surface of the desk. She slid the paper out. The word "KillerBot" was scrawled across it.

Was this your screen name or something else?

"Watson?" Lara spoke into her smartphone. Her screen lit up with the image of a man with a thick beard and mustache.

"Yes, Ms. Kingsley? How may I be of assistance to you this evening?" Watson replied in a singsong English accent.

She'd named her AI voice assistant after Sherlock Holmes' famous sidekick and customized him to sound overly polite and cooperative. It made it easier for her to work with a computer; otherwise she'd start arguing, speaking too fast, and then lose her patience with the muddled response. She still didn't trust AI with any complex queries.

Lara took a picture of the paper with her smartphone. "I found this piece of paper in Sully's safe room. What does it mean?" Lara said and waited for an answer.

Let's see how you do with this one, Watson.

"That's quite an odd query, Ms. Kingsley." Watson paused for several seconds. "Based on my comparative analysis of the writing in the photo and your files on the cloud, the handwriting sample belongs to Mr. Phil Sullivan, a PI and your best friend."

Belonged. Lara swallowed hard and suppressed an intense surge of emotion.

"The literal meaning of the word killerbot is a small robot designed to kill people, which are illegal in the U.S." Watson continued. "However, in this context, I believe the word is most likely a pseudonym for communicating over the Dark Web. Unfortunately, you have disabled my ability to search the Dark Web. With your authorization, I can change the settings now and look further."

That's what I thought. "No, that's okay. Thanks, Watson."

"My pleasure." The smartphone screen went dark.

Lara left the piece of paper on the desk for the cops to find. She'd have Vik search the Dark Web for any references to the pseudonym when she returned to her office. Lara combed the rest of the area but found the desk drawers and the tall filing cabinet empty.

Sully was obsessed with keeping detailed records. *Where are all the case files he kept here?* He typically used written logs to record his prolific notes. If she could get her hands on his most recent journal, she might be able to find out who wanted him dead.

Someone must have cleaned them both out. But who?

Obviously, the house had been torn apart but the intruder didn't appear to make it into the safe room. *Had there been a second intruder, or had Sully cleaned out the files himself?* That thought kept repeating in her mind. If he had cleaned out his records, it could only mean one thing.

You felt your safe room was compromised. But where did you put your records?

As she peeked over the edge of the top file drawer, a tiny glint in the back corner of the drawer caught her eye. She grabbed the foot stool from underneath the desk and placed it next to the cabinet. Even with the additional inches, she needed to stand on her tiptoes to reach all the way to the back corner.

Lara reached inside the filing cabinet and found a small metal box held in place by a magnet. Carefully, she slid the box toward her with the tip of her finger until she could grasp it. She slid the top off to find a key engraved with the number D110. She looked around the office for a lock that the key might open, but it didn't match any of the keyholes in the office. Lara tucked it away in her pocket.

She put the foot stool away. As she headed toward the door, she spotted a business card stuck under the corner of the filing cabinet. Getting down on her hands and knees, she slipped the card out with her fingernails.

It named a Dr. Anton Stepanov at DARPA as Director of Robotics Research. Between the card and the forged ID, there was a good chance the renowned defense agency had something to do with Sully's case. She made a note on her smartphone to pay Dr. Stepanov a visit.

In the storage room, the sleeping area appeared to be untouched with blankets neatly folded on the bottom bunk. Next to the bed stood an oak cabinet with glass doors holding Sully's weapons cache. The pristine glass bore no marks of any kind— no smudges, fingerprints, or scratches. She tried opening the door, but it was locked, and the key in her pocket didn't match.

Lara opened the metal lockers stationed up against the wall. They were fully stocked with bottled water, canned food, other non-perishable items, and medical supplies. The shelving unit next to the lockers contained a small hot plate, pots and pans, tools, a hand-crank radio, and board games. A fold-up table and two chairs stood in the corner.

Lara walked into the bathroom to find the toilet seat left up.

Typical man.

The bathroom was spotless and the shower dry, leaving her no clues about Sully's last few days. She glanced at the toilet again. Nature was calling. She shrugged, put the seat down, and answered the call.

When you gotta go…

She grabbed a handful of toilet paper and pondered her next

move. Then something light tickled her forehead and crawled up into her hair.

What's that?

She reached up, expecting to swat away a fly. Lara sat up a bit straighter to see into the mirror on the wall across from her and yelped. Panicking, she nearly fell off the toilet. Something like a large bug moved in a circle on her head. She jumped up from the toilet, pulled up her pants, and ran into the office.

Lara frantically danced around, trying to shake it off. Instinctual terror shot through her veins as she imagined it crawling down her back. She dug her fingers into her hair, shaking it out and patting it down. The bug was no longer there. In a frenzy, she searched her clothes and every inch of the room to see if the bug had fallen on the floor. It was nowhere to be found.

Cautiously, she inched back into the bathroom and searched every inch. Behind the toilet, she caught a glimpse of the huge metallic golden-colored beetle. Its wings buzzed as it inched slowly toward her and stopped at her feet. She got the impression it was staring up at her.

Well, now that's odd.

Trembling—but insanely curious—she bent down to get a better look. She'd never seen a beetle so large. But it was also stunningly beautiful, for a bug. The golden beetle had hints of green, brown, and red on its iridescent body.

But something else struck her as out of the ordinary. Nearly camouflaged by its color, the beetle wore a tiny backpack with circuits and wires.

Is that…?

She couldn't believe her eyes. On top of the green circuit board was a small disk with a tiny aperture. The miniature camera was smaller than her pinky fingernail. Her heart skipped a beat.

Someone's watching me.

Remembering the plastic container, she ran back to the desk

and returned to the bathroom. Getting down on her knees, Lara held the container and the lid in her sweaty hands.

Now comes the tricky part.

Lara's hands shook, but she used the lid to lift the body of the beetle upwards just enough to flick it into the container. Then she pressed the lid down tightly to seal it shut and breathed a sigh of relief.

You're not getting out of there anytime soon.

In spite of her military training, Lara reacted to bugs with intense fear, something she blamed on a traumatic experience during her childhood. At five years old, Lara had been sitting on her mother's lap when a large beetle crawled down her forehead to rest on the end of her tiny nose. Ever since, she suffered from a bad case of entomophobia—something her team in Afghanistan had way too much fun with.

Her phone vibrated in her pocket.

"Hey Vik, Tor doesn't have a browser history, right?"

"No."

She gave herself a mental high-five. "Awesome, I—"

"Boss, the cops really want to talk to you. They're demanding that you come down to the station right away."

"Yeah, uh…" A shadow crossed one of the monitors, drawing Lara's attention. Within seconds, several dark forms appeared on the screen for the front porch. "Vik, I've got company. Tell them I'll get there as soon as I can."

Five armed men wearing familiar navy blue jackets with yellow FBI lettering were on the front landing.

Now, what are they doing here?

FIVE

The Safe Room

LARA WATCHED the video feed from the front door. Sweat formed on her brow as the agents came inside. She drew a deep breath, but the air in the safe room suddenly felt stuffier. The walls appeared to close in around her. She stole a glance at the safe room door, but it was too late for her to escape undetected.

Unsure of her next move, Lara sat rigid and watched as five FBI agents stacked up along the front of the house. After picking the lock, one of them gave a signal, and the first agent barreled through the front door of Sully's townhouse and burst into the entry hall. Three additional agents slipped through the door, one by one, staying close to the walls with their guns drawn.

"FBI, show yourself! FBI, put your hands in the air!" the first agent shouted, his voice barely audible through the thick walls of the safe room.

For a moment, Lara contemplated exiting the safe room and simply announcing her presence to the FBI. It was the right thing to do. But it would be a bold and risky move, putting her at the mercy of the Feds. If they wanted to be spiteful, they could accuse her of interfering with a federal investigation. And in her experience, FBI agents were not too fond of meddling private investigators.

Although she'd not technically broken into Sully's place, Lara didn't stand squarely on the right side of the law. Her fledgling PI firm couldn't afford a misunderstanding with law enforcement.

"Front room and hallway clear!" the first agent yelled, proceeding into the living room.

Lara turned up the volume on the audio and clicked the mouse to switch between cameras in order to follow two agents as they went upstairs. The other one made his way through the rooms on the first floor.

"First floor, clear," an agent reported over his comms.

"Second floor is clear," another agent said.

"Third floor is clear."

Movement on the second screen brought her attention back to the front door. Another agent walked in, presumably the team lead. He brought his hand to his mouth to speak into a mic on his wrist.

"Copy that, first floor, second and third floors clear. Droneman entering on first floor."

Lara sat up straight in her seat. *No way! It can't be him.*

"Boss, someone turned this place upside down real good."

"That's an understatement," the team lead said. "I'm gonna take a look around on the first floor. Make sure you sweep two and three. And don't forget to check the basement."

The voice sounded muffled over the surveillance audio, but she thought she recognized it. She stared at the monitor, trying to catch a clear glimpse of his face, but the resolution was too grainy. Glued to the camera, she watched him as he moved about the space.

The blood drained from her face, and a rush of adrenaline shot through her veins. She shook her head, realizing her deepest fear. The team lead was her ex-boyfriend, Special Agent Robert Martin.

Still walking around with that ridiculous swagger. Lara had never seen Rob at work before, and she wondered about the story behind his new call sign. *Droneman?*

She regained her composure and watched him barking directions to the other agents. Lara rubbed her eyes in disbelief at the situation unfolding before her. Given the overlap in their jobs, she knew a run-in with her ex was inevitable at some point, but what were the chances of that happening here, now, at this very moment?

"We're starting decon on two and three now."

Decon? What do they need to decontaminate?

"Roger that," Rob said into his wrist. "Make sure you find every one of them, okay? And be quick. D.C. cops are likely on the way. And I'm not about to lose a year of my life because the fat blue line messes up our investigation."

Each of the agents replied in the affirmative.

"And Chimbo, try not to spill your DNA all over the place this time. I don't want to clean up the bureaucratic mess afterwards."

What are you cleaning up, Rob?

Lara clicked on the third-floor cameras to see what the other agents were up to. One agent dragged a chair to the center of Sully's bedroom and appeared to be removing the fire alarm from the ceiling. Wearing plastic gloves, he pulled something small from the alarm. The other agent, also wearing gloves, fiddled with a lamp next to the bed. After a few seconds, he removed the base and pulled out something that looked identical to the first.

They're removing bugs. But why were they listening in on Sully? And why the secrecy from the D.C. police?

Maybe the FBI didn't have probable cause to justify the surveillance operation. Or perhaps they simply didn't want the cops knowing about their investigation.

Lara switched to the first-floor camera in the library. Her stomach twisted violently in circles, and a lump grew in her throat. Rob's rugged face stared into the camera as if he were looking straight at her. With his ruffled curly brown hair slightly out of place, he looked as handsome as when they first met.

"Hey, I found a camera hidden in these bookshelves. Agent

Carter, you don't suppose Sullivan has a safe room, do you?" Rob asked. Both of them peered into the camera with curious faces.

"His file indicates he suffered from paranoia, so it wouldn't surprise me," Agent Carter said.

"Well, if you're being bugged by the FBI, and your townhouse gets ransacked by God knows who, I'm not sure I'd chalk that up to paranoia," Rob said, chuckling. "Plus, he's handled some nasty cases in the past—some of them working for us."

"And this is how we repay him?" Agent Carter scoffed. "I sure hope *we* didn't get him killed tonight."

Rob shook his head. "If he'd come to us with what he knew, he wouldn't have been anywhere near our sting operation."

Sting operation?

From the looks of it, Rob and his team were removing illegal bugs from Sully's townhouse in reaction to his death at the ballpark. But it didn't make any sense to her. It wasn't like her ex-boyfriend to bend the rules, much less do anything illegal. Rob was a rule follower to his core.

Lara's success as an investigator required her to bend the rules on occasion. Her habit of breaking the rules in her job had been a sore spot in their relationship, but watching him now, Lara once again questioned how well she really knew him.

"I'm glad we caught it when he died, before anyone else could come in here."

"Yeah, I didn't see Sullivan's death coming," Rob said. "No warning, just huuukk," he made a vomit face, "and gone. KillerBot means business, that is if this is *his* work."

Rob was at the ballgame? KillerBot wanted Sully dead? Lara's mind raced as she wondered what else the FBI knew about Sully's death.

"Who else could it be?" Agent Carter asked.

"Who knows? Sullivan could've pissed off some crazed Brave's fan in the men's room or maybe he had a heart attack."

Lara shook her head at the screen. *If you'd seen Sully convulsing on the concrete, you'd know it was murder.*

"Carter, do you still have your contact at the medical examiner's office?"

"Dr. Stevens? I haven't called her in months, though. She's a little pissed at me."

"Well, I need you to call her tonight and make up."

Carter groaned.

"I don't want to hear it. Take one for the team. Send flowers, chocolates, giant teddy bears, whatever it takes. Make things right because we *have* to get our hands on that autopsy report. I want to know how Sullivan died."

Both agents stepped back from the camera and surveyed the book cases.

"Didn't we pick up some interesting creaking noises on the surveillance tapes?" Agent Carter asked. "Do you think one of these books here opens the secret door?"

"Nah, that's too obvious. Plus, there's at least a thousand books in here," Rob replied. "It would take us days to find the right one… unless…"

Lara's heart nearly stopped. *Did I push the book back flush with the others?*

Rob peered at the bookshelf containing the secret button, his lips pursed, his head cocked to one side. He narrowed his eyes, and then the corner of his mouth turned up in a cocky grin. "This has to be it," Rob said as he reached up and lifted a book, feeling underneath with his fingers.

Dammit I, Robot! Lara bit her lip, praying they wouldn't be able to figure out the code. Her palms were sweaty, and the sound of her heart pounded in her ears. *What if they find me in here, watching them?*

Seconds later, a high-pitched creak sounded through the speaker as the bookshelves opened to reveal the safe door.

Agent Carter gasped. "You found it! I can't believe it. How did you know which book?"

Rob gave a half shrug and lightly pounded his chest twice. "I am Droneman."

Lara rolled her eyes.

"Besides, the book seemed out of place. Now, how are we going to crack this code?" He squinted at the keypad and stroked his chin. He tried a combination, and then another one, and another. Each time, the electronic panel beeped loudly, signaling an incorrect entry.

Three agents from upstairs joined Rob and Agent Carter in the library. "Boss, we've cleared the upstairs of all the bugs. Did you decon the first floor and the basement?"

"No," Rob said, pointing at the safe room door. "As you can see, I've been a bit distracted."

The agents looked at each other. "No problem. We'll get it cleaned up right away."

"Swell, but don't expect a medal for doing your job."

Frustrated much? In his work interactions, Rob had an edge she'd never seen before. Perhaps he'd hidden some of his less flattering traits from her when they dated.

The other agents disappeared from the screen.

"I wonder what Sullivan was hiding in there?" Agent Carter asked, putting a hand against the vault door as if he could feel its contents by osmosis.

Rob shrugged his shoulders. "We'll have to come back later with a code breaker. We need to finish this job now and get out of here before the cops arrive."

He leaned forward and pressed the button. The bookshelves slid shut, hiding the entrance to the safe room once again. Lara exhaled sharply.

"We got the last one, boss," an agent yelled from the front of the townhouse.

"Okay, let's get outta here," Rob said.

Switching between cameras, she watched as the FBI agents departed the townhouse through the front door. When she was certain the coast was clear, she leaned back against the chair and breathed a huge sigh of relief.

That was way too close for comfort.

Agent Carter's question replayed in her head: "I wonder what Sullivan was hiding in there?"

Yeah, me too, buddy… Knowing Sully, he probably stashed something in the safe room for safekeeping. *There's at least one place I haven't looked.*

She walked cautiously into the small bathroom again, scanning the walls for any unwanted beetles. Lifting the cover off of the toilet tank, she peered into the water, looking for something that didn't belong. And she found it. Lara stuck her hand inside and pulled out a small, sealed Ziploc bag containing a key linked to a Star Wars Darth Vader keychain.

Another key. Now, what does this unlock?

She thought for a moment, and then an idea surfaced. Lara ran into the storage room and put the new key into the door of the oak cabinet holding Sully's weapons cache. *Voila!* The cabinet door opened, revealing twelve rifles standing vertically. Several pistols hung on the back of the cabinet. Lara reached inside, searching behind and around the guns.

Nothing out of the ordinary here.

Opening the storage area underneath the display, Lara found several wooden boxes. Sully had shown her these before; they held his collector weapons. Opening the first box revealed a Colt Python revolver with pearl grips cradled on a wine-colored velvet lining.

Sully's favorite.

She remembered when he showed it to her, full of pride. It belonged to his birth father, and his foster family had kept it for him until he turned eighteen. The box weighed more than she expected. The body of the gun boasted an intricately engraved floral and leaf design. As she laid the gun back into its slot, the edge of the velvet lining crinkled. She tested the loose edge with a fingernail, and it easily pulled away from the box. Lara carefully set the gun on the floor and pulled back the lining to reveal a folded manila envelope.

What's this? What an odd place to hide something.

But it felt like Sully wanted *her* to find it, like he guided her here from beyond the grave.

Did you know your life was in danger?

Inside the envelope, she found two newspaper clippings that appeared to be scanned from microfiche at a public library. When it came to his case research, Sully was old-school and avoided leaving any digital trail to the best of his ability.

"Nothing is secret on the Internet," he'd told her time and time again. He refused to use cloud computing or regular email for anything he needed to keep confidential and warned her to do the same.

The first clipping from the *San Francisco Post* was dated November 1979. The headline read:

U.S. ARMY COMES CLEAN ON BIOLOGICAL WEAPONS TESTS OVER THE BAY AREA

The article explained that the U.S. Army had conducted a series of secret tests in the 1960s in which they dispersed a plume of aerosolized, nonpathogenic bacteria into San Francisco from a small military vessel. The test was intended to judge the effectiveness of bio-weapons against a large urban target.

To conduct the tests, the Army used the bacteria *Serratia marcescens*, useful for simulating *Bacillus anthracis*, the cause of anthrax disease. They believed the bacterium was harmless to humans. It was ideal for such an experiment because it grew in bright red colonies—easily visible on surfaces. This way, the Army could assess the extent of coverage caused from the dispersal by taking samples throughout the city.

From these tests, the Army concluded that a bio-attack using aerosol dispersal on a large city would expose and infect most of its citizens. This meant American cities were extremely vulnerable to a bioweapons attack from the Soviets.

The article also stated that right after the tests, local hospitals reported an unusual spike in urinary tract infections caused by an unknown bacterium. Years afterward, the Army admitted the bacteria were not harmless and may have led to several illnesses.

The second clipping from the same paper was dated May 1985. The headline read:

COURT FINDS FOR THE U.S. GOVERNMENT IN BIOWEAPONS CASE

The article detailed a lawsuit brought by Jan Speelman against the U.S. Government. The twenty-five-year-old man had lost his mother, Anita Speelman, in 1965 when he was just five years old. She died from a urinary tract infection that her doctors suspected was caused by the *Serratia marcescens* bacteria released by the Army.

The Court determined that the government could not be sued for injuries resulting from the experiments since they were a critical part of national defense planning. The Court also stated that the plaintiff's case failed to provide sufficient evidence. To definitively prove the Army caused Mrs. Speelman's death, researchers would need a DNA fingerprint of the Army's strain for comparison with existing microbes. Conveniently, the original strain no longer existed.

Lara stuffed the newspaper articles in her coat pocket, wondering what they meant. Locking up the weapons cabinet, she sighed heavily as she absorbed the hypocrisy of it all. The government killed people under the guise of saving lives, and that made the deadly tests legal?

She tucked the plastic container under her arm and sent a text message:

I HAVE SOMETHING YOU NEED TO SEE

SIX

The Bionic Bug

October 20, 2027

SOMETHING KEPT NAGGING AT LARA, something she was supposed to do or remember in the morning, but she didn't have time to figure it out. Right now, she was on a mission. She marched into the genetics laboratory of the Department of Entomology at the University of Maryland in College Park, eager to get rid of the wretched beetle.

The lab bustled with activity. More than a dozen graduate students in white lab coats scurried about. Some held pipettes in their hands, transferring small volumes of liquid onto glass plates while others sat at laptop workstations, entering data and running tests.

As Lara proceeded, a male lab technician glanced up from his station and gave her an inquisitive look. His eyes darted from her black leather jacket and ripped stonewashed jeans to the plastic container in her hands. She held the closed container in front of her like a contaminated object.

"Can I help you with something?" the technician asked.

"I'm looking for my friend Maggie. She's expecting me."

The technician frowned at her and shook his head. "I don't know anyone by that name."

"Sorry, I meant Margaret Brown."

"Oh, you mean Dr. Brown, our lab director," he said, leaning toward her with a grin on his face. "She's over there in the back corner, tinkering with the new gene sequencing machine." His eyes were bright, and he looked to the corner. "We're all waiting to see what she thinks about it."

Lara nodded and moved carefully through the laboratory, trying not to knock anything over. For a university facility, the lab was much larger and more modern than she expected. Spotless, silver-trimmed, white lab benches separated the workspace down the middle of the room. Glass cabinets lined the walls on either side, providing ample storage. The countertops were covered with petri dishes and glass tubes, which were filled with brown liquid and what appeared to be small bugs.

A rather foul smell, like rotten food mixed with sulfur, permeated the lab and made Lara cringe. The odor was an odd contrast to her pristine surroundings.

An itching sensation spread as she imagined the tiny bugs crawling all over her skin. Her imagination started to get the better of her, and she double-checked the container.

Still there. In a few minutes, I'll be rid of you, beetle.

Maggie was bent over the gene sequencing machine, oblivious to everything else around her.

Not wanting to startle her, Lara called out when she was several feet away. "Hi, Maggie."

"Hey Lara, how's it going?" Maggie said in her silky Australian accent, waving her hand for Lara to come closer. "I just got my new top-of-the-line gene sequencer, and I'm about to give it a whirl." Her smile couldn't be contained, and she nearly jumped as she rocked onto her tiptoes. She clapped her hands together once and spun back to face the machine. Maggie adjusted a few knobs as her long, auburn hair swayed from her ponytail.

Even without a stitch of makeup, Maggie looked stunning in her plain white lab coat. "What sort of prezzy did you bring me?" she asked, clasping her hands together under her chin. Her eyes were wide in anticipation.

She was the only woman Lara knew who got a thrill from studying insects. For her Ph.D., she'd used new gene editing tools to render fleas incapable of carrying the plague, thus contributing to a decline in naturally occurring cases around the world. It was groundbreaking research, and her fifteen minutes of fame led to her current position as the entomology lab director at the University of Maryland.

Despite her earlier success, Maggie seemed unable to relax and enjoy it. She often spoke about the pressure of filling her parents' shoes and the need to make another research breakthrough. Maggie's parents were both preeminent scientists in the field of genetic engineering in Australia and had won Nobel Prizes for their discoveries related to gene splicing. Unlike Maggie, Lara didn't have any shoes to fill.

I guess there's at least one advantage to having no parents. No expectations.

Lara handed Maggie the container and wiped her sweaty hands on her jeans. "I'm working on a case for a friend and found this beetle in his home." She hated to tell a lie, but this way she avoided Maggie's efforts to comfort her over Sully's death. She needed answers. Comfort could wait. "I don't know what kind of beetle it is, but it has an electronics package on its back. I was hoping you could take a closer look."

Pushing her glasses up her nose, Maggie opened the container and inspected the beetle. Her light blue eyes widened. "What have we here? Oh my, I haven't seen one of these in years. What a beauty!" She gently picked the beetle up out of the container with her fingers to get a closer look, its wings trembling at her touch.

Instinctively, Lara backed away, placing a palm on her gun as if the beetle might jump out at her as punishment for its captivity.

"Now, don't tell me you're bothered by this peaceful little beetle." Maggie chuckled heartily. "Beetles are truly peace-loving creatures. There are only one or two species of beetles that cause problems for humans."

"Sure, tell that to my tomato plant," Lara smirked. She looked closely at the beetle. In the bright light, its shiny green head matched the flecks on its golden body. "I've never seen anything like this one. Is it even a living beetle?"

"Oh yes, it's alive. Christmas beetles belong to the *Scarabaeidae* family, which—"

Lara gave her friend a blank look. "Huh? Can you give that to me in layman, please?"

"Sorry, a force of habit. Have you heard of scarab beetles?" Maggie asked.

"Aren't those the beetles Ancient Egyptians made into amulets?"

Maggie nodded. "Yeah, the Ancient Egyptians worshiped them because they spontaneously emerged from the soil like the creator god. Egyptian hieroglyphs often depict Khepri as a scarab beetle or as a man with a scarab beetle head. Ancient Egyptians wore scarabs as charms, which were thought to have magical powers for warding off evil and bringing good fortune. Anyway, the Christmas beetle is endemic only to Australia. Every winter, they emerge from the soil and form swarms to find food. A beetle swarm can strip several whole eucalyptus trees bare in a feeding frenzy."

Lara grimaced.

"C'mon… don't you think it's beautiful?" Maggie looked at the beetle like it was a newborn baby. "It reminds me of Chrissie. We could hear the beetles buzzing loudly the night before we would open our presents. They're notoriously clumsy. They fly around like wind-up toys—crashing into walls, windows, trees, and even people. I can't tell you how many times I've found one of these stowed away in my clothing drawers as a kid. Sadly, they've come to be viewed as pests given their voracious appetites for eucalyptus trees."

"So, how did the beetle get all the way here then?" Lara asked, her foot tapping the floor.

"You mean from Oz? It must be part of someone's live collection. Though I wonder how they got it through customs." Maggie furrowed her brow and studied the beetle carefully.

"What's the contraption on its back?" Lara asked. "It looks like some sort of micro-sized surveillance camera to me, but does it do more?"

"Oh sweet, I've heard about the research they're doing on these," Maggie said, her smile on full throttle as she continued to examine the beetle. "But I've never seen one in person. This tiny backpack on its thorax contains microelectronics designed to control the beetle's flight. See there," she pointed to a small cube, "that's the tiny lithium battery powering the electrodes that are implanted into its wing-folding muscles."

"How does it work?" Lara asked.

"If you look closely, you can see the electrodes are connected to a microprocessor which has a built-in wireless receiver. The human operator sends radio signals via a handheld transmitter. The electrical pulses trigger the beetle to take off, cease flight, and swerve to the right, left, upwards, or downwards, providing full control over the beetle's flight. The camera records everything and transmits the video feed wirelessly to the operator."

Lara frowned. "What do you think these beetles would be used for?"

Maggie wrinkled her forehead. "DARPA funded this research for years, so it must be defense-related. Surveillance? Search-and-rescue missions?"

"But why not just use micro-drones or micro-bots?"

Maggie shrugged her shoulders. "I reckon a live beetle would draw less attention than a small robot? Plus, a beetle of this size can carry an impressive amount of weight on its back and doesn't require a large external energy source. Perhaps it's a payload issue. And why not take advantage of the beetle's natural abilities by blending insect and machine, creating the ultimate bionic bug? This is absolutely incredible, Lara."

Nightmare cyborg is more like it.

"Now that's interesting…" Maggie said, raising an eyebrow.

"What?" Lara asked.

"I'm not sure. Let me have a closer look." Maggie walked over to the counter, placed the beetle on a glass slide, and situated it under the microscope. "Huh. I don't think I've ever seen this before." She reached for a nearby tablet and opened an insect identification app. She typed in Christmas beetle and compared the pictures to the beetle on the slide.

"What is it?" Lara craned her neck around Maggie's shoulder to try to get a better look.

"Well, the mouthpart of this beetle appears to have been slightly modified…"

"Why would someone modify the mouth of a beetle?" Lara asked.

Maggie kept her eyes glued to the microscope. "Possibly to give it the capability to bite. Unlike many other insects, most beetles are plant feeders and unable to bite humans or animals or feed on blood."

Lara cringed.

"Blood-feeding insects are quite common nowadays. Entomologists believe they have been around for about two hundred million years. Flies evolved first, followed by our favorite, the mosquito. But for an insect to feed on the blood of humans or animals, they need a specialized mouthpart."

"Are you saying this beetle could have… bitten me?" Lara asked, shivering as if a chill went through her.

"Possibly. If so, that means the beetle may also be able to transmit disease through its saliva. But lucky for us, most beetles aren't able to carry human pathogens. I'd have to take a closer look and run some gene sequencing. Do you mind if I keep the beetle for now?"

"By all means, keep it. Could you have one of your techs

download the camera footage and send it to me? I want to see what that beetle was looking at."

"Sure thing. Don't worry. I'll get to the bottom of this." Maggie continued to stare into her microscope.

"Lara Kingsley?" A gruff voice called from a few feet away.

Lara turned to find two Maryland police officers walking in her direction, followed by a familiar dark-skinned man in plain clothes. *Crap.*

Detective Mario Sanchez of the D.C. Metropolitan Police had locked her up in a cell the last time she'd "interfered" in a police investigation.

"Detective," Lara acknowledged Sanchez as he approached, stopping in front of her with crossed arms. His shorter stature had never interfered with his intimidation techniques. The certainty in his eye, the way he set his jaw, even the way he chose to stand with his feet planted squarely shoulder-width apart—it all made her recoil. This was not going to go well for her.

"Ms. Kingsley, we meet again." He pasted on a smile and then wiped it away with a scowl. "You need to come down to the station with me to answer a few questions. Now."

Maggie's eyes grew wide as she stared at Lara.

"Aren't you out of your jurisdiction, Detective?" Lara asked, her eyes narrowing.

"Not at all. These fine officers are here to make sure everything is on the up and up. We work closely with other police departments to prevent suspects from crossing state lines to evade detection and capture." The detective motioned for her to follow. "Let's go for a walk."

"Do I have a choice?" Lara asked.

"Not really," Detective Sanchez said, a grimace on his face. "I can use handcuffs like I did last time."

"Is everything all right, Lara?" Maggie asked, giving the detective a onceover.

"Yeah, no problem. I'll call you later, okay?" Lara squeezed Maggie's shoulder and nodded.

Maggie breathed out, shrugged, and—now that everything seemed to be fine—proceeded to ogle the handsome detective. Lara rolled her eyes. Sanchez was nice to look at, but he could be a real jerk when he wanted, which was most of the time.

"All right, let's go," Lara said.

"After you." The detective motioned for her to go first.

Holding her head down to hide her face, Lara followed the officers toward the exit through the maze of graduate students and equipment. All eyes were on her, some staring outright, while most stole glances sideways. The detective walked behind her as if to prevent a last-minute escape.

"One last thing," Detective Sanchez said.

Lara stopped and looked over her shoulder. "What?"

"Gun and phone please."

She closed her eyes, shaking her head, and handed them over. "How did you find me?" Lara muttered under her breath.

Sanchez gave her a triumphant look. "Your assistant, Vik Abhay."

Lara wanted to punch something but kept her cool.

I'll have a few words with Vik when I get back to the office.

He unloaded and placed her gun and phone in an evidence bag. "You know these work better when you charge them," he snickered, shaking the phone at her before dropping it in the bag.

Crap, that's what I forgot…

SEVEN

The Police Station

THE INTERROGATION ROOM at the First District police station in Capitol Hill barely fit the small wooden table, two metal chairs, and the people sitting in them. Lara shifted around in the unforgiving seat. The table wobbled just a bit when she tried to rest her arms on it, so she left her hands folded in her lap. Everything in the room seemed designed with discomfort in mind. Even the air itself, stale and thick, felt like the work of some maniacal interrogation genius.

She glanced at the rust-stained vent above the door where a tiny paper tag, like the kind they put on cadavers, fluttered against the musty, lukewarm air. Beads of sweat rolled down Lara's cheek onto the table.

Detective Mario Sanchez glowered at her with his dark brown eyes, which matched the five o'clock stubble on his face. His muscular arms were tightly folded across his chest. He'd been like that for five minutes.

Lara had learned in a business class at MIT not to speak first if she wanted to win a negotiation, but this wasn't a negotiation. This was a game, and she was done playing. "I know a good repairman who could fix your AC problem."

Sanchez jumped from his chair and slammed the murder book for Sully's death on the table in front of Lara.

"What do you know?" he yelled, his face tight and his eyes narrowed. "This isn't a joke, Ms. Kingsley." He beat his fist on the table. "You were at the scene of the murder, and then you left. Looks awful suspicious from where I'm standing."

Lara watched as he railed against her, pointed his stubby finger in her face, and made a lot of noise. It was all for dramatics, but even if his temper had been genuine, Lara didn't care. She'd been through this drill with the detective before, and like the last time, she'd done nothing wrong.

Well, except for taking the beetle. And the key. And the newspaper clippings.

Stealing evidence from a scene of interest in a police investigation was technically against the law. Of course, she'd eventually hand them over, but right now the only thing that mattered was solving Sully's murder, and to do that she needed clues.

Sanchez could keep her there for hours if she didn't figure something out. He still held a grudge from years ago when Lara's involvement in a case had fudged his plans to make an arrest. He'd never forgiven her for the shit he had gotten from his boss.

This time, however, she had critical information and specialized skills to help solve his case. She figured the D.C. police didn't have the resources to keep a drone expert on hand, and in fact, she was banking on it. Otherwise, she'd be in trouble.

The hard metal chair made her thighs sore, so she stuck her hands under them for extra padding. She glanced at her reflection in the one-way mirror on the wall behind the detective. Her long, blonde hair looked embarrassingly unkempt.

Did I also forget to brush my hair this morning? Ugh. What about my teeth?

As she reached up to smooth out her hair, Lara sensed a presence lurking in the next room. Her intuition told her

Commander Jamison was watching the showdown from his hidden perch.

Sanchez pounded his fist on the table again, bringing Lara out of her daze and returning her attention to the interrogation room. A muscle in Sanchez's jaw twitched repeatedly.

"Are you fucking listening to me?" the detective screamed. He must have been shouting at her for several minutes now, but she'd spaced out. She continued to ignore him. His rants could take a while, and it was best to keep quiet until he finished.

Or until I'm ready for the fight.

"Can I get a bottled water?" Lara asked sweetly, eyes wide and docile.

Shaking his head and putting both of his hands on the metal chair in front of him, the detective leaned toward her, making sure she looked into his fiery eyes. "You're gonna tell me what you know now or later. Either way, you're gonna fucking cooperate with me."

"Cooperation? Oh, so you want me to cooperate with you now?" Lara asked, crossing her arms and raising an eyebrow. "You come all the way out to Maryland with two police officers, treat me like I'm a person of interest in my friend's murder and escort me to your cruiser under threat of being handcuffed. If you were trying to put me in a cooperative mood, I gotta tell you, that was a big, fat fail."

"Ms. Kingsley, we've tried to reach you for the past twenty-four hours." Sanchez rubbed his temples. "We relayed multiple messages through your assistant asking you to come down to the station. And you never. Fucking. Showed."

"I never received any messages," Lara said. She waved a hand to dismiss his accusations. "Besides, you saw my phone was dead when you picked me up. I was going to come by the station, but I had some personal things to take care of first."

"Like dumping the implicating evidence?" Sanchez ground his teeth and squeezed the back of the metal chair so hard his knuckles turned white.

"Seriously?" Lara rolled her eyes.

"Do you have any idea how much trouble you're in right now? I have an empty cell with your name on it!"

Lara sat up straight and stared into the mirror, hoping Jamison was listening on the other side. "I've never asked before, but last time we did this dance and you put me in jail, how did that work out for you?" She raised a defiant eyebrow at the detective.

I can play this game, too.

"You think you're special, don't you?"

Lara didn't respond.

He took a stack of photos from the folder and spread them out across the table. *Sully.* His lifeless body filled each picture.

"You were there when it happened."

"Yes," Lara said, studying each photo for a small clue she might have missed.

"You knowingly left the scene of a crime. Why?"

She clenched her jaw tight and didn't reply.

"I don't like private investigators interfering with my cases."

Lara looked up at him. "Except of course, when we do the work, and you get credit for solving the crime."

"Look, we can do this the easy way or the hard way," the detective said. "The easy way is you cooperate with us fully without any conditions. If you choose the hard way, we'll file charges for obstruction of justice. And then it's another night in the fucking slammer. No FBI agents to bail you out this time."

Lara chuckled. "Don't try to bluff me. This isn't my first rodeo. You know full well those phony charges won't stick. I'm not required to assist you in your investigation, and I've done nothing to obstruct your case."

It was obvious. He was playing hardball with her, most likely as a show for his boss behind the one-way mirror. Jamison despised her even more than Sanchez did. As the detective took the seat across from her, a vein popped out of his reddened neck. He was clearly not accustomed to women of her ilk. He wiped his sweaty forehead with his sleeve.

I've gotten under his skin.

She suppressed a smile and looked over the photos again. "What did you do with the remote control?" Lara asked, mostly out of idle curiosity.

"What remote control?" He rubbed his temples again.

"The one I found at the scene next to Sully's body…" Lara's voice trailed off.

Oh shit, had it gone missing? Why didn't I just let him run the interview?

He glared at her intensely and enunciated every word. "There was no remote control when we arrived."

"What do you mean?" Lara asked, feeling the blood drain from her face.

"We found nothing resembling a remote control. Perhaps you're the one who took it from the crime scene?" Sanchez's eyes narrowed.

Lara scoffed. "Why would I do that and then ask you about it? If my phone was charged, I'd show you."

"Here, I fucking charged it for you." He turned it on and tossed it to her.

She caught the phone just in time and shot the detective an angry glare. The screen showed forty-seven missed calls and texts.

Whoops.

Ignoring them, she scrolled through the photo album on her smartphone and showed him pictures of the remote control at the scene. "See, there's the remote on the ground next to Sully. I didn't take it. You can check the surveillance tapes at the ballpark, which will show me leaving the hallway empty-handed except for my motorcycle helmet and a baseball glove. Hell, get a warrant and search my apartment for all I care. You're barking up the wrong tree and wasting precious time. Meanwhile, Sully's killer is getting away."

"You're just trying to throw suspicion off yourself."

"That's utterly ridiculous," Lara said, her jaw clenched.

"Maybe your assistant took it from the scene," the detective fired back.

Lara's eyes flashed with fury, but the notion gnawed at her. Did she know for certain Vik didn't take it?

Please don't let him be right.

Vik was the last person to see the remote. She'd told him to keep his eye on it. More than once. *Hopefully, he didn't take her order literally and take it with him.*

Lara wiped the sweat off her face. "Would you like my help, or would you prefer to squander more time playing testosterone games in this hotbox?"

Sanchez fell silent and shifted restlessly in his seat. He looked as if he were considering all his options.

"It might interest you to know that several FBI agents visited Sully's townhouse the night of his death…" Lara dangled the teaser.

The detective sat up straight in his chair.

I've got you now.

"So, are we going to work as a team and cooperate?"

Sanchez cleared his throat. "Okay, fine. Tell me about the FBI traipsing all over my crime scene."

She knew he didn't like surrendering so easily. Lara looked him directly in the eyes. "So, you're not going to try to arrest me or threaten me with charges?"

He nodded.

"And I have your word on that?"

"You want me to get that in writing for you or something?"

"Just give me your word." Lara pressed.

He let out an exasperated sigh and uncrossed his arms, leaning forward, trying to give her some sense of authenticity. "Fine, you have my fucking word. Now just tell me what you know. From the beginning."

Lara breathed a little easier and folded her hands on the table in front of her. She left out the parts where she pocketed potential evidence, but she told the detective how she found Sully dead just after the seventh inning stretch, how she wanted to find his killer and went to Sully's townhouse to look for clues, how she had been the one to install his surveillance system, and finally how the FBI came over for some light housecleaning.

When she relayed the juicy details of the FBI's "decontamination" mission, the detective sat on the edge of his seat, listening intently to every word.

He jotted something down in his notepad and then flipped back a few pages. He cleared his throat. "Know anything about those cursed drones at the park?" he asked.

"Not yet, but I suspect DARPA might have something to do with it, or at least know something about it."

"DARPA? My guys found a business card. Do you know what they do over there?"

Lara nodded. "It's the Defense Advanced Research Projects Agency. They fund research on defense-related science and technology. Cutting-edge, futurist stuff. Maybe Sully was investigating something there."

"Did you find anything else?" the detective asked.

Lara retrieved the newspaper clippings and Sully's house keys and slid them across the table.

"You took these from the townhouse?" Sanchez's nostrils flared. "You know that—"

"I know I crossed the line," Lara interrupted. "But I'm only trying to help you. Sully handed me his keys right before he died, and he left those clippings for me in a hiding place only I would find. If you think I did it to keep evidence from you, then arrest me."

The detective crossed his arms, glaring at her. "What hiding spot?"

"I found them under the case lining of his favorite revolver."

Sanchez nodded, looking somewhat satisfied with the explanation. He let her indiscretion slide and read the newspaper articles slowly while she waited. "If this Jan Speelman is still alive, he'd be sixty-something by now. We'll see what we can find out. Anything else? Last chance to avoid trouble."

"You know how you found me in the lab?" Lara asked.

"Yeah?"

"I also found… well, it actually found me…" Lara searched for the right words to tell him about the bionic bug that was part machine, part nature, with possible genetic modifications. "Um, I was in the bathroom, and a large beetle landed on my head."

"A bug? Not the surveillance kind. A real bug?"

"Well, it was no ordinary bug," Lara said, taking a serious tone. "It wore a backpack."

"A backpack?" Sanchez's tone became incredulous.

"Yeah, I know… it sounds crazy—"

"I suppose the bug also wore a hoody and little sneakers?" He smirked. "Maybe it was late to a night class at GWU." The detective laughed at his own joke.

Lara stared at Sanchez until he quieted. "Well, you're not too far off. The beetle wore a tiny camera."

The detective's eyes nearly bulged out of their sockets. "Are you messing with me?"

Lara shook her head. "No," she said firmly. "Anyway, I took it to my entomologist friend at the University of Maryland. That's where you found me. She says it's a bionic bug, a beetle hooked up to a tiny electronics package that allows a human operator to control its flight patterns and receive video feed from a surveillance camera. She's gonna take a closer look at it."

"Lemme get this straight. You're telling me someone out there," Sanchez waved his hand around, "is flying a beetle around with a fucking camera on its back?"

Lara nodded. She didn't have the heart to tell him about the genetic modifications and their potential for disease transmission. That information would likely send him off the edge. She would wait for confirmation before stirring things up further.

Suddenly, the door flew open and slammed against the wall behind her. Startled, Lara jumped in her seat. Sanchez glanced up expectantly at a young officer.

"Sorry, Detective, we have preliminary autopsy results in the Sullivan case. I thought you'd want to review them right away."

"Thanks." Sanchez motioned for him to hand over the file.

"Uh, sir, this isn't the report. The medical examiner isn't quite ready to move forward. She wants to speak with you first."

The detective threw his hands in the air. "The examiner needs to do her fucking job. What does she expect me to do, bring my pocket knife and remove a pancreas for her?"

Lara rolled her eyes. *Boy, he sure thinks he's clever.*

"Sir, she's stumped on the cause of death." The officer's voice quivered slightly. "Not really on the cause, the victim died of asphyxiation, but the medical examiner doesn't know why. She thinks it might be some sort of poison, and she's tested for everything she can think of."

Lara recalled the seizure-like movements and the foaming around the mouth she'd seen right before Sully died. For her deployment to Afghanistan, she'd been trained on the full range of chemical and biological agents. "Tell her to test for biological toxins… maybe ricin or botulinum toxin?"

"Doesn't sound like a typical homicide…" The detective pondered audibly. "Why do I always get the fucking weird cases?" Turning to the officer, he said, "Have the medical examiner do the test and get me results ASAP."

The officer nodded nervously and closed the door quietly behind him.

"Ms. Kingsley, this has been… uh, very helpful. The department could really use you on this case."

"Is that a formal request for assistance?" Lara asked, grinning at the detective. His expression fell flat and remained static. "The answer is yes. I'll be glad to help you out for the usual fee." Lara knew the payment would amount to small change, but anything would be better than nothing. Of course, she would have worked Sully's case for free, but the detective didn't need to know that.

Sanchez nodded. "One more question."

"Yes?"

"Is your friend Maggie single?" He grinned sheepishly.

EIGHT

DARPA

October 21, 2027

LARA TAPPED her fingers nervously on the table while she waited in the windowless conference room at DARPA in Rosslyn, Virginia. She'd stashed her phone in the lockbox outside the room and felt awkward without a screen to stare at.

When he'd finally stopped asking about Maggie, Sanchez agreed that Lara should handle all the technology-related leads, and he'd focus on the basic crime elements. He asked her to visit DARPA and get some answers about the drone show at Nationals Park.

Lara didn't know what to expect from her meeting with DARPA officials, or even what she was searching for. She knew the agency developed technology similar to what she had found on the beetle and that Sully carried a fake DARPA ID the day he died. Most private investigators didn't view the law as she did—particularly not Sully, so his indiscretion must have been for a good reason.

Her thoughts drifted to Vik and the missing remote control. She'd been trying to reach him by phone to ask about it, but he had suddenly become mysteriously unavailable. He claimed to be busy with midterm exams, but Lara sensed something else was afoot.

Why would he take the remote?

As a green card holder, Vik could get himself in real trouble and jeopardize his plans to make America his permanent home. It wasn't likely Sanchez would tolerate another violation of the law from her or anyone associated with her.

Lara stared at the barren walls of the conference room. The long walnut conference table stretched out before her. A classified conference phone sat in the center, along with a Secure Video Teleconference System (SVTS) placed at the far end.

She'd attended meetings in a Sensitive Compartmented Information Facility (SCIF) several times before. During her years on active duty, she'd held Top Secret clearance with regular access to classified information.

Lara remained in the National Guard mostly for the extra income, but with her military rank of Army Captain, her status allowed her to keep an active Top Secret clearance. This came in handy for her job as a private investigator when she occasionally consulted for the U.S. government.

Lara fidgeted with her clothing as she crossed and uncrossed her legs. She loathed wearing a formal business suit, but somehow she didn't think her usual leather jacket and leggings would make the right impression.

The conference room door opened. A balding man with a white beard and a slightly bulging stomach walked into the room with a younger woman at his side. Lara stood to greet them.

"Ms. Kingsley," the woman said. "I'm Justyne Marsh, DARPA's Director of Public Outreach. And this is my colleague, Dr. Anton Stepanov, Director of Robotics Research."

Lara nodded and sat back down as they both took seats across from her at the conference table. Stepanov looked like a typical engineer. He wore a red bowtie that clashed with his tan tweed suit and stared at Lara awkwardly through his thick-rimmed glasses.

Unlike Stepanov, Justyne seemed rather out of place in the drab federal building. An attractive woman with striking blue eyes, she had unusually smooth, silky skin and black, straightened hair. With the way she carried herself, Lara judged her to be in her forties, though she could pass for thirty-five, easy. The bold, floral scent of Justyne's perfume wafted in Lara's direction, tickling her nose.

Justyne smiled warmly. "Detective Sanchez called and asked us to meet with you about the drone show that took place during the Nationals game a few days ago. What is it that you would like to know?"

Lara cleared her throat and flipped open her notebook. "We're investigating a homicide that occurred at the ballpark shortly after the drones arrived. We would like to know if you have any information regarding who was behind the drones. It's possible the two events are connected in some way."

"DARPA is not an intelligence agency," Stepanov said, revealing a slight Russian accent. He crossed his arms defensively and glowered at Lara. "We don't track users of drone technology. So, I'm not sure what *we* can tell you about it."

"But we want to be as helpful as possible to your case," Justyne said, ignoring her colleague's rude attitude. "Dr. Stepanov is correct. We don't know that much."

Lara nodded. "Based on your expertise, surely, you must have some ideas about the type of drone technology that was used?"

A moment of silence followed.

Justyne elbowed Stepanov, and he nodded reluctantly. "Obviously, I didn't see the drones myself. What I say is almost entirely based on speculation and inference. But I believe the drones at the ballpark must have been off-the-shelf commercial products, possibly with a few defense-related modifications."

"What sort of modifications?" Lara asked, scribbling furiously in her notebook.

"Some years ago, DARPA funded a project to develop drones with military-like capabilities from off-the-shelf parts," Stepanov said. "These drones ended up being so cheap and effective that the U.S. Army decided to employ them in the field for surveillance missions. The Army added some advanced modifications including a visual-aided navigation system and the capability to use encrypted frequencies for data transmission. We believe the drones at the ballpark benefited from both of these modifications."

Lara raised her eyebrow. "How do you know that?"

"Detective Sanchez told us the D.C. Metropolitan Police followed the drone squadron out of the park. The police officers used sophisticated jamming technology to try to take the drones down, and—"

"What type of jamming technology?" Lara asked.

"They used shoulder-mounted rifles that attack drones with radio waves. These rifles are designed to safely stop drones in the air by disrupting the radio and GPS signals controlling the drones. When a drone loses its radio and GPS signals, it is programmed to enter into its safety protocols, which usually means it will either hover in place, attempt to land, or return to its original location. But if the drones don't transmit any signals—"

"What does a typical jammer look like?" Lara asked, a possibility popping into her head. The U.S. Army now used high-power microwave weapons to counter IED drones controlled by insurgents. She'd never seen the equipment used by domestic police.

"A police jammer looks like a semi-automatic rifle with a long, spiky antenna attached. The typical jammer on the street is more like a large remote-control device with thick antennae."

That sounds exactly like Sully's remote control. So, maybe he was trying to jam the signal to the drones, or even hijack them, depending on how he modified the remote.

"How were the drones able to defend themselves against the rifles?" Lara asked.

Stepanov's frown deepened. "Yes, that's the key question. As I was saying before, we suspect the drones were using encrypted frequencies, which would protect them against the jamming signals. Either that, or they were designed with visual-aided navigation systems and didn't require GPS in the first place. Perhaps both. Most off-the-shelf drones depend on GPS for navigation and use unencrypted frequencies for data transmission, which makes them vulnerable to jamming and interception."

Lara decided to test out her theory. "The victim was found with a device that sounds like the street-level jammer you've described. Do you think our victim might have been attempting to spoof signals and hijack the drones?" she asked.

Stepanov sighed heavily. "Without inspecting the remote, it's impossible to know what capabilities it encompassed. But if the drones benefited from some level of encryption, they would be protected against false GPS signals intended to hijack a drone's navigation system."

Lara rubbed her chin. *If Sully was trying to steal a drone—or jam the signal—he failed. But, why would he try either of those things in the first place? How did he know the drones would even be there?*

"Why do you think Sully didn't show you the remote when he met with you, Dr. Stepanov?" She spoke on impulse to see how he would react, if it would startle him to learn she knew about their meeting.

Lara watched his face turn ashen and his mouth open and close. His eyes bulged from his pudgy face, and he cast a nervous glance in Justyne's direction.

"Eh, I don't know what you're talking about. I've never met him." Stepanov avoided eye contact and readjusted his tie.

"You mean you didn't meet with Phil Sullivan and give him your business card?"

"Not that I recall," Stepanov said curtly.

Why would he lie about this?

"If you could bring us the remote you found, we could compare it to—" Justyne started.

"I think we should end this conversation right now," Stepanov said, turning to Justyne. "Ms. Kingsley does not have the appropriate clearance to hear more on this matter."

Justyne shrugged her shoulders and waved off her colleague's objections. "Anton, I've already cleared us to share Top Secret information, and we haven't even gotten to that point yet. Everything we've said thus far is unclassified."

"Ms. Marsh, with all due respect, I think we need to stop here," Stepanov said forcefully. He pointed at Lara with his index finger. "*She* doesn't have clearance for compartmentalized information. And frankly, I don't care what the higher-ups think… this technology belongs to the Department of Defense, and it's my duty to ensure information doesn't fall into the wrong hands."

"You're being unreasonable. She's not asking for anything dangerous, just help in solving a murder," Justyne said.

He gave Justyne a death glare. "If you continue, I will have to report you for a security violation."

Justyne returned the glare with a frosty look that could freeze hell over. She then turned to Lara with a warm smile. "Do you have any other unclassified questions?"

Lara glanced down at her notepad. "Yes. Do you think there was a single perpetrator, or a group behind the drone show?"

Stepanov gritted his teeth. "Even if the drones were pre-programmed, it would be next to impossible to launch and maintain effective control over that many drones with only one or two people. They'd have to have perfect line of sight the entire time."

Lara furrowed her brow. "What if the drones were outfitted with the latest swarming software? I assumed this feature had already entered the mainstream. In that case, couldn't a single operator be able to control an entire swarm consisting of hundreds of drones?"

"I can't answer that question," Stepanov growled.

Lara didn't intend to press his patience any further and instead changed the subject. "There's another issue I wanted to raise in the interest of full disclosure. When I searched our victim's townhouse, I found a beetle with… well, essentially, it's a bionic bug."

"What?" Justyne's eyes widened, her interest clearly piqued.

"I took it to an entomologist, and she identified the bug as an Australian Christmas beetle with an embedded microelectronics package to control its flight patterns."

"You don't say…" Justyne said. "DARPA funded that research many years ago, but the tech you're describing sounds a bit outdated. What was the beetle being used for?"

"Mostly surveillance, I think… but we're looking into a few other issues," Lara said.

Stepanov looked at his watch. "Sadly, I don't have time to hear more. I have another meeting to get to." He placed his hands flat on the table to lift himself to his feet.

Lara stood up, following his lead. "Sir, thank you so much for your help on our case. It was extremely useful." She reached out her hand, but he refused to take it.

Stepanov grimaced, turned on his heel, and walked briskly halfway toward the door, then stopped and turned back. "Ms. Marsh, are you coming?"

"In a moment."

"I'm serious, don't give her any classified information."

Justyne rolled her eyes and gave Lara a disbelieving look.

"Of course, we would be interested in hearing further developments about the beetle," Justyne said loudly so Stepanov would hear her. He shook his head, spun on his heels, and marched off. When her ornery colleague was out of sight, she turned to Lara and whispered in a low voice. "I'm very sorry about his rude behavior. I hate to say it, but it's not entirely out of character for him. He's on a detail assignment from the NSA, and I'm not sure he's happy here."

Lara shrugged her shoulders. "It's no problem at all. I got what I came for."

Justyne paused. "Actually, I'd really like to hear more about this case, if you're willing. Do you have time to grab lunch?"

"Now?" Lara wrinkled her nose as she tried to recall if she had anything on her schedule. She was hopeless without the calendar on her phone.

Justyne nodded.

Lara glanced at her watch. "Uh... sure." She didn't know what more she could tell Justyne about the case, but maybe she could learn more about Stepanov.

"Okay, wait here. I just need to run to my office to get my wallet. Also, don't forget to take your cellphone," Justyne said, pointing to the set of lockboxes hanging on the wall. Then she turned and hurried down the hallway.

As Lara retrieved her cellphone from lockbox number D107, she froze. A sense of déjà vu washed over her. But she'd never been here before.

Something feels familiar.

She carefully studied the small keys in each of the empty lockboxes, and her eyes darted to D110. The box was locked, and the key was missing. From her wallet, she pulled out the key engraved with D110 she'd found in Sully's safe room. Her hands trembling, she fit the key into the lock... and it turned. She opened the box to find a low-tech cellphone—possibly a burner.

Could this be Sully's phone? The detective had Sully's personal and work cellphones in the evidence lock-up at the police station. *Did Sully leave the cellphone here for safekeeping? Is that why he made himself a DARPA ID?*

Lara rubbed her finger across the screen. Nothing. She pressed the power button. Still no response. *Just my luck, dead battery.*

* * *

PHO 75, a hole-in-the-wall Vietnamese restaurant located a few blocks from Justyne's office, was packed with people sitting around rickety folding tables in red-stained wooden chairs. The majority of the customers were Asian, which Lara considered a good sign. With its white linoleum floors and drab ceiling panels, the bland and unrefined atmosphere didn't do justice to the quality of the food.

Lara's stomach growled as she enjoyed the full-flavored beef broth. After a few unsuccessful attempts at using chopsticks, she surrendered to eating her rice noodles with a fork and spoon. Across from her, Justyne handled her chopsticks in one hand and her ceramic ladle in the other, like an expert foodie, effortlessly lifting the noodles from the beef broth into her mouth.

"I couldn't tell you before, but I actually also used to work for the NSA until recently," Justyne said, her voice barely above a whisper, though they sat in the far corner where no one seemed to be paying attention to them.

Lara's eyes widened. "Oh really?"

Justyne nodded. "Dr. Stepanov doesn't suspect anything, and he can't know about it," she said, lowering her voice even more. "The NSA sent me to DARPA on a temporary assignment. I'm conducting an internal investigation on a major leak of classified information. We think someone working at DARPA may be collaborating with someone from the NSA community to sell Top Secret encryption technology on the Dark Web."

Lara sat up straight in her seat. *Dark Web again?* "Are you in counterintelligence or something?"

Justyne shook her head. "No, I'm assisting the NSA lead counterintelligence investigator. My boss thought sending me here might help us pry loose useful information from my unsuspecting colleagues at DARPA. Lately, we've had our eye on Stepanov, who has engaged in some suspicious behavior. You saw how upset he got about anything remotely classified? Something's not right there."

"What other sorts of behavior is he exhibiting?" Lara asked as she spooned broth into her mouth, grimacing as it spattered on the table. A little old lady in Lara's line of sight shook her head in disapproval as she lifted her bowl and scooped the broth and noodles into her mouth. Lara brought her own bowl to her mouth, this time managing to eat without a mess.

Justyne swallowed a large spoonful of noodles. "Well, we're

cooperating with the FBI, and they put a light tail on him and…" she paused and glanced across the room, "on several occasions, he met up with your victim before he died. Obviously, I couldn't tell you that when we were with Stepanov."

Lara's mouth dropped as she tried to absorb the new information.

Stepanov knew Sully? So, he did lie.

From the business card, she already knew Sully had contact with Stepanov, but to learn Sully had met with him several times surprised her. "Where did they meet?"

"At a bar called Wicked Bloom in D.C.," Justyne said. "You know it?"

Lara nodded, the blood draining from her face. *Sully met Stepanov at our place?* "What FBI agent are you working with?"

"My primary contact is Special Agent Martin from the Washington D.C. field office."

Another freak coincidence.

Lara kept a straight face, but her heart began to race. "Why are you sharing all of this with me? Surely, it's highly sensitive stuff."

"I'm, well… I feel like I can trust you." Justyne looked away for a moment and then stared directly at Lara with uncertainty. "And you're working with the D.C. police. I figure we can help each other out. If we pool our information, maybe we can find…" Justyne turned her face away again.

Her eyes glistened with tears, and Lara cringed internally. She always found it unsettling when people cried around her. Partly because she never knew how to behave. *Should I console them? Or would that make it worse?* She didn't understand why anyone would express their emotions so openly.

As a kid stuck in the foster care system, frequently traded between families, Lara learned to cope internally with her own emotions and rarely cried without prompting from someone else. Seeing the tears of another made her feel things she'd rather ignore.

"It sounds like it's a bit more than that," Lara said.

Justyne wiped a tear from her cheek. "Yes, I'm personally invested in this case. I suspect the person who killed Sully also bears responsibility for the death of my colleague at NSA." She paused for a moment. "Well, Frank was much more than a colleague. We were very close."

"You were romantically involved?" It wasn't really a question, Lara could see it in her eyes.

Justyne nodded. "Yes. He was killed about a year ago. I think by the same person behind the technology leaks. I've been helping the NSA track down the scumbag ever since. If you could tell me anything else about the case, I'd appreciate it."

Lara shook her head. "There's not much, I'm afraid. I've already told you everything I know."

Justyne's face fell, and she closed her eyes for a moment. "But, would you be willing to work with me moving forward?" she asked cautiously. "Please?" Tears formed in Justyne's eyes again, and Lara could feel her stomach knot.

"Sure. Why not? Putting our heads together could be helpful."

Relief fell across Justyne's face. "You've no idea how much hope that gives me. We've been floundering lately in the investigation. Every lead has come to a dead end. We desperately need a breakthrough. And I'm sure with all of your amazing expertise, we would crack the case very soon."

Lara shrugged halfheartedly, her cheeks growing hot. She didn't take compliments well. They made her feel awkward and added pressure.

"With all of NSA's resources at your disposal, I'm not sure how I can help," Lara said.

Justyne shrugged her shoulders. "NSA doesn't have jurisdiction on domestic counterintelligence, so I've been relying on the FBI for my information." The waiter stopped by their table to clear the food. Justyne glanced at Lara. "I'll get the check, okay?"

"That's really not necessary, but thank you." Lara smiled. She waited while Justyne took cash from her wallet and left enough to cover the bill and tip on the table. "If you would, please keep me in the loop on any developments on your end." She handed Justyne her business card.

"Sure, and same for you. Do you need to call a cab?" Justyne asked as they got up from the table and headed toward the door.

"No, my motorcycle is parked right there." Lara pointed to her shiny blue bike gleaming in the sun as they walked out.

"You ride?" Justyne asked as she fixed her eyes on Lara's bike. "I've always wanted to try it, especially now that we can't manually drive cars anymore. But I'm a bit intimidated by the size and weight of a bike. I'm not sure if I could keep it balanced and avoid tipping over."

"It takes some practice, but once you get the hang of it, it's easy. Plus, the self-balancing technology does most of the work for you. If you want, I could teach you sometime."

Justyne gave Lara a wide grin as she stood on tiptoes for a moment. "Oh, that would be great."

As Lara stashed her wallet in the seat compartment, she turned back to Justyne one more time. "I'm curious. How did your partnership with Special Agent Martin come about?"

Justyne stepped back, surprised by the question. "I suppose his boss assigned him the case when the NSA called the FBI for assistance."

Lara nodded, wondering if there was more to it. She waved goodbye to Justyne, who turned around and strode quickly down the sidewalk back to her office. Then she took out her smartphone. Hands shaking, Lara typed out a text:

WE NEED TO TALK

Her thumb hovered for several minutes before she finally hit send.

NINE

Coffee

THE AROMA of freshly brewed coffee filled the air, lifting Lara's spirits. For a weekday morning, an unusual number of students packed the Georgetown coffee shop. Three baristas bustled around the chrome espresso machines to fill the long list of coffee orders. Their equipment whirred and buzzed as they frothed milk, ground coffee beans, crushed ice in blenders, and waited for espresso to trickle from the machines.

She took small sips of her frothy cappuccino and savored the feeling of warmth in her chest, hoping it would calm her nerves.

Dammit, what the hell am I doing?

Lara fidgeted with the zipper of her leather jacket. When she texted her ex-boyfriend, she wasn't certain he would be interested in talking, but he'd responded immediately. They'd texted back and forth, Lara hinting that she knew something about a case of his. It finally piqued his interest enough for him to agree to meet.

She bit her lip at the thought of seeing him again. It had been six months since the breakup, and she had been lucky to be

84

spared any run-ins with him in D.C.—well, except for on camera at Sully's townhouse.

Maybe I should've picked a different place.

The Grind Coffee Shop stood just around the corner from her townhouse. It had been one of their favorite spots to spend a slow Sunday morning together, and she'd spent months exorcising the painful memories. But it was also the one place where she felt secure enough to handle the intense discomfort of their encounter.

Lara had snagged the last bistro-style table with two wrought-iron chairs positioned next to the large glass window. With a good view of the street and front entrance, she'd be able to see him coming and prepare for their first greeting.

Next to her, an old, white-haired man with silver spectacles flipped noisily through the tall, thin pages of his daily newspaper—a notable contrast to the college students glued to their smartphones and tablets.

Her phone buzzed with a text from Vik:

I HAVE INFORMATION ON KILLERBOT FOR YOU WHEN YOU GET IN THE
OFFICE

Lara texted back:

GREAT, I'LL SWING BY IN ABOUT AN HOUR

Finally. Although she and Vik hadn't seen each other since the baseball game, they'd been exchanging notes on the case. Lara got the sense Vik was avoiding her since the ballpark, and she wondered why he deflected her questions about the missing evidence. *I need to find out what happened to the remote.*

A dark shadow fell across the table. Looking up from her smartphone as she took a drink, Lara jumped in her seat and nearly choked on her coffee. Rob stood over her, with his ruffled, curly brown hair and familiar handsome, goofy grin.

"Hey," Rob said as he leaned over for an awkward side hug.

"Sorry, I didn't see you come in," Lara said, willing the blush creeping up her neck to go away. Her chest tightened as she avoided direct eye contact, calling to memory how he'd hurt her. This wasn't a friendly get-together. This was about Sully's murder.

Rob knew she didn't like people sneaking up on her, but he'd always found it funny. Now, he grinned like he'd won a prize for making her jump. He sat in the seat across from her, taking a sip from his iced coffee through a plastic straw. Lara almost rolled her eyes out of habit. The season didn't matter. Summer or winter, he insisted on drinking iced coffee. When they were dating, she would tease him about drinking coffee from a straw, like a little kid.

Taking a long sip, he gazed at her playfully with his warm, brown eyes. She placed her hands on the table, and then folded them in her lap, fidgeting with the hem of her t-shirt. The blush had reached her cheeks; she could feel them burning.

The lingering feeling of familiarity stung. After a year together, Lara thought they'd been close. As a private investigator, she prided herself on deciphering people's motivations and character from only a few details and scattering of behavioral patterns.

And yet, Rob cheated on her for several weeks without any of her prized instincts kicking in. She'd planned to ask him about some odd behavior, but she never anticipated infidelity from a guy like him. He was supposed to be one of the good ones. The betrayal hit her like a ton of bricks. Besides breaking her heart, it shook her confidence in her own instincts about people. And that was her bread and butter.

With him sitting across from her, her heart ached like it happened yesterday. She could still remember how she felt during the moment of truth, like her stomach was punched by an iron fist and the air was squeezed from her lungs. Clutching her coffee cup tightly, the thought crossed Lara's mind that it was too soon to see him again, but she had important business.

Time to woman up, Lara. You can do this.

"How are you doing?" Lara smiled brightly, trying to hide her discomfort.

"I'm good." Rob grinned.

"And how's Bimbo Barbie?" The initial warmth between them chilled immediately. She hadn't meant to say it, but it had been spinning in her mind for months and just rolled off her tongue.

Rob winced and frowned at the same time. "Alexa is okay, I guess." He shifted uncomfortably in his chair, like he was trying to reset. "I was surprised to get your text after the way we parted. But then you said you knew something about a case I'm working. I'm rather intrigued. How in the world do you know what cases I'm working at the moment?" He pasted a fake smile across his face.

"Yeah, so actually, I was hoping you could give me information about a case *I* am working on," Lara said, grimacing.

Rob's smile disappeared instantly. "I hope you didn't lure me here under false pretenses, Lara."

She raised her eyebrow. "Even if you're just telling me what you know about KillerBot?"

He scowled. "You know I'm not at liberty to discuss any of my ongoing investigations with you."

"Oh, I thought you might say that… but I think the circumstances might change your mind." She gave him a knowing look.

"And what circumstances might those be?" Rob leaned away from her, crossing his arms.

"Let's just say I know you and your team removed illegal bugs from Phil Sullivan's townhouse last Thursday."

Rob gaped at her, his eyes narrowing. "And how would you know that?"

"Does it matter?" Lara asked, toying with him.

Rob's glare could kill a cat. "I don't know who your source is, but that's utterly ridiculous."

"Being honest for once wouldn't hurt, don't you think?" Lara's tone lashed at him like a sharpened dagger.

A flicker of anger shone in his light brown eyes. His stone-cold face returned, and he looked as if he wouldn't budge.

"It might help to know that I was in Sully's safe room watching you." Lara looked him directly in the eyes. It felt good to have something to hold over his head. "So, I'm the source. And I think Detective Sanchez would be very interested to know that the FBI showed up at Sully's house on the night of his murder to clean up an illegal surveillance operation. How about I call him right now?"

Lara took out her smartphone and pretended to look up his number. Rob didn't need to know she'd already told the detective everything.

Rob put up his hands in surrender. "No, no… Lara, that's not gonna be necessary. You don't need to blackmail me into cooperating with you. But I'm going to need you to protect my investigation, okay? I can't have D.C.'s donut patrol messing up a sting operation that took months to put into place."

"Oh yes, the sting operation you mentioned…" Lara said. *Now I'm getting somewhere.* "Against Sully, a known hardened criminal…" She let sarcasm drip from her mouth and narrowed her eyes.

Rob shot her a defensive look. "We've been tracking KillerBot's activities on the Dark Web for months and were just about to figure out his true identity."

"He?" Lara asked.

"We don't know for sure, but we suspect KillerBot is a man. We found him on a message board called *TechNow* on the Dark Web, trying to purchase high-end drone technology as a potential delivery system for something."

"Delivery of what?" Lara asked.

"We don't know yet. Based on his desired specs, maybe a biological weapon. He regularly interacted with a person, screen name CyberShop. He also communicated with us while we hid our identity under the pseudonym Droneman."

Droneman? Lara gave him a that's-a-bit-obvious smirk, and Rob shrugged in response. She wanted to laugh out loud, but feared it would disrupt the flow of information. *He used his call sign for his secret pseudonym?*

"We offered to sell him drone technology as part of our sting operation, hoping to draw him out into the open," Rob continued. "But KillerBot demanded we first make a public demonstration of our capabilities."

"A demonstration?" Lara lowered her voice to a whisper, asking, "You don't mean the drone show at the ballpark, do you?"

Rob rubbed his forehead and loosened the collar of his starched white shirt. "Yes, *we* were behind the drones at Nationals Park."

Lara's jaw dropped as she absorbed the information. "Yeah, come to think of it… that makes sense. And because it was a sting operation, you couldn't inform stadium security or the D.C. police."

"Correct. The whole thing had to look legit to KillerBot, or he'd know something was wrong."

"But how the hell did you get authorization to fly so many drones in the District?" Lara stared at him intently. "Is that how you got your call sign?"

Rob winced, his face turning slightly pink. "Well, sort of. My boss gave me the nickname because of the sheer audacity of the stunt. The op was a bureaucratic nightmare, but we argued that KillerBot may be plotting something big, a terrorist attack of some sort, so we were able to get it approved. No one wants another 9/11 on their hands. Anyway, the sting operation turned out to be a bust. We weren't able to get KillerBot to come out into the open. And then Sullivan died in the park."

He took a long sip on his straw.

"So, what were you doing *illegally* monitoring Sully?" Lara asked, pressing one of this well-known buttons.

Rob blanched. "Huh?" He paused, searching for words. "It wasn't illegal per se… well, it's a bit of a gray area. Initially, from our investigations on the Dark Web, we thought Sully was KillerBot. Turns out we were wrong."

Lara raised her eyebrow. "Since when does Special Agent Martin operate in a gray area?"

Rob shrugged. "I was following my boss's orders, so it appeared pretty black and white to me."

Well, this is new. Lara had to stop herself from drawing too many conclusions. Before he cheated on her, she thought Rob the rule-follower would never deviate from the letter of the law—no matter what. Of course, that notion went out the window when he betrayed her. He was clearly capable of crossing the line when it suited his interests.

Lara crossed her arms. "In other words, you should have ended the surveillance once you knew Sully was not your suspect, but you continued the operation anyway?"

Rob nodded.

Lara frowned, the link to Sully continuing to nag at her. "But I thought activities on the Dark Web are anonymous. I mean, that's what that Tor thing is for, right?"

Rob sighed and looked like he was launching into a lecture. "Normal web traffic travels across well-defined and efficient pathways over private servers around the wor—"

"Yeah, yeah… Tor covers the tracks of its users. That much I know. Thanks for the Dark Web 101." Lara rolled her eyes. "What I don't understand is how you could find out who anyone is, or where they are located, if Tor is truly anonymous. What's your hack?"

Rob ran a hand through his curly hair. "The Dark Web is quite the boon for law enforcement. Using Tor, we can blend in with everyone else. It's the perfect environment for setting up a sting operation. You never really know who's on the other end of a conversation or a deal struck over the Dark Web. But you're right, it's considerably more difficult for the FBI to detect physical locations or browsing habits on Tor than the surface Internet."

"Difficult but not impossible?" Lara pressed.

Rob frowned. "I'm not going to say more than that. Let's just say we have ways of circumventing the anonymity feature of Tor."

Feeling a growing sense of irritation, Lara brought the subject back to her case. "Rob, how could you think Sully was KillerBot? He was one of my oldest and dearest friends. And you've worked with him on several cases. You can't tell me you actually thought Sully was part of some evil terrorist plot."

"I know. It surprised me too, but we had to follow the evidence. You know how it works. Sully was posting actively on the TechNow message board under the pseudonym RoboTech and interacted with CyberShop, asking all sorts of technical questions. We assumed KillerBot might be using multiple screen names to disguise his activities. We hacked Sully's computer, discovered his physical address, and began monitoring him using the bugs you saw us removing. That's when we realized Sully was not KillerBot."

"What was Sully doing on the message board then?" Lara asked.

"We now think he was actually investigating *us* for KillerBot. He tried to hack our computers several times, but our encryption was too powerful."

Sully was working for KillerBot?

"Investigating you? Didn't he know you were FBI?"

"Maybe. We're not sure," Rob said.

"I saw him at the ballpark right before he died," Lara said, with a shudder. She didn't like thinking about Sully's lifeless body lying on the cement floor. It made her emotional, and right now she needed to keep it together. She focused on maintaining her game face.

"You were at the game, too?" Rob looked at her sideways. "Where *weren't* you that night?"

Lara nodded, ignoring his jab. "I didn't know it was him at first. He was operating some sort of remote control—likely a spoofer or jammer."

Rob rubbed his chin. "Huh, that's interesting. I'm surprised he smuggled something like that into the ballpark, or even dared to operate it in public. It's a federal crime for civilians to operate a jammer, and there are stiff penalties."

Now there's the Rob I know! "I'm sure Sully had his reasons." She paused to consider her next question. "Do you have any other leads on KillerBot's identity?"

Rob shook his head. "We're still trying to piece together how we were misled into following Sully as our lead suspect. Once we trace back our path, we'll find out where we went wrong and rediscover the scent. We did find one clue I can't make sense of. Maybe it relates to Sully's murder."

"What did you find?" Lara asked.

"When we arrived at the townhouse, it was trashed… well, I guess you know that. You were there before us. Was it you?" Rob chuckled at his own joke, forgetting his anger. "Anyway, we found a prescription bottle in his waste basket."

"What for?" Lara asked.

Rob pulled out his notebook and flipped through several pages. "It was for Streptomycin. I think that's a common antibiotic?"

Lara nodded. "Who prescribed it?"

Rob rubbed his forehead, paging through his notes. "I didn't write that down. I'll have to check the bottle in the evidence locker and get back to you."

"That would be great. I really appreciate your help on this." Lara glanced at her watch. "I need to get back to the office. I'll let you know if I discover anything further about KillerBot."

When Lara got up to leave, Rob banged his knee on the table in an effort to stand up at the same time.

"Are you okay?" Lara asked, crinkling her nose.

Rob nodded. "Yeah, I'm fine," he said. Then, he stepped toward her and began to raise his arms.

Lara's heartbeat quickened. *He's not going to hug me, is he?*

When he kept going, she panicked. Lara shoved her hand out, accidentally punching him in the gut. Her eyes widened in horror as Rob flinched and grimaced. His face scrunched up, and he gave her a what-the-hell look.

Lara shot her hand out again, this time to shake his hand. Rob raised an eyebrow as his pained look subsided, but he shook her hand. Lara gave it one solid shake and bolted from the coffee shop without another word, not wanting him to see the fresh blush forming on her cheeks.

I'm such a moron. She sighed as she slowed her steps about a block away from the coffee shop.

The air outside was crisp and refreshing. Squeezing her eyes shut, Lara stood still for a moment and took a slow, deep breath. *I survived the first meeting.* The next encounter would be easier. And eventually, she'd be able to put the past with Rob behind her.

When she opened her eyes, something metallic landed on her shoulder. She yelped out loud and flicked whatever it was off her shoulder. She squinted in the sunlight, but only caught a flicker of gold.

That better not be what I think it is.

Seconds later, a faint buzzing reached her ears and something in the air approached from behind. Slowly, she turned her head to the right and recoiled. Perching on her shoulder, a golden beetle with a green backpack fluttered its shiny wings. The beetle stared blankly at her as if it were frozen in place by its unknown operator.

Trembling, she reached up, grabbed the beetle, and put it in her shaky hand. *Hmmm, that's strange.* The backpack looked different. The tiny cube battery was missing, and she thought she detected a small solar panel in its place. Unless the operator was nearby using wireless control, the microelectronics package must enable autonomous navigation.

Her eyes wandering up and down the street, she didn't see anything out of the ordinary. No one that looked like they were directing the beetle.

A tiny ring attached to its backpack bore a small scroll of paper. As soon as she slid off the scroll, the beetle took flight again, buzzing in front of her face for a few seconds, and then disappearing into the sky. Her hands still shaking, she unrolled the paper.

In tiny print, she read:

MEET ME AT THE NATIONAL CRYPTOLOGIC MUSEUM

TEN

KillerBot

_____

CLIMBING the steps to her brick townhouse, Lara caught a glimpse of something buzzing overhead along with a falling object. She reacted immediately, seeking cover against the base of the door by crouching on the ground and shielding her head. Nothing happened.

When she finally looked up, a few harmless brown oak leaves drifted downward in a circular motion, floating onto the step beside her. Whatever might have been flying above her head had disappeared into thin air.

Even without visual confirmation, Lara knew she'd seen a drone flying in her periphery. She would never forget that feeling. During her tours in Afghanistan, she'd served on a special reconnaissance team that would travel behind enemy lines to gather intel. Her team would often use drones of varying sizes and capabilities to scope out enemy hideouts.

And then one day, insurgents began using sophisticated off-the-shelf drones converted into IEDs against her unit. The U.S. Army didn't anticipate this development, and they were not equipped to counter the attacks from their position. Drones armed with powerful explosives appeared out of nowhere and dove toward her unit, dropping their payloads and killing all of them, except her.

For the past several days, Lara had the distinct impression she was being surveilled from above by a drone. With the rise of drone package delivery in D.C., however, she had no way of knowing whether the drones flying above her belonged to one of several online retailers, or to someone using the drone to track her activities. Admittedly, recent encounters with bionic bugs and the strange note demanding a meeting had put her on edge.

Who wants to meet at the National Cryptologic Museum? Sully's killer?

When she first read the note, her immediate instinct was to jump on her motorcycle, speed over to the museum, and meet the mysterious person in control of the bionic bugs. But Vik's voice rang in her head, nagging her about her tendency to race toward danger instead of stopping to think and assess the situation first.

But I wouldn't be in any real danger.

The National Cryptologic Museum was one of the safest places to meet, so it shouldn't pose too much of a risk. Located next to the NSA on Fort Meade, the museum crawled with federal police, surveillance cameras, and detection dogs.

In the end, Lara decided not to go. She didn't like the notion of obeying a stranger's command to meet at a remote location without any reason.

What precedent would that set?

Plus, the note was rather vague. Without an actual meeting time, the "invitation" seemed open-ended. She could always go later If she changed her mind.

When she opened the front door into the shared foyer of her townhouse, Lara stumbled over a pile of mail lying on the worn oak floor in the hallway. The postal worker must have hastily shoved the stack through the slot in the door, rather than enter the building and separate the mail into the correct boxes. Sighing audibly, Lara bent down to scoop up the mail and caught a whiff of onions and garlic coming from her office on the first floor.

Vik must be cooking again.

Lara sorted the mail into two neat stacks—one for her and the other for her landlord. Her heart sank at the red envelope with a past due notice addressed to Kingsley Investigations.

Crap. Another collections notice.

She still wasn't sure how to tell Vik the whole truth about her financial misfortunes and the pending eviction. Stuffing the red envelope in her pocket, Lara walked through the door carrying the rest of the mail.

Steam wafted up from a black pot on the stove, and the smell of freshly cooked food permeated the air. Vik sat at his computer, staring intently at his screen. Lara put the stack of mail on the kitchen island and walked over to the stove.

"I just finished cooking a fresh pot of Greek bean soup if you are hungry," Vik said, not looking up from his computer screen. "Also, there's fresh tabouli salad on the counter."

Her stomach growled. She hadn't eaten all day, and it was almost lunch time. "Thanks, I think I'll grab a bowl. Remind me to thank your mother someday when she visits the U.S."

"What for?" Vik asked, his eyes widening.

"For teaching you to be a great cook." Lara gave him a half-smile.

"You should instead thank her for making me a genius with computers." Vik gave her a forced laugh. His parents were both computer programmers who worked for a major firm in New Delhi.

"That too." Lara chuckled in an attempt to break the tension. She didn't know what she'd do without his computer savvy. She bit her lip.

Something was off between the two of them. She hadn't seen Vik for more than a few minutes in over five days, and when she did, he wouldn't make eye contact. He was avoiding her for some reason.

I sure hope he didn't take that remote.

"Did you get the text I sent you?" Vik asked with a note of caution in his voice.

"Yes, I did. Sorry for not responding. I met with Special Agent Martin. Turns out he is investigating KillerBot as well."

Vik looked up from his computer tablet and stared open-mouthed at Lara. "You met up with Rob?" His eyebrows knit together, and he frowned just a little.

"Agent Martin," she corrected sharply.

He shook his head. "Why Rob? You can't go through this again."

Vik had been at her side throughout the painful breakup and tried everything he could to help her pick up the pieces Rob had left behind. Lara was grateful for Vik's patience while she dragged her feet, unable to take on any new cases for several months.

Lara still paid him for his time, but he was too smart to sit around doing nothing. When Vik became restless and showed signs of looking for another job, Lara finally snapped out of her comatose state. Financially, she was still trying to recover from that episode.

"Vik, don't worry. I'm fine. It was all business. He was the lead FBI agent conducting surveillance on Sully. I had to talk to him to make progress on our case."

"Okay, if you say so…" Vik was clearly not convinced. "So, what did he tell you?"

"Well, the FBI initially thought Sully was KillerBot, which is why they bugged his townhouse from top to bottom. The biggest news is that the FBI instigated the drone show as part of a sting operation."

His eyes widened. "Really? Very interesting…" he said, rubbing his chin. "That seems to match up rather well with what I've discovered in my own research."

"Oh, what did you find?" Lara asked, taking a large bite of the bean soup.

Vik moved his fingers quickly across the screen of his tablet. "KillerBot interacted with a number of people disguised by pseudonyms on the TechNow message board on the Dark Web. He put out several feelers to acquire drones capable of carrying several pounds each. Based on what you've told me, I'm now thinking Droneman was the FBI working undercover."

Lara nodded.

Vik smirked. "That was actually pretty obvious. There are two other pseudonyms, RoboTech and CyberShop, that I have not identified," Vik said.

"Rob told me—"

"I thought it was *Agent Martin*?" His tone was sassy, and his brown eyes twinkled.

She grimaced, taking another bite of the soup. "He told me the FBI identified Sully as RoboTech. Apparently, Sully was trying to figure out the true identity of Droneman and CyberShop before he died, allegedly working for KillerBot."

Vik's mouth fell open. "Sully was working for KillerBot?" His eyes darted back to his tablet. "And Agent Martin claims he doesn't have a clue about CyberShop's identity?"

Lara nodded.

Vik narrowed his eyes, and his lips formed a firm line as he thought for a moment. "That's interesting," he said. "CyberShop claims to be a professional hacker and supplier of military-grade technology. Based on the communications I've read, he or she collaborated with both Droneman *and* KillerBot. CyberShop offered to sell both of them advanced encryption technology to protect against jamming and spoofing."

"Well, that's an interesting coincidence," Lara said, with her mouth a bit too full. She continued to gulp down her lunch like a ravenous animal.

"What do you mean?" Vik asked.

"The folks at DARPA think the drones must have used encrypted frequencies for data transmission, protecting them against jamming. That means CyberShop might have sold the tech to the FBI to pull off the demonstration."

Did Sully also get the remote from CyberShop?

"And?" Vik asked.

"That means Ro—I mean, Agent Martin wasn't entirely straight with me. If the FBI got the tech from CyberShop for the drone show, they must have some idea about his or her identity. He knows more than he's telling me." A fresh sense of betrayal made her blood boil.

What should I expect from a cheater? He also never mentioned working with Justyne, now that I think about it.

"Don't worry, Lara. We'll find out who is behind this without help from that loser G-Man."

Lara's mouth turned up at the corners. "He actually calls himself Droneman now."

Vik returned an eye roll.

"So, what's your plan?" Lara asked.

Vik straightened his shoulders and met Lara's eye. "I'm going to find out the true identities of CyberShop and KillerBot," he said as his chest puffed out.

"But how? You're not going to start hacking computers again, are you?" Lara asked, worried about him getting into trouble.

Vik shook his head. "Even people on the Dark Web need to use the surface Internet on occasion. They don't realize it, but they leave behind digital breadcrumbs that can help shed light on their true identities. For example, if they use Bitcoin for their transactions, they still have to convert cash into Bitcoin and vice versa at some point."

"Why would using digital currency help you track them?" Lara asked, furrowing her brow.

"Many people don't realize that Bitcoin is not completely anonymous and fail to take appropriate steps to hide their personal identity."

"So, you can track them?" Lara asked.

Vik nodded. "At some point, you need to show an ID to purchase Bitcoin from a reputable source, unless you want to take your chances with a private seller or rely on a lesser-known cryptocurrency. All transactions are stored in a public record called a blockchain and can be viewed by anyone. In other words, to maintain your anonymity across these transactions, it's critical to separate your personal identity from your digital wallet by using disposable email addresses and using a new one for each payment. It's also a good idea to use a digital coin mixer."

"Coin mixer?"

Vik grinned. "Coin mixing is a bit like money laundering in the physical world. Before actual money is transferred to your digital wallet and into your bank account, the amount of Bitcoin is mixed with a larger amount of coins first before moving to its final destination, to disguise the actual source of the transaction."

Lara frowned.

Vik smiled. "Don't worry. Money always leaves a trail. If we follow the money, we'll find them."

"Oh, I almost forgot," Lara said, placing Sully's cellphone on the counter. "I would have given this to you sooner, but you've been hard to track down lately."

Vik picked up the burner phone and turned it over in his hands. "Is this what I think it is? Where did you get it?"

"I found it in a lockbox at DARPA using the key from Sully's filing cabinet. He must have left it behind for a reason. I need to see what's on the phone. It could have clues pertaining to our case."

"Sure, boss. I'll get right on it." His long, skinny arms dropped to his sides. "Is there something else?"

Lara put her spoon on the counter and gave Vik a serious look. "Uh… yeah, there's something I need to talk to you about."

Vik stared at his feet. "I'm sorry I haven't been around lately. I don't want you to think I haven't been putting in the hours. I'm in the middle of midterms at school and have been swamped. And my aunt and uncle want to bring my fiancé over from India for a visit. They keep asking me when I'm going to be done with school and get a real job. I need to start getting my ducks in a row."

"Vik, I'm not concerned about your hours." Lara hesitated, pressing her lips together. It was best to cut to the chase. "Did you take the remote from the crime scene?" There. She'd asked him. However, as soon as she uttered the words, a wave of guilt followed. A long moment passed where neither said a word.

How could I distrust Vik of all people?

Lara opened her mouth to apologize.

"Yes," Vik said, not looking at her.

"What?" Lara shrieked. Her head spun. "Do you realize D.C. police will press charges against you if they find out? They could press charges against me too! How could you do that? How could you be so careless?"

Vik pressed his palms to his cheeks. "Oh Lara, I didn't mean any harm! I wanted to take it apart, study the code, and see if I could find something that would lead us to Sully's killer. And you did tell me to keep an eye on it. I was afraid the police would leave it untouched, hidden away in an evidence locker, and we would miss any evidence it could provide."

"When I said keep an eye on it, I didn't mean for you to remove it from a crime scene." Lara clenched her jaw and glared at Vik. She knew he meant well, but this would put her in more hot water with Sanchez—that is, if he found out. She wasn't about to tell the detective. At least not now.

"I'm so sorry. Lara, I didn't mean for..." Vik's eyes glistened. He smacked himself in the forehead. "By our actions, we create our destiny."

"What?" Lara asked, confused.

"For every action, there is a consequence. Hindus believe in karma, the law of cause and effect. In the end, we are defined by our thoughts, words, and deeds. I will accept whatever comes my way. No regrets."

"Vik, it's okay. I know why you did it." Her expression softened. "But from here on out, we need to be straight with one another. It's just you and me against the world, right?"

Vik nodded.

"So that's where you've been hiding the past few days? Taking the remote apart?"

Vik nodded again and his shoulders slumped. "But I was also

telling the truth about midterms and my family. It has been a most hectic week."

"And have you found anything interesting?" Lara asked.

"No, not yet."

Lara rubbed her forehead. "If you actually get a lead from that remote, I'm going to have to figure out how to share it with the police without getting us both locked up."

Vik gave her a slight smile and returned to his computer. "Like I said, karma…"

Lara began sorting through the pile of mail. Thankfully, there were no additional past-due notices or bills. But she did find something strange.

Tucked inside her new issue of *Scientific American*, she discovered a large manila envelope addressed by hand to Kingsley Investigations. No return address or postmark.

Someone must have delivered this in person.

Lara ripped open the envelope and slid out several large photographs. Her heart raced as she flipped through them, one by one. Several photos of her in Sully's safe room the night she found the beetle. Photos of her meeting with Rob less than an hour ago.

How the hell? Shoving the pictures back into the envelope, Lara's eyes darted anxiously around the office. *Is there a camera in here as well?*

"Are you okay?" Vik asked, noticing her sudden movements.

"I'm fine… uh, I'm just going to get some fresh air. Be right back."

Lara closed the office door behind her and sprinted out the front of the townhouse, down the steps, and onto the sidewalk. Her chest tightened. Gasping for air, she bent over, put her hands on her knees, and tried to calm herself by breathing deeply.

Her smartphone buzzed. A text from an unknown caller popped up on the screen:

MEET ME AT THE NATIONAL CRYPTOLOGIC MUSEUM

NOW

Her heart pounding in her ears, she scanned the neighborhood, searching each car. There were no signs to garner suspicion, nothing out of place. But, somehow, she was being watched. A helpless feeling overwhelmed her for just a moment, but then her determination and instincts kicked in. Someone might be one step ahead for now, but there was no way in hell she was going to let it stay that way.

ELEVEN

The Museum

COLORFUL FALL LEAVES stood out against a clear blue sky. The afternoon sun gently illuminated the world in natural light. Despite the bright weather, a dark cloud loomed above Lara as she rode out to Fort Meade.

Instead of basking in a blissful ride on her bike, tension riddled Lara's entire body. On top of Sully's murder and dealing with Rob, her head swam with the fact that someone was stalking her. And underlying all of that, she now felt a pang of guilt for not telling Vik where she was going.

He would likely give her another earful when she returned—especially after her little speech about being honest with one another. But she couldn't risk putting him in danger. At least she had the good sense to call Justyne, who agreed to meet her there. There was a good chance this stalker was Sully's killer.

There's safety in numbers, right?

Revving her engine for the last time, Lara pulled her Harley into the nearly empty parking lot of the National Cryptologic Museum. Only a few cars were parked near the museum entrance. Did one of them belong to her stalker? Lara scanned the entire area.

Where's Justyne? She said she'd wait in the parking lot.

Lara decided to check for her inside and give the place a quick onceover.

The museum was nestled in a far corner of Fort Meade, near the overflow parking for the NSA. In the near distance, barbed-wire fences cut through the landscape. Shrouded in secrecy and designed like a fortress, the NSA was guarded by armed federal agents and dogs. A fleet of visible, in-your-face cameras monitored every inch of the grounds.

This fortress had two critical missions: protect the nation's secrets from potential adversaries and listen in on the communications of terrorists and foreign nations. And unless you were a VIP with the appropriate level of clearance, there was no such thing as a behind-the-scenes tour of the NSA.

The National Cryptologic Museum held the honor of being the first public museum associated with the intelligence community. Inside, the general public could learn about the fundamentals of signals intelligence and America's cryptologic history.

Lara walked up to the entrance, noticing a placard. It described the nature of the exhibits, which among other things contained old equipment used to encrypt, decrypt, and secure information. Words like "uncleared facility" and "no classified talk" stuck out in bold on a large sign positioned above the placard to remind NSA employees and visitors that the museum was not the place for sensitive conversations.

Lara stepped inside the building. Minimal lighting provided a dark and mysterious atmosphere, with spotlights focused on the individual exhibits. At the front desk, the museum docent, a white-haired woman in her sixties, introduced herself to Lara and offered to show her around. Lara politely declined and made her way into the exhibition space where a few people milled about.

Justyne was not there yet. Lara studied the few museum visitors carefully, trying to determine if one might be the author of the cryptic note.

A young man with brown hair and glasses, dressed in a business suit, stood near the secure phones exhibit. He carried a slim briefcase and looked like he might be waiting for a job interview. Perhaps he'd arrived too early and decided to stop at the museum to kill time. Lara walked by him, but he didn't even notice.

He's not the one.

In the corner, a young couple, dressed in souvenir T-shirts depicting the Washington Monument, stood in front of the signals intelligence (SIGINT) exhibit and posed for a selfie.

Definitely tourists.

Walking around to the next exhibit, Lara stopped cold when she saw an older man lingering in the darkest corner of the cyber exhibit. On the wall in front of him hung a descriptive plaque about the Dark Web. With his back to her, the gray-haired man slouched his shoulders, fidgeted with the sleeve of his tattered corduroy jacket, and glanced at his watch.

Maybe that's him?

Her pulse picking up speed, Lara approached the man with caution. When she was within five feet of him, the man turned to face her.

He gave Lara a warm smile. "Ma'am, can I help you with something?"

Her eyes darted to the name tag on his blazer, which identified him as a museum docent. She exhaled. "No, but thank you."

She weaved a path around the docent and finished searching the rest of the museum. It was empty. The stalker was a no-show.

For the next ten minutes, Lara sat on a bench in-between exhibits. She tapped her foot on the matte-black floor and glanced at her watch. It had been several hours since the delivery of the manila envelope and over an hour since she'd received the text. Perhaps she had arrived too late and missed the window for the meet-up. Either way, it looked more and more like a fool's errand.

She decided to wait a few more minutes before giving up. At

least she and Justyne could exchange any new information on the case.

As she let her eyes wander, the cipher device display caught her attention. Walking toward the exhibit, she remembered learning in school about the German Enigma machine captured during WWII. The Americans and the Brits had cracked the Nazi code with the U.S. Navy's Cryptanalytic Bombe, decrypting thousands of internal messages between German leadership and military forces. This breakthrough led to many Allied successes in WWII and ultimately to their victory over the Third Reich.

A figure appeared in the display's reflection. Trying to appear subtle, she turned her head slightly to get a glimpse. A tall, dark-haired woman wearing a black trench coat, sunglasses, and high heels passed by the docent's counter.

Lara stood and turned, offering a little wave. Justyne returned the wave, walked over, and smiled warmly.

"You made it," Lara said, reaching to shake Justyne's hand. "It's good to see you again. Thanks for having my back. Doing this alone didn't seem wise."

"No trouble at all. I had plans to meet up with a friend at the NSA anyway. It's easier to pop over here instead. We'll just meet up here when she gets off work. I can avoid the hassle of going through security, and I don't have to give up my cellphone. It's so much easier to coordinate things on the outside."

Lara nodded. She'd been at the NSA once before and remembered to leave her cellphone in the car, but had forgotten about the small USB drive stowed in the pocket of her bag. The security guard confiscated it and gave her a onceover for having the *audacity* to bring such a thing anywhere near the building. The NSA lived under the constant threat of leaks by malicious insiders, and USBs were ideal for stealing classified information or installing intrusion malware.

"So, has our suspect shown up?" Justyne surveyed the museum as she pulled Lara aside into a dimly lit hall. Her grip was a bit too tight.

"Not yet," Lara said, rubbing her arm.

"Anything new on the case?" Justyne asked.

"Should we talk about the case somewhere more private?" Lara asked.

Justyne grabbed Lara's arm again, this time pulling her even closer. "No one else is here, Lara… besides, we're not going to talk about classified details." Despite her vice-like grip, her voice remained gentle and reassuring.

"Uh…" Lara's senses were overwhelmed by Justyne's perfume, the same tropical flower aroma she had picked up at DARPA. After years in the military, she didn't care for small spaces any more than she liked beetles. And with a nose like a bloodhound, she detested most artificial fragrances.

Justyne smiled. "Okay, I'll go first. I learned from the FBI that the drone show you witnessed was actually a sting operation to draw out someone who calls himself CyberShop on the Dark Web."

Lara nodded. "Actually, I heard the same thing." She studied Justyne's fixed facial expression. Justyne smiled, but her skin remained unbelievably smooth. Not a single wrinkle.

Some people have all the luck.

"Well, did you know KillerBot paid the FBI one hundred K as a deposit toward the purchase of drones? He was going to pay them twice that much on delivery." Justyne raised her eyebrows and tilted her head.

Lara gritted her teeth. *Rob, what else did you hide?* "No, I didn't. That's a shit ton of money for drones."

"Especially since KillerBot ended up reneging on the drone purchase," Justyne added. "I hear the FBI pocketed the deposit for their slush fund."

"What?" Lara's jaw dropped.

Why would KillerBot pay the deposit, order up the drone show, and then cancel the sale?

Justyne crossed her arms and leaned closer. "It gets even weirder than that. Apparently, CyberShop provided encryption technology to the FBI to support the operation."

Lara took a step back. "What?" She hadn't expected to be

right about her suspicion that the FBI accepted assistance from a spy. *What is Rob playing at?* This didn't sound like standard protocol for the FBI. None of it did. "Are you sure?"

Justyne nodded. "We've honed in on my colleague Stepanov as the key suspect for CyberShop. It makes the most sense to us. His home agency is NSA, and now he's on detail to DARPA. He's perfectly positioned to leak both encryption technology and the advanced drone modifications he knows so much about."

Lara rubbed her chin. "Huh, that's interesting. What would be his motivation?"

"Money… what else?" Justyne tossed her long, black hair behind her shoulder. "So?" She looked at Lara expectantly.

"You seem to know a lot more than I do at this point. I met with Special Agent Martin earlier today, and he said nothing about collaborating with you. In fact, he didn't even mention the money from KillerBot. You think he might be involved somehow?"

Justyne frowned. "I hadn't thought about that. Is it possible his higher-ups don't know about his activities as Droneman? That's strange he didn't mention me, though. I talked about you with him."

Lara furrowed her brow. *He's never honest with me, but I keep believing him. Fool me once.* "One thing I did learn today: the FBI originally thought Sully was KillerBot."

A confused look fell across Justyne's face. "Why would they think that?"

Lara shrugged. "No idea. I guess they thought Sully was using two different pseudonyms on the Dark Web."

"Huh. Strange." Justyne bit her lower lip for a moment before looking at her watch. "Ugh, I didn't realize the time." Her smile returned. "My friend is expecting me out by the NSA employee parking lot, which is a bit of a walk from here. Do you think you'll be okay? It doesn't look like this guy is going to show."

"Yeah," Lara said. "I think you're right. He's not coming."

"It was a good idea to call me. Let me know if your stalker

ever shows up. I'll be in touch." Justyne waved to her and turned the corner into the main room of the museum, disappearing from sight.

Lara let out a deep breath and stepped into the open. She rotated her shoulders back and forth and stretched her arms as if she'd just spent a week packed into a tight cylinder. She appreciated the intel from Justyne, but why did the woman insist on invading her personal space?

Lara scanned the various exhibits; the other patrons had all left the museum. Still no sign of her stalker. She glanced at her watch. It was past time to get back to the office and fill Vik in on what happened.

When she exited the building, the museum parking lot was empty except for her motorcycle and a black BMW convertible. As she approached her bike, something white peeked out from underneath her handlebar, almost out of sight. Another scroll waited for her there, like the one attached to the beetle, except bigger. Her hands shook as she pulled it off the handlebar. She rolled it open and read the tiny print:

IF YOU WANT TO MEET ME, YOU'LL HAVE TO LEARN TO FOLLOW
INSTRUCTIONS
NEXT TIME, COME ALONE

That's it? Looking up at the sky for a surveillance drone, she shook her fist and shouted: "Really? That's all you've got? Maybe next time be more specific. Put times, dates, and important instructions. You never said come alone! You're the world's worst stalker!"

Her impulse to shout fulfilled, she grimaced and glanced around her, thankful to find no one watching. Lara searched for any indicators as to who had placed the note on her bike. Cameras were posted all over Fort Meade, but there was no way she could go up and ask the security guards to pull footage.

Another dead end.

Frustrated, Lara put her helmet on and mounted her bike. When she turned the ignition, nothing happened. She tried again, but the engine wouldn't start. Dismounting the bike, she examined the engine. Everything looked intact—except for the cut fuel line. Lara kicked the curb. She pulled her helmet off and almost pitched it across the parking lot, but took several deep breaths instead. Her stalker had stranded her.

But why? Why sabotage my bike?

She considered her options for getting back to D.C. Since Vik insisted on taking public transportation like it was his patriotic duty, he didn't own a car. Justyne could still be in the area, but Lara didn't want to interrupt her meeting. Only one option remained: driverless cab. She chewed her lip as she looked at the GoGoCab app.

You're a big girl, Lara. Push the button.

Before she could, the screen changed to an incoming call. "This is Lara."

"Ms. Kingsley, Detective Sanchez here. I need you to come down to the station. The medical examiner finished the autopsy, and she wants to talk to you."

Lara put her hand on her forehead. "Uh… I'm actually out at Fort Meade."

"How soon can you get here?"

"You see, that's the problem… someone cut the fuel line on my motorcycle. So, it might be a while."

After a momentary pause, Lara checked her screen to see if she lost the call. She hadn't. "Helloooo?" Lara asked.

"I'm here," Sanchez said. "Let me come get you."

"You'd do that?" Lara asked.

"Sure. Consider it an apology for trying to arrest you again."

A little smile crossed her lips. "That'd be really nice. Thank you."

"I'll bring an evidence kit with me. We'll brush down your bike for prints and find the perp that did this."

"You don't have to go to all that trouble."

"It's no trouble."

After saying thank you again, Lara hung up the phone, opened the seat compartment and removed her worn-out leather baseball glove.

No way I'm leaving this behind.

* * *

DETECTIVE SANCHEZ DUSTED her bike for prints, collected some skin cells from the fuel line, and put the scroll in an evidence bag for forensics testing. "That should do it. If the perp has a record in one of our databases, we'll nail them for this and maybe more…" As they headed toward the patrol car, Sanchez turned to her. "You'll ride in the back, okay?"

Lara's mouth fell open. "What? You offer to pick me up and now you want me to sit in the back like some common criminal?" She glanced at the mesh screen made of steel, aluminum, and plexiglass separating the front seats from the back and pulled up her nose. She didn't want to think about what kind of body fluids had covered the rear seat at one time or another. Lara shook her head. "Oh no. I'm not sitting back there. Not unless you're arresting me for something."

"Don't tempt me." Sanchez crossed his arms and glared at her over the roof of his cruiser for a few seconds, as if he were trying to find an excuse. "I don't want you messing with my stuff in the front."

Lara rolled her eyes and reached for the handle of the front door. "I won't touch your stuff. I promise."

Sanchez grunted and frowned at her.

Lara tried to open the front door, but it was still locked. She motioned for him to unlock it, and he sighed heavily. When she heard the click, she opened the door and climbed inside before he could change his mind. Sanchez slammed his door shut, grunted again, and started the engine.

On the way back to D.C., they hit major traffic, barely inching forward on the George Washington Parkway for more than twenty minutes with an awkward silence between them.

Although Lara had won the argument, the radio equipment and computer terminal in the front of the vehicle now crowded her. She stared sullenly out of the passenger-side window of the patrol car, hoping desperately traffic would clear up soon.

"Uh, did your guys find anything interesting when you searched Sully's townhouse?" Lara asked, attempting to build a bridge.

Sanchez kept his eyes glued to the road. "Not really. We found some latent prints inside the safe room, but there were no matches in the fingerprints database. We have excluded you as a match, so we know more than one person had access to the room besides Sully."

Lara frowned. "Did you find anything on Sully's computer or in his video archives?"

"The high-tech crime unit analyzed the contents of Sully's electronics. The computer was wiped clean, even the Internet browser history. And someone tampered with the video footage, erasing everything five days prior to Sully's death."

"Why only five days? Why not destroy all the video files?"

Sanchez shrugged.

"What do you think of Stepanov as a potential suspect?" Lara asked cautiously.

Sanchez sneered. "We're playing detective now, are we? Think you're so smart, you can do my job, too?"

Lara grimaced. "I'm playing investigator, which is my job. I'm just trying to help. I'm merely asking what you think about the idea."

"Well, it's a fucking stupid idea."

She had planned to fill in the detective on her meetings with Rob and Justyne. But if that's how he wanted to play, she was happy to play his game.

Lara clenched her jaw. "Well, okay then, who's on your list?"

"Until you're off the fucking list, I'm not telling you shit."

"You still think I had something to do with Sully's murder? I thought we were working together."

Sanchez said nothing. He just stared out the window.

Lara adjusted her body away from him as best as she could in the claustrophobic seat and stared out her window. *Let me come get you. It's no trouble. I'd love to treat you like an idiot.* She turned, ready to fire another shot, and then shifted back, folding her arms tight across her chest. *He's not worth it.*

TWELVE

The Autopsy

A PUTRID ODOR rushed toward Lara as she walked into the autopsy room, assaulting all her senses. Her stomach churned violently in anticipation of the onslaught. She gagged, and the taste of bile made it worse.

Don't throw up in front of the detective.

Lara barely tolerated the smell of decomposing flesh mixed with formaldehyde. Still, she couldn't decide what was worse—an hour in the car alone with the detective or a visit to the morgue. She'd never been to an autopsy before.

The brightly lit room was furnished with white tile floors and smooth white walls. The temperature ran uncomfortably cold in order to keep bodies from decaying too quickly. Three stainless steel operating tables were placed down the center. Sully's stiff and naked body lay on the middle table, the lower half of his body draped with a sheet. The customary identification tag hung from the big toe on his right foot.

Though his lifeless body was before her, Lara couldn't shake the feeling that she could go to Wicked Bloom tonight, and Sully would be waiting with a drink in his hand, an enormous smile on his face, and a friendly ear to listen to her terrible day. But that would never happen again. Lara swallowed hard, suppressing her emotions.

I'm sorry, Sully.

Dr. Caroline Stevens, the medical examiner for the D.C. Metropolitan Police, hunched over Sully's body. She wore blue scrubs with her brown hair tied up in a bun and a face mask. On the cart beside her lay some instruments Lara had seen before—a saw for ripping bones and scalpels for cutting cold flesh. At the head of the table, there was a long, stainless steel sink for washing and rinsing body parts. Above the sink, a scale hung from the ceiling for weighing them. On the counter next to the sink stood several jars filled with organs.

Lara shuddered at the sight of it all, focused on taking short breaths to minimize the smell, and pulled her leather jacket tighter around herself. Sully's waxy, gray-blue-tinged brown skin made him look like a character from a bad zombie movie.

Sully's corpse reminded her of the fragile nature of life and her own mortality, but it also brought up distant and painful memories of her mother, lying lifeless on a stretcher, carted away from the accident that took her away from Lara forever.

Dr. Stevens looked up from the body. "Detective Sanchez, glad you came by. And you must be Ms. Kingsley. Here…" She handed them both face masks. "Helps with the smell."

Lara tried to smile though her nose wrinkled of its own accord. She took the mask and hooked it over her ears.

"Have you determined cause of death?" Sanchez asked as he also put on his face mask.

"Yes, the cause of death is clear… but I'm rather mystified by something else I've found. And that's why I wanted to talk to you, Ms. Kingsley, since you were so helpful with your suggestion to test for toxins."

"What do you think killed him?" Lara asked.

"The cause of death was asphyxiation. Apparently, the killer injected the victim, right here." Dr. Stevens pointed to a small red wound on Sully's right leg.

Lara shot a quick glance and then looked away. Referring to Sully as the victim sounded callous, but she had to remember that the doctor didn't know him. Lara imagined the medical examiner had to keep emotional distance to do her job.

"Thanks to Lara, we know the victim died from a botulinum toxin injection."

"What?" Lara furrowed her eyebrows. The case grew stranger by the second.

First drones, then bionic bugs, and now biological weapons?

"What exactly is botulinum toxin?" Sanchez asked as he shifted his weight and looked from Lara to the doctor and back again.

Dr. Stevens handed a clipboard to the detective. "The top sheet has a full profile. It's one of the most powerful toxins on earth. Less than a microgram is lethal. And it's produced by the bacterium *Clostridium botulinum,* which can be found in the soil or in spoiled food. Don't you remember being warned about bulging cans of preserved food when you were a kid?"

Sanchez's eyes widened. "How does the toxin work? I mean, how does it kill?"

Dr. Stevens nodded. "The toxin blocks healthy nerve function by inhibiting a neurotransmitter and causing paralysis in the body. When the muscles in the chest cease to function, breathing becomes difficult and then stops, leading to respiratory failure and then respiratory arrest."

"That tracks with the symptoms Sully had at the baseball park," Lara said. "Before he died, Sully stumbled up the stairs, rubbed his eyes, and then he vomited. In the hallway, I found him convulsing. He died so suddenly."

"Symptoms of botulism can include blurry or double vision," Dr. Stevens said, nodding. "That's probably why he rubbed his eyes."

"You're certain someone injected him?" Sanchez asked.

"Yes, we found the toxin in his bloodstream, which suggests injection rather than ingestion. There was also the injection site, and we didn't find any evidence of the bacteria in his stomach or digestive tract."

"How would someone get a hold of botulinum toxin?" Lara asked.

"Well, as I mentioned, the bacteria that produce the toxin are quite common. However, it would take some skill to isolate a virulent strain from the soil or from spoiled food and then grow it in a makeshift lab, but it's definitely possible for someone to do that at a low cost, even in their basement. A more sophisticated perpetrator might decide to produce synthetic bacteria."

"Synthetic?" Sanchez crossed his arms.

"Man-made. If we know the genome of a living organism, a scientist can reproduce it synthetically in a lab environment. This is, of course, no easy task and would require a great deal of scientific expertise. In my research, however, I found there is an easier route for gaining access to botulinum toxin."

"And what's that?" Sanchez uncrossed his arms and leaned toward the doctor a little.

"It's available on the commercial market as a cosmetic product called Botox. Injections of botulinum toxin are the most common non-surgical cosmetic procedure in this country. The toxin is used to paralyze muscles of the face where wrinkles can form. Any dermatologist office or cosmetic surgeon that performs Botox treatments would have a supply of the toxin on hand."

Lara stopped herself from telling the doctor to lead with that sort of information first. *They do love to show how much they know.*

"That's crazy shit," Detective Sanchez said, rubbing his forehead. "What some people do for beauty."

"So, if he died of botulinum toxin, when do you think his killer injected him?" Lara asked.

Dr. Stevens rubbed her forehead with her arm. "The average incubation period for the toxin is anywhere from twelve to seventy-two hours. He could have been injected on the day he died or up to three days prior."

"That means in order to isolate suspects, we need to trace back his contacts for the last three days of his life." Sanchez looked up at the ceiling for a moment, as if thinking of how they would accomplish the task.

Dr. Stevens nodded.

"If only Sully could tell us…" Sanchez grumbled.

If only I had Sully's journals.

"You mentioned when we first arrived that you were mystified by something you found," Lara said. "What was it?"

Dr. Stevens pulled back the sheet to expose Sully's upper legs. "I found an unusual rash on his skin."

So that's why Sully was scratching himself at the bar.

The red and black patchy rash was unlike anything Lara had seen before. Each of the red bumps had a small white dot in the center, reminiscent of an insect bite.

"I also found some unusual bleeding in the skin and organs." Dr. Stevens pointed to Sully's hand. "Underneath his nails, his fingers are a purple color."

Lara remembered seeing something strange about his nails. "What does that mean?"

"It means your friend likely came down with a form of the plague, which is caused by *Yersinia pestis*, a different type of bacteria."

"What?" Lara asked.

"And what's the incubation period for the plague?" Sanchez asked.

"About one to six days," Dr. Stevens said.

"So, the victim was likely infected with the disease before he was injected with the toxin," the detective said. He nodded once and folded his hands in front of him, puffing out his chest as a smile spread.

Dr. Stevens nodded. "The symptoms I found are consistent with septicemic plague, which is a life-threatening infection of the blood, most commonly spread by bites from infected fleas. In his case, however, the plague did not cause the victim's death.

But it might have done so if the toxin hadn't finished the job first."

"I didn't think the plague could be spread by fleas anymore," Lara said. "I personally know the scientist who led a team in editing the DNA of fleas. Maggie—that's my friend—said they used a gene drive to transmit the new genetic sequence through the reproductive process, making it impossible for fleas to carry the disease. Then, they released large batches of the new fleas into the environment around the country. The genetically altered fleas mated with wild fleas, and the new traits passed to succeeding generations."

The detective shot her a you-think-you-know-everything look. Lara didn't understand why it had to be a competition between them.

Dr. Stevens nodded. "I know of that project. I found it fascinating. As for this victim, I don't really know how he picked it up. Another mystery to be solved, I suppose."

Did one of those beetles bite Sully?

Lara remembered what Rob's team found in Sully's trash. "Actually, I think Sully was taking some antibiotics, so he must have known he was sick."

Sanchez eyed her suspiciously. "Do you know who prescribed the medication?"

"No, my friend at the FBI found it in Sully's trash and couldn't remember the doctor's name," Lara said. "I need to follow up with him. That could lead us to some answers."

As soon as she mentioned the FBI, she knew she'd said something wrong. The look on the detective's face shifted instantly from wary to enraged. His nostrils flared, and he clenched his hands. Without warning, he turned on his heel and marched toward the door.

"Detective! Stop and let me explain!" she called after him.

He ignored her, walked out of the room, and slammed the door behind him.

Startled, Dr. Stevens took a few steps backward and tilted her head at Lara.

"Don't worry. It's me, not you," Lara said, trying to reassure her as she rushed from the room. She should've told Sanchez about her recent conversation with Rob. In her defense, she'd been kind of busy. Somehow, she didn't think this would appease the detective, especially after their hour-long road trip.

Crap.

THIRTEEN

Jail Time

LARA WEAVED her way through the crowded patrol suite of the First District Metropolitan Police station toward the squad room. The faint stench of sweaty socks hung in the air. Patrol officers rushed about to prepare for the shift change and hit their beat. Others departed the station in plain clothes, carrying gym bags, heading home for the evening.

A line of D.C. residents waited at the service counter to apply for parking permits or to file complaints about their neighbors. A young boy with a tear-stained face grasped a broken toy drone under his arm and stood next to his stern father.

Lara flashed her ID to the officer at the desk. He nodded and waved her by as if he knew who she was. With knots in her stomach, she walked down the long hallway past several interview rooms. She cringed as she passed the holding cells. She'd been stuck in there once or twice, and the memories weren't fond ones. She'd been working a case for the FBI and found herself in the detective's crosshairs. Sitting and doing nothing while leads ran cold had been pure torture for Lara.

At the end of the hallway, she entered the squad room filled with about ten cubicles. The detective's office was located on the far end with the door cracked open. The blinds on the panel window were tightly shut, and she couldn't see inside. A one-sided conversation clued her in to the fact that Sanchez was on the phone, so she knocked lightly and peeked inside. When he motioned for her to come in, Lara's spirits lifted. Maybe she misread the source of his anger in the autopsy room.

She opened the door and froze in place. Commander Kenneth Jamison, Chief of the First District police station and Detective Sanchez's boss, sat quietly in the corner of the office. Lara jumped a little at the unexpected sight; her throat suddenly felt dry. As Lara and the chief locked eyes, she took a step back. His unrelenting, steely glare coupled with his deep, serious frown gave Lara a shiver down her spine.

Jamison was a well-built black man in his fifties, dressed in a decorated uniform that befitted his many years of service and stature within the D.C. police department. That alone was intimidating, not to mention the actual power he could wield.

Swallowing hard, Lara took the seat next to the Commander and waited for Sanchez to get off the phone.

Now I've done it.

She wiped her clammy hands dry on her pants. This time, she was on her own. There'd be no FBI agents coming to her aid.

Maybe he's gotten over what happened last year?

Commander Jamison leaned closer and whispered, "Lara Kingsley, you don't know how happy I am that you're here. How long has it been? A year now?"

Dammit.

He made a face as if trying to remember. He kept his voice low so Sanchez wouldn't be able to hear. "Yes, it was a year ago, because I was up for promotion, and your little stunt took all that away." His eyes narrowed.

It hadn't been a stunt. A year ago, Lara was assisting the FBI with a money laundering case. Her special agent then-boyfriend had connected her to several of his colleagues who hired her to set up electronic surveillance on a confidential informant, with the informant's permission of course. By recording all communications between the informant and his organized crime network, the FBI hoped to incriminate a bigger fish—a local kingpin known for laundering money for corrupt politicians.

While meeting with the informant, a thug confessed to the murder of a local girl—a case Sanchez was investigating. Somehow the D.C. police got wind of the recording and learned the name of the PI behind the surveillance operation.

Commander Jamison tried to pressure Lara into giving up the tapes by throwing her in jail for a night and threatening her with a long list of charges. Thankfully, Rob came to the rescue and bailed her out.

The FBI refused to turn over the recordings to protect their informant. When the FBI Director himself complained about the interference to the D.C. Police Commissioner, Commander Jamison was suspended for his bullying tactics and skipped over for a promotion.

The Commander had made his own bed. He should've known better. The last time she'd seen him, he'd uttered under his breath that he'd make her pay.

Lara glanced back at Detective Sanchez. A few veins were visible, popping blue against his tan complexion. His emotions must have escalated after leaving the autopsy room. Perhaps the detective had gotten a severe lecture from his boss for trusting her.

Sanchez hung up the phone. His eyes were cold and hard as he spoke, his voice laced with spite. "Commander, you remember Ms. Kingsley?"

"Indeed, I do," the Commander said, his upper lip curling up into a snarl. "We were just catching up. So, what has she done this time?"

"Well, we caught her snooping around on the Sullivan case. Against your advice, I made a deal with her not to press charges in exchange for her help. And until recently, she was assisting me on the case."

"Until recently?" Lara said, interrupting him.

"The Commander and I have decided to take you off the case since you no longer offer any value to the D.C. police—"

Commander Jamison cleared his throat, interrupting the detective. "Moreover, we've decided to convince the district attorney to file charges against you for tampering with evidence and interfering with a police investigation."

"Charges? Tampering with what evidence?" Lara asked, staring wide-eyed at the detective.

Sanchez crossed his arms angrily. "You removed the remote control from the scene of the crime and are now in possession of it."

Commander Jamison nodded in agreement.

"I don't know where it is. I swear." Lara preferred not to lie, but she didn't want to get Vik in trouble. With Commander Jamison breathing down her neck, out for blood, this wasn't the right time to tell Sanchez about the remote. Plus, she wanted to give Vik more time to extract clues from the device.

Commander Jamison glowered at her. "Ms. Kingsley, we've reviewed our chain of custody, and there is no other logical explanation for its disappearance. You and your assistant were the last people to come into contact with the remote. I watched you show the detective the photos you took."

So, he was watching from the other room as I suspected.

"Well, sorry to call your chain of custody into question, but I don't have it." Lara shifted around in her seat. That part was true. She didn't have the remote.

"I don't buy it." The detective pointed at her. "You've been interfering with this case from the beginning. You say you're helping, but then you withhold critical information from me. And it makes me wonder if you killed Sully and are trying to cover it up by sticking your nose where it doesn't belong. You were at the ballpark the night of Sully's death. Coincidence?" The detective shook his head. "I think not."

He rose from his seat and paced. "And then somehow you notice him using a remote in a massive crowd of people. Then he leaves the stands, you follow him, and he dies in the hallway. You tell the medical examiner to look for toxins. And the remote mysteriously disappears. There's a shit ton of evidence against you… and I think the remote is the smoking gun."

"Circumstantial!" Lara threw up her hands in exasperation. "If as you say, the remote *is* the smoking gun, why would I implicate myself by showing you pictures of it? You wouldn't have even known of its existence if it weren't for me. Do you really think I'm that stupid?"

Sanchez rubbed his temples. "You burned us once with the FBI, and now you're going behind my back with them. I've had enough."

"Is that what this is really about? My conversation with the FBI? I assure you I only acted in the interest of this case and the D.C. police department. And I've been upfront with you about the FBI's involvement. The agent in question is my ex-boyfriend. He was the lead agent who bugged Sully's house."

She continued. "And I'd like to note for the record that I leveraged that information on behalf of the D.C. police to gain critical intelligence related to our case. I was going to share that information with you immediately, but I got a bit preoccupied when a suspected killer began stalking me, writing me notes transmitted via flying beetles, sending me on a wild goose chase out to Fort Meade, and sabotaging my motorcycle.

"You say you're cooperating with me, but then in the car, you tell me I'm on the top of your suspects list. What's the point of sharing what I know if it only makes you more suspicious?" Lara paused to catch her breath. "I'm sorry if it looked like I went behind your back to involve the FBI. I assure you, I did not. If you want to throw me off the case, go ahead. But I think you need me more than I need you, so you might want to keep that in mind. Your ego isn't worth losing this one."

"Ms. Kingsley, we're not interested in your apology or your services anymore." The Commander waved off Lara's explanation. "Bring us the remote, and we'll drop the charges. Otherwise, you're going to spend another night in jail. This time without your knight in shining armor coming to your rescue."

When the Commander wasn't looking, Sanchez squirmed in

his chair. Lara thought she detected an apologetic glint in the detective's eyes. As soon as their eyes locked, it disappeared.

Commander Jamison wants his revenge. It's the only explanation for this.

"Detective, you gave me your word." Lara shot him a what-the-hell look.

Sanchez avoided eye contact and said nothing.

They apply the law whenever it's convenient for them.

She'd learned the hard way that this is how things worked in the real world. Her second tour in the military had shattered Lara's rose-colored glasses about government and the law.

"Clearly, you've been planning this little ambush all along," Lara snapped as her whole body tensed. Her blood simmered, her cheeks growing hot. She pointed a finger at Jamison. "You've been waiting for the right time to screw me over." Then she turned to Sanchez. "And you pounce as soon as I say something to set off your temper and confirm your suspicions. I'm sorry if you feel I've overstepped my bounds, but pressing charges against me is ridiculous, and it won't get you anywhere."

Commander Jamison scoffed and shook his head. "If anything, the detective has developed a soft spot for you. I saw the two of you pull into the station earlier, sitting next to each other in the front seat like long-time buddies. I warned him about trusting you, but the fool didn't listen to me. Now he knows what's good for him."

"Do you have the fucking remote or not?" Sanchez asked, his face turning a darker shade of red.

Lara shook her head.

The detective stood up and approached her, pulling out handcuffs.

"Detective, don't do this," Lara pleaded, raising her voice and rising from her chair. "I've done nothing but provide you with new leads to advance your case."

The Commander gave an eager nod to Sanchez who grabbed her arms and snapped the handcuffs around her wrists.

Jamison sneered at her, stood up, and grinned as if he'd been dreaming of this for months. "Lara Kingsley, you are under arrest for tampering with evidence and interfering with a police investigation. You have the right to remain silent. Anything you say can and will be used against you in a court of law. You have the right to an attorney. If you cannot afford an attorney, one will be provided for you."

"Boss, I'll take her to lock-up." Sanchez pulled her roughly by the arm into the hallway. The Commander followed them into the hallway, presumably to watch them and savor the moment of her demise.

Lara tried to make eye contact with Sanchez over her shoulder. She wasn't above a little pleading, not this time. "Detective, please don't do this. You're going to make me miss Sully's funeral tomorrow." Sully didn't have any family to speak of, and she desperately wanted to be there for him.

This can't be happening.

"I don't care about the fucking funeral. That's on you. You should have considered the consequences of your actions." The detective yanked her arm, dragging her down the hallway.

"Do I at least get to make a phone call?" Lara asked as they turned the corner, wincing as his fingers dug into her flesh.

FOURTEEN

The Journal

OCTOBER 23, 2027

DESPITE A STEAMY HOT SHOWER, Lara couldn't completely rinse away the stench of jail. Some things required more time to forget. The tantalizing smell of fresh coffee wafted through the floorboards of her apartment, increasing her desperation for her morning caffeine fix.

Wearing a sweatshirt, yoga pants, and her favorite bunny slippers, she shuffled down the wooden stairs from her second-floor apartment to her office, the steps creaking. Once she caught up with Vik, she planned to walk over to Sully's funeral, which would take place a short distance away in Georgetown's Oak Hill Cemetery.

Thank God, I got out in time.

Her back aching, she grasped the railing for extra support. After the detective allowed her to use the phone, she'd spent most of the night in jail on a hard cot. Lara had made her one call to Vik, who apologized profusely for not owning a car during her time of need but promised to do his best to get her out.

She hadn't realized "his best" meant calling the last man on the planet she'd want to see and asking him for help. Being bailed out of jail by her ex-boyfriend only added to her humiliation. At the bottom of the stairs, Lara stopped short. The front door of the townhouse was cracked open.

That's strange.

Her landlord and Vik were pretty good about closing the door to avoid unwanted strangers in the building. The District was home to a large homeless population, and several regulars lived in the Georgetown area on side streets. Lara did what she could to help them out, giving them food and water. She preferred not to give them money, just in case it would go to support some kind of addiction like drugs or a gambling habit. One evening, she came home to a gross-smelling man lurking in the front hallway, pulled her gun, and nearly shot him dead. Ever since, they made sure to keep the door shut at all times.

Lara peeked outside, but there was no one in sight. As she closed the door, the sight of the empty spot where her motorcycle usually parked made her stomach lurch. The drama of the previous day came rushing back.

"Gah…" Lara hit herself in the forehead. Her pulse spiked.

I forgot about my bike. By now, she was certain that NSA security guards would be all over the abandoned motorcycle. *Hopefully, it's still there.*

Lara walked into her office to find Vik hunched over the counter, clutching a cup of coffee. He'd picked up warm croissants from The Grind Coffee Shop, his way of softening her up before he laid on something really serious. Silently, he poured her a cup of coffee and slid the mug and a plate with a chocolate croissant in her direction.

Uh oh.

She grabbed the mug, took a generous bite of the pastry, and washed it down with a gulp of coffee. "Thanks. Jail food is so bland, and I think the coffee is made with recycled grounds." She thought that might bring a smile to his face. *Nope. Nothing.*

Vik looked like he was going to burst. "Lara, I was so worried about you. Yesterday morning I watched you through the window as you completely freaked out and then just sped away on your motorcycle like a crazy woman. You were gone for hours, and I didn't even get one text. And when I did hear from you, you were calling me from jail. Jail!" He threw his hands in the air in a what-the-hell motion.

Lara placed a hand on her chest and squared her shoulders. "I would've texted you or called, but everything happened so fast."

He shook his head with displeasure. "I cannot believe you would put yourself in harm's way when you could have taken me with you. I thought we were a team." Vik stared sulkily down at the floor.

Lara ignored the accusation. Vik tended to forget she'd been deployed to Afghanistan and was trained in hand-to-hand combat. She could manage just fine on her own and didn't like to be coddled. Vik grasped his coffee cup tightly and looked away. He opened his mouth and then closed it again. They stood in tense silence for several minutes.

"Uh… there's something…" He hesitated as he avoided eye contact. He took a deep breath. "There's something else I need to talk to you about."

"I figured as much," Lara said, pointing to the plate with crumbs on it. "What's wrong?"

"Well, for one, there's no money in the Kingsley Investigation expense account. I had no car and no money to get you out. Sully's gone. I couldn't call my uncle without facing a long interrogation, I didn't know who else…"

Lara's face fell. She'd wanted to be straight with Vik about her financial status, but there had never been a good time to tell him she was flat broke.

Vik gave her a miserable look. "That's why I had to call Rob last night… otherwise, I never would…"

"I'm so sorry, Vik. I shouldn't have put you in this situation. I should've told you about my money problems sooner." A rush of guilt washed over her.

Vik frowned. "At least now I know why my paycheck

bounced. I'm not able to pay my rent, and my roommate has asked me to move out by the weekend."

The blood drained from her face. "Oh no, Vik... I never meant—" She thought for a few minutes. "You should definitely move into the office until we can figure something out."

Hopefully, we won't lose this place too.

Vik gave her a half-smile, pointing to his suitcases in the corner. "I didn't really have any other options."

Lara smirked.

Vik wrinkled his forehead. "I don't understand. I thought things were going well for you. We just closed that big case, and the Langstons will be a great job for us."

Lara looked away as Vik tilted his head at her, like he had just solved the world's most difficult riddle. She didn't say a word.

Vik continued. "The baseball game—you said they were going to reschedule."

"I didn't know how to tell you." She looked him in the eyes. "I lied. I'm really sorry. I just didn't want you to worry. That last case paid for all the past due bills stacked up from several months of me wallowing in self-pity. Even if the Langstons had signed the contract, it wouldn't have mattered. Sully's dead, and I need to do this for him."

He frowned. "I liked Sully, but why are you sacrificing your livelihood for the dead? I'm not sure Sully would be happy about this. The police and FBI are both investigating the case. Shouldn't you focus on getting a new client? One that pays?" He took a sip of his coffee and shook his head.

"Vik, Sully floated Kingsley Investigations for several months... if it hadn't been for Sully, you and I would no longer have our jobs. And I still owe him money." She paused. The pain of his absence sliced through her heart. She swallowed hard, holding back the tears. "Owed... he's one of the most loyal friends I've ever had. He's family. I couldn't live with myself if I didn't at least try to find his killer."

Vik nodded. "All right then. I'm in," he said, shoving his

hands into his pockets. A moment of silence passed before he spoke again. "So, are you going to tell me what happened yesterday?"

Lara nodded, relieved at the change of subject. "Yeah, I think I'm being stalked."

"By whom?" Vik's eyes widened.

"I don't know. Maybe Sully's killer? Yesterday, another one of those beetles landed on my shoulder with a small scroll attached to it. It was a note instructing me to go to the National Cryptologic Museum."

Vik furrowed his brow, taking a sip of coffee. "Now that's an interesting place to meet."

"I thought so, too. I decided to ignore the demand. And then I received a second message. This time, the stalker put a manila envelope containing pictures taken of me in Sully's safe room on the night of his murder and several during my meeting with Rob. To get those pictures, the stalker had to have been right by the coffeehouse and printed the photos directly from a car or something. Then he—"

"Or she," Vik added.

"—managed to put the envelope in the mail slot before I even returned home. That's why I panicked."

Vik scratched his forehead. "Wait. You said there were pictures of you in Sully's safe room. Didn't you say the beetle you found there had a camera on its back?"

"I did, but…" Lara gave him a confused look.

"And you took it to your friend, the bug lady. Maybe she printed the photos."

"Come on, that's ridiculous. I'm sure the camera broadcasts the footage wirelessly, and besides, Maggie is my best friend," Lara said.

"So, naturally, you went out to the museum?" Vik shot her a look of disapproval.

Lara took a gulp of her coffee. "Yes, but I called Justyne Marsh from DARPA for backup. Anyway, the stalker was a no-show and when I came out of the museum, I found another note. And someone cut the fuel line on my bike."

"Holy crap, Lara. That's terrifying. Did you tell Detective Sanchez about your stalker?" Vik asked.

Lara shook her head. "He knows someone cut my fuel line, but we didn't really get a chance to delve into that on the car ride. When we got back, the detective was more focused on helping his boss put me in my place. They wanted to know about the missing remote and my knowledge of its whereabouts."

"Oh," Vik said with a slight grimace.

"Yeah, and let's just say they were very displeased." Lara let the matter drop, not wanting Vik to feel any worse about her night in jail. She redirected the conversation. "Did you get any clues from Sully's burner phone?"

Vik nodded and smiled, perking up for the first time that morning. "In my distress, I forgot to tell you the good news."

"Good news? I need some of that right now. Spit it out." Lara finished the last sip of her coffee and set the mug down on the quartz countertop.

"I cracked the password on Sully's cellphone."

Lara's eyes grew large. "And? Did you find anything interesting?"

His face lit up. "Oh yes. The phone contained what appeared to be journal entries."

Vik found Sully's journal.

"That's huge news!" Lara clapped her hands together once. "Tell me everything. Start with the last few entries. I want to know who Sully met during his last three days. Someone injected him with the toxin during that timeframe. If Sully recorded all his interactions, we'll be able to make a list of possible suspects."

"Okay. He wrote the last entry the day before he died."

Lara frowned. She'd hoped to find out what Sully had been doing at DARPA when he hid his phone in the lockbox, presumably on the day he died.

"Did you know Sully had an assistant?" Vik asked.

Lara nodded. "Yeah, he mentioned hiring someone a while back, but he never said anything about him."

"Ashton Grant, a recent graduate of American University, worked for Sully for several months. Sully met with him the day before he died. Two months ago, Sully learned Ashton was trying to get involved with the KillerBot case behind his back. A guy named John Fiddler, aka KillerBot, was paying Sully huge sums of money, and his assistant wanted a bigger piece of the pie."

Lara raised her eyebrow. *Huge sums of money?*

"Anyway, Sully was determined to keep him out of it for the kid's sake. Apparently, Ashton wouldn't listen because he needed the money desperately. So, the kid broke into Sully's safe room and figured out how to get in contact with KillerBot, aka John Fiddler. Sully fired Ashton but remained concerned the kid was still working for Fiddler and had ongoing access to his townhouse and safe room."

"Maybe that's why he emptied the safe room, and why Sully used weird hiding places—the toilet tank, weapons case, and the lockbox. Sully thought the safe room was compromised." She thought for a moment and then added, "But why not just change the code?"

"Sully wrote in several entries that he thought the kid was in over his head and was going to get into serious trouble. I believe he tried to keep an eye on him, maybe even help him. So, instead he just moved everything of importance out of the safe room."

"Did the journal say where?" Lara asked. She recalled the videotape of Sully frantically trying to find a hiding spot for a cardboard box.

I need to find that box.

Vik shook his head.

"We need to find Ashton," Lara said. "He might have information on Sully's last days." She was pretty sure Rob must have known about Sully's assistant from the FBI's surveillance operation.

Another thing he didn't tell me.

Vik scrolled through the journal entries. "Two days before Sully died, he met with Fiddler."

Did Fiddler kill Sully?

Lara crinkled her forehead. "KillerBot hired Sully to do what exactly?"

"Based on what I can infer from the journal entries, Fiddler hired Sully as a private investigator six months ago. He asked Sully to investigate the identities of Droneman and CyberShop for him. Fiddler wanted to buy drone tech and needed to know if they were legit suppliers or not."

"Hmmm… so, Rob posing as Droneman and the NSA spy posing as CyberShop offered to sell him technology. Fiddler must have suspected something."

Vik nodded. "Apparently, Fiddler was extremely paranoid. He thought the FBI was coming after him. He agreed to pay several hundred thousand dollars for the drones and put down a sizeable deposit. Sully claimed Fiddler planned to use the drone show to lure CyberShop out into the open."

Well, Fiddler was right about the FBI.

"Yeah, Justyne mentioned that Fiddler paid a one-hundred-thousand-dollar deposit. Can we track the money?" Lara asked.

"I don't think so, but I'll see what I can find out."

Lara stood up and stretched her neck. "So, walk me through the events leading up to the ballgame." She grabbed her baseball glove and began punching into it while she paced the room. Even though Lara's hands were small, the kid's glove barely fit her anymore. But that didn't matter. It was her lucky charm.

"Okay. Fiddler challenged Droneman and CyberShop to a tech demo at the baseball match. Sully was under the impression that CyberShop supplied Droneman with an encrypted frequency scatter device to make them resistant to jamming and spoofing."

Lara stopped in the middle of the room and rubbed her chin. "Ah, yes. I've learned about that recently. It's a device that enhances signal security. I think they said it changes the encryption key and frequency every five seconds. Something about staying ahead of hackers and signal disruption. Pretty advanced tech."

"CyberShop also sold Fiddler a combination jammer/spoofer. Sully wrote in his notes that CyberShop guaranteed it would work." Vik paused to think. "That must be the remote Sully used to try to take control of the drones, possibly to steal one of them. Obviously, that plan failed."

Lara frowned. "Or was Fiddler just testing to see if the drones were immune to signal interference?" She punched her glove a few times. "Okay, Sully confirms that CyberShop, our suspected NSA spy, sold tech to the FBI *and* to Fiddler?" Lara asked, trying to piece it all together.

Vik nodded.

"So, if KillerBot is John Fiddler, then who is this Fiddler?" Lara asked.

"I'm not sure yet. I'm still reading through the entries. Sully didn't write any further details about Fiddler in the journal. And it's impossible to find any information about him online. I may have to break my oath and make a few phone calls."

"There has to be another way," Lara said with a dramatic flair and a toothy grin. Vik always insisted the Internet had all the answers, and he hated talking on the phone. She shook her head and moved on. "What else did you find?"

"Shortly before he died, Sully met with a Dr. Anton Stepanov from DARPA. Isn't that the man you met to talk about drone technology?"

Lara raised her eyebrow. *Now that's interesting.* "Yes. Dr. Stepanov is a colleague of Justyne's. Rather gruff and unfriendly. Justyne said some negative things about him. He's at the top of her suspect list. Anyone else?"

Vik nodded. "Three days before he died, Sully met with Dr. Margaret Brown at her lab... wait—that's bug lady! She could have—"

"Could have been having lunch," Lara said, cutting him off. "I was supposed to introduce Maggie to Sully at his party.

Maybe since they didn't get time to talk, they set up a date. Anyway, is that it?"

Vik bobbed his head. "At least, that's all Sully recorded in his journal in his final days. We have Ashton, Fiddler, Stepanov, and your friend." Vik paused when Lara furrowed her brow. "Of course," he continued, "the killer may not even be on this list."

Lara rubbed her chin. "You're right. Maybe Sully didn't actually *meet* with the person who injected him. During the Cold War, a Soviet agent stabbed a Bulgarian dissident with an umbrella containing a pellet filled with ricin. To get pricked, Sully just had to come into contact with his killer. It's possible he didn't even notice when it happened."

Vik scrunched his face, turning his head toward the storage room. "Lara, do you smell something funny?"

"It smells like… something is burning," Lara said with alarm. "Do you have anything going on in the kitchen?"

"Just the coffee maker," Vik said, walking into the kitchen area to double check. "Wait… there's smoke in the hallway."

Lara's eyes widened. "Where's it coming from?" Suddenly, a loud bang and the sound of breaking glass came from the storage room. Instinctively, Lara dove for cover behind the island.

"Oh my God, there's smoke coming from underneath the door to the storage room." Vik pointed at the crack under the door.

"Quick, grab the extinguisher!" Lara shouted, scrambling to her feet and running over to the storage room. When she touched the door handle, she shrieked in pain from the scalding hot metal. She raced back to the kitchen to grab oven mitts from the drawer. She yelled at Vik to unhook the fire extinguisher from the wall. His feet pounded behind her as they ran back down the hallway.

Wearing an oven mitt, Lara turned the handle of the door, and a thick ball of black smoke barreled out of the room, filling the hallway. Black smoke ate up every inch of air, surrounding them completely. Lara's eyes stung, and she reached out to try to find Vik.

"What's that smell?" Lara coughed uncontrollably as acidic smoke rolled into her mouth. Unable to breathe, she dropped to the floor, trying to get away from the cloud of smoke.

A few seconds later, she could feel the heat of flames bearing down on her. The fire licked her arm, singeing her skin. She screamed at the pain and scrambled away from the fire. It felt as if someone was sticking her with a hundred needles. She tried to scream again, this time to shout for help, but nothing came out. Her chest tightened as if there were a ton of bricks pressing on her lungs. A heavy thump came from behind her. At first, she thought Vik had collapsed, but then a hand gripped her arm, pulling her away from the door.

"Lara, the fire is too big. We need to go now!"

Someone shouted in the distance, but Lara couldn't turn her head or move her body to see who it was.

"Lara, can you hear me?" A muffled voice cried out.

Lara desperately gasped for air but could find none. Her head spun and her stomach churned as vertigo took over her senses. She fought against the darkness as her vision continued to blur, but the fight was too hard. The world slipped away.

FIFTEEN

Hospital Room

October 25, 2027

WHEN LARA OPENED HER EYES, panic overtook her at the unfamiliar surroundings. She gasped and scanned the room for information. The generic white walls, sterile environment, and rhythmic beeping of the heart monitor were unmistakable. Her stomach lurched.

What happened to me?

Her heart pounded in her ears as her mind returned to a similar setting from decades ago. Memories flooded into her head—images of her father in a hospital bed, helplessly trapped in a coma. Lara snapped out of it, banishing the memories, and looked around the hospital room for answers.

Flower arrangements sat on a table at the foot of her bed. An intravenous drip hooked into her left hand, causing some pain at the entry point. Several layers of bandages had been wrapped around her right arm. Her throat was scratchy and her lungs heavy. With her left hand, she felt plastic tubing sticking into her nostrils.

Oxygen?

After a few minutes, the memory of the fire and smoke rushed back to her. She sat up straight in bed, her heart racing.

Where's Vik?

Panicking, she pressed the call button on the remote sitting in her lap.

"Ms. Kingsley, you're awake," a white-haired nurse said pleasantly, popping her head in the door. "I'm Betsey Jenkins. I'll be looking after you today." The nurse fiddled with Lara's IV drip to make sure the feed was working.

"Where's Vik?" Lara asked, her eyes darting back and forth. Her voice was raspy and weak. The beeping of the heart rate monitor sped up. Gasping for air, Lara coughed several times, her throat burning hotter with every dry bark.

"Sweetie, I'm going to need you to calm down," Betsey said. "You're having trouble breathing from the smoke inhalation. If you get upset, you're only going to make things worse."

"Where's Vik?" Lara repeated, this time with increased intensity.

"Oh, do you mean that nice, young Indian boy?" the nurse asked.

Lara nodded.

Betsey set a tray of bland-looking food next to her bed, and the familiar institutional smell made Lara pull up her nose. "He spent all of yesterday and the whole night here, watching you like a hawk. I sent him down to the cafeteria to get some breakfast an hour ago. Poor thing didn't sleep a wink. He brought you some things from home." Betsey motioned to the duffel bag on the chair next to the window. "You're lucky to have such a loyal friend."

Lara breathed a sigh of relief and then coughed several times. Vik was more than a loyal friend.

He saved my life.

"What's this?" Lara said, raising her right arm.

"You burned your arm pretty badly in the fire," Betsey said, grabbing the chart. "You were lucky, though. It's only a second-degree burn, and you didn't need a skin graft. It should heal up in about two to three weeks. I wouldn't expect any scarring, but you could see minor changes to the surface of your skin."

Lara nodded. For a moment, she remembered the searing, stinging pain as the hot flames devoured her flesh. She shuddered and her eyes wandered to the side of her hospital bed. A recent issue of *Wired* magazine sat on the table.

Perfect distraction. She reached for it and pushed the painful memories away. *Vik must have brought this from home.*

"Is there anything I can get you?" Betsey asked.

Lara shook her head and flipped through the pages of the magazine.

"Okay, if you need anything, you know how to reach me." Betsey smiled warmly at her before leaving the room.

It only took about fifteen minutes before she got bored with the issue she'd already read three times. Lara leaned back in the bed and closed her eyes, exhaustion taking over. Just as she started to drift off, a soft knock on her door brought her back to full consciousness.

"Ms. Kingsley, do you mind a few visitors?" a familiar voice asked.

Lara's eyes fluttered open. *Oh great.*

Sanchez stood in the doorway, looking sheepish and holding a plush teddy bear. Rob followed him into the room with a huge bouquet in his hands. The blood drained from her face.

Oh God, what's he doing here?

Tempted to make a run for it, she glanced sideways at the machines next to her and followed the wires and tubes to where they hooked into her body.

No way I'm getting out of here fast.

Rob set the arrangement on the table at the end of her bed and turned to face her.

Lara forced a weak smile. "Did you both come here together or something?"

Rob nodded. "Detective Sanchez and I met when I bailed you out, and we ended up discussing Sully's murder case. Since the case involves biological weapons, it comes under federal jurisdiction. I assured the detective that we'll work together to solve the case… but only on one condition."

"Oh? And what's that?" Lara winced as her voice squawked from her dry throat.

"That the D.C. police department drop the ridiculous charges against you," Rob said firmly.

Lara's eyes widened. "I see." Relief came over her, mixed with irritation. It was one less thing to worry about, but she didn't like the thought of Rob saving the day—twice in twenty-four hours.

"Are you feeling okay?" Rob asked. His face was pale, and his curly hair rather unkempt.

Huh. He looks like hell…

Lara straightened up a little, and her cheeks warmed.

Is he worried about me?

Lara played it cool. "Oh, I've had better days, I suppose," she said, her voice raspy.

Sanchez held out a thin file for her to take. "Here's what we have on Jan Speelman, the man mentioned in the newspaper clippings you found."

Lara gave the detective an angry look. "Oh, are we working together now?" Rob's shining-knight-in-armor gesture didn't erase her anger with the detective. His ambush with his boss and the long night in jail still lingered fresh in her memory.

Sanchez cleared his throat. "Yes, about that. I think we went a bit too far."

"Oh, you think so? What changed? You realize you need my help now?" Lara put on her best scowl, satisfied just a little when the detective flinched at her harsh tone.

Lara snatched the file from his hand and flipped through it, landing on a page with photos of Jan as a child and a young adult. He had bright, twinkling blue eyes, rosy skin, and light blond straight hair, a towhead with Dutch ancestry. He looked healthy and happy. In the other picture, Jan posed with his violin as a teen. In the later pictures, his hair had grown darker, becoming a dull brown. As a young adult, Jan grew into a thin man, almost gaunt. His eyes were dark gray and haunting. His expression portrayed an eerie foreboding. She handed the file back to the detective.

"Hey, Rob, hand me a few pieces of paper from your pad," she said, picking a pen up off the side table. Rob tore out a couple of pages and handed them over. She mumbled her thanks, annoyed she had to ask him for anything.

"It's not much," Sanchez said as he nodded at the file. "Speelman was born in 1960, an only child to a single mother. When his mother died in 1965, he was five years old. With no immediate relatives to take him in, he became an orphan and entered the foster care system. All we have from his childhood is that he was a prodigy violinist and joined the San Francisco Symphony at the age of fifteen."

"Wow. That's impressive," Lara said, scribbling some notes.

The detective continued. "His mother took out an insurance policy on herself, leaving him a great deal of money when he turned eighteen. It was enough to live on for many years if spent frugally, or longer if he invested in the stock market. After the court found in favor of the U.S. Government in 1985, Jan Speelman moved to Maryland, somewhere near Silver Spring. We couldn't find an address under his name. In fact, we couldn't find another piece of information about him. He just vanished into thin air. He must have assumed another identity."

"Huh… that's interesting," Lara said. "Sully wouldn't have hidden the newspaper clippings if they didn't matter. I mean, it was all that was left in his safe room. Obviously, he'd gone to great lengths to find the articles and maybe even worried that if someone destroyed them, they would never be found again."

She paused for a few moments, the detective stared at the floor, and an awkward silence fell between them. It was time for a change in subject, something Lara had been wondering since she woke up and remembered what happened.

"Detective, do you know how the fire started?" Lara asked.

Sanchez perked up. "We found some evidence of arson. Someone stuck a small incendiary device in your storage room and then dumped all the paper from your files onto the floor. The device had a timer and was triggered with a cellphone signal. There was plenty of fuel in the room, so the fire grew like crazy."

Another period of awkward silence. Lara wished she could avoid eye contact, but she was stuck in her bed between the two of them.

"Lara, Vik told me that someone is stalking you?" Rob asked. His face went all puppy-dog as his brow furrowed, like his feelings were hurt. "Why didn't you come to me?"

Lara stared blurry-eyed at both men and shrugged awkwardly.

Why wouldn't I go running to you, Rob? Take an educated guess.

She ignored his question and turned to Sanchez. "So, what else did I miss, locked up in this place? How long have I been out?"

The detective crossed his arms. "The doctors put you in a medically induced coma for two days. But you didn't miss much. We did fingerprint analysis on the coffee cup and DNA traces on the half-eaten sandwich found in the safe room. We got no print matches in the D.C. or FBI databases. We also couldn't get a match from CODIS on the DNA profile."

"So, someone else was drinking coffee and eating a sandwich in Sully's safe room? Who could have the codes?" Lara asked.

"That's what I'd like to know," Sanchez said. "We don't know who the prints belong to, but we did discover an interesting match."

"Really?" Lara sat up a bit straighter.

"The prints on the tiny scroll of paper you found… the one attached to your bike out at Fort Meade." She leaned forward in anticipation. "Well, they matched the print on the coffee cup."

Lara scratched her forehead with her good hand. "Wait a sec, the person who left me the note on my bike was also in Sully's safe room?"

The detective nodded. "Even stranger, remember we found

no prints on your bike, but snagged some skin near the fuel line?"

Lara nodded.

"At first, I didn't get it. Why would someone leave a print on the note and then nothing on the bike? Did he or she put on gloves after touching the note or wiping down the bike? Why not be more careful with the note?"

"That is a bit puzzling," Lara said. "Maybe we're talking about two people? One person cut my fuel line, and the other person left behind the note."

Sanchez nodded. "That's exactly what I thought. And that's where the DNA results come in. While the prints on the note match the print from the coffee cup, the DNA we found on the bike doesn't match the DNA profile from the safe room. After conducting a thorough search in CODIS and local databases, we found our first possible lead."

Lara's pulse sped up. "What is it?"

"The DNA profile from the skin belongs to a woman by the name of Martje Hussny. The Fairfax police found her DNA on a crime scene for a money laundering case ten years ago. There's an outstanding warrant for her arrest as a person of interest, but the Virginia State Police weren't able to find her or any other evidence of her involvement. Honestly, they couldn't find anything substantial about her life before the crime. There were no pictures of her, no eyewitnesses, and she disappeared into thin air after the crime. The only thing the Fairfax police know about this Martje person is that she seemed to be deaf in one ear."

"Really?"

The detective nodded. "A vendor who spoke on the phone with her said Martje mentioned it in the conversation."

"Huh… weird. What sort of name is Martje Hussny?" Lara asked, writing the name down on paper and studying it.

"It's an alias."

"No, I mean where does the name come from?" Before the detective could answer, Lara pulled up a website on her smartphone. "See, the first name is Dutch for Martin. The last name is Arabic for beauty. What do you suppose that means?"

"A random coincidence, I'm sure." The detective continued, clearing his throat. "We also put a tail on Dr. Stepanov and have mostly come up empty. I'm not surprised. Anyway, we did get one lead from it. Dr. Stepanov met up with a young kid in his twenties, glasses, probably in college. The meeting between the two of them seemed off, strained. They got into it with each other. Rather heated. That's all we got."

Lara's head snapped up to look at the detective. Her head was still foggy, but she remembered the kid from Sully's party. And then Vik telling her about Sully's assistant, Ashton.

Sanchez tilted his head and raised an eyebrow. "Does that mean something to you?"

Lara nodded. "Before the fire broke out, Vik and I were reading through Sully's journal entries. Sully had an assistant named Ashton Grant. That could have been him."

The detective took a step back, his eyes narrowing. "What's this journal?"

Crap, here we go again.

"Uh, I found Sully's burner phone while I was at DARPA. Vik finally hacked the password, and Sully had kept his journal on the phone. We were reading the journal entries when the fire broke out. We also have a name for KillerBot."

Rob leaned in, suddenly interested in the conversation. "Who?"

"John Fiddler. It turns out this Fiddler character hired Sully to investigate potential tech suppliers." Lara looked directly at Rob to see his reaction, but her ex remained stone-faced.

Just like when he snuck around with Bimbo Barbie.

Sanchez crossed his arms and glared at Lara. "Why didn't you tell me sooner?"

Lara sighed. *So much for our détente.*

"Um, I've been a little occupied," she said, pointing to the medical equipment she was attached to. "And besides, I didn't know if I had anything at the time. Now I do. And look, I'm telling you right away." She hoped this would satisfy him. It was mostly true.

A muscle twitched in the detective's jaw. He looked like he might lose his temper at any moment.

"And if you're going to go there, I'm not the only one holding out on you. Special Agent Martin knew about Ashton all along. Didn't you, Rob?" She added a little bite to her tone.

Rob said nothing, probably to avoid a confrontation with the detective, who was bursting at the seams. Suddenly, a wave of fatigue came over her, and she struggled to swallow, her throat a little swollen and quite raw. She tucked the notebook paper into the magazine, set it on the table next to her, and closed her eyes. When she opened her eyes again a few minutes later, she could see the concern on Rob's face.

"We're going to find whoever did this, Lara," Rob said. "But right now, you should rest. Get better, okay?"

Lara nodded.

Sanchez looked uncertain as he handed her the brown teddy bear with a pink bow. "I wasn't sure what to get you in the gift shop. I hope you like it."

Lara forced a smile of appreciation. "Thanks. It's the thought that counts."

The detective followed Rob out of her room and shut the door. Lara set the bear on the table next to her. It didn't take long for her to fall into a deep sleep.

* * *

LARA WOKE up in a cold sweat. The light of early morning poured through the hospital window. A dark shape lurked over her hospital bed. Through the haze in her eyes, all Lara could make out was a woman with long, dark hair. After blinking several times, she recognized blue eyes, always intense but glowing bright.

"Lara, I'm so glad you're okay," Justyne said. "I heard about what happened from Vik. I've been so worried about you."

"Oh hey," Lara said, her voice barely above a whisper. "Thanks for coming by." She rubbed her eyes, trying to get rid of the blur.

Justyne wore a black Burberry trench coat, a silk blouse, and a matching pencil skirt. Her Armani sunglasses were pushed up onto her forehead, holding her slick, black hair in place.

She towered over Lara in the hospital bed. "I was hoping we might have a conversation about the case, but I see you're in pretty rough shape."

"Yeah," Lara said halfheartedly. She wasn't really in the mood for talking even if she could muster the words.

"Did you find out anything about Sully's killer?" Justyne asked, lowering her voice to a whisper. She was standing too close.

Why doesn't this woman understand personal space?

Lara reached for her magazine and pulled out her notes and pen. "A few things, I guess." She put a hand to her throat as it burned when she spoke. She might have overdone herself with Sanchez and Rob. "The autopsy showed Sully was killed by a botulinum injection."

Justyne's mouth fell open. "You mean Botox? Like the stuff I get injected in my face?"

So that's why she has no wrinkles.

Lara nodded. "We're not yet certain about the source, but it could have been cosmetic Botox."

"Have you checked out the local clinics? I could set you up with my dermatologist, Dr. Grayson at Heavenly Cosmetics. Maybe he knows something that could help you."

Lara gave her a weak smile as she jotted down the information. "Yeah, that would be great." Her voice was down to a coarse whisper.

Just then, Vik appeared in the doorway holding an iced latte and a chocolate croissant. Lara grinned at him from ear to ear, relieved to see his smiling face. "You need to give your vocal cords some rest," he said with a smile.

"Ah, you must be the infamous Vikram," Justyne said. "We spoke over the phone about Lara's bike."

Lara perked up.

"Ms. Marsh, thank you again for your help rescuing Lara's motorcycle from NSA's security personnel. I am sure Lara feels extremely indebted to you."

Lara bobbed her head up and down. "Yes," she whispered. "Thank you."

"Happy to help," Justyne said. "I was just asking Lara if you learned anything new about the case."

"Uhhh…" Vik looked at Lara, his eyes wide. "No, ma'am, we don't have any new information. I'm sure Lara will follow up with you when she gets better. If you don't mind, I think she needs to get some rest."

Justyne patted Lara's arm and nodded. "Yes, of course, I don't want to overstay my welcome. Lara, please give me a call when you're feeling up to it."

Lara agreed and watched Justyne leave the room. She motioned to Vik to close the door. He did so gently and came to sit next to her bed. Lara smirked, pointing to the plastic coffee cup.

He grinned. "I know you hate iced coffee, but I figured you would make an exception this time. What was that all about?"

"She wanted…" Lara started out at regular volume, but grabbed her throat when a sharp needle-pricking pain assaulted her. She motioned urgently to him.

Vik handed Lara the iced coffee, and she sipped eagerly, grimacing as the cool liquid went down. Her shoulders and neck relaxed almost as soon as the caffeine reached her stomach.

"She wanted an update on the case. She seems to think her colleague Anton Stepanov might have something to do with Sully's death," Lara said.

"I know she helped me recover your bike, but there's something off about that woman."

Lara agreed that Justyne seemed a bit off, but she liked her. "How long do I have to stay locked up in here?"

"The doctor said several more days."

"But why?" Lara pouted. She'd rather jump from the hospital window than lie in the bed for another minute.

Vik sighed. "He said the damage to your lungs from smoke inhalation makes you susceptible to infections. They have to keep you for observation and administer antibiotics intravenously for a few days."

"Why didn't *you* suffer from any smoke inhalation?" Lara asked defensively.

"Oh, the doctors said I was lucky. But before I ran down the hallway after you, I grabbed a damp towel to hold in front of my face."

"Smart thinking, Vik." Lara frowned, wishing she'd done the same. "How bad is the townhouse?"

"Pretty bad… the first floor has a lot of damage from the fire, the water, and the chemicals they used to put it out. We're not going to be able to get back in there for several weeks until the contractors repair everything."

"Did we lose the hardware?" Lara asked. She didn't have the money to replace any of it. Thankfully, she hadn't let her payments on her rental insurance lapse.

Vik nodded gloomily. "Even Sully's cellphone didn't survive."

"And my apartment?" Lara flinched, anticipating the response.

"Mostly intact with some smoke damage. I had the insurance guy come over to start a claim. We should have it cleaned up for you soon."

Suddenly, Lara's stomach lurched.

What did I do with my baseball glove?

"Do you remember if I brought my glove to the office?" she asked.

Vik's eyes widened. "Uh, yeah. You were using it like you always do when we were going through the information on Sully's phone."

"I hope it's okay." Then another realization hit Lara square in the stomach. "Oh crap, Vik. I totally forgot you'd moved into the office with all of your belongings. Did you lose all your stuff?"

"Yeah. It's gone." Vik hung his head and his eyes watered up a little.

"That's terrible. I'm so sorry," she said.

And here I'm worried about my own stuff.

Vik shrugged. "It's not a big deal. I didn't lose anything sentimental or valuable. Just clothes and my school books."

"But where are you going to stay, Vik?" Lara asked, guilt washing over her. It was her fault he had to move into the office in the first place.

"I'm crashing at a friend's place until we get the office in better shape. I'll move back in as soon as it passes the safety inspection."

Lara sighed. She was thankful the fire had not reached her apartment. She always backed up her work files digitally in multiple places, but she still didn't like losing her paper copies. She preferred using papers and photos for her work rather than digital files. Hard copies were somehow more steadfast.

"Lara, I hate to bring this up right now... but in light of losing everything... we didn't finish our conversation about Sully's journals."

There's more?

"Toward the end of Sully's entries, he became increasingly focused on CyberShop. He was convinced CyberShop was a double agent of some sort."

"What do you mean?" Lara asked.

"He seemed to think CyberShop worked for the U.S. Government and was selling military-grade technology for cash on the side, possibly in collusion with someone else."

"You realize CyberShop was part of the sting operation, right?" *Rob could be involved somehow.*

"Yeah," Vik said. "I'll keep searching the Dark Web and see what I can find." He rose to his feet. "Hey, before I forget, the executor of Sully's estate left a note for you at the townhouse."

"Huh? Who?" Lara wrinkled her brow.

"I don't know. Some lawyer by the name of Wyatt Turner. Anyway, he said he's been trying to get a hold of you, but doesn't think he has the right number." Vik pulled a slip of paper from his pocket and handed it to her. "His contact information is on this note he left."

"Did he say why he wanted to talk to me?" Lara asked.

Vik shook his head.

Lara studied the writing and slid it into her magazine for safekeeping with her other notes. *Sully had a will?* "I feel terrible about missing his funeral." Her face fell, and her eyes welled up with tears. Quickly, she pulled her emotions back.

Not in front of Vik.

She hadn't had a free moment to mourn the loss of her best friend. She knew she was still in shock and feared waves of grief would soon consume her. When she'd finally let herself grieve her relationship with Rob, it had knocked her out for months. It terrified her to think of putting down her walls to grieve Sully's death.

How long until I feel normal again?

Vik nodded, his eyes downcast. "I'm sure Sully would understand… and be glad you made it out of that fire alive. Lara, you should get your rest. I'm going to go to my friend's place and get some sleep, but I'll be back soon."

"Okay." Lara paused. "Thanks for saving my life." Her eyes glistened. A thank-you wasn't enough, but it was all she had at the moment.

"Anytime, Lara." Vik smiled.

SIXTEEN

Black Death

OCTOBER 29, 2027

LARA WATCHED Maggie pull out a sofa bed while wearing a black Gucci cocktail dress and matching Jimmy Choo high-heels. Her one-bedroom apartment in Fort Totten was so different from what Lara was used to. The high ceilings that exposed the ductwork and electrical wiring above, the tall industrial windows, and the open concept made the apartment feel much larger than the actual square footage.

The urban, modern feel of Maggie's apartment did not appeal to Lara, with all its harsh corners, hard surfaces, and cold colors. It made her miss her cozy traditional townhouse with creaky wood floors and antique furnishings even more.

"Thanks so much for taking me in," Lara said with an uneasy smile. Every bone in her body screamed for her to stop intruding on Maggie's space. She wished she could go back to her apartment where she wasn't dependent on someone else.

I don't have a choice. Where else would I go?

Even after five days in the hospital, investigators hadn't finished examining the crime scene at Lara's townhouse. Sully was gone, Vik had been kicked out of his apartment, she didn't have anyone from her old Army unit nearby, and she had no family to speak of. There was Rob, but asking him would be pushing it. He'd already done too much.

Although seeing the look on Bimbo Barbie's face might be worth it.

"No worries, mate. It was the least I could do," Maggie said, opening her sliding door a crack to let in some fresh air. The chilly night air smelled of a wood-burning fire from a nearby chimney. "You've been through a lot lately… and frankly, I'm not here all that much."

"I don't mean to keep you from your event." Lara frowned. Maggie was the keynote speaker at a scientific fundraiser that evening. "Don't worry about me, I can handle myself." She looked down and fidgeted with the buttons on her shirt. "I feel awful, like I'm butting in."

Maggie threw up her hands to wave off Lara's worries. "Oh please, those bloody people can wait. I don't have to give my remarks until an hour after it starts. Plus, it's customary to be at least thirty to forty-five minutes late to these bloody things. If I showed up on time, everyone would get all fussy and feel like they had to entertain me or something."

Lara laughed.

Maggie's expression turned serious. "Anyhoo, how's your case going? Did they find out how Sully died?"

Sully? Lara hadn't planned on bringing him up and was taken aback by Maggie's familiarity with him. *Did they meet up after the party or something?* Her stomach stung with a pang of jealousy. That would mean Maggie got a chance to see him before he died at the park. *Does she know something?*

Pulling herself together, Lara took a moment to decide what to say. "The medical examiner found signs of the plague during Sully's autopsy." She watched Maggie's reaction closely.

"What?" Maggie froze in place, eyes wide, mouth slightly hanging open. "What kind of plague?"

"Septicemic plague," Lara said, hoping she pronounced it

correctly. "There was a rash on his body and bleeding underneath his nails."

Maggie frowned. "I'm not sure how that's possible… the bacteria must enter the bloodstream to cause an infection. But that type of plague usually occurs as the result of untreated bubonic or pneumonic plague."

"Bubonic?" Lara stared at her blankly.

"Sorry, most cases of the plague are bubonic and caused by the bite of an infected flea. And as you know, that's no longer possible."

"What about pneumonic plague?" Lara asked.

"Pneumonic plague is very rare, but you can get it from untreated plague infections, or if you inhale infectious droplets from someone who has it. Septicemic plague is difficult to get on its own. You can still get it through insect bites or handling infected animals, but it's very unusual these days."

"Do you think the beetle I gave you had anything to do with it?" Lara asked, stroking her bandaged arm.

Maggie furrowed her brow. She began pacing about the room, her fists clenched tightly. "That's what I'm worried about. I've been studying it. I'm not yet certain about what I've found, and I'm hesitant to jump to conclusions. Testing an insect to find the different genes that allow it to carry a particular disease is like looking for a needle in a haystack. The consequences of my findings would be so profound that it could change the field of entomology as we know it. I need to be sure before I give you an answer." She took a deep breath and added, "This could be the breakthrough my lab needs to keep its funding."

"I understand you need to be sure, but what do *think* you've found?" Lara asked.

Maggie hesitated for a minute. "I *believe* the beetle you gave me was genetically modified to bite humans and perhaps to carry a dangerous pathogen… maybe the plague. I think the scientist used CRISPR, a powerful gene-editing tool, to snip out sections of the beetle's genetic code and replace it with new code, allowing it to bite and carry disease."

"What do you mean by snipping out DNA?"

"A genome refers to the entire genetic code for any living organism. Each of us has unique genetic code or DNA made up of A's, C's, G's and T's, like our own personal software. In the same way we can edit computer software code, we can also edit your DNA. We can cut, copy, and paste pieces of code."

Lara's eyes widened. "And you think someone edited the genetic code of the beetle?"

Maggie nodded. "Whoever modified the beetle left behind some crude genetic markers. I can tell the beetle's genome has been tinkered with, but I'm not certain about the exact impact of the changes. Each gene codes for different functions. I don't know enough about the beetle's original code to determine what genes and functions have been altered. For example, I can't confirm for sure if the beetle is actually capable of transmitting a disease. If I did, it would be a huge discovery that would shake up my field. Beetles are not known for being vectors of human diseases. My colleagues in Oz are going to send me a dataset for Christmas beetle genomes by email to establish a baseline for comparison. Then I can get some specific answers."

Lara rubbed her chin, trying to absorb what she was hearing. "What do you mean by crude genetic markers?"

"I mean the scientist did a messy job of cutting, copying, and pasting, and that might indicate the changes to the beetle you found at Sully's place were experimental rather than a final product." Maggie sighed. "I'm sure going to miss that bloke."

Her stomach lurched. "I didn't realize you and Sully connected so well," Lara blurted, looking intently at her friend.

Maggie shot her a guarded look. "What are you getting at, Lara?"

Lara crossed her arms. "I thought Sully left the bar long before you got a chance to hang out. Why didn't you tell me you met with him before he died? I had to learn about it from Sully's journal of all things."

Maggie frowned. "It's really none of your business. I left the bar shortly after Sully on the big night. We bumped into each other on the street corner. He was piss drunk. Well, maybe we both were off our faces. Anyway, the bloke got cheeky, ended up hitting on me, and I went home with him."

Lara gaped at her.

"What? He's hot," Maggie said.

"And then what? Why did you meet up again?"

"He called me several days later to ask for my help."

"Why didn't you tell me this before?" Lara asked, the blood draining from her face.

Why didn't he ask me for my help?

Maggie crossed her arms. "Okay, you're the one who couldn't be bothered to tell me about Sully's death when you came to me with that beetle. I didn't think Sully's call was pertinent. I didn't even know he was dead until a few days ago."

"What did he want?" Lara asked, though a sense of guilt for distrusting Maggie surfaced.

"He came to me in confidence and didn't want anyone to find out. He thought he'd been bitten by something and popped around for me to take a look at it." Maggie looked at her watch and walked toward the closet to get her coat.

"And?" Lara pressed.

"I didn't recognize the bite marks, but I suggested he get a prescription for antibiotics from his doctor. Now I realize it could've been the beetle that bit him."

"Do you think that beetle could have given me the plague, too?" Lara asked, as terror shot through her body. Twice now, such a beetle had landed on her. As much as she disliked beetles, she never thought them to be harmful or deadly in any way.

"No. The beetle you gave me doesn't carry any human pathogens, but it appears to have the genetic code that would allow it to do so. The carrying gene was turned off."

"But the beetle was modified to carry the disease?" Lara asked.

Maggie nodded.

"And what if the gene was turned on?" Lara asked.

"If the gene was turned on *and* the beetle carried the plague, presumably, it could infect you with the disease."

Lara contemplated everything she'd learned. "Do you think Sully's killer might be planning to do something terrible with the plague?"

"I don't know what to think," Maggie said, wringing her hands. "You're the detective. Talk to your coppers about it."

Lara wrinkled her forehead. "But why else would a scientist go through the trouble of modifying a beetle to bite humans and carry the plague?"

"Like I said, the consequences of my findings, if correct, would be profound for my field. The plague has caused three of the greatest pandemics in human history. The disease was so greatly feared that it was called Black Death. If someone wanted to cause death and widespread panic, the plague would be a bloody good way to go."

"Why?" Lara asked.

"Well, it's fairly easy to get a hold of *Yersinia pestis* from a lab, and there are strains of the bacteria that are resistant to antibiotics. The fatality rate of untreated pneumonic plague is extremely high, so if someone were to target an unsuspecting population, there would be significant casualties. The dose for causing infection is quite low. Also, pneumonic plague is contagious and can spread from person to person. All of this is why, in the past, some countries developed the plague as a weapon of biological warfare." Maggie glanced at her watch and shrugged her shoulders. "And on that positive note…"

"Go, go," Lara said, waving her friend out the door. "I don't want you to be *too* late."

"Oh, I almost forgot." Maggie reached into her purse, pulled out a USB drive, and tossed it to Lara.

Lara caught the USB drive and turned it over in her hand. "What's this?"

"That's the camera footage we were able to get off the micro camera on the beetle. I haven't had a chance to look at it."

Could this USB have evidence of who might have murdered Sully?

Lara's heart pounded quickly. She'd completely forgotten about the camera. "Thanks, I'll check it out. Have fun tonight."

Lara didn't wait for Maggie to close the door before she reached for the new MacBook she'd purchased with her credit card, walked over to the bar stool at the large island in the kitchen, and put her shiny new computer on the marble counter. She shoved the USB in the slot.

The video footage started on the evening of Sully's death. At the beginning of the recording, the beetle appeared to be perched on top of a bookshelf in the library and the camera looked down below. The grainy footage made it difficult to distinguish the details. Lara carefully forwarded through hours of blank footage.

About the time of the drone show, a tall person wearing a baseball cap came into the townhouse from the back entrance. Though it was difficult to tell, the person looked like a woman. Her movements were too lithe to be a man, and her frame too curvy. Her hair was tightly tucked underneath the cap, and she wore sunglasses. Lara couldn't make out any defining features from the grainy images. The woman appeared to be searching through everything, tossing books off the shelf and searching under and behind chair cushions.

What is she looking for?

When the beetle flew to the other side of the room to get a better shot, the woman appeared to catch a glimpse of it. She bent down to grab a book and began swinging toward the beetle, trying to swat it. The beetle flew away from the bookshelf into the middle of the room.

Suddenly, the video went blurry. When the picture came back, the beetle was near the floor as if it had been swatted downward. The shape of the woman hovered over it, and the closer footage showed her features. Wisps of light-colored hair poked out from underneath her baseball cap and her amber-colored brown eyes stared into the camera.

The beetle flew straight up into the air at a steep incline and landed on an antique cast-iron air vent. The video showed the woman coming straight for it. She slapped down the book just as the beetle slipped into the wide crack in the air vent. Her dark eyes peered through the grill into the air duct.

So that's how the beetle got in the safe room. Is this woman Martje Hussny?

Lara fast-forwarded through a couple hours of blank video from the safe room. About the time of Sully's death, a young man with dark hair and glasses entered the safe room, carrying a plastic container and a cup of coffee. The kid looked eerily familiar. Then it came to her. He was the strange kid from Wicked Bloom. Her pulse spiked.

Could this be Sully's assistant, Ashton Grant?

Since the fire, Lara had not yet had a chance to follow up on the lead. She watched as he logged into Sully's computer, ate a bite of the sandwich, and drank from the coffee cup.

Did he leave the note on my bike? The fingerprint evidence said yes. But why would Ashton do it? Was he working for Fiddler?

After searching around on the Dark Web for an hour, the man got up from the desk and disappeared from the picture frame. Then the video went black. Lara had reached the end of the footage.

Did the camera battery run out? Or did he know about the camera?

Something metallic glinted in Lara's periphery. A familiar buzzing brought her to a standstill, frozen with fear. She looked up, her expectation met when she recognized the bionic bug. It carried a small scroll on its back and landed on the counter next to her computer. The little beady eyes stared at her expectantly. When the creepy creature remained in its place, her curiosity pushed her fear aside. She reached out and gently pulled the scroll from its back. Her hand trembled as she read the note:

I'M GLAD YOU'RE OKAY

With that, the beetle launched itself into the air, hovered for a few seconds, and then flew out of the crack in the sliding door.

Lara ran to the door, following the path of the beetle.

Did Maggie leave the sliding door open on purpose?

Walking out onto the balcony, Lara shivered from the cool night air. For a few minutes, she tracked the beetle's flight with her eyes, as it reflected the streetlights. And then it disappeared into the darkness. The balcony revealed no sign of any intrusion. Down below, she caught a glimpse of a woman climbing into a dark-colored car.

Is that Maggie?

In the dark of night, it was impossible to tell. Lara looked at her watch. Thirty minutes had passed since her friend left for the event. It couldn't be Maggie... unless her friend had waited outside for some reason. Walking back into the apartment, Lara closed the sliding door behind her and warmed herself with her hands.

A framed picture on the bookshelf in the far corner caught her eye. Walking over to it, she picked up the picture. Her hands trembled. It was a recent picture of Maggie posing with a Christmas beetle nestled in the palm of her hand.

SEVENTEEN

Botox Clinic

November 2, 2027

LARA STEPPED off the metro bus on M Street NW in Georgetown and looked at her watch. She was not the type of person to run late, but she'd vastly underestimated the commute into the city from Maggie's apartment in Fort Totten. With her motorcycle still stuck in the shop and her dislike of driverless cabs, she reluctantly decided on the metro system to get around.

Vik waited for her patiently on the front steps of Heavenly Cosmetics beauty clinic, holding an extra coffee cup. At Justyne's recommendation, they were visiting the clinic to investigate the source of the botulinum toxin that killed Sully. Heavenly Cosmetics was known, among other things, for its renowned expertise in administering Botox.

"You're late," Vik said, smirking as he handed her the coffee.

"And you're funny," Lara said.

Without a car of his own, he knew all about metro woes. Lara often got on his case for being late, claiming there was no excuse for his lack of planning. After her own tardiness, she had the feeling she'd never hear the end of it.

"Before I forget, Maggie downloaded the video footage of Sully's townhouse captured by the beetle's camera." She dug the USB out of her pocket and handed it to him. "I've watched all of it, but I want you to take a look. Maybe you'll see something I missed. Also, the quality of the video is suspicious. I think someone might have tampered with it."

"Anything juicy on this?" Vik asked, arching his eyebrow as he held up the drive.

"Not really. There's footage of an unknown woman searching Sully's townhouse. And some clips of Ashton in Sully's safe room. At least, I'm assuming it's him." She decided not to mention the note she received the previous evening via courier beetle.

He doesn't need more to worry about.

"Did you get a chance to call that lawyer?" Vik asked.

"What lawyer?" Lara scratched her head.

Vik rolled his eyes and sighed. "The one I told you about… Sully's executor… Wyatt… last name starts with a T. I gave you the information in the hospital. You didn't lose it, did you?" His eyes narrowed.

Lara grimaced. "No, of course not. Been busy. I'll get to it." She quickly turned away from Vik and walked toward the clinic entrance.

Now where did I put that note?

Only a few seats remained empty in the large waiting room, tastefully decorated in relaxing tones of beige and pastel green. Gentle and soothing music played in the background. Vik plopped down on a seat in the corner, next to a table piled with magazines.

As she walked up to the reception desk, Lara surveyed the women sitting in the plush chairs of the waiting room. They were all of a certain class—well-dressed and quite beautiful.

Trying to get more beautiful.

Lara rolled her eyes. The receptionist swiped left on her phone repeatedly and didn't seem to notice Lara. She leaned in and cleared her throat. The receptionist jumped in her seat, a hand flying to her chest as she looked up at Lara. She hurried to put the phone away and offered a resentful smile.

"Yes?"

"I have an appointment with Dr. Grayson at ten," Lara said. She had Justyne to thank for getting onto his calendar. Normally, Dr. Grayson had to be booked at least three months in advance.

"Please sign in here and have a seat. We'll call you when he's ready for you." As Lara went to sign in, the receptionist shook her head and patted Lara's hand. "You're going to be so happy with the results."

Lara glared at the receptionist, but the woman was already swiping left again. Lara's mouth hung open for a moment, but she decided it wasn't worth the trouble to put this woman in her place. Instead, she finished signing in and went to find a seat next to Vik. Except something stopped her dead in her tracks.

In the opposite corner, a familiar handsome man with curly brown hair sat in a chair, reading a *Sports Illustrated* magazine.

"Rob, is that you?" Lara asked hesitantly. *What were the chances?*

Rob looked up, and his face went a bit pale. She'd clearly caught him red-handed doing something he didn't want anyone to know about.

"Lara… what are you doing here?" He fidgeted with the magazine in his hands.

"I should ask the same of you…" Lara grimaced.

"I'm… uh… here with Alexa."

Lara's stomach dropped. *Of course.* Bimbo Barbie was the last person she wanted to see, especially dressed down in her regular black leather jacket, t-shirt, and stone-washed jeans. She expected Alexa would be decked out in the latest fashions.

"It's her birthday today, so… I took the day off and am treating her to a facial thingy." He motioned awkwardly at his face.

"I see," Lara said in the iciest tone she could muster.

"What are *you* doing here? I didn't think you… um… were interested in this sort of thing." Rob waved his hand around, pointing to the various poster advertisements offering unrealistic guarantees for defeating wrinkles and the aging process.

"I'm not. Vik and I are investigating Sully's murder," Lara said.

"Oh really? Murder... I didn't realize you had the cause of death already."

Lara gave him a toothy grin. "Botulinum toxin. You know, the stuff your *girlfriend* is getting injected in her face at the moment."

"Wait a minute." Rob raised his eyebrows, and his face became stern. "You knew the cause of death, and you didn't *tell* me?"

He's got some nerve.

"What, wasn't Agent Carter able to make up with the medical examiner to get a copy of the autopsy report?" Lara asked, crossing her arms. "And aren't you all buddy-buddy with Detective Sanchez now? I would have told you myself, but then I almost got burned to death and spent several days recovering in the damn hospital, in case you don't remember." Her nostrils flared and her blood began to boil, but she wasn't ready to let up quite yet. "And don't you dare tell me you have been straight with me because I will call bullshit on you—right now. You've been hiding all sorts of interesting tidbits. What about the money from KillerBot, Rob? And would you like to tell me about CyberShop's deal with you? And what about your working with Justyne? When were you going to share that interesting detail?"

Rob flinched. "Dammit Lara, I'm not lying to you," he shouted. "You weren't in the 'need to know,' but a lot has happened since we met at the coffee shop. So yes, I withheld information from you back then. But I did it for the right reasons. And now it sounds like you're fully informed about everything, anyway." Rob's face turned red, and a vein appeared in his neck.

His outburst rendered Lara speechless for a few minutes. He never used to lose his cool so easily. In the silence, the gentle music playing in the background reminded Lara of her surroundings. The poised, beautiful women in the waiting room were all staring at them with wide eyes, some with disgusted expressions. Vik buried his face in his hands and refused to look at her at all.

"Sorry," Lara said, apologizing to everyone in the room. She sat down next to Rob and tried to regain her composure. Smelling his cologne made her feel as if nothing had changed between them. She'd bought him that scent for his birthday. It was one of the few masculine scents her sensitive nose could tolerate.

Rob's expression softened. "Lara, I'm sorry. I didn't mean to raise my voice… it's just that… it's just…"

"It's just what?" Her voice was unintentionally sharp.

"Well, you still get under my skin sometimes." Rob's cheeks turned red as he avoided eye contact.

Lara's face flushed. "Rob, I didn't mean to come at you guns blazing, but I really need some answers for my case. Sully died. I need to find his killer." She paused, swallowing hard and holding back tears. "I believe Fiddler and possibly this CyberShop character have something to do with it. I know you're not supposed to talk about an ongoing investigation, but…" Her lip quivered as she looked away.

"Okay, what do you need to know?" Rob asked, his voice calmer than before, almost tender.

"I know Fiddler paid a hefty deposit for the drones and later reneged on his deal to buy them. Do you know why?" Lara asked.

Rob crinkled his forehead. "We're not really sure… maybe he was on to us? When he cancelled the order, he did ask us to do something odd for him."

"Really? What?"

"He wanted us to send the NSA all the paperwork and evidence related to the drone show. Said he didn't need the deposit back, but this was of the utmost importance."

Lara furrowed her brow. "Huh… and did you send it over?"

Rob nodded. "Yeah, that's why Justyne and I are cooperating so closely now." He paused, as if trying to remember something.

"I keep forgetting to tell you that a doctor by the name of Anita Fiddler prescribed the antibiotics to Sully. Interesting coincidence, isn't it? Could she be Fiddler's wife? Or maybe his daughter?"

Lara's mouth fell open. "What the hell, Rob. This news didn't warrant even a phone call to me or Detective Sanchez? Whose side are you on?"

Rob's face suddenly became tense.

"Rooobbb?" A familiar female voice grated on Lara's ears.

She turned to see a stunning, tall, thin, blonde-haired woman walk toward them. Alexa wore black high-heels, cropped camo-green pants with a sparkly cream shirt, and a military-style jacket.

Bimbo Barbie.

"Uh… Alexa, this is… uh, my friend, Lara." His tone turned stiff and unnatural.

"*The* Lara?" Alexa asked. Her voice was high-pitched, and she didn't try to hide her irritation.

Lara stood up to shake Alexa's hand, though Bimbo Barbie's grip was limp and noncommittal.

"What is *she* doing here?"

She's actually jealous of me. Lara couldn't help but smirk.

"Honey, she's here to meet with the doctor," Rob said, jumping to his feet.

Alexa looked closely at Lara, scrutinizing her face. "Oh, I see. Well, I want to leave now. You promised to take me shopping."

A mortified look fell across Rob's face.

He traded me in for that?

"Keep me in the loop, and let me know if you find out anything about Anita, okay?" Rob said as he followed Alexa out the door, holding her purse. He dragged his feet a little; it was almost painful to see his confidence dwindle in his girlfriend's presence.

Almost. You reap what you sow, I guess.

Lara nodded. "Will do," she called out as Alexa opened the

door and let it slam in Rob's face. He took a deep breath and glanced over his shoulder at Lara.

Lara shrugged her shoulders. *She's your problem, not mine.*

"Ms. Kingsley, Dr. Grayson is ready to see you," the receptionist called out, eyes still glued to her phone.

Vik followed Lara down the long hallway into the doctor's office. Dr. Daniel Grayson sat behind the desk in a black leather executive chair, wearing a long white lab jacket over his clothes.

Despite his salt-and-pepper hair, Dr. Grayson looked young for his age, but in a slightly unnatural way. His skin was just a little too tight. Lara suspected he might have helped himself one too many times to the anti-aging procedures he administered. She took a seat in the plush armchair next to Vik.

"Ms. Kingsley, how can I be of help to you today?" Dr. Grayson said. When he smiled, there was hardly a wrinkle on his face. It was uncanny, on the border of disturbing.

"I would like to learn anything you can tell me about Botox," Lara said. "The case I'm working on involves a murder caused by Botox injection."

Dr. Grayson pursed his lips. "Well, I don't know what you're suggesting. Our clinic administers Botox as approved by the FDA and—"

"Sorry, I should've clarified upfront. The murder was not caused by a Botox treatment from a clinic. Rather, the perpetrator acquired a sufficient quantity of Botox and injected the victim with the toxin with the intent to kill. I'm here to understand everything I can about the toxin and how this could've happened."

"Oh, I see," Dr. Grayson relaxed his shoulders. "Well, Botox injections are the most popular nonsurgical cosmetic procedure in the country. Some people live by them. Administered properly, the toxin typically wears off after three to four months."

"How does the toxin work?" Lara asked.

"It paralyzes the muscles in your face and prevents repetitive movements whenever you make facial expressions. Those movements cause unwanted wrinkles."

"Could a cosmetic Botox injection cause death?" Lara asked.

Dr. Grayson pursed his lips. "I've heard of a few cases where the toxin was improperly administered at an unlicensed clinic. However, the doses approved for cosmetic treatment are too low to cause botulism. If the toxin is highly concentrated or administered in doses higher than permitted by the FDA, then illness can occur and death is possible. In those cases, the patient would have suffered from what is called iatrogenic botulism. But otherwise, no. The procedure is as safe as they come."

"How might someone get a hold of significant quantities of the toxin?" Lara asked.

"Botox is a commercially available product, so it's possible to purchase from any number of suppliers. That said, suppliers typically verify the legitimacy of end-users and their licenses to administer the toxin. We get our inventory from a company called Beautific Creations. They complete a background check with every order. I doubt someone off the street could go and buy a large supply without raising suspicions."

Lara lowered her head in disappointment. "Are you sure you don't have any other ideas?"

Dr. Grayson rubbed his chin and looked up toward the ceiling, as if he were trying to retrieve a lost memory. "Come to think of it, about a month ago, I heard about a stolen Botox shipment to Beautific Creations that impacted deliveries across the region. Fortunately, our clinic had plenty of the toxin on hand, and our treatment schedule was not disrupted. I didn't think much of it at the time, but that might be your source of the toxin."

Lara perked up and wrote it down in her notebook. "But how would someone know a truck was carrying small bottles of deadly toxin?"

"I'm not really an expert on security practices, but I'd imagine they knew what they were looking for."

Lara nodded. "Thanks, that's really helpful. I think we've

used up too much of your time, but I really appreciate your assistance."

As Lara stood up to leave, Dr. Grayson strode quickly around his desk and came uncomfortably close. As he moved in, she leaned away. Up close, his skin appeared waxy, almost like plastic.

"Do you mind me taking a look?" he asked, grabbing her chin before she could respond, inspecting her face, and moving his hand across her cheek. "My, my, you do have exquisite bone structure. However, there are some things we could do if you wish to preserve your youthful look." He took out a piece of chalk from his pocket and sketched a few lines on her face. "Are you sure you don't want a treatment on the house? Justyne is one of my best clients, and I'd be happy to do it as a favor to her."

"Uhhh, I don't really do that sort of thing. Thanks for the offer, though." Lara rubbed her face and squirmed away from Dr. Grayson's hands, squeezed around him, and headed toward the door, motioning to Vik to follow her.

Once they were clear of the doctor and safely in the hall, Vik tapped her shoulder. "Lara, I looked up the address for Anita Fiddler. Her office is not far from here. We should check it out."

"Good idea." Lara couldn't get out of the clinic fast enough.

EIGHTEEN

The Fiddler

As Lara traversed the narrow streets of Foggy Bottom with Vik, she made a quick call to Detective Sanchez to fill him in on her new leads. The neighborhood, home to George Washington University, crawled with college students going to and from their afternoon classes. The students clutched their coffee cups in one hand and their smartphones in the other, often not looking where they were going. Others spoke into the air, writing emails or texting using voice recognition software. To avoid a collision, Lara and Vik had to weave around them.

She cringed while delivering the news to Sanchez about the Beautific Creations tip and the information on the doctor who prescribed Sully the antibiotics, fully expecting another shouting match. Glad to have timely info for once, the detective spared her the usual scorn, gave her his blessing to interview Anita about the prescription, and promised to check in with the Virginia police about the missing Botox shipment. He'd even offered to fill in Rob on the new lead.

Exactly what I was hoping for. There was always a method to her madness. *I'm in no mood to talk to my ex again.*

As she ended the call with Sanchez, Lara contemplated John Fiddler's role in the homicide case. Even if Fiddler had nothing to do with her friend's death, she was certain that finding him was key to identifying the killer. Maybe Anita could shed some light on his whereabouts.

When the crosswalk light illuminated, Lara stepped into the street. The squealing of tires made her pause. A black BMW convertible careened around the nearby corner and raced toward them at high speed. She pushed Vik out of the way. As she spun around to hop back up onto the curb, she tripped over her own foot and fell toward the street. A hand grabbed her bandaged arm and tugged her so hard she stumbled up the curb and onto the sidewalk, landing squarely on her knees. Seconds later, the BMW hurtled within inches of the back of her feet. A heavy gust followed, sending dirt and exhaust into Lara's face.

Reeling from the momentum, Vik fell backward onto the sidewalk and landed on his free arm. Lara inspected herself. The pressure of Vik's hand on her burned arm stung and throbbed, but she had no further injury, and the bandages were intact.

"That was too close for comfort," Vik said, sitting on the cement and clinging to his arm, which had a nasty, bloody scrape. He rocked back and forth, grimacing as he inspected the injury.

"Are you okay?" Lara asked.

"I am not entirely sure. I hit my elbow on the pavement when I fell. There was a weird cracking sound… Lara, I think I busted up my arm pretty badly." Vik's eyes watered, and he bit the inside of his cheek.

Curious bystanders had already gathered around them, some to ask if they were okay and others with their phones out, apparently having filmed the near accident.

Lara looked down at her knees, both of which were scraped and bleeding through newly-made tears in her jeans. "Well, aren't we a pair?" She chuckled. The two of them certainly had experienced their share of bad luck lately.

Within minutes, the sirens of an ambulance blared nearby. She assumed it was heading toward the university hospital located right around the corner, but it screeched to a halt right in front of them. "Oh, that's for us?"

Someone must have called 911.

She glanced at the small crowd standing around them, but didn't see anyone take responsibility. Two uniformed EMTs jumped out of the ambulance, one with a bag of medical supplies and the other with a stretcher.

"What happened here?"

"We nearly got run over by a car. They ran a red light," Lara said, trying to catch her breath as she dabbed her bloody knees with Kleenex from her purse. Her injured arm pulsated angrily, and her chest tightened. She had not yet recovered her full lung capacity since the fire.

"That's not possible. Self-driving vehicles are programmed to stop at red lights," the EMT said.

Lara scowled at him for stating the obvious. "Well, this one didn't stop. So, either the software failed, or someone was driving the car manually."

"Ma'am, that would be illegal."

Not the brightest bulb…

"Exactly." She brushed his hands away. "I'm fine, but I think he might have a broken bone."

"Let me just bandage up your knees, miss. We can't have you getting an infection. The city is a dirty place."

Lara rolled her eyes but let him clean her up.

"What happened to your arm?" He pointed to the bandages.

"Oh, just a burn from another accident," Lara said. The EMT shrugged and got right to work cleaning, disinfecting, and bandaging the scrapes on her knees. The other medic attended to Vik, stating he should take a ride to the hospital for an X-ray to confirm the suspected fracture. "Load him up," the medic said.

Lara watched as they helped Vik climb onto the stretcher.

"Lara, you go on without me," Vik said, shoulders slumped and face downcast, looking miserable. "Trust me. I'll be fine. Come meet me at the hospital after you're done. But please… could you stay out of trouble for once?"

Lara frowned. "Okay, but only if you're sure." It didn't feel quite right letting him go to the hospital alone. But Lara desperately needed to talk to Anita Fiddler to get some answers.

Vik had already emailed her a rundown on what he'd found online. Lara opened it as the ambulance drove off and began to read.

Anita was a 33-year-old family physician who had studied medicine at George Washington University. From her online presence, Anita didn't appear to have a husband or any children. Given her age, Lara assumed she must be John Fiddler's daughter.

Lara hustled toward the address of the small medical practice located on a side street near the university hospital. Her knees protested every second of the five-minute walk to Fiddler's offices.

The placard read: Johnson and Moore Family Practice.

Huh. Staring up at the sign, she scratched her head for a moment. *Where's Dr. Fiddler's name?* She double-checked the address. *Well, this is the right address.* Perhaps Anita had not yet made partner.

Lara surveyed the brownstone surrounded by taller, more modern buildings. She walked up the steps and rang the buzzer.

"Good afternoon," a voice called out through the intercom.

"Hi. My name is Lara Kingsley. I'm here to see Dr. Fiddler," Lara said into the speaker.

The door buzzed promptly, allowing Lara to walk into the building. The hallway had old hardwood floors just like Lara's townhouse and a winding staircase leading up to the second floor. The main part of the practice was located on the first floor with a reception desk in a waiting room, directly off the entry hall.

A young woman with long, mousy brown hair and glasses looked up and smiled at Lara. Then her eyes drifted down to the blood stains on Lara's jeans, and her smile disappeared. The name tag on her shirt said "Lindsay." Dressed in preppy clothing and holding a college chemistry textbook, Lindsay had the look of a student working part-time to help fund her studies.

"Um, Ms. Kingsley... did you have an appointment?" Lindsay asked, scanning the scheduling book with her finger.

Lara shook her head. "No, I'm a private investigator working a homicide for the D.C. police. Dr. Fiddler treated the victim before he died, and I have a few questions."

"Oh." Lindsay's face became serious. "She stepped out for a few minutes. I think she'll be back shortly. You can have a seat right there while I text her to see where she is." Lindsay pointed to a row of plastic chairs lined up under a big picture window.

Outside, a silver Honda pulled up and a stunning woman with Scandinavian roots stepped out. Lara recognized her from her headshot on the website, though the picture hadn't done her justice. Dr. Fiddler was an extraordinarily beautiful woman, tall and trim. Her blonde hair and blue eyes were framed by high cheekbones and peachy skin.

Minutes later, Anita appeared in the doorway of the waiting room, even before Lara had a chance to sit down. She walked over, greeted Lara, and shook her hand firmly. "Please follow me, Ms. Kingsley. My office will be a good place to chat."

Looking past her beauty, Lara detected a deep sense of melancholy in her eyes, as if she'd lived decades beyond her real age. She followed the doctor down the Victorian-style hallway on the first floor, the old floorboards creaking under her feet.

She entered a large office with generous windows opening onto a small, lush courtyard in the back of the townhouse. Dark-stained wooden bookshelves lined the walls around Dr. Fiddler's ornate mahogany desk. Medical texts and journals filled each shelf. Anita motioned for Lara to take a seat in the leather chair across from hers. A rich, sweet, calming scent filled the air from the incense burner on Anita's desk, tickling Lara's nose.

As Lara sank into the deep, cushy chair, a strange necklace hanging around Anita's neck caught her eye. At the end of the silver chain hung a scarab beetle pendant covered in what appeared to be Egyptian hieroglyphics.

"My assistant told me you're investigating a homicide of one of my patients?" Anita asked.

"Yes, I'm Lara Kingsley of Kingsley Investigations. I'm supporting Detective Mario Sanchez's investigation into the murder of Phil Sullivan."

Lara watched Anita's face for any recognition, but the doctor didn't show any recollection of Sully's name.

"I don't think I have a patient by that name," Anita said, rubbing her forehead.

"We found an antibiotic prescription with your name on it."

Anita wrinkled her forehead and closed her eyes, as if she were searching the recesses of her memory. When her eyes popped open, Anita folded her hands on her lap and nodded. "Phil Sullivan! Ah yes, now I remember. I prescribed the medication as a favor to my father. Mr. Sullivan was working for him in some capacity."

"When did you prescribe Mr. Sullivan the medication?" Lara asked.

Anita tilted her head. "I actually never met him. My father wanted to have the medicine on hand a couple months ago in the event that Mr. Sullivan was accidentally exposed to something in his lab."

"So, he must have gotten the prescription bottle from your father?"

Anita nodded slowly, her eyebrows knitted together, her consciousness seeming to be somewhere else. She reached up and fidgeted with the beetle pendant, rubbing it in circles with her thumb. Finally, she looked at Lara. Her face had grown paler in the few seconds since Lara's question. Anita cleared her throat. "Did he die of a bacterial infection?" she asked.

Lara shook her head, watching the doctor closely, trying to figure out what was going on inside her head. "Would the antibiotics you prescribed be effective for treating the plague?"

Anita's eyes went a little wide, and she sat up in her chair.

Her hand dropped into her lap, leaving the beetle to rest on its chain. "You don't think my father was working with *Yersinia pestis*, do you?"

"I'm not sure. Sully—" Lara stopped when Anita pressed her lips together and leaned forward with confusion written all over her face. "Sorry, I mean Mr. Sullivan. Anyway, he appears to have picked up the plague, but I don't know how he got it. That's why I'm here. We need help to figure out exactly how he died. Talking to your father would be helpful."

Anita hesitated and broke eye contact. "I don't really see him anymore. He doesn't like to see people, not even his family. Over the past year, he's gone off the grid. I'm not even sure where he's living at the moment." Anita spoke too fast, too dismissively. And whereas before she'd gripped the armrests of her chair, she now gestured nervously.

What are you holding back?

Lara followed Anita's gaze toward the corner of her office, where an old, clunky desktop computer and a boxy, tube-style monitor sat on a small desk. It had been years since Lara had seen such a computer, and the last time had been in a museum exhibit. *What is Anita using that old thing for?*

Lara turned her eyes back to Anita and leaned forward. "We really need to speak to your father. Any information you can give us—anything at all—would be a big help."

Anita paused, opened her mouth as if to speak, but closed it again. She repeated this twice more before she spoke. "He's not in any trouble, is he?"

"No. I'm trying to figure out what Mr. Sullivan was doing for your father before someone murdered him." Lara intentionally neglected to mention that Anita's father was a person of interest in the case. She seemed like a nice woman, and Lara didn't like lying to her, but she needed information.

"Well, every other week we have coffee, and I give him his mail."

"When will you see him next?" Lara asked carefully, staring at her notebook.

Play it cool. Don't scare her off.

"We're scheduled to see each other next Monday."

"What sort of job does your father have?" Lara scribbled notes, recording everything Anita said. This was going better than she'd thought it would go, and she didn't want to miss anything.

"None that I know of. He's been retired for a couple of years now. He just tinkers around in his shop on occasion. When he asked for the prescription, I was actually surprised to learn he's working in a lab again."

"Why did your father retire?"

Anita looked away. "It's actually embarrassing. He was fired from his last job."

"What did he do?"

"He worked for more than thirty years as a molecular biologist at the U.S. Army Medical Research Institute for Infectious Diseases up at Fort Detrick. I think he specialized in genetic engineering. He didn't talk much about his work since it was Top Secret and all."

Lara sat up straight. "Why did he get fired?"

"I'm not sure."

Hearing about the U.S. Army reminded Lara of the newspaper clipping, but she couldn't recall what specifically jogged her memory. "Is he still married?"

Anita's face fell. "No. My mom died about two years ago."

Her pulse accelerated. Lara had a hunch, and she decided to go with it. "Do you have a picture of your father… one you can give to me?"

Anita's eyes widened. "Why do you need his picture? I thought this was about Mr. Sullivan?"

"Well, I knew Mr. Sullivan quite well. Maybe I've seen him with your father." Lara knew the truth would scare her off. "Again, I'm just trying to understand the nature of their relationship. Any information might help us catch the killer."

Anita walked over to her bookshelves. She paused for a few minutes and then pulled a book that looked like an old travel guide for Australia. From the book's spine, Lara could tell it originated from a library. Anita flipped it open to the front page, pulled out an old photo, and handed it to Lara.

"This was my father at fifty. He's aged some, but he pretty much looks the same as he did then."

"Yes, I might have seen him before," Lara said.

The photo looked familiar, and she remembered exactly where she had seen the face before. Fiddler's hair was a mousy brown color with patches of gray, and his eyes were a light blue-gray. A curious look on his face suggested he had just asked the photographer a question.

"How does your father support himself without a job?" Lara asked.

"He inherited quite a bit of money from his mother and invested it wisely. She died when he was young. He never told me much about his childhood. It was too painful for him, I think."

Dead mother. Orphan who inherited a large sum. It's too close to be a coincidence.

"Has your father ever changed his name?" The usual adrenaline rush that accompanied a revelation made Lara perk up a little.

Anita furrowed her brow. "Not that I know of…"

"Did your father play the violin?" Lara's heart pounded.

Anita's face lit up. "Why yes, he did. He used to be an amazing violinist. He could have played professionally. It's been a while, though."

"Does the name Speelman ring a bell?" Lara held her breath.

Anita thought for a moment, but then shook her head. "No… not at all. Should it?"

Lara didn't need any further confirmation. Jan Speelman and John Fiddler were one and the same. As she wrote an equal sign between the names in her notebook, the meanings of the names hit her squarely in the face. Speelman was Dutch for fiddler. And they both played the violin.

Duh! The facts were in front of her the whole time. *That must be why Sully hid those newspaper clippings. He wanted me to learn the truth.*

"I'm curious," Lara said, pointing to the scarab beetle necklace around Anita's neck. "Where did you get that necklace?"

Anita looked down at her chest and smiled slightly. "My father gave it to me. Said it would ward off evil spirits."

Lara paused for a moment. When Anita moved her head forward, a family photo on the bookshelf behind her came into view. It appeared to be of Anita, her husband, and her son.

"Does your father spend any time with his grandson?" Lara asked.

Anita's face went slack, and she became silent. Her eyes welled up with tears. "My son is dead. And I'd rather not talk about it right now." She grabbed for a Kleenex and blew her nose. The tears started falling, and her sniffles increased in intensity.

Lara shuffled her feet and closed her eyes for a moment. "I'm sorry… I didn't realize."

Poor woman. Ugh. Me and my big mouth.

"Hey, we can finish this another time, okay?" Lara said.

Anita nodded and turned away. "I think that would be best."

"Of course. I'll come by again soon."

The doctor didn't say anything more, only walked to her window with her hand over her mouth, tears trickling down her face. Lara was convinced Anita could help unravel the mystery behind Fiddler, which could lead to solving Sully's murder. But for now, the doctor was too distressed to be of much help.

"I'm sorry about your son," Lara said softly as she slipped out the door.

* * *

LARA WEAVED through the thick crowd at the entrance to the hospital. The automatic sliding doors whooshed open for patients, visitors, and staff. An ambulance pulled up outside and medical personnel raced to the door, forcing Lara to jump out of the way. Seconds later, EMTs wheeled a patient into the ER.

She detested everything about hospitals—the intensity of emotions on people's faces, the jarring sounds, the disgusting smells, and sick people coughing up their germs everywhere.

Lara followed the signs to the ER where Vik was being treated for a broken elbow. He'd been texting her with minute-by-minute updates, albeit with one hand, and the messages were full of typos. She felt bad for leaving him alone.

Walking up to the admission desk, Lara said to the nurse, "I'm here to see Vikram Abhay. He came in with a broken elbow."

"Are you family?" the nurse asked, looking her up and down.

Lara shook her head.

"Family only." The nurse glared at her and then looked down at her digital charts briefly. "The doctor is finishing up with Mr. Abhay. You may wait over there."

Lara turned away from the desk and walked over to the row of beat-up chairs along the wall. When she sat down, the feet of the chair slid an inch, making a high-pitched screeching sound and startling the other people in the waiting area. The nurse looked up and frowned at her.

Several seats over, a woman used a plastic trashcan to vomit. Lara shuddered as the sour tomato-like odor wafted past her, causing her to gag. Next to her, she heard incessant scratching of a pen on paper as an elderly man filled out paperwork. Across the room, a crying child nagging his mother for apple juice added to the unwelcoming atmosphere of the room. A desperate urge to walk out rose within Lara, but she couldn't leave Vik there by himself. She wrapped her arms around her body, terrified of touching anything.

Lara texted Vik:

I'M IN THE WAITING ROOM. EVIL NURSE LADY WON'T LET ME COME SEE YOU

Her cellphone buzzed. She thought the message was from Vik, but it was a text from an unknown caller:

MEET ME IN ONE HOUR AT THE
BASILICA OF THE NATIONAL SHRINE OF THE IMMACULATE
CONCEPTION
I WILL BE IN THE LAST CONFESSIONAL
DON'T BE LATE

Her heart racing, Lara jumped up from her seat. She began pacing up and down the waiting room and biting her nails. If she didn't leave now, she'd be late for the meeting. But she couldn't leave Vik behind without an explanation.

This could be the breakthrough I need in the case.

Lara texted Vik:

HEY, SOMETHING URGENT HAS COME UP
WITH STALKER MAN
I FEEL REALLY BAD BUT I SHOULD GO

Vik texted her back:

I DON'T WANT YOU GOING OFF ALONE AGAIN
WE WERE JUST NEARLY KILLED

She rubbed her forehead and sighed. Lara didn't like being babied.

SORRY. I'LL PAY FOR YOUR CAB, OKAY?
AND YOUR MEDICAL EXPENSES

Vik texted:

IT'S OKAY, LARA
REMEMBER, YOU DON'T HAVE ANY MONEY

Lara texted back:

I'll let you know what I find out

Lara pocketed her phone and raced out of the hospital as guilt pricked her conscience for leaving Vik alone.

The street outside was crowded for the rush hour, but she quickly spotted an empty driverless cab. She swallowed her discomfort and got inside. The people she cared about were being targeted. It was time to overcome her distaste for self-driving cars.

There's no way I'm losing anyone else.

She punched in instructions on the screen in the back of the cab. She was ready to do whatever it took to close this case, find Sully's killer, and protect the people she loved.

NINETEEN

The Proposition

THE DRIVERLESS CAB pulled up to the right side of Harewood Street, which ran adjacent to the Basilica of the National Shrine of the Immaculate Conception. A toneless robotic voice announced Lara's arrival.

She'd admired the church many times from different vantage points throughout the city but had never actually visited. She looked up in awe at the blue and orange mosaic-covered dome, the regal entrance, and the giant tower of the limestone building. From every angle, the Basilica was simply breathtaking.

The impressive structure sat high upon a hill on the grounds of the Catholic University of America and held the honor of being both the largest Catholic church in the United States and the tallest inhabitable building in the nation's capital.

Passing through the front doors, Lara found the interior of the shrine eerily quiet. A few priests meandered silently through the corridors. A handful of tourists lingered in the main sanctuary, admiring the architecture and masterpiece works on display. Otherwise, the Basilica was empty.

Lara had used her phone to learn more about the Basilica on the way. The confessionals were located next to the crypt on the basement level in the Chapel of Our Lady of Hostyn. She trod carefully down the stone stairs, the clacking sound of her shoes echoing off of the granite walls. She shivered as the damp, cool air of the basement drifted up toward her.

I'm about to meet the man behind the beetles. I hope he's ready for me because I'm ready for him.

Though a potential suspect, Lara couldn't piece together any reasonable motivation for Fiddler to kill Sully. Still, he was up to something, of that much she could be sure. At the very least, Fiddler might be able to give her some information about Sully's killer.

The floors and walls of the large confessional room were made of polished granite. Empty pews stood in the center of the room, a waiting area for busier times. Only a few people were making their confessions. It had been years since Lara made her last confession, and she had no intention of changing that anytime soon.

Across from the entrance, there was a total of nine confessionals with unmarked wooden doors, three on each wall. Lara looked left to right, trying to figure out what the message had meant. She took a step toward the first confessional on the right wall and then stopped in her tracks. Turning her head, her eyes darted to the first confessional to the *left* of the door.

Which one is supposed to be the last confessional?

The confessional designated as the last one depended on the direction. *Did Fiddler mean left or right?* Most people tended to turn right when they entered a room, but Fiddler was not most people. She turned to the left and grabbed the handle. If she'd chosen correctly, the first confessional would be counterclockwise from her position.

Lara opened the wooden door and stepped inside. The dimly lit stall was constructed entirely out of dark, grainy wood and contained a bench and a shelf with an open Bible. Lara sat on the bench and looked expectantly at the screen on the side wall. No one was there. After a few minutes of silence, a cool burst of air passed through the screen, and she detected a rich, sweet fragrance that reminded her of Anita's office.

Jasmine? The pleasant smell gave her the chills.

"I was worried you wouldn't make it," a cold, smooth voice said from behind the screen. The voice sounded different than she'd expected—younger.

"Are you John Fiddler?" Lara asked, her voice quivering slightly.

"Yes."

Lara rubbed her clammy hands together. "What do you want from me?"

"I want to get to *know* you better. I feel like we haven't had that chance… and yet, we've spent so much time together."

The thought of him watching her made her flesh crawl. "What do you want?" Lara asked again, this time more loudly.

"Why must you always cut to the chase?" His voice became sharper. "Patience is a virtue you should learn to value more. I've been watching you. I'm fascinated by how you work."

"Did you kill Sully?" Lara asked, her voice strained.

"Why would I do that? Sully *worked* for me. He was helping me."

"Did you try to burn down my townhouse?" Lara pressed.

"*I* called you here. *I* will ask the questions and direct this conversation. Do we have an understanding?" His tone switched from cold to hostile.

"Yes." Lara's body stiffened, and she shot a glance at the door. If she needed to, she could make a run for it. It was a straight shot from the confessional room to the staircase. Fiddler was a sixty-year-old man and would be no match for her, even with her weakened lungs. Plus, there were still people milling about in the room, going to and from the confessionals. And there would be priests waiting in some of them. Fiddler wouldn't attack her in public.

Would he?

Lara licked her lips and folded her hands together to stop them from trembling.

"Good," Fiddler said. "Now, I want to clarify further rules of our engagement. I know you met with my daughter today. You will not speak with her again."

Lara remained silent.

"I would like an answer from you that indicates you've heard me and understand what I've said. Do you understand that you are *not* to speak to my daughter or involve her in any way?" He said each word carefully.

"Yes," Lara said.

"Good. I also know you're working with the FBI."

"Actually, I'm not working with—"

"Do not take me for a fool," Fiddler hissed. "I know full well you're cooperating with that miscreant Special Agent Martin. You will no longer have any more dealings with him. Do you understand?"

The hairs on her arms stood on end, and her skin prickled. "Yes," Lara replied in a placating voice. The Feds had jurisdiction over incidents involving biological weapons. It wasn't really her choice anymore. But she'd tell Fiddler whatever he wanted to hear.

"Okay, let's get down to business. I have done my research. I know about your finances and fledgling business, that you have accumulated over ten thousand dollars' worth of debt, and that you can't pay the bills. And now you're working Sully's homicide case, practically for free."

Lara winced at the reminder. He was right. If she didn't do something quick, she wouldn't be able to pay the rent, and her landlord would evict her.

"What do you want?" Lara asked.

"I want you to take Sully's place," Fiddler said.

"What do you mean?"

"I want to hire you as my private detective."

Lara furrowed her brow. "To do what?"

"I want you to investigate CyberShop and discover his or her true identity."

"And what if I'm not interested?" Lara asked. She pulled a tissue out of a box by her feet and dabbed her skin. Despite the chilly air in the basement, beads of sweat formed on her forehead.

"Oh, you'll be interested if I pay you one hundred thousand dollars," Fiddler said. "Fifty K up front and another fifty K when CyberShop is in custody."

Lara paused, unsure how to respond. The money was tempting, but could she work for him? "Suppose I agree to work for you. What can you tell me about CyberShop?" Lara knew it was a long shot, but maybe she could get useful information out of him.

"I've met CyberShop before."

"Oh?" Lara nearly jumped up from the bench. "What does CyberShop look like?"

Fiddler remained silent for several minutes. Lara could hear sounds of scratching on paper coming from his stall. *What's he doing?*

"CyberShop set up my son-in-law as a traitor and killed my family." His voice trailed off.

Lara did a double take. "What do you mean killed your family?"

"Will you take the job or not?" Fiddler rasped.

"Who did CyberShop kill? Your grandson?"

"Last chance. Yes or no?"

Lara thought she heard a tremor in his voice this time.

She sat in silence and contemplated what the amount of money would mean for her. For her business. It would literally change her life. *Technically, I'm already investigating CyberShop. What's the harm in taking money for it? But work for Fiddler?*

If Rob was right about him, he was a criminal or worse—a madman planning a massive biological attack. Any affiliation with Fiddler would be risky for her career and might even jeopardize her freedom.

No, the money isn't worth the risk.

"I'm not interested," Lara said firmly. She put her hands on the bench next to her, ready to spring into action if needed.

"You will come to regret your decision," Fiddler said, his

voice quivering. "If you don't take my offer sooner or later, I'll make sure of it."

Lara bit her lip. She didn't like the sound of the threat, and the shift in the atmosphere between them puzzled her.

A loud thump came from Fiddler's stall. She jumped up and opened the door. The door to the priest's stall beside her squealed as it swung back and forth.

Lara searched the stall, but Fiddler had left nothing behind, except for the sickly, sweet smell of jasmine. Before she left, she glanced at the open Bible. The heading on the page read Exodus 8. The verses 20-23 were underlined in pen:

"THE LORD COMMANDS YOU TO LET HIS PEOPLE GO, SO THEY CAN WORSHIP HIM. IF YOU DON'T, HE WILL SEND SWARMS OF ~~FLIES~~ TO ATTACK YOU, YOUR OFFICIALS, AND EVERY CITIZEN OF YOUR COUNTRY. HOUSES WILL BE FULL OF ~~FLIES~~, AND THE GROUND WILL CRAWL WITH THEM. THE LORD'S PEOPLE IN GOSHEN WON'T BE BOTHERED BY ~~FLIES~~, BUT YOUR PEOPLE IN THE REST OF THE COUNTRY WILL BE TORMENTED BY THEM. THAT'S HOW YOU WILL KNOW THAT THE LORD IS HERE IN EGYPT."

Growing up in the Catholic church, Lara was familiar with the ten plagues God had sent against Egypt as punishment for not letting his people go.

Did he cross out the word "flies"? To replace it with... Lara shuddered at the idea of a plague with deadly beetles. *Is Fiddler planning on punishing someone for something? If so, why would he tell me?*

Lara's ears perked up at the sound of footsteps echoing from the stairwell. She pushed out the swinging stall door, exited the room, and raced up the stairwell two stairs at a time in pursuit of Fiddler. By the time she got to the top step, her lungs burned as she struggled to catch her breath, but she kept running down the hallway as fast as she could without collapsing into a coughing fit.

Damn that fire.

As she rounded the corner toward the main doors, she collided with a nun dressed in formal garb. At the force of the impact, the nun fell to the floor in a heap.

"Oh my gosh, I'm so sorry, ma'am," Lara said.

"What in the world are you rushing about for, young lady? Death comes soon enough. We shouldn't bring it upon ourselves with haste," the old woman said as she straightened her skirts to cover her legs.

"I was—are you okay?" Lara asked as she craned her neck around the nun, only to see an empty hall.

I've lost him.

She pushed aside her frustration and turned her attention back to the nun.

"I think so," the woman grumbled, feeling her arms and legs as if to inspect for injury. Lara reached out to help the woman to her feet using her one good arm. Still, her chest burned and her other arm throbbed as the nun used Lara to steady herself as she stood.

"Again, I'm so very sorry," Lara said. "You wouldn't have happened to see a man run by here?"

"Well, if you mean a young man racing toward death as quickly as you, he ran past me and out the front door." The nun glared at Lara, lips pursed as if expecting a few more apologies. But what she'd said piqued Lara's interest, distracting her from any attempt at exaggerated platitudes.

Young man?

"Thank you. Again, very sorry about bumping into you," Lara said, adding the second apology as an afterthought.

She ignored the nun's open mouth and crossed arms as she stepped around her. She jogged to the door, stopping on the outside landing. She searched the landscape until she spotted a man sprinting across the grounds, perhaps a tenth of a mile away.

That's way too fast for a sixty-year-old.

TWENTY

Malware

MOONLIGHT POURED into the industrial-style loft apartment, reflecting off the many metallic surfaces and creating an unearthly vibe. Lara stood in Maggie's kitchen, waiting for the coffee pot to finish brewing. She tapped her fingers on the counter, staring aimlessly at the steel ductwork on the ceiling.

Am I still considering Fiddler's offer?

With one hundred thousand dollars, she could pay the bills for Kingsley Investigations, replace the scorched electronics, and perhaps even upgrade a few things in the office. And still have plenty leftover to pay Vik.

As the gourmet coffeemaker whirled and gurgled, the rich aroma of fresh coffee filled the entire apartment.

A professional-grade espresso machine sure would be nice.

Lara sat on a stool at the marble-topped island and admired Maggie's glamorous kitchen. The exposed red brick and the high-end stainless steel appliances reminded her of the massive chef's kitchen in her childhood home, when her parents were still alive. Nothing else about Maggie's place felt like home.

Her thoughts returned to Fiddler.

It couldn't have been him at the confessional. Whoever he

sent in his place was working with him—or for him. *Maybe it was Ashton Grant?*

The coffeepot hissed. Lara reached for the carafe, poured two large cups of French dark roast, added some cream, and paused for a moment to lean against the counter. Her body ached all over. She didn't know whether her exhaustion was physical or emotional. Maybe a bit of both. Every movement drained her. Her limbs dragged as though tied to weights. She took a deep breath. It had been a long day—the near-death accident, her interview with Anita, waiting for Vik at the hospital, and then chasing after the man at the Basilica.

No wonder I feel like a dead woman walking.

"Hey Lara, is the coffee ready yet?" Vik called out from the living room.

Lara snapped out of her daze. "Coming right up."

She navigated the oversized yet sleek furniture, carefully balancing two full mugs of coffee. Lara had pulled out the queen-sized sofa bed and replaced the bedding to accommodate Vik.

He'd already nestled himself into the plush cushions, leaning against the back of the couch with his laptop next to him. His broken elbow was propped up on a stack of pillows, and he wore a pair of digital glasses. They were blocky, oversized, and transparent. A faint image of a computer screen displayed on the lenses. Lara couldn't help but do a double take. "What are those?" she asked, trying not to laugh.

Entranced by whatever he was seeing from behind the glasses, Vik didn't move.

"Vik!"

He peered at her over the rim. "Sorry. These are the new DigiSpecs, the latest hands-free, voice command computing platform for accessing my devices and working online. They are simply amazing. Even more useful now that I'm one-handed."

Lara gawked at him suspiciously. "Yeah, and don't they cost a fortune? Where did you get them?"

Vik winced and cleared his throat as he took off the glasses, folded them up, and put them safely by his side. "You're not going to like the answer."

Lara's heart sank. "Just tell me."

"As I left the hospital, a delivery man came up to me and asked if I was Vikram Abhay. I said yes, and then he handed me a small box and asked me to sign for it. When I realized there was no sender or recipient information on the box, I tried to call for him to come back. But he was gone. Like he vanished into thin air." Vik made a poofing gesture with his good hand.

"What did he look like?" Lara asked, handing Vik the cup of coffee.

"Probably sixty years old, grayish brown hair, gray-blue eyes. He looked more like a professor than a delivery guy. Now that I think of it, the whole thing seems odd to me. He wasn't wearing one of those polo shirts with a name tag, but he had a package and a scanner so I just assumed he worked for a delivery company." He paused, focusing on the air in front of him, his face scrunched up. "But how did he know exactly where to find me?"

"And you're just thinking about that now?" Lara rolled her eyes and sighed heavily. She reached into her pocket and pulled out the photo Anita gave her. "Was this him?"

Vik studied the photo for a moment and his eyes grew wide. "Yeah, I think so… he looks a bit younger here."

"Well, congratulations. You met John Fiddler. And now you're using the tech he gifted you. For all we know, he is recording this conversation right now."

Vik's eyes widened even further. He set down the coffee on the side table and slowly picked up the glasses to inspect them. "Do you think he has infiltrated them somehow?" Vik held the glasses between two fingers as if they were contaminated. "Should I stop using them?"

Lara shrugged, thinking through the pros and cons. *What would be Fiddler's motivation behind the glasses? He already tracks us with his drones and beetles.*

If Fiddler wanted to hurt either of them, he would've already done so. Maybe the glasses would help them solve the case. If CyberShop killed Sully, as whoever she met with had indicated, then she and Fiddler were on the same page. "Go ahead and use them. But first you might want to use your computer-whiz skills to find out why Fiddler gave them to you. Maybe he inserted a surveillance program or a bug. In the meantime, let's turn them off. I don't want him listening to this conversation."

As he shut down the glasses, Vik breathed a sigh of relief. "So, if I met Fiddler at the hospital, who did you meet after your interview with Anita?"

"I think Ashton was the man I met at the Basilica."

Lara settled into the lounge chair and tried to relax her body. She told Vik about Ashton pretending to be Fiddler, the strange Bible passage, and the interview with Anita. The connection between Jan Speelman and John Fiddler shocked him the most, and he laughed about the truth staring them in the face. Lara didn't tell him about the offer or Ashton's threat.

Did Fiddler send Ashton on a mission to convince me to take the job?

"Are you going to talk to Anita again?" Vik asked.

Lara nodded. "I'm going to try. What have you been up to?"

"I'm working on finding the location of Fiddler's computer, at least the one he used to log in as KillerBot," Vik said. "I'm getting close to cracking it."

"Not on those glasses, I hope?"

Vik shook his head. "I'm trying to remotely install malware on Fiddler's computer. It's a bit of a minefield, but I think I can pull it off."

Lara furrowed her brow. "But how?"

Vik chuckled. "The TechNow message board used by Fiddler and CyberShop for their conversations was misconfigured and was routing some traffic to several unsecured http links."

Lara scrunched her face. "But I thought Tor was for the Dark Web and doesn't access the surface Web."

Vik shook his head. "Tor is a browser like any other. You can use it to surf the Internet anonymously, but it's a dangerous game. Https websites use end-to-end encryption. However, http websites are unprotected. If you click the wrong link using Tor, you could expose yourself."

"So, Tor doesn't work a hundred percent of the time?" Lara asked.

Vik nodded. "Tor routes traffic and encrypts it within the Dark Web, but if you wander outside the network and click on an unencrypted *http* website, all bets are off. Whoever logged in as KillerBot clicked on a few of these links and compromised their anonymity. I'm this close to getting the IP address." Vik held up two fingers. "To nail KillerBot, I've set an irresistible trap. If Fiddler or his proxy clicks the delicious link I just uploaded to the message board, it will install malware and send me the IP address. Then we can decipher its location."

"Wow, that's brilliant, Vik. I hope it works. But I'm not sure Fiddler is that stupid."

Vik grinned. "Oh, it will work. He's a scientist, not a computer guy. I'm sure he missed something. Or maybe Ashton will click on it by mistake."

"You think Ashton is logging in as KillerBot on behalf of Fiddler?"

Vik nodded. "That's what I'd do if I had an assistant running around doing my dirty work. It's called layered defense. Even if we locate the computer, then we still don't locate Fiddler."

Lara sat silently for a few minutes, drinking the rest of her coffee.

"It's real good of the bug lady to take us both in like this," Vik said.

"Well, she wasn't going to let you fend for yourself with a broken elbow in a half-burned townhouse. Plus, I'm already here and can wait on you hand and foot. But if you're staying here, can you please try to call her Maggie from now on?"

Vik gave her an embarrassed look. "Okay, sorry." He wrinkled his forehead. "But if you're taking her bedroom, where is Maggie going to sleep?"

Vik didn't like putting anyone out any more than she did. "She said she's spending the night at a friend's place."

Whatever that means.

A knock at the door startled her.

Who might that be?

Lara set her coffee cup down, heaved her achy body up from the chair, and plodded over to the door to look through the peephole.

Detective Sanchez? What's he doing here?

When Lara opened the door, a look of surprise crossed the detective's face. She couldn't tell if it was a happy surprise or not. He was better dressed than usual, wearing a newly ironed button-down shirt and pressed khaki pants and holding a bouquet of white roses. His recently applied cologne overwhelmed her nose, forcing Lara to sneeze.

"Sorry," she said, wiping her face on her sleeve. "Detective Sanchez, what are you doing here?"

He didn't answer, leaving an awkward pause between them. "Well," he finally said. "I'm here to see you. Um, Mag—Dr. Brown told me you would be here, and I wanted to make sure you're okay. I heard you almost got hit by a car today. Here, these are for you." With an awkward motion, he handed her the flowers.

Lara's mouth hung open slightly as she took the bouquet. "Uh, thanks. They're beautiful." The words came out monotone and cumbersome. The gesture had caught her off guard.

"They're get-well flowers."

Lara nodded. "All out of teddy bears?"

Sanchez cleared his throat. Something told her the detective was not there to see her.

Or is he? She recalled the Commander making a snide remark about a soft spot.

"Is that it?" Lara asked.

"Actually, there's something more." The detective shoved his hands in his pockets. "I've been investigating Stepanov since you're so hot on him for our suspect."

"You have?" Lara asked.

Why is he suddenly being so nice to me?

Sanchez shifted his weight back and forth. "I called the NSA and verified his work status. The operator transferred me to Justyne Marsh, who said she's working with you and Rob on the case."

Lara nodded.

"Ms. Marsh said Stepanov is on a detail assignment at DARPA, but she wouldn't tell me why. Something about it being classified, need to know, blah, blah, blah bullshit... Anyway, I searched through our intelligence database and found out Stepanov was a Russian national up until five years ago when he gained U.S. citizenship and joined the NSA for his language and technology skills."

Lara nodded. Stepanov had a slight Russian accent, but his recent naturalization surprised her. His English was nearly flawless.

The detective continued. "Back in Russia, he worked for a defense contractor with close ties to the FSB."

"Holy shit, the Russian espionage agency? You think he might be a double agent?"

Sanchez nodded, his awkwardness giving way to excitement. "I also had my computer guys do some digging into CyberShop's activities on the Dark Web. Get this, many of CyberShop's customers appear to be—"

"Let me guess. Russian?"

"Exactly," the detective said as he puffed out his chest a bit and grinned.

"Wow, that's really good stuff. I appreciate you taking my suspicions seriously."

"It's no trouble... really. It's my job." The detective stared down at his feet. "Um, it's getting late. I'd better go."

Lara nodded. "Yeah, I've had a long day. We should catch up on the rest of the case soon. Maybe you could swing by the townhouse tomorrow? I'm stopping by there to see how the repairs are coming."

"Okay, I'll see you tomorrow then." Sanchez gave her a half-smile.

Lara waved goodbye and closed the door behind her.

What was that about?

From across the room, she could see Vik beaming at her. He burst into laughter until he couldn't breathe. He'd obviously been on the edge of his seat the whole time, listening to every word.

"Well, that was some sticky wicket," Vik said, grinning from ear to ear. "Did the detective actually try to hit on you?"

"Ew, Vik. I don't think so." Lara shivered at the idea. "He stopped by to give me information on the case."

"What are the flowers for then?" Vik smirked.

Lara shrugged, trudging toward the kitchen to search for something to put them in.

Was he really here to see Maggie?

After finding a suitable glass vase, Lara opened the utensil drawer to look for scissors to trim the stems. Then something caught her eye. At the back of the drawer, she found a single key linked to a Star Wars Yoda keychain.

What's this doing here?

She recognized it immediately; it was part of the set she'd given Sully for his birthday.

Why does Maggie have this?

TWENTY-ONE

Arson

AS LARA EXITED the cab with keys in hand, she glanced up wistfully at her townhouse. She'd not seen it since before the fire. Vik left Maggie's apartment first thing in the morning and called her with the good news that the contractors were finished de-smoking her apartment. She had the green light to move back home much earlier than originally projected.

They were ahead of schedule, which was perfect. After finding Sully's key, Lara couldn't get out of Maggie's place fast enough. She couldn't shake a growing sense of distrust in her friend. She fingered Sully's Yoda figurine, now attached to her own set of keys. She didn't know what this key would unlock, but she was determined to find out.

Inhaling deeply through her nose, she could detect subtle remnants of smoke in the air.

How could such a small fire do this much damage?

The first-floor windows, broken by firemen in their desperate efforts to suppress the blaze, were still boarded up. The blackened frames gave the lower level the appearance of an abandoned building. Vik said the contractors planned to replace the windows the next day. That couldn't come soon enough. She dreaded the idea of working in the office with no natural light.

Carrying her suitcase up the steps made her injured arm ache. When she reached the landing, Lara sensed something hovering above her. She tilted her head slightly and listened to the whirring coming from above. Pretending she didn't notice, she unlocked the front door. Right before stepping into the building, Lara looked up quickly and caught a glimpse of a quadcopter drone equipped with a surveillance camera. In a flash, the drone hid from sight.

So, I'm not imagining things. That was no delivery drone the other day.

Someone was monitoring her every move. She wondered how many times she'd missed the stalker's drone in plain sight. Once inside her townhouse, a huge wave of relief came over her.

Home at last. At least for a bit longer.

The hallway looked untouched by the fire except for the slight odor of burnt wood. The door to her office stood wide open, and a crew busily worked to finish up the repairs. Lara set her suitcase by the stairs and walked into her office.

The living room and kitchen were more of a construction zone than a living space. Black soot and ashes covered the hardwood floor. The contractors blocked off portions of the room with "do not enter" tape, where they were still replacing the floorboards. Lara peered around the corner at her old storage room; the walls were completely reframed with new wood. A stack of drywall sat on the floor at the end of the hallway, waiting for installation. The amount of work left to be done shocked Lara; she'd hoped they would be farther along.

Vik sat at the charred countertop with his back toward her. The new piece of granite leaned against the wall in the kitchen. He typed awkwardly with one hand while his casted left arm rested in a sling. The DigiSpecs and USB drive with the beetle video footage lay on the counter next to him.

Despite her objections, Vik insisted on coming into work to

keep an eye on the contractors and make sure they wired the new electronics correctly. Earlier that morning, he had texted her:

OMG, THESE GUYS ARE WORSE THAN PIE BOWLERS
THEY DON'T KNOW WHAT THEY ARE DOING
I NEED TO WATCH THEIR EVERY MOVE

"Morning Vik, how are you feeling?"

Vik didn't look up from his computer tablet and continued typing furiously with one hand on the virtual keyboard projected onto the countertop. "Still a bit achy, but otherwise I'm doing okay, boss."

"Did you get a chance to look at the video feed from the beetle?" Lara asked, pointing to the drive.

"Yeah, the footage was doctored all right. Someone with access to the USB damaged the file. Either that or someone corrupted the video wirelessly, which would require some mad skillz."

Lara paused for a few minutes, wondering who might have damaged the file and why. "And the DigiSpecs? Did they check out clean?"

Vik shook his head. "No, but they're clean now. I found the program Fiddler installed to monitor the glasses and disabled it. It wasn't easy to find, but pretty simple to remove."

I knew it.

"Are you absolutely sure they are clean now?" Lara furrowed her eyebrows.

Vik bobbed his head. "One hundred percent certain."

Lara narrowed her eyes. *I sure hope so.* "Did you find my baseball glove anywhere by chance?" she asked with a glimmer of hope.

Vik shook his head and frowned. "Either you put your glove somewhere else, or it burned up in the fire. I'm really sorry."

The pit of her stomach dropped and her expression went

slack. Vik avoided direct eye contact. As her eyes moistened, the initial pang in her chest changed to a dull ache.

Get a grip, Lara. It was just a glove.

She decided to change the subject. "You took the remote, though, right?"

Vik hung his head in shame. "You're never going to forgive me," he mumbled. "The remote is gone too… destroyed in the fire, I think. And I didn't get enough time to take it apart for clues."

Lara grimaced. This was not good news. She hadn't told Sanchez she'd found the missing remote. And now the smoking gun was a dead end.

Maybe what he doesn't know won't hurt him?

A light knock on the office door startled her. She turned to see the detective followed by Rob, stepping over a pile of blackened wood. Her stomach did a flip, and the blood drained from her face.

Speak of the devil. That was close.

"Hey Lara," Rob said with a smirk. "Is this a good time?" He surveyed the damage with raised eyebrows and a low whistle. Sanchez avoided looking at her altogether.

"Sure, come in," Lara said, surprised by her lack of discomfort. After their recent interactions, Rob felt familiar and strange to her at the same time. She couldn't remember why she'd dated him in the first place. Of course, there was his brown curly hair and irresistible grin.

Am I finally over him?

For the first time since their breakup, there was no painful stab in her chest at the sight of him. Maybe crossing paths with him on Sully's case had been a good thing.

Vik waved at the two men. "Can I get either of you a coffee or tea?" He paused before adding, "Or a flower vase?"

Vik! She gave him a look, but he just grinned back mischievously.

Sanchez shoved his hands deep into his pocket and stared at his feet.

Rob looked at Vik with a sideways grin as he scratched his temple. "Um, I'm okay, Vik. Thank you."

The detective is acting like he didn't stop by last night.

Lara wasn't sure if she could adjust to the idea of Sanchez *not* being angry with her. She couldn't figure out what had changed, but she was relieved they were getting along. Though she prayed the detective had not somehow developed a crush on her. The thought gave her the heebie-jeebies.

An awkward pause hung in the air until the detective asked, "Say, was it a black BMW convertible that tried to run you down?"

Lara nodded.

"I remember you also mentioning a similar car out at Fort Meade when your fuel line was cut." Sanchez rubbed his chin. "Do you think it was the same car?"

Lara shrugged. "I don't know. Maybe? The D.C. area is chock-full of BMWs, so it could have belonged to anyone."

"Convertibles are pretty rare, though. It's too bad you didn't get the plate," Sanchez said.

Lara sighed and held up her hands. "Sorry, I was too busy trying not to get dead. Next time, I'll try to do better."

The detective snickered. The half-smile on his face made his brown eyes twinkle in a way she hadn't noticed before. "We put out a bulletin to the general public requesting personal video or pictures taken of the car that tried to run you down. We discovered there's a black BMW convertible registered to Stepanov. If we can get a plate number from a bystander video, that could be evidence for his involvement…"

Lara tilted her head at the new information.

He's actually pretty good-looking. That is if you could get past the chip on his shoulder.

"Is that all?" Lara asked. "I've got some unpacking and inspecting work to do here."

Sanchez shot her a stern look, as if he disliked her tone. "No, that's not all. I received the fire inspector's report yesterday and wanted to go over the evidence with you."

"Oh?"

"There were uh… the inspector found some abnormalities that suggest attempted murder."

Murder?

Lara's eyes grew big. While in the hospital, the detective had told her there was evidence of arson. So, she knew the fire was set intentionally, presumably to destroy her files, or so she thought. But she hadn't considered it to be yet another attempt on her life.

Someone is rather determined to kill me.

"What abnormalities?" Lara asked.

"The incendiary device in the storage room contained napalm."

"Napalm? That would explain the weird smell," Lara said. Militaries had used napalm in the past to burn people alive. "How would someone get their hands on that stuff?"

"I looked it up, and it's pretty easy to make," Sanchez said. The instructions are online. You mix a few common ingredients, and you get a jelly-like substance that sticks to almost anything and burns for a very long time. Once ignited, it burns at more than five thousand degrees Fahrenheit. A napalm fire is almost waterproof."

"So that's why there was so much damage here?" Lara asked.

"Yep," Sanchez said.

Lara furrowed her brow. "But, how did someone set off the device?"

"The device was similar to a Molotov cocktail on a timer. The timer started wirelessly by a remote cellphone signal. When the timer ran out, a lighter released a flame that burned through a long wick. The inspector found glass everywhere, so we think the device was a glass bottle containing napalm and a long wick soaked in kerosene. When the flame reached the inside of the bottle, it exploded, spreading napalm all over your case files and walls."

Molotov cocktail? Could Stepanov have done this?

"Did you find any evidence of who might have done this?" Lara asked.

Sanchez shook his head. "If there was any evidence left behind, it burned up in the fire. However, we did find a few things."

Lara raised her eyebrows. "Oh?"

"Someone returned to the townhouse after the fire. We found shoe prints in the ash. The shoe tread shows minimal wear and indicates a woman's size ten or a men's size nine."

"Does that help us?" Lara asked as she ran her fingers through her hair.

"Not really. We'd need to match the shoe print to the shoe of a suspect."

Lara threw up her hands. "And we don't have a solid suspect. So, we still have zilch."

The detective huffed. "I wasn't finished. We found a few strands of hair stuck to your kitchen window, which was left open."

"In my apartment?" Lara searched her mind to remember if she'd forgotten to latch the window.

"Yes, the intruder climbed the fire escape and entered the townhouse through your kitchen window. We found ash footprints on the floor that were identical to those downstairs."

"Is that it?"

Sanchez scowled at her. "I'm. Not. Done. The lab analyzed the hair from your apartment and found a match to the mitochondrial DNA of the person who cut the fuel line on your bike. It belongs to Martje Hussny. Of course, because hair does not contain nuclear DNA, it could have been this woman, any of her siblings, or her mother. But we're pretty certain Martje is our suspect. Unfortunately, the name is an alias and hasn't come up in the system for ten years."

The woman who cut my fuel line tried to burn down my apartment?

"Okay, so, we still ultimately have nothing," Lara snorted. "Because we have no idea who this woman really is."

Sanchez looked like he was about to implode.

"Lara, have you or Vik dug up any new leads on the case?" Rob interrupted, probably in an attempt to defuse the situation. "We could really use a hit on Fiddler's location."

Lara nodded. "By the way, when I spoke with Anita Fiddler, I finally linked those strange newspaper clippings to the case."

"And?" The detective was all ears as his tense shoulders relaxed a bit.

Lara smiled. "Jan Speelman changed his name to John Fiddler when he moved out here to the East Coast."

"Huh, that is interesting, but what does that really tell us?" Sanchez asked with a half-cocked grin and a sarcastic tone.

"It gives us a motive, I suppose." Lara ignored his jab. "Fiddler's mother died because of the U.S. Army's negligence."

"Motive for what?" the detective pressed.

"I'm not really sure. I learned from his daughter that he worked for the U.S. Army at Fort Detrick for several decades. He was fired recently, but I didn't find out why."

"So, do we think Fiddler killed Sully or not?" Rob asked.

Lara shook her head. "I don't think so."

"Well, if Fiddler didn't kill Sully, then who the fuck did?" Sanchez asked.

Martje Hussny?

Lara preferred not to engage in wild speculation, but humored him. "My gut tells me this CyberShop character, whoever he or she is, killed Sully. And I think CyberShop is the one trying to hurt me, too. But I don't have the faintest clue why." Lara glanced at the others to see what they thought.

"What do you think CyberShop's motive might be?" Rob asked.

"No idea. I'm still trying to make sense of why Fiddler hired Sully to investigate CyberShop's identity." Her thoughts drifted for a moment to the $100K.

Stop it, Lara. It's not worth it. No money is worth that kind of compromise.

"Lara, I think I have something," Vik said in an excited tone, looking up from his tablet. The detective and Rob walked over to the counter and huddled around the screen.

"What did you find?" Lara asked, standing on her tiptoes behind Rob and the detective.

"I've been working around the clock to determine the location of KillerBot's computer, and I think I finally did it. He has been a bit sloppy in covering his tracks on the Internet, and I successfully installed malware on his computer. This morning, someone clicked on the link, and I got the IP address, which appears to be assigned to a building in Takoma Park. Of course, the IP address could be spoofed, so we need to check it out to be sure."

"Where is it?" Lara asked.

"My best guess is the computer is located in *this* abandoned storefront." Vik pointed to a map of Takoma Park in D.C. "I did some digging and found that the space is not in use at the moment. But it used to be a violin shop."

Lara raised an eyebrow. "A violin shop? Fiddler played the violin. Perhaps he ran the shop before changing his name…"

"Let's go check it out now before the lead goes dead," Rob said. "My cruiser is out front."

Lara agreed and followed the guys out of her office.

Finally. A solid lead. Let's hope this one doesn't dead end, too.

TWENTY-TWO

The Violin Shop

AFTER THEY PILED into the FBI cruiser, Rob took off at high speed with his sirens blaring and lights flashing. The traffic on North Capitol yielded obediently to the FBI vehicle. Rob quickly shifted back and forth between lanes, jerking his passengers to the left and then to the right. Lara reached up for the handle above her door to steady herself. For once, a driverless cab didn't seem too bad.

"It's much easier to navigate the streets these days," Rob said, grinning at her in the rearview mirror. "Engineers programmed the software in self-driving cars to force civilian cars to move to the right side of the road in an orderly fashion whenever they receive a signal from an active emergency vehicle. No more dodging cars and driving on the opposite side of the road when traffic refuses to yield properly."

"That doesn't mean you need to drive like a crazy person," Lara said, gripping the handle tightly.

She glanced over at Vik, who shared the back seat of the cruiser with her. Every time the SUV's tires squealed, Vik grinned from ear to ear.

He clapped his hands together a few times. "It's like we're in some kind of police chase," he said as he steadied himself against the window.

Lara rolled her eyes. *Only Vik would think this is fun.*

After about twenty minutes, the SUV screeched to a halt in front of an abandoned storefront on Butternut Street in the northwest quadrant of the District. City parking meters lined the street, shaded by large maple trees. A broken neon sign hung above the window:

TREBLE PITCH

Not waiting for the others to exit the vehicle, Lara jumped out and raced across the street. An old woman exited the rundown laundromat next door, holding a large basket of freshly folded laundry. She gave Lara a dirty look and then hurried to her car parked on the side of the road as if she smelled trouble.

By the time the detective and Rob approached the building, Lara was already peering through the window. Vik had remained in the cruiser, glued to his DigiSpecs.

"I can't see much from here," Lara said to Sanchez and Rob as they joined her. "There's some stuff covered in plastic and a few cardboard boxes lying around. It looks abandoned."

"Let's get a better look," Rob said, taking out a lock pick from his pocket.

"Shouldn't we get a warrant first?" Sanchez asked.

"Lara, do you see anything suspicious in the shop?" Rob grinned at her.

She followed his cue. "I guess so?"

"Good enough for me." Rob picked the lock, and they entered the shop one by one. Out in front, Rob and the detective pulled out their guns. "FBI, show yourself! Put your hands in the air."

A rustling of papers followed by a loud thud came from the back room.

"Shsst," Rob said, holding his finger to his lips. He shouted again. "FBI, come out now!"

A door opened, followed by a loud bang and then footsteps heading toward the back of the shop.

"I'll go after the suspect," Rob said as he ran toward the noise, his gun drawn. "You stay here and check out the rest of the place."

Lara followed Sanchez, checking behind the front desk, the storage room, and another small room being used as an office. She placed a hand on the computer sitting on the desk; it was warm to the touch. Next to it, a laser printer. Lara sniffed and smelled a hint of toner in the air.

It was just used.

"Everything's clear," the detective announced, holstering his gun.

Lara caught a whiff of an intensely sweet aroma. "Do you smell that?"

Sanchez nodded. "Jasmine?"

Lara did a double take. *The detective is full of surprises today.*

She nodded in agreement and continued. "Anita burned incense with the same fragrance at her practice. And I detected—"

A sudden noise from the front of the shop startled them. A pile of boxes tumbled to the floor. They both turned to see Vik wandering into the shop, wearing his DigiSpecs and not paying attention to his surroundings.

"Vik, wireless Internet appears to be working. Come check to see if KillerBot used this computer." Lara pointed to the blinking router.

Vik plopped down at the computer, grinning like a kid in a candy shop, and began typing one-handed. "It will take me a few minutes to hack the password, maybe longer, depending on its strength."

Lara nodded and began searching the shop more carefully. From the thick dust layer covering everything in the store, Lara assumed it hadn't been cleaned in years. Large sheets of plastic draped over the furniture and shelves as protection from the dust buildup. Random sheets of music were scattered on the floor.

In the front corner of the shop, a piece of plastic hid what appeared to be a small shaped case. She knelt on the floor and carefully lifted up the plastic to avoid disturbing the dust. She pulled out a black violin case with an antique finish.

What have we here?

Lara opened the case. The violin was missing. Inside, the case had a thick red velvet lining. An orphan violin bow rested in the slot in the lid. Pulling out the bow and inspecting it closely, Lara could tell it was no ordinary bow. She took a picture of the bow and then spoke into her smartphone: "Watson, could you please identify the violin bow in this picture?"

"Of course, Ms. Kingsley." Watson paused for a few seconds. "I've identified the bow. Based on a quick comparison, the bow is made of Pernambuco wood, very rare and high quality. The tip plate appears to be made of solid gold. Here are some images of similar violin bows."

Lara scanned through the images and clicked on a matching photo. The bow was worth a fortune.

Why was such an exquisite bow left behind, separated from its violin?

A piece of paper sticking out of the bow's pocket distracted her. Setting down the bow, she pulled out the slip. The words were printed by an old typewriter:

IF LOST, PLEASE RETURN TO JAN SPEELMAN, 3300 WHITE OAK DRIVE, SILVER SPRING

"Detective Sanchez, I think I found something," Lara called out. "This violin case belonged to Speelman, aka Fiddler, and there's an address. It tracks approximately with Fiddler's known whereabouts by his daughter."

"I found something, too." Sanchez walked over to Lara with two large scrolls of paper. He rolled out the first scroll to reveal a detailed map of Fort Detrick.

"That's where Fiddler worked before he got fired," Lara said. "What's the other one?"

"It's a detailed map of the NSA at Fort Meade," Sanchez said, rolling out the second scroll.

"Huh?" Lara frowned. "What do you suppose that means?"

"Maybe Fiddler is planning something with the beetles, and these are his targets?" Sanchez shrugged.

Lara bit her lip as she thought about the possibility.

"I also did a quick check on the ownership of Treble Pitch," the detective said.

"And?" Lara asked.

"The business is registered to an Anita De Vries, born in the 1940s. Without confirmation, I'd guess that name belonged to Fiddler's mother, and De Vries must have been her maiden name. That's why we didn't find the shop when we investigated Jan Speelman."

Lara nodded. "Fiddler sure likes using aliases. He must have bought the place right after he moved out here from California, maybe before he changed his name from Speelman to Fiddler."

They both turned to see Rob come running back into the shop, his chest heaving. "I chased him—for ten blocks… but… he had… a head start." Rob bent over, trying to catch his breath.

"What did he look like?" Sanchez asked.

Rob breathed heavily. "Didn't get a close look… maybe six feet tall, regular build, brown hair. He looked young… in his twenties, I think."

Could that be Ashton?

"While you were running after the suspect, we found another address," Sanchez said. "It's not far from here. We should check it out while Vik attempts to break into the computer."

Rob wrinkled his brow and glanced at Lara. She returned his worry with a what-is-your-problem look. *Is he concerned over Vik's hacking or about my safety? Either way, I don't need a knight in shining armor. Especially if it's Rob.*

Rob's face went deadpan at Lara's glaring. "You two okay here, for a bit?" he asked. "We'll be right back."

Lara gathered all the sarcasm she could possibly muster. "No, Rob. This is *so* much scarier than freaking Afghanistan."

Rob rolled his eyes and held up his hands in surrender. "Fine," he said. "I was just asking. You've had a rough few days. Just call us if you have any problems, okay?"

"Yeah, sure." Lara crossed her arms.

"Lara…" Rob gave her that puppy-dog face that used to make her cave every time.

She shook her head. "I promise. I'm not stupid. If I need you, I'll call."

Lara watched the two men hurry out of the violin shop. Then she laid out both maps on the front desk and studied them, hoping they would tell her something.

What are you up to, Fiddler? What do you know about Sully's killer?

On the map of Fort Detrick, Fiddler had circled in red marker the lab where he had worked.

Is the detective right? Is this your target?

She thought about the Bible verse she'd read, about the plague of insects sent against the Egyptians. Something didn't add up. Revenge would have been a great motive decades ago, before he ever set foot in the lab that caused his mother's death.

But why now?

"I did it!" Vik shouted.

Lara's head popped up from studying the map, and she ran over to see what he found, peering over his shoulder. Vik had accessed the computer and was checking the IP address.

"This is it. *This* is the computer KillerBot used to communicate on the TechNow message board."

"Fiddler sent his emails from here?" Lara asked.

"I don't know about that. But I'm absolutely certain KillerBot sent emails from here. I have no way of telling if Fiddler ever logged in as KillerBot at this location, or if he simply had someone else manage his comms for him."

"Oh, right. Is there anything useful on the computer? Any files? Internet search history?"

"Let me see." Vik opened up the browser. "You see, this is where KillerBot went wrong. To maintain anonymity on Tor, never use the Internet on the same computer. I set him up with malware, and he couldn't resist clicking my link, which led him straight to an insecure site on the Internet. And voila, we found him!"

Vik loaded up the last Internet link that was opened. When the page appeared on the screen, Lara's mouth fell open. It was an old newspaper article from a year ago.

One Survivor In Car Crash On The Chesapeake Bay Bridge

The article reported that a local doctor, Dr. Anita Moore, had survived the car crash that killed her husband and son, Frank and Jayden Moore. Their car collided with the railing of the Chesapeake Bay Bridge, breaking through the steel barrier and plummeting into the cold water below.

Although the family survived the impact of the fall, only Anita escaped the car in time and swam to shore without complications. Frank drowned at the scene. Jayden was resuscitated and brought to the hospital, where doctors discovered severe brain damage and were unable to save his life.

In her report to the police, Anita claimed her husband dodged a car barreling toward them on the wrong side of the bridge. When the other driver didn't stop, her husband swerved, lost control of his car, and crashed through the railing. Police couldn't find any evidence of another car. The article noted that the husband worked as a senior cryptologist at the NSA.

Vik rubbed his chin. "It's been a while since I've read about a major accident, you know, since we can't drive manually in D.C. anymore."

"Yeah, but the law doesn't apply outside the District," Lara mumbled absentmindedly, lost in her thoughts.

Justyne's lover was named Frank. He worked at the NSA. This is too coincidental to not be connected.

Lara connected the dots. Anita's husband and Justyne's lover were one and the same. She stared intently at the article, rereading it several times.

"Does the article mean something to you?" Vik asked.

Lara scrunched her face. "I didn't realize Anita's husband worked for the NSA. And when I visited Anita at her office, I asked her about her son, but she couldn't talk about him. This accident happened only a year ago. No wonder she got upset. This could explain Fiddler's retreat from society as well."

"As a doctor, Anita must feel overwhelming guilt at not being able to save her husband or her son from drowning," Vik said.

"Strange." Lara stared at the computer screen.

"What's strange?" Vik asked.

"Anita goes by her maiden name now, but her married name remains on her practice and is used in this article. Why would a widow change her name back to her maiden name?"

Vik's eyes lit up, and he typed "Anita Moore" into the Internet browser window. She peered over his shoulder. The search results exceeded her wildest expectations, one scandalous headline after another about Anita Moore and her husband. Vik clicked on the first article. The headline read:

SENIOR CRYPTOLOGY ANALYST SUSPECTED OF LEAK AT NSA

Lara's jaw dropped as her eyes raced back and forth, digesting the content. "It says Frank Moore was suspected of leaking classified information and selling advanced defense technology over the Dark Web under a pseudonym. NSA officials claim it found massive amounts of evidence to support the allegations, so they suspended Frank's clearance and launched a formal investigation. That's when Frank allegedly drove his family over the Chesapeake Bridge in an effort to commit suicide. They later cleared him of the charges when the Dark Web activity continued after his death."

The NSA thought Frank was CyberShop.

Lara nodded grimly. "If you read further, you'll see that the

NSA then suspected Anita was his accomplice, carrying on the activities after her husband's death. However, after months of harassment, interrogations, and searches by authorities, they finally cleared her name as well."

Vik pressed the back button and selected the next link. The article's headline read:

ANITA MOORE, WIFE OF DEAD NSA SENIOR CRYPTOLOGIST, PRIME SUSPECT IN COLLUSION WITH THE RUSSIANS

Vik grimaced. "This could explain why she changed her name back to Fiddler—to avoid further spotlight and negative press."

"Yeah… and now we've established a clear link between Fiddler and the NSA," Lara said. "And we have a motive. I think Fiddler might be planning something with the beetles. It seems he's chosen two targets. Fort Detrick and Fort Meade. Fiddler is likely seeking revenge on the Army and the NSA for ruining his family."

Lara heard the front door of the shop open.

"Ms. Kingsley?" Sanchez called out.

"In the back room," Lara shouted.

The detective and Rob walked into the room.

"Did you two find anything?" Lara asked.

"No. It was a complete bust," Rob said. "A house once stood at that address, but not anymore. A massive commercial development took its place about two years ago. We checked out the lobby. No suspicious tenants, mostly tech startups. It must have been Fiddler's old home address. Unfortunately, we can't search it further without a warrant. A judge won't grant us one without any evidence establishing probable cause. I think it's a dead end."

"Any luck with the computer?" Sanchez asked.

"Vik cracked the password." Lara filled them in on what they had learned.

"Why would someone search online for Fiddler's dead

family members from this computer?" Rob asked, scratching his head and staring at the screen.

"Good question." Lara shrugged her shoulders.

Is Ashton trying to send me another message? But why?

"Vik, what's that paper peeking out from underneath the keyboard?" Rob pointed at the edge of the keyboard.

Vik lifted it and pulled out map directions to a company called Beautific Creations. At that moment, Lara's suspicions were confirmed.

"Hey, didn't you hear about that place from that dermatologist you visited?"

"Yeah," Lara said. "And now I'm convinced that's where the toxin came from. The one that killed Sully."

TWENTY-THREE

Beautific Creations

NOVEMBER 4, 2027

AS LARA FOLLOWED the curves of Highway 395-South on her motorcycle, the bitter air blew hard against her face. *Oh, how I missed this!* She relished in the splendid freedom of the open road and the power between her legs.

After spending the previous evening trying to get a warrant to search Beautific Creations, Rob gave up and suggested they drive out there on his day off and have a friendly chat with the owner. Sanchez passed on the trip, claiming he was up to his eyeballs processing evidence from the violin shop. His team had scoured the premises for additional leads, but so far only turned up prints and DNA evidence that matched those found in Sully's safe room.

The prints and DNA must belong to Ashton.

The forensics team was still trying to make sense of all the boxes of tiny electronics parts found in the storage room. So far, they hadn't found much in the way of new information.

The cold air refreshed her scratchy, raw throat. Wearing her leather biker jacket, a wool sweater, thick cargo pants with generous pockets, and a cashmere scarf to keep her neck warm, she finally felt like herself again. A sudden gust of wind whisked up falling leaves on the road in front of her. The leaves swirled around in circles and danced about, hovering a few feet above the pavement. The fall weather lifted her spirits.

Lara exited the highway at King Street and drove West on Route 7 for several miles. Compared to D.C., she found the suburbs of Virginia idyllic with their windy roads, gentle hills, wooded neighborhoods, and stately homes. She passed a row of tall trees on her right. For a second, Lara was certain she'd spotted a swarm of golden beetles resting in a nearby tree. She looked up again, but all she could see were golden maple leaves fluttering in the breeze, reflecting the morning sunlight. The dazzling fall colors were playing tricks on her eyes.

Great, I'm seeing things now.

When she pulled into the parking lot of Beautific Creations, Rob's FBI cruiser was already there. In a far corner near the side door sat a shiny black BMW convertible, exactly like the one from the parking lot in Fort Meade. Alarm bells went off in her head at the sight of the vehicle. Lara froze, her heart thumping against her chest.

She kicked herself for not getting a closer view of the plates at the museum or in Foggy Bottom. She killed her engine and wiped her palms on her pants.

Calm down, Lara. It's just circumstantial evidence.

Lara gathered herself together and parked her bike next to the FBI cruiser in visitor parking. Rob and Vik were chatting on the sidewalk. As she dismounted her bike, they waved and headed her way. Rob had offered to swing by the office to pick up Vik. Normally, he would just hop on the back of Lara's bike, but his broken elbow made that impossible.

She glanced across the street at a lonely, dull silver Honda idling under a tree, white smoke billowing from its exhaust. A woman sat in the back of the car, wearing sunglasses and a headscarf. She appeared to be looking out of the opposite window in order to avoid Lara's gaze.

"So, we meet again," Rob said, his eyes twinkling.

Still distracted by the woman, Lara halfway turned toward him. "Yep, good to see you, too."

She didn't know what to make of her ex-boyfriend's warmth. Maybe Rob was having second thoughts about his high-maintenance girlfriend, or maybe he was relieved things were normal between them again. Lately, she'd experienced moments where it seemed like they were still together. And each time she was lulled into a false sense of intimacy, she reminded herself that he'd dumped her, with no warning, for a girl like Bimbo Barbie. Lara wouldn't be fooled into thinking he had feelings for her. Even if he did, it was too late for that. She couldn't forget what he'd done.

"Shall we?" Rob led the way to the front door of the building.

Lara nodded. "Did you see the BMW parked over there? It has a Maryland plate. Convertible. 3B5 7JH." She grinned and lifted her chin.

"Yes, I've already run the plate," Rob said.

Lara deflated, her grin receding. *Show off.*

Rob continued. "The car belongs to Linda Maxwell, the owner of Beautific Creations. With the exception of an arrest when she was a teen, she has a clean record. Another dead end."

"Perhaps…" Lara said, her eyebrow raised. The coincidences related to black BMW convertibles were beginning to mount.

They walked toward the entrance. A nondescript sign with the Beautific Creations logo hung on the left side of the front door. The plain, brick building betrayed no evidence of the types of products contained within its walls. In fact, the posters in the window showed young women, smiling and looking their best.

Lara scoffed now that she knew better. *One of the most dangerous toxins on Earth is stored here. I wonder how many women would be smiling about that.*

Once inside the building, they found themselves in an unfurnished and empty lobby with a basic front desk. A heavy stainless-steel door with an electronic PIN pad stood to the right of the desk. A few tacky pictures hung on the wall, and surveillance cameras were mounted to the corners of the room ceiling. Elevator music played softly in the background. Lara found the ambiance of the place rather unsettling.

"This place looks cleaned out," she said. "Like it's going out of business or something."

Rob gave her a puzzled look and nodded.

Vik seemed oblivious to the peculiar scene. As of late, he'd spent most of his time staring intently into the DigiSpec glasses and speaking to the voice command system, or typing fast into a companion virtual keyboard with one hand. Vik had assured her the glasses were clean. Still, she couldn't shake the feeling Fiddler might be tracking their every move.

Maybe I shouldn't have approved of him keeping them. Too late now, I guess.

An intercom box sat on the counter with a small sign next to it.

PLEASE PRESS THE BUTTON FOR ASSISTANCE

Rob pressed the intercom button.

"May I help you?" a female voice answered.

Rob furrowed his brow. "Yes, I'm Special Agent Robert Martin with the FBI. I'm here to talk to Linda Maxwell."

"Do you have an appointment?" the voice asked.

Lara looked around the empty office, expecting a secretary or an assistant to come talk to them in person, but no one showed. It was just the voice on the intercom.

"Uh, no. I just have a few questions for her. It will only take a few minutes."

Silence followed for several minutes. Rob and Lara exchanged anxious glances.

"I'm sorry, but Linda's quite busy at the moment," the voice said. "You'll have to come back another time when it's more convenient."

Rob clenched his jaw. "Would you prefer I get a search warrant?"

Silence.

He's bluffing. They had already tried and failed to get one. This was their last shot.

"We can do things the hard way if you want," Rob continued, "but I promise it will be quick and easy if she talks to me now."

They waited in silence for a few minutes before the voice returned. "Linda is out in the warehouse. I'll buzz you in. When the door opens, walk all the way down the hall. The warehouse is the last door on your left."

Vik motioned to Lara that he wanted to stay in the lobby and continue his work on the DigiSpecs. When the door buzzed, Lara hurried to open it. Holding the door for Rob, she could sense his growing discomfort with the negligible level of security in the building. Under these circumstances, it was no wonder someone was able to access and steal the toxin.

The long hallway, painted plain white and unadorned, led to four unmarked doors.

What is hiding behind those doors?

As if he read her mind, Rob tried each of them, but they were locked.

They proceeded toward the end of the hallway and Rob opened the last door, which to Lara's surprise gave access to a huge warehouse with many rows of empty shelves.

At the far end of the warehouse, the garage door stood open, revealing a moving truck with its back door hanging ajar and a ramp leading up into the trailer. It was already nearly packed to the brim. Next to the ramp, a tall, curvy woman stood by a dolly loaded with three boxes piled on top of each other. She waved to them, took off her gloves, and began walking toward them.

I was right. Going out of business.

Near the front of the warehouse, two rows of shelves were still stacked with cardboard boxes. Lara moved closer to inspect them. They were labeled with item numbers and barcodes, but there was no indication of their contents. The shelf above each stack of boxes had matching item numbers and barcodes.

A thief would need more information than what's printed on these boxes to know what he was stealing.

The attractive woman dressed in gray jeans and a designer t-shirt approached them. Her face flushed red as sweat beaded her brow. The color of her cheeks matched her auburn hair. "Hi, I'm Linda Maxwell, the owner of Beautific Creations. You must be Special Agent Martin. And you—"

Rob nodded. "Nice to meet you. This is Lara Kingsley. She's helping me with my case."

Linda wiped her forehead with her hand. "Sorry I'm such a mess. As you can see, I'm in the middle of some heavy-lifting at the moment. I'm shipping out most of my current inventory to customers. That happens every few months. Most of my products have expiration or sell-by dates."

Lara detected a slight edge behind the woman's smile. She was hiding something, and Lara would figure out what it was. First, her voice sounded almost identical to the one over the intercom. Almost. It seemed suspicious that Linda would refer to herself in the third person.

Unless she were afraid of something.

As she shook Linda's clammy hand, a sense of familiarity came over Lara.

Where have I seen her before? Lara searched the recesses of her memory. She couldn't recall meeting her, but Lara was sure she'd seen Linda somewhere. *On the beetle video feed, maybe?*

Linda peered at them expectantly. "So, what are you investigating?"

Rob frowned. "I can't share the details of an ongoing investigation. We're working a homicide case in which the cause of death was botulinum toxin."

Linda's eyes grew wide. She took a step backward and shifted her stance. "What? Is that why you're here? Botox is completely safe." Her voice had a defensive ring to it. "Side effects are rare, reversible, and last only a few weeks. Of course, the extent depends upon the location of the injection."

Lara stared at Linda closely. She had almost no wrinkles. The lack of expression on her face was strangely disconcerting.

She must be using her own product. Suddenly, Lara made the connection. She saw Linda in the lobby at the Botox clinic.

"Didn't I see you at Heavenly Cosmetics the other day?" Lara asked.

Jerking her head, Linda gave her an incredulous stare. "I don't remember."

Lara pointed her finger at her. "You were there. I remember you sitting in the waiting room when I came in."

"And your point being?" Linda's eyes were cold when they met Lara's. "Getting a Botox treatment is not only safe, it also happens to be perfectly legal."

"Ma'am, we're not suggesting Botox treatments are dangerous or illegal, at least not if administered properly," Rob responded calmly, subtly shaking his head at Lara.

Oh, yes, we are doing this, Rob. Try to stop me. Lara didn't trust her. *This woman is involved somehow. She could be Sully's killer.*

"The homicide victim died from a lethal injection of the toxin, not the kind you'd get at a beauty clinic," Rob continued. "Over the course of our investigation, we learned about a stolen shipment of the toxin from your company. We're wondering if you might be willing to answer a few questions about the theft."

"But I already spoke to the Feds at length about the incident. We were completely cleared of negligence." Linda became flustered and took out a pack of cigarettes from her pocket, tapped on the side of the container until a cigarette popped out, and then dumped out the lighter hidden inside. "Do you mind?" Linda's face paled, and she looked a bit unsteady.

Rob shook his head.

Then she lit the cancer stick.

Yes, I mind. Lara hated second-hand smoke and detested anyone who made her suffer through it. If some people wanted to choose a slow and painful death, that was their business. But Lara drew the line in the sand when it came to her own health.

Rob continued. "Ma'am, we understand you've been through

a great deal of questioning. But now the stolen shipment appears to be tied to at least one murder, so we're looking for more information to clarify a few things."

Lara glared at Rob, but he didn't notice. He also acted oblivious to the ongoing activity in the warehouse. This didn't look like a routine inventory shipment to her. She was pretty sure they'd walked in on Linda cleaning out her entire operation. In a hurry.

After lighting the cigarette and taking her first puff, Linda sighed. "Do you mind if we sit down?" With her trembling hand, she pointed to a round table and three chairs next to a kitchenette in the far corner of the warehouse.

Rob nodded. "Of course."

Lara walked in a wide circle around the cloud of smoke Linda left in her wake and headed toward the chair furthest from the woman. "Where are all your employees today? Do they have the day off or something?"

"It's always been just me running the show," Linda said dismissively. "Of course, all the automation we have these days helps with that. Would you like something to drink? Water, soda, coffee?" She reached into the refrigerator for a bottle of water, opened it, and took a few generous gulps.

They shook their heads and sat down at the table. Linda crossed her legs, her dirty, rugged-style boots a stark contrast to her brand name gray jeans. Lara stared at them and pressed her lips together to keep her mouth from falling open.

"So, who was the other woman on the intercom?" Lara asked, still staring down at Linda's feet.

Her shoe size could be a women's 10. Eyeballing it, they appeared to be the same print the police found in Lara's apartment.

"Oh that…" Linda took a long drag on her cigarette and blew the smoke up toward the ceiling in Lara's direction. The large fan above spread the smoke around the warehouse, filling Lara's nose with the stench. "I'm just overly cautious."

Lara grunted. *Yeah, right.*

"Tell us what happened with the shipment," Rob asked, giving Lara a get-back-on-task glare.

"Beautific Creations distributes cosmetic products to support the full gamut of surgical and non-surgical procedures for high-end clients. We supply plastic surgeons and cosmetic clinics with everything from mud facials to breast implants to Botox. As I told the Feds several weeks ago, someone intercepted a shipment en route to our warehouse from the manufacturer."

"You mean it was stolen?" Lara asked.

Rob gave her a dirty look, but she didn't care. To her, Linda's oversensitivity felt like an act. And she wouldn't be winning an Oscar any time soon. The security measures in the building were lax. The woman had to know their company would be vulnerable to thieves. Something didn't add up.

"Yes, stolen," Linda said, rubbing her forehead.

"Was the truck stolen too or just the toxin shipment?" Rob asked.

"The toxin was stolen from the truck while it was sitting at a rest stop," Linda said.

"But the boxes are unmarked," Lara said. "How would a thief know which boxes to take?"

"The thief must have known the item numbers on the barcodes," Linda said flatly. She'd clearly repeated the story over and over.

"And how exactly did the thief get a hold of the item numbers?" Lara asked.

Rob kicked her from under the table, and Lara raised her eyebrows at him. *What?*

"The Feds explained to me several weeks ago that my computer system was hacked. That's how the thief knew about the shipment schedule and the item numbers on the barcodes for the inventory on the truck. All the thief needed was a barcode scanner like the ones delivery drivers use, and they could identify the contents of each box." She shook her head. "But honestly, I don't know how they hacked us."

"Was there any video footage of the theft?" Rob asked.

"No, the thief disabled the cameras in the back of the truck before taking the toxin. According to the Feds, there was no evidence left behind. Not a stitch."

"You keep saying 'thief'… how do you know there was only one person involved?" Lara asked, unable to hide her skepticism.

Linda shrugged.

A box crashed to the floor on the other side of the warehouse, startling them. Everyone jumped out of their seats.

"Who's there?" Rob called out, drawing his gun.

"Is there anyone else here besides you?" Lara asked, narrowing her eyes.

Linda shook her head, her eyes wide.

Footsteps padded in quick succession between the aisles, and Lara drew her gun.

"FBI, come out and show your hands!" Rob shouted, running toward the noise and checking every aisle and corner before advancing. Lara followed closely behind, her gun drawn.

Suddenly, a tall pile of boxes came tumbling toward them. Rob ducked out of the way. Lara jumped backward to avoid getting hit. Seconds later, a man with dark hair and thick-rimmed glasses dove out from behind the boxes, pulled open the door, and sprinted down the hallway. Rob chased after the man. From behind, Lara thought he looked rather familiar. She'd run after him before.

It's the man from the Basilica.

The man grabbed the door handle to the lobby and tried to open it, but it wouldn't budge. He turned to face Rob and Lara with his hands up. His ragged, pale face and blue eyes sent a shiver down Lara's spine.

"Don't shoot! I give up. Please don't shoot." His eyes bulged out of their sockets.

A moment of recognition flashed through Lara's head from the bar and pictures she'd seen on the Internet of Sully's assistant. "Ashton Grant?"

The man nodded.

From inside the warehouse, Lara heard a truck engine start up. She stared at Rob in a panic. "Linda! She's getting away."

"You go after her. I'll stay here with Ashton and make sure he doesn't go anywhere. And remember to get the license plate of the truck."

Lara raced down the hallway at top speed, bursting through the door and into the warehouse. The moving truck backed away from the open garage door and did a tight U-turn, tires squealing. Lara sprinted as fast as she could, jumping to ground level from the warehouse, struggling to breathe through her weakened lungs. Then the truck came to a screeching halt. Gasping for air, she stopped and bent over for a moment to catch her breath.

The driver's side window rolled down slowly. Linda gazed out, her eyes ablaze. Her mouth slowly twisted into a grimace. Suddenly, Lara caught a glimpse of a gun barrel. Seconds before the loud *crack, crack* pierced the air, Lara dove behind the dumpster. The bullets ricocheted off the metal, inches from her head. Then, the truck pealed out of the parking area, sending the smell of smoke and rubber into the air.

Lara peered around the dumpster, squinting to get a read on the license plate before it turned the corner.

Crap, I only got four digits.

TWENTY-FOUR

The Assistant

WEARING a black hoodie wrapped around her waist, Lara leaned against the cold cement wall in the back of the room and wiped the sweat off her face. The interrogation room at the FBI Washington Field Office, though clinical and spacious, was primed for the confession of suspected criminals by the lack of air conditioning. A video camera rested atop a tripod stand, staring down the suspect and creating a disquieting atmosphere.

Ashton Grant stared numbly at the table in front of him, his left wrist bound by a handcuff attached to the table. He wore the same jeans and t-shirt as the previous day, but they were grubbier after spending the night in a holding cell.

Lara fidgeted with her pen and notebook, waiting for Rob to arrive and begin the interrogation. Right before they headed into the room, he'd received a call about the location of Linda's moving truck.

The timing of events at Beautific Creations stumped her. Lara had tried to piece together everything she knew about Ashton, but couldn't figure out how he'd ended up at Beautific Creations at the same time as them.

Ashton looked up at her, his face twisted with worry. "Lara, are we off the record?" He stared anxiously at the camera.

She nodded and gave him a warm smile.

"If I were you, I wouldn't bother Anita again."

"Why?" Lara asked, her eyes widening.

"Fiddler was furious when he learned that you visited her practice. He literally hit the ceiling. I don't think it would be a good idea to test his patience. He's... somewhat unstable."

"Thanks. That's good to know. Um, Ashton—"

"Yes?" Ashton looked at her expectantly.

"What happened to Sully's case files? When I searched his safe room, it was cleaned out."

"He moved them somewhere, probably because of me." Ashton looked down and away. "Sully knew I gained access to the safe room. Perhaps he was worried about me snooping around."

"Do you have any idea where he might have hidden them?" Lara asked. The likelihood Ashton would know was slim to none. Sully would've made sure his assistant hadn't a clue, but she still had to ask.

Ashton shook his head.

"Why were you trying to help me?" Lara asked.

He looked at her wide-eyed and said nothing.

"You left me clues. Why?"

He remained silent.

"The Bible verse at the Basilica? The article about the car accident on the computer at the violin shop, and the directions to Beautific Creations? Do you know something about Fiddler's plans? Are you trying to tell me something?"

Before Ashton could answer, the door flung open, and Rob barged into the room. Ashton's face turned pale, and terror flashed through his light blue eyes. Rob took the seat across from Ashton and scowled at him. Lara wanted to kick Rob for being such an oaf.

Who knows what kind of information I could've gotten from Ashton.

"You understand you're entitled to have a lawyer present?" Rob pushed a written statement and a pen across the table toward Ashton, who nodded grimly. "And you understand you're forgoing that right to cooperate fully with the FBI?" Ashton nodded. "You also realize we're not offering you any deal in the event that you're formally charged with a crime. If you cooperate with us, however, we will put in a good word for you with the District Attorney."

Ashton readjusted his thick-rimmed glasses and then hesitated for a moment. He read and reread the statement, but the pen remained on the table, and his free hand didn't move.

Rob glared down at him. "Sign this statement indicating you understand that your rights have been read to you," he demanded. "If you refuse, we'll put you back in the holding cell and work up some charges for aiding and abetting a criminal."

Sighing heavily, Ashton scribbled his signature on the line and dropped the pen on the table, returning Rob's glare. It rolled to the edge of the table and fell to the floor.

"Do you understand this session will be recorded and can be used against you in a court of law?" Rob asked.

"Yes, I do," said Ashton.

"Great, let's get started. Tell me how you know Linda Maxwell."

Apparently surprised by the direct question, Ashton's eyes narrowed. "I don't know anything about her."

Rob folded his arms across his chest. "Then why were you at Beautific Creations yesterday?"

"Uh... I was following Fiddler's orders to track Lara's movements."

Lara shifted and her eyes shot from Rob to Ashton. *What the hell?*

Ashton was at the warehouse before their arrival. He must have been up to something else, possibly for Fiddler, but Ashton didn't want them to know about it.

Maybe he was tracking CyberShop? It doesn't make sense for him to have only been tracking me.

"So, you were trespassing," Rob said.

Ashton gave Lara an uncertain look. She nodded slowly as if to encourage him.

"I guess so."

"How did you know Lara would be at the warehouse?" Rob asked.

"I figured you'd show up when I left the directions to Beautific Creations for you to find at the violin shop." Ashton gave Lara a half-smile.

So, was he helping me by giving me directions? Or leading me into a trap?

"Who drove off in the BMW?" Rob asked.

Ashton shrugged his shoulders. "I don't know. You had me in handcuffs at the time."

Lara still couldn't believe someone had escaped without Vik noticing.

If Linda was in the moving truck, who drove the BMW?

Vik claimed he'd been sitting in the lobby, glued to his glasses, and didn't realize what was happening until he heard the squealing tires outside. He apologized profusely for responding too late and failing to get a glimpse of the driver.

"So, you're telling me you showed up at Beautific Creations, snooped around, and didn't see anyone else there besides Linda?"

Ashton bobbed his head.

"How did you get to Beautific Creations?" Lara asked, catching a look of disapproval from Rob.

"I took a GoGo cab," Ashton said, looking down at his cuffed wrist.

"But how were you planning to leave?" Lara asked, her eyebrow raised.

Ashton scratched his temple with his free hand. "Um, I guess I didn't think that far ahead."

His explanation made no sense. It was foolhardy to rely upon cabs that far outside the city in a potentially dangerous situation.

Who is Ashton protecting? Was Fiddler there too? Did they track CyberShop to the warehouse together?

"I thought you might be interested to know we found Linda's moving truck abandoned in a church parking lot in Alexandria," Rob said, retaking control of the interrogation. "There's an FBI evidence team out at the warehouse right now, combing the facility for evidence. Things will go much better for you if you confess everything now."

Ashton stared blankly at Rob and remained silent, not moving a muscle.

"Did you steal the botulinum toxin?" Rob asked.

Ashton shook his head vigorously. "No, I didn't know anything about that until I overheard your conversation in the warehouse. Is that what killed Sully?" His eyes grew large with desperation.

"I can't comment on an ongoing investigation," Rob said dismissively.

Ashton slumped in his chair. Lara could tell something weighed heavily on him.

He cares about how Sully died...

"How did you come to be Mr. Sullivan's assistant?" Rob asked.

Ashton rubbed his neck with his free hand. "Sully put out an advertisement to local universities, including mine. He wanted to hire a grad student for part-time investigative work. I saw the notice on the American University career board, so I applied and got the job."

"What are you studying in school?" Rob asked, scribbling in his notebook.

"Electronics engineering with a specialty in microelectronics."

Lara perked up. *Now we're getting somewhere.*

"Why were you interested in doing investigative work?" Rob asked.

Lara leaned against the cement wall.

Why do you keep dropping the interesting issues, Rob? He must know something about the beetles.

Ashton shrugged. "The money was good, much better than I

could earn working for an engineering professor. And I'm trying to avoid massive student loan debt after I graduate."

Relaxing a bit, Lara realized Rob avoided going deeper at first to build momentum and make the kid feel comfortable. Answering a few harmless questions usually got suspects primed for the really important ones. Classic interrogations move. Shock and awe, followed by easy questions. Ashton didn't know it, but they already extracted a motive. The kid desperately needed money.

Yeah, but so do I. That's circumstantial at best... unless we find out more.

"When did you begin working for Fiddler?" Rob asked, changing the subject. Another interrogation tactic.

"Several months ago." Ashton wiped beads of sweat from his forehead. "I figured out that Sully was bringing in huge amounts of money from a client with the pseudonym KillerBot. Sully wouldn't let me get involved in the case. So, I broke into his safe room, searched through his files, and figured out a way to get in touch with Fiddler, aka KillerBot. Then I offered him my services directly."

"I'm curious. How did you break into Sully's safe room?" Lara interjected. Out of the corner of her eye, she caught an irritated look from Rob.

Ashton glanced up at Lara while he scratched at the back of his head and swallowed loudly.

Lara gave him another encouraging smile. "It's okay. From Sully's journals, we know you were in there, even after he fired you. You might as well tell us what you were doing."

"I dusted the code panel for fingerprints and left a recorder in the room to catch the tones of the buttons. The fingerprints narrowed the combination possibilities, and the tones gave me the order of the numbers. Quite simple, actually."

Lara was impressed.

"And how did Fiddler respond to your offer to work for him?" Rob asked.

"Well, at first, he was skeptical and asked me what I could do for him that Sully wasn't already working on. I told him about my specialized expertise in microelectronics. That seemed to catch his attention right away."

"How so?" Rob asked.

"He asked me if I could develop a microelectronics package small enough to fit on the back of a beetle. He was trying to develop a delivery system. He didn't say what for. Before I came along, he'd initially been looking for drones to meet his needs. But he said he preferred something smaller, more agile, and less detectable."

"Why do you think Fiddler pushed forward with the drone show if he'd moved on to something else?" Lara asked, catching some shade from Rob.

"Fiddler wanted to lure CyberShop out of hiding," Ashton said. "The old man hoped CyberShop would make a mistake, leaving us a trail of breadcrumbs or something that would help determine his or her identity."

"Why?" Rob asked.

"Fiddler has a personal beef with CyberShop," Ashton said, his eyes darting briefly toward Lara. He'd told her about CyberShop killing Fiddler's family at the Basilica. He'd also told her he'd met CyberShop while impersonating Fiddler.

Had Ashton met CyberShop?

"Did you get any leads on CyberShop?" Lara asked.

Ashton shook his head.

"Did Fiddler know about our sting operation?" Rob asked.

Ashton laughed. "Yeah, he was on to Droneman for a long time. You guys aren't as sneaky as you think."

Rob readjusted just slightly, and Lara smirked. *Yeah, Droneman. Not as smooth as you want everyone to believe, are you?*

"Why were you at Sully's townhouse the night of his murder?" Rob asked, apparently trying to catch Ashton off guard.

Ashton stared at Rob uneasily, visibly unsettled by the dramatic shift in the conversation. "I wasn't there that night," he stuttered, avoiding direct eye contact.

"We have the DNA evidence to prove you were," said Rob, staring intensely at him across the table. "We know you had access to the safe room. You just admitted it."

"What evidence?" Ashton asked.

"You left saliva on a coffee cup and an unfinished sandwich," Rob said. "I thought you said you were willing to cooperate."

Lara knew Rob was bluffing about having the DNA evidence in hand and was counting on the fact that these items did indeed come from Ashton. They'd not yet had a chance to collect a DNA sample from Ashton to make the final comparison.

"Okay, okay. I was there." Ashton rubbed his forehead nervously.

"And what were you doing there?" Rob asked.

"Communicating with Fiddler."

"About?"

Ashton shrugged. "I don't remember. It wasn't that important."

"How much did Fiddler pay you to work for him?" Rob asked.

"About two hundred thousand dollars in total."

Enough money to pay for his entire graduate education. She couldn't really blame him for being tempted.

"How did he pay you?" Rob asked.

"Bitcoin."

"Did you ever meet Fiddler in person?" Rob asked.

Ashton shook his head, pushed his glasses up, and looked away. Lara knew he must be lying. *How else could they work together?*

"Do you know where Fiddler's laboratory might be located?"

"No. He never gave any hints about his home base," Ashton said, shaking his head again. "I communicated with Fiddler from Sully's safe room a few times and later from the violin shop."

"Okay, back to the topic of microelectronics; how did you respond to Fiddler's question about their potential?" Rob asked.

"I told him engineers had succeeded in using electronics to

control the flight of beetles years ago and claimed I could do it, too." Ashton fidgeted with his shirt.

"And were you able to pull it off?" Rob asked.

"Yeah. It was no problem. I developed a microsystem capable of directing the flight of a beetle."

Lara leaned forward, interrupting Rob's interrogation again. "I found your bionic bug. At first, I thought it was pretty impressive, but then I discovered the upgraded version Fiddler made. Now that was a masterpiece. The backpack looked smaller, and the flight control seemed to be more advanced."

Ashton's eyes narrowed. "That was mine too. I made it, not Fiddler."

Lara shook her head in disbelief. "No, you're good, but not that good."

"Oh yes, I am. I figured out a much better way to control the beetle's flight, leveraging Fiddler's expertise with gene-editing tools. Fiddler genetically modified the nervous system of the beetles to make them capable of responding to pulses of light delivered through optrodes. Rather than control the beetle's flight through electrical stimulation of the muscles, the light pulses activate steering neurons in the beetle's brain. This is a much more direct pathway to flight control and taps into the insect's natural abilities."

"What about the smaller backpack?"

Ashton nodded eagerly. "By removing the battery and adding a tiny solar panel to harvest energy from the sun instead, we reduced the overall weight and were able to integrate a navigation system into the backpack. The system enables autonomous navigation without wireless control. All of this means the beetles have the capacity for heavier payloads, longer ranges, and extended use."

Lara scoffed and waved him off dismissively. "Sounds like a bunch of fancy talk to me. Your beetle doesn't work very well. When I downloaded the video from your beetle, the footage turned out to be too grainy to identify anyone."

Ashton shot her a defiant look. "That's not possible. I

designed my prototype system to capture and transmit high-definition video wirelessly. If the footage was grainy, someone doctored the video after the fact."

"Did you do it?" Lara pressed.

Ashton jerked his head back and let out a bark of laughter. "Why would I do that?"

Rob let out a frustrated sigh. "This is interesting, but I'd prefer to get back to the case if you don't mind, Lara?"

Lara frowned. "Okay… sorry." She didn't understand Rob's haste. Though technical, she was convinced the information Ashton provided would be essential to discovering Fiddler's plans.

"Do you know what Fiddler is planning to do with the beetles?" Rob asked.

"I'm not sure." Ashton shifted around in his seat and avoided direct eye contact.

"Do you know if the beetles are infected with the plague?" Rob asked.

Ashton shook his head.

Lara didn't believe him. *Not with the clue he'd left in the Bible at the confessional.* She decided to drop it. Maybe she could use it to elicit his trust later.

"Did Fiddler ask you to do other things for him besides develop the microelectronics package?" Rob asked.

"Odds and ends. He often asked me to communicate with Sully and sometimes with CyberShop under his pseudonym. He asked me to keep an eye on you, Lara, and deliver notes by beetle courier."

Lara's cheeks flushed red as anger flashed inside her chest. She shoved her hands in her pockets and paced the room behind Rob.

Ashton looked directly at her. "For example, he asked me to meet you at the Basilica, to impersonate him and—"

"Do you know anything about CyberShop?" Lara interrupted, brashly redirecting the conversation away from her. She didn't want Rob to learn about Fiddler's offer.

"Fiddler was convinced CyberShop worked for the NSA and peddled Top Secret encryption and drone technology developed by DARPA to the highest bidder over the Dark Web. CyberShop sold some sort of remote control to Sully."

So, I was right. Sully tried to take control of the drones.

"How did Sully get the device from CyberShop?" Lara asked.

"CyberShop mailed the package to his townhouse," Ashton said. "I was there when Sully got it and opened the box. Much smaller than I thought it would be…"

Lara made a mental note to return to Sully's townhouse to look for the box she'd seen on the video footage. Maybe it had a return address or some other clue to CyberShop's whereabouts and identity.

"Did you know Sully was ill?" Rob asked, probably trying to startle him.

Ashton averted his gaze. "No… no, I didn't have any idea."

"Did you have anything to do with Sully's death?" Rob's jaw tightened.

"Uh… I think I want a lawyer." A look of fear crossed Ashton's face.

"Just answer the question." Rob raised his voice.

"No. I had nothing to do with Sully's death. I'm not saying anything else without a lawyer."

"You let the right to a lawyer go when you signed those papers," Rob shouted.

Ashton glared at Rob defiantly, pressing his lips together, and shook his head.

Rob pounded his fist on the table, got up out of his chair, and stomped out of the room, slamming the door. When he left, she breathed a sigh of relief. Maybe she could get something more from Ashton. For a few minutes, Ashton sat in awkward silence while Lara made notes in her notebook.

"Lara, I swear I didn't doctor that video. You have to believe me."

She gave him a half-smile. "I think if you'd done it, there

wouldn't be any footage of you in the safe room on the day of Sully's murder."

Ashton looked stunned. "The beetle made it into Sully's safe room? But I releas—" He shut his mouth and stared at the floor.

"It's okay," Lara said in a soothing voice. "I'm not going to tell Rob you released the beetle, or that you know about it carrying the plague." Ashton relaxed slightly. "You're covering for someone at the warehouse, aren't you? You weren't there by yourself." Lara thought of the idling silver Honda parked across the street. She had a theory.

Ashton shifted around in his seat.

"Fiddler was there with you, wasn't he?" Lara asked. His eyes flicked upward at her for a mere second, but then he turned them back at the floor, staring intently at nothing. "I saw the silver Honda parked there. You were both tracking CyberShop, weren't you? You said you'd met her before when we were talking at the church. Were you speaking for Fiddler or yourself?"

Ashton gave a slight nod, but still avoided her gaze.

Yes? To which question?

"Is Linda Maxwell CyberShop?" Lara asked. "Is that why you were both at the warehouse?"

Before she got an answer, the door opened a crack. Rob poked his head in and motioned to her with a stern look on his face to come with him. Ashton clammed up immediately and pressed his lips firmly together again.

Reluctantly, Lara followed Rob out of the room, closing the door softly behind her.

Walking briskly down the hallway, Rob turned to her and said, "We have video footage from the warehouse, and the techs think they've found an important lead."

Well, I sure hope so.

Because she had the feeling Ashton was about to tell her something big, and she wasn't sure she'd be able to get him to the point of spilling the truth a second time.

TWENTY-FIVE

The Stakeout

NOVEMBER 5, 2027

KEEPING one eye on the door of Anita's townhouse, Lara pretended to read a newspaper while sitting on a bench at the edge of a quaint city park in D.C.'s Petworth neighborhood. She contemplated the events of the previous day. The silver Honda she'd seen at Beautific Creations haunted her mind. It looked just like Anita's car.

Her thoughts drifted to the interrogation. She shook her head in disbelief. Rob had prevented her from learning what Ashton knew about CyberShop, all for some useless video footage.

Well, almost useless.

After Rob pulled her from the interrogation room and dragged her to the FBI's video processing center, they'd watched the footage seized from the cameras at Beautific Creations. From an outdoor closed-circuit camera, they observed the black BMW pealing around the corner of the building and racing into the street, followed closely by the moving truck.

The angle of the camera made it impossible to get a visual of anyone in the BMW, but they were able to see the license plate of the moving truck. Sanchez had offered to pull footage from nearby traffic cameras to see if they'd have better luck identifying the driver of the BMW. But he'd also come up with nothing.

To Rob's annoyance, Lara asked the techs to replay the video several times and demanded they stop every time something silver flashed across the screen. Finally, they were able to isolate the partial image of what she thought was the same silver Honda she'd seen idling on the street. Without the license plate, a full image of the vehicle, or images of its passengers, Rob dismissed her gut instinct that they should investigate further.

Lara had a strong feeling the Honda belonged to Anita, and that she'd come along with Fiddler and Ashton to investigate Linda Maxwell. It infuriated her to think Rob wouldn't believe her without further evidence.

Anita had mentioned she always took a day off from the medical practice on Mondays, and Lara decided to conduct a stakeout. She hoped the doctor would also follow her biweekly ritual of picking up her father's mail and meeting him for coffee. If Anita met with her father, Lara could kill two birds with one stone.

Perfect day for Operation Fiddler.

Most people would have already gone to work for the day, which made Lara sitting on the bench stick out like a sore thumb. The newspaper was not the most inconspicuous disguise, but she couldn't wait on her motorcycle or hide her face behind her smartphone. If Anita got even a quick glimpse, she would recognize her immediately.

A scrappy-looking man in his twenties with a yellow Labrador passed by her bench and gave her a strange look. Given the mid-morning hour and the treat bag around his waist, the man probably worked as a dog walker or trainer. But she couldn't take any chances on being recognized and raised the paper higher, hiding her face.

Perusing the headlines, Lara waited patiently for Anita to leave her townhouse across the street. Lately, the news media were stoking fears across the country about the many technological changes looming on the horizon. The rise of artificial intelligence, the restructuring of commerce due to advances in 3D printing, and the emerging drone traffic control system had all recently captured the public's attention. Incessant media coverage only intensified speculation about a future war between humans and machines.

Lara didn't understand all the hysteria. Most people wanted things to stay the same so they could remain in their safe little comfort zones. Even when reluctant to adopt certain types of new tech, she found the pace of change to be thrilling, like an old-school Wild West adventure.

As if we can stop the pace of technological advances, anyway. She laughed. *No, that drone has left the station.* And if it ever came to a war with Skynet, she was pretty certain the machines would win due to their superior aptitude for adaptation.

Hearing a front door open and close across the street, Lara looked up to see Anita race down the front stairs of her townhouse and climb into the back seat of a silver Honda. The same car from the street at Beautific Creations.

I was right.

The car gradually inched out of its parking spot. For such maneuvers, Lara knew the light detection and ranging sensors must be working hard to identify nearby obstacles on all sides and make the smallest corrections to avoid collision.

Time to play ball.

Lara got up from the bench, tucking the newspaper under her arm, and strode toward her motorcycle parked only a few feet away. As the car proceeded slowly down the street, Lara snapped a photo of the license plate, put the newspaper in the seat compartment, and then mounted her motorcycle. She put the bike in neutral and moved it into position.

She waited until the Honda reached the next intersection before turning the ignition, and she winced at the loud rumble of her engine. That unmistakable noise was the number one downside of riding a bike as a private investigator. Of course, following a lead in the pouring rain would be even worse.

Keeping as much distance as possible, Lara followed Anita's car as it weaved mechanically in and out of traffic, finding the most efficient route. The drive to the cozy community of Takoma Park on the border of Northeast D.C. and Maryland took about fifteen minutes. Anita's car parked itself on Laurel Street in front of the Takoma Park post office. After climbing out of the back seat, Anita went into the post office building. In full view of the entrance, Lara waited patiently a block away with her engine idling.

After a few minutes, Anita came back out with a thick stack of mail under her arm. Instead of returning to her car, she walked down Carroll Street for a few blocks until she arrived at a storefront. Anita paused for a moment and turned her head to see if anyone followed her. Then she ducked into a small coffee shop.

Lara parked her bike, dismounted, and grabbed her newspaper from the seat compartment. Crossing the street, she made her way toward a park bench next to an old stone church directly across from the coffee shop. She sat and opened the newspaper to hide her face, then put on the DigiSpecs she'd stolen from Vik's desk.

The thin-rimmed glasses provided full Internet connectivity and displayed useful information about objects within her line of sight. Other advanced features included a camera and zoom lens. The glasses could be operated over her smartphone, a Bluetooth keyboard, or voice-recognition software.

"Enter command, zoom in," Lara said under her breath. The camera zoomed in. Peering around the side of her newspaper, she had an unbelievably close-up view of the coffee shop. "Enter command, record."

Too bad it can't pick up sound from behind glass.

Inside the café, Anita sat at a table across from a man who looked to be in his sixties. His hair was mostly gray with a bit of brown. He had a slender frame and wore a corduroy suit jacket with patches sewn onto the arms.

So, that's Fiddler. The man behind the beetles. And Sully's former client. What does he know about Sully's killer?

Anita slid the mail across the table to her father, who sipped his coffee and glanced anxiously out the window as if he were looking for someone. His eyes locked on her position, and chills spread throughout her body. For a moment, she thought Fiddler had spotted her. Through the magnification of the DigiSpecs, she detected a flicker in his blue-gray eyes, a flash of anger. Her hair stood on end.

Does he know I'm here? She still didn't trust the DigiSpec glasses. *Maybe he's tracking the usage somehow...*

Her heart pounding, Lara hid herself behind her newspaper. After a few seconds, she peeked cautiously over the edge of the newspaper. Fiddler appeared to be deep in conversation with his daughter, no longer paying any attention to things outside the shop.

I must be imagining things again.

After about thirty minutes, the atmosphere between Anita and Fiddler appeared to deteriorate. Anita threw her hands up in the air and seemed to be speaking in a raised voice. Fiddler crossed his arms and scowled at his daughter and then shook his finger at her. Suddenly, Anita got up from the table, exited the coffee shop in a huff, and marched back to her car, slamming the door shut. Her face was contorted with rage, and tears streamed down her cheeks.

A few minutes later, Fiddler got up from the table and disappeared toward the back of the store. Anita drove away, and Lara waited on the bench for about twenty minutes, expecting Fiddler to exit through the front door. He never did.

Crap.

She had waited too long and lost her lead. Folding up the newspaper and shoving the DigiSpecs into her pack, Lara jogged across the street toward the café. The bell hanging at the top of the front door rang merrily as she entered. The barista at the counter looked up at her and smiled.

Lara surveyed the café. Except for a couple patrons sipping their coffees and staring at their computer screens, the café was empty. She walked toward the back of the store and pushed open the door to the men's room. Also empty. Lara walked back to the counter and ordered an iced coffee.

Rob would laugh at me if he saw this.

Of course, the purchase was just for show. She couldn't quickly gulp down a hot coffee, and her throat was still sore from the smoke inhalation.

Or maybe iced coffee was growing on me.

She pushed the picture of Fiddler toward the barista. "Have you seen this man? His name is John Fiddler."

The barista nodded. "Sure, John's a regular here. He was actually just here with his daughter. Things got kind of heated this time, and they both stormed off."

"What were they arguing about?" Lara asked.

The barista shrugged. "Honestly, I tried not to pay attention. Didn't catch that much. Something about a warehouse. I think she was angry about him making her go there. He wanted her to go somewhere else, and she was refusing."

"Did you overhear where?"

"Maybe the Chesapeake Bay?"

"Do you know where he went?" Lara asked.

"Oh, he left out back about half an hour ago." The barista pointed to the kitchen.

Dammit.

The barista continued. "Every time, he asks one of us if he can leave through the back door. He tips us well, so we let him do it. What's the harm, right?"

"Do you know anything about him?" Lara asked.

The barista shrugged. "Not really. He meets up with his daughter here like clockwork every two weeks. Nice guy, but somewhat strange. That's all I know."

"Thanks for the info," Lara said, gulping down the rest of her coffee and dumping the plastic cup into the trash.

Outside the coffee shop, there was no sign of Fiddler. It was as if he had vanished into thin air. Lara headed over to the post office to see if she could get any information on Fiddler's post office box account.

As she pulled open the glass door, she didn't expect the Takoma Park post office to be so small. Lara knew the U.S. Postal Service was phasing out all of its remaining postal workers and replacing them with automated machines, which lined an entire wall in the next room. Hours had been cut back severely, and the quality of customer service had suffered. She'd grown tired of the messy piles of mail tossed in the slot of her townhouse.

At the small bulletproof kiosk, a frazzled and overworked postal worker handled a long line of impatient customers, who were stopping in on their lunch hour to buy stamps and send packages.

Lara scanned the rows of metal post office boxes, which were located on several adjacent walls in the back corner next to the automated machines. She studied them for a few minutes, wondering which one might belong to Fiddler, when a familiar waft of floral fragrance passed by her nose and made her sneeze.

"Bless you," a voice said from behind her, causing her to jump slightly.

Lara turned to see Justyne standing there, her head tilted and her arms crossed. Dressed in her usual black Burberry trench coat, sunglasses, and Louis Vuitton shoes, Justyne was stunning as usual. Her black hair was tied up in a neat bun, and her skin was flawless. Lara checked the status of her own hair in the reflection of the post office window and shuddered.

Okay, not my finest moment.

She shook off her insecurity and smiled. "Justyne, what are you doing here?"

"I could ask the same of you." Justyne's voice had a shrill edge to it. She narrowed her piercing blue eyes. "I have to say I'm a bit disappointed in you. I thought we were working the case together, and you haven't called me since I visited you in the hospital. And now I see you're out tracking down leads again."

Lara gave her an apologetic look. "Yeah, uh… sorry. I've been kind of busy."

"That's okay. I'm just giving you a hard time." Justyne smirked, relaxing her shoulders. The sudden change in demeanor gave Lara a chill. "How did your visit to the Botox clinic work out?"

Lara gave her an uncertain smile. "Really good. We got our first big lead. Thank you for getting us in to see Dr. Grayson so quickly. We definitely owe you one."

"Great! I'm so glad." Justyne lowered her voice to a whisper. "Did you learn anything interesting?"

Lara hesitated for a minute. "Yeah. We discovered the source of the botulinum toxin that killed Sully. It's a cosmetic supply company called Beautific Creations."

"Wow. You weren't kidding about big leads. That's huge news. Do you have a suspect?"

Lara nodded. "We think Linda Maxwell, the company owner, was behind the theft of the toxin and possibly Sully's death. If we're lucky, maybe we'll learn that she's involved in your colleague's death as well."

Justyne leaned in toward Lara, her interest piqued. "And did the FBI apprehend the suspect yet?"

Lara shook her head. "No, she escaped without a trace. The FBI is still digging through the warehouse, though, so perhaps we'll get another lead on her whereabouts. We think she had an accomplice."

Justyne raised her eyebrow. "Oh really? Do you think it could have been Stepanov?"

"Not sure. We saw a black BMW convertible on the scene when we arrived, but we checked the plates, and it belonged to Linda. But someone else drove it away, so—"

Justyne gaped at her. "I'm pretty sure Stepanov drives the same car."

"Huh…" *Interesting coincidence. Did Stepanov try to run me down?* Lara's eyes narrowed. "By the way, how did you know to find me at this post office?"

"By coincidence, actually. I was inside the café watching Anita meet with her father. And then I saw you sitting on the park bench, doing the same thing. I ducked into the women's restroom when you entered the café, in case Fiddler was watching us. Then I followed you into the post office, hoping we could catch up."

I never checked the women's room. Rookie mistake.

"But why would you… how did you…" Lara stuttered, unable to finish a thought.

"I've been tracking Anita's movements for a while. At first, I thought she might have had something to do with her husband's death. Maybe she found out about our affair and had someone run her husband off the road."

Anita would never cause an accident with her son in the car.

Lara's eyes grew large. "So, your Frank *is* Anita's husband."

Justyne nodded. "I didn't tell you that up front?"

Lara shook her head and said nothing for a moment as she absorbed the information. "You also never mentioned that before he died, Frank came under suspicion by the NSA for leaking the classified information. Or that authorities suspected Anita to be his accomplice for several months."

Justyne clenched her jaw and bared her teeth. "I didn't tell you because it was not worth mentioning. Complete bullshit." Her eyes flashing with fury, she looked like she might kick something. "The Agency wasn't interested in the truth. Instead, NSA officials misconstrued the evidence and then made up a bunch of lies about Frank to protect the Agency's reputation in the press." She took a deep breath, trying to calm herself. "My Frank was a true patriot and would've never betrayed his country. If anything, he died because he was trying to expose the real traitor—CyberShop."

"But the NSA seems interested in the truth now," Lara said.

"I mean, if they assigned you to the case and asked you to collaborate with the FBI."

"Yes, but only because the leaks continue to happen, not because they want to clear Frank's name. That's why I volunteered to help. I want to make this right for Frank."

Lara crinkled her nose. "I still don't understand why you're spying on Anita and Fiddler."

"Good question. I quickly dismissed my theory about Anita and began to wonder about her unstable father as a potential suspect for Frank's death. John is definitely capable of murder. Maybe he killed Sully too?" Justyne paused and studied Lara's face for a few seconds. "Anyway, after following Anita around for months, I knew she picked up his mail and met with him every two weeks. I'd stopped spying on their meetings two months ago. But working with Special Agent Martin and hearing about the bionic bugs, it occurred to me that John might be the one sending those nasty beetles after you. So, I decided to check him out again. At the very least, John knows something about CyberShop."

"But why would Fiddler kill Frank?" Lara asked flatly.

Justyne shrugged. "I don't know... maybe he found out about Frank's affair with me?"

Lara furrowed her brow, shaking her head. "I don't think Fiddler killed Frank or Sully, but you're right. He's definitely capable of something. Did you overhear anything interesting in the café?"

Justyne shook her head. "Not really. I had to sit in the back corner because the tables next to theirs were already full. I couldn't make out any words until they began fighting. Anita was angry with her father about tricking her to drive out to some warehouse. John said he wanted to prove to her they were still in danger from an NSA analyst posing as CyberShop."

"Do they have any idea who CyberShop is?" Lara asked.

Justyne moved her head from side to side. "I heard their attempt to learn CyberShop's identity got cut short by something... I didn't catch that part. Toward the end, it sounded like John was trying to warn Anita about something he was planning. He urged her to leave town, to go out to the Chesapeake Bay and stay with her mother-in-law for a few days. Not sure why. Anita became quite agitated. She argued with him, refused, and then left in a hurry."

Would Anita skip town?

Lara was too tired to hide her dismay. Every time she made progress on the case, she hit a wall.

"Would you be less disappointed if I told you I got Fiddler's street address from the postal worker?"

"What? How did...?" Lara was baffled.

"I flashed my Department of Defense badge, and the postal worker gave me the information." Justyne smiled triumphantly.

Lara grimaced. "They're not supposed to give out that information." She glanced at the postal worker, who looked exhausted and worked to the bone.

"Well, I got it." Justyne shrugged. "Do you want to come check it out with me or not?" She turned on her heel toward the exit.

Lara nodded eagerly and followed her, but something caught her eye through the glass window—a strange metallic glimmer. "Wait," Lara said, grabbing Justyne's arm right before she opened the door.

"What?" Justyne looked back at her, brow furrowed.

"Do you see what I see?" Lara pointed to the large maple tree next to the park bench where she'd been sitting. A swarm of metallic beetles flew around in circles at the top of a tree, glistening in the sun.

"Those aren't... like the beetle you found, are they?" Justyne asked.

"Yes, that's a swarm of bionic bugs." Lara's voice quivered. "Fiddler has been using his beetles to spy on me. Apparently, now he's using swarms. He must know we're here. And something tells me the swarm might be dangerous. We have to get out of here. Now!"

"Oh my God." Justyne cringed, and her face went pale.

Lara motioned to her. "Come, we need to slip out the back."

Lara walked calmly to the back entrance and opened the door. Justyne followed closely behind. Before exiting, Lara looked all around for any metallic gold color. "I don't see anything out here… but just to be safe, I don't think we should hang around for much longer. Do you have wheels?"

Justyne shook her head. "No, I took a cab."

"Do you mind riding on the back of my bike?"

"Sure. It's not what I had in mind for our first driving lesson, but anything to get me out of here… and fast."

"C'mon, let's go." Lara raced around the back of the shops toward her bike.

She was thankful she'd parked only a block away from the post office. Behind her, Justyne struggled to keep up in her high heels.

Serves her right for wearing those silly stilettos.

As soon as Lara mounted the bike, she revved her engine. With some effort, Justyne finally climbed onto the back of the bike and grabbed Lara tightly around the waist. Gunning the engine, Lara sped away, dodging in and out of traffic as fast as she could to get as far away from the beetles as possible. She had no idea what kind of range they had and didn't want to find out.

TWENTY-SIX

The Library Book

Traffic wasn't bad for a Monday afternoon. It took Lara only twenty-five minutes to reach downtown D.C., even with the extra weight of a passenger. Slowing to a near stop, she pulled up in front of a convenience store and tipped the bike gently toward the sidewalk to let Justyne dismount.

"I hope this is a good place to let you off," Lara said, tilting her head behind her.

"Where are we?" Justyne asked.

"Foggy Bottom, near the George Washington University Hospital. You should be able to grab a cab from here if you want to head home."

Justyne looked around, somewhat uncertain of her surroundings. She recoiled as a scraggly old woman with a reddish face, drinking from a poorly hidden bottle in a paper bag, stumbled by. Even from several feet away, Lara could smell the telltale odor of alcohol on her breath. The old woman dragged her dolly full of groceries behind her and took no notice of the two women sitting on a motorcycle.

Lara waited until the old lady passed and then rested her right foot on the curb to steady the motorcycle. Just then, a city bus whooshed by, nearly knocking her off balance. Its brakes screeched as it approached the bus stop just a few yards away.

"Okay, this is fine." Justyne dismounted in a hurry and shook herself out.

"A bit shell-shocked by the speed of the ride?"

"That and the narrow miss by the bus."

Her neat bun had come completely unraveled. For once, Justyne wasn't perfectly put together. If Lara didn't feel sorry for her state of mind, she might have laughed out loud.

"Are you okay? I'm sorry if I took the roads a bit rough." Lara winced at the idea of Justyne's terrified face as they'd hugged a corner or whipped down the highway. She'd been focused on driving and on getting away from the beetle swarm; she'd barely noticed how tightly Justyne had been holding on.

Now that I think of it, though, my sides are kind of sore from where she squeezed me.

Justyne gave her a half-smile. "I'm fine… just glad to be far away from those beetles."

"Yeah, me too. Do you mind giving me that address you found for Fiddler?"

Justyne's eyes narrowed. "You don't want to check it out now, do you?"

Lara shook her head. "No, not without police backup. I've had enough beetle swarms for one day."

Breathing a sigh of relief, Justyne pulled a piece of paper from her purse and showed it to Lara.

3300 White Oak Drive, Silver Spring

Lara's face fell. *Another dead end.*

"What's wrong?" Justyne asked.

"The address isn't valid anymore. We already checked it out, and Fiddler's house is no longer there. It was replaced by a commercial development."

Justyne frowned. "Well, that's a shame. I thought we had something. So, where are you headed next?"

Lara paused before telling her. "I was thinking of paying Anita another visit at her medical practice. It's only a few blocks from here. Doctors never really take the day off, and she doesn't have any family waiting for her at home. Maybe she headed back to the office after meeting her father in the café to take care of paperwork."

She might let something slip from the conversation she had with her father.

Justyne's face lit up. "Do you want me to come with you? Maybe for some unofficial backup like last time?"

Lara thought for a moment and remembered what Ashton told her about Fiddler. "Actually, that's not a bad idea. Let me park my bike, and we'll walk over together." Several feet away, she found a tiny spot next to the convenience store.

After walking for a few blocks in silence, Lara pointed up to the townhouse with the metal sign *Johnson and Moore Family Practice*. "That's it." She climbed the stairs to hit the buzzer. Fidgeting with her leather jacket, she waited for a response.

"Hello?" a female voiced answered.

Lara recognized the voice.

"Hey Lindsay, this is Lara Kingsley from the other day. I'm here to see Dr. Fiddler."

She grabbed the door handle as soon as the lock buzzed open. Justyne followed closely behind as Lara walked into the front office. Lindsay looked up and greeted her with a smile and then glanced nervously at Justyne.

"You're Lara Kingsley, right?" Lindsay's voice was tentative, as if she were trying to remember Lara's face.

"Yes, that's me. This is my colleague, Justyne. Is Dr. Fiddler by chance in the office today?"

"No... actually... it's rather strange. Dr. Fiddler came in here about an hour ago in a mad rush and told me to cancel all her appointments for the next few weeks. I don't know what happened, but she told me she was leaving town indefinitely. She said she'd be in touch and left about twenty minutes ago."

"What?" Lara gasped.

Anita left town? What did her father say to her?

"I'm as surprised as you are, believe me. She didn't even give her partner any notice. He's livid."

"Has she done anything like this before?"

Lindsay shook her head. "Never. She rarely leaves town and hasn't taken a single vacation day the entire time I've worked for her. She didn't even take time off after her husband and son died in a tragic accident. She's very dedicated. Anyway, I've been on the phone for the past hour, trying to explain to her patients that I don't know when... or if... she's coming back. They're all shocked and disappointed."

"Do you mind if I sit down for a minute?" Lara asked, trying to take in what she'd learned. Her mind raced with possible explanations.

"Be my guest," Lindsay said, picking up the phone, probably to call another patient.

Justyne wandered into the waiting area and began picking through the magazines on the coffee table. "Oh no, a little boy must have left his baseball glove behind... I'm sure he'll wonder where he lost it."

Lara turned to see the glove Justyne held, and her mouth fell open.

"What's wrong?" Justyne asked, walking the glove to the reception desk.

Lara's head spun in circles as she tried to make sense of what she was seeing. "That's my glove."

Justyne stopped and looked at the glove and then at Lara. "Are you sure? They all look the same."

"Yes, I'm sure," Lara said and reached for the glove. "Why the hell would it be here? Where did you find it?"

"I found it on the chair over there and wanted to make sure it got into lost and found. How do you suppose it got here? Did you leave it here the last time you visited Anita?"

No, someone must have stolen it from my townhouse.

Her mind raced. Lara had it with her when she and Vik were discussing Sully's journals. Someone had to have taken it after

258

the fire. *Did Anita steal it from her? Did Anita start the fire? Was Anita Sully's killer?* Nothing made sense. Something didn't compute.

"Lara?" Justyne waved a hand in front of her face.

"Sorry, I don't know how it got here." Lara kept the truth to herself, though she wasn't sure why her instincts had put a wall up with Justyne. She shrugged to play off any tensions she'd created and smiled. "I must have forgotten it."

"Oh, I almost forgot," Lindsay called from the desk. "Dr. Fiddler thought you might come by. She left something for you." She came around the desk and handed Lara an old tourist guide for Australia.

Lara stared at the book, turning it over in her hands. "Thanks. Did she say anything about it?"

"No. She said you'd know what it meant."

Lara returned to the chair in the waiting room. Justyne sat next to her as Lara ran her fingers over the embossed title. *A Guide to Australia for Insiders.*

Wait… I've seen this title before.

It was the same book that had contained the picture of Anita's father. Lara opened the book and flipped through all the pages. There were no pictures, scraps of paper, or even writing in the margins. *Nothing.*

Frustrated, Lara studied every detail of the book. It was an old library book published ten years ago. Out of date now, practically useless. Tucked in a sleeve in the front cover, the book had a slip of paper with date stamps. Lara pulled it out and looked at the last entry. Justyne shot her a confused look.

JOHN FIDDLER - DUE ON SEPTEMBER 8, 2017

"I think I know why this book is important. Fiddler checked it out, most likely to prepare for a trip to Australia. He must have traveled there to bring back a live specimen of a Christmas beetle to breed them in his lab."

Justyne rubbed her chin. "Do you think Anita knew about all

of that? If so, it sounds like she's involved in Fiddler's plot somehow. God knows she has motive."

"No, I think she left the book as a clue for me. She knew I'd understand its significance. She's trying to tell me something."

A thin film of plastic wrapped the cover of the book. Turning it over, Lara read a sticker on the book spine:

TAKOMA PARK NEIGHBORHOOD LIBRARY

"That's it! Fiddler must have had to give a local address to get a library card. We might actually have a new lead on his location." Lara relished the rush of adrenaline that came with a new lead. She jumped up out of her seat and rushed to the reception desk. "Lindsay, thanks so much. If Dr. Fiddler comes back, tell her to call me." Lara grabbed a pen and scribbled on a piece of scrap paper. "Here's my cell number and just in case, this is Detective Sanchez's number. We desperately need to talk to her."

"Sure, no problem." Lindsay said with some hesitancy in her voice. She furrowed her brow at Lara's business card, but took it and placed it on the desk.

Lara dashed out of the doctor's office with the book and her baseball glove under her arm. Justyne followed closely behind, her heels clicking frantically.

When Lara reached her motorcycle, she turned to Justyne. "Do you want to come to the library with me and see if we get a location on Fiddler?"

Justyne glanced at the bike and then her watch. "No, that's all right. I think I've had enough for today. But keep me in the loop, okay?"

Lara nodded and watched Justyne walk down the street and turn a corner. In some ways, she was relieved to be on her own again. Before mounting her bike, Lara paused to survey the area, making sure no one was tailing her. Several pedestrians, mostly students, walked about, but Lara didn't see anyone suspicious. She packed the library book and her baseball glove into the seat compartment and took out her smartphone to text Vik:

WON'T MAKE IT BACK TO THE OFFICE TODAY. DON'T WORRY ABOUT ME. EVERYTHING'S FINE.

The moment she pressed the send button, a buzzing noise made her jerk her head up as her heartbeat picked up pace. Before she had time to react, a swarm of golden beetles swooped down toward her. Lara ducked and tried to scream, but no noise came out. Within seconds, hundreds of beetles enveloped her, swirling in circles around her. Beetles smacked into her face, thumped her on the head, and clattered against her bike. Trembling, Lara squeezed her eyes shut, stopped squirming, and clutched her arms tightly around her stomach. Letting out a primal scream, she gasped for air.

A sharp pinch, small but painful, punctured her arm. And then another and another. Her muscles tensed as she swatted the air, hitting a few beetles to the ground. Seconds later, the swarm stopped buzzing and disappeared. When she opened her eyes, a single beetle sat on her arm, staring at her as if someone were watching her through its camera.

She grabbed the beetle with her other hand. *Gotcha, you little bastard.* The beetle's legs quivered, and it tried to fly away from her. Lara opened the seat compartment underneath her legs and shoved it inside, closing it quickly, and then sat back down on her bike. Shuddering, Lara patted down her body, inspecting a few of the little bite marks they had left on her arms.

What if they are carrying the plague...

Lara didn't plan on wasting any time to find out. She would have to make another stop before visiting the library. She tried Maggie's cellphone, but no one answered. She called the genetics laboratory at the University of Maryland's Department of Entomology. It was after 5 p.m., and a technician told her Maggie had left for the day.

Lara contemplated going to the Emergency Room, but she

was keenly aware of what type of national crisis would ensue as public health officials and law enforcement authorities struggled to understand how she may have contracted the plague from a genetically modified beetle.

No, I can't show up at the ER.

Her hands shook, and she was lightheaded, still reeling from the horror of being surrounded by the swarm of beetles. She didn't know how many times she had been bitten, or where to go for help. Her skin tingled painfully where the beetles had pierced her flesh. Taking a few deep breaths, she accepted her only good choice.

She needed to see Maggie and get the beetle tested for the plague. Lara mounted her bike, revved the engine, and headed out to Fort Totten as fast as she could.

TWENTY-SEVEN

Infection

LARA STOOD outside Maggie's apartment door, ringing the doorbell over and over. No one answered. She pounded her fist.

Come on, answer.

The bites on her body tingled, itched, and stung all at the same time. It took all the restraint she could muster not to scratch at them. Her cheeks flushed hot, and she put a hand on her clammy forehead.

Is it even possible for a plague infection to set in so quickly?

She had already tried Maggie's cell several times. It was unlike her friend not to answer her phone. She kept it in her pocket at all times. Lara's arms hung from her body like weights. She stared down the door, imagining boring a hole straight through the gray steel, but it seemed her superpowers were on hold today.

I might have to go to the ER after all.

Lara rested her head against the door. The metal felt cool against her cheeks.

That feels nice.

The thought crossed her mind that she probably looked ridiculous, leaning with her face on Maggie's door, but she didn't care. Just as she was about to give up, she heard something unexpected.

Is that... wait. Did I just hear someone giggle? Does Maggie have someone over?

Lara rang the doorbell again. Finally, a shuffling of feet approached the other side of the door, and the lock disengaged. Opening it a crack, Maggie peered out. She wore a plush green bathrobe, but it was her flushed face and tousled auburn hair that really grabbed Lara's attention.

"Lara? What are you doing here?" Maggie's voice sounded tense. Lara tried to look inside the apartment, but Maggie intentionally blocked the view.

"I'm sorry to bother you... but I... had nowhere else to go."

Maggie glowered. "That didn't stop you from leaving my apartment the other day without saying a single word. What gives, Lara?"

Lara shifted her weight around on her feet. She didn't know how to raise the fact that she found Sully's keys in Maggie's kitchen, so she'd avoided her friend altogether.

"The beetles... I was... surrounded by... by..." Lara's voice trembled slightly, her eyes filling with tears. Her clothes were soaking through with sweat. A single tear rolled down her cheek. Maggie's stern disapproval melted slowly as her eyes scanned Lara from head to toe.

"What happened? You look terrible. Here, come inside and tell me everything. I'll make you a good strong cuppa and some biscuits." Maggie's Australian accent soothed Lara as she took her arm gently and pulled her into the apartment. "Do you want English breakfast or Earl Grey?"

"Earl Grey is fine, thanks."

When the door opened wider, Lara's mouth fell open at the sight of Sanchez sitting on Maggie's couch, half-dressed. He fumbled awkwardly with the buttons on his shirt and gave her a sheepish smile.

"Detective?" Lara continued to gape at him.

Sanchez looked back at her with big brown eyes as his cheeks flushed, but then he shrugged and waved off his embarrassment. It was obvious what she'd walked in on, but she was too distraught to have an opinion. She sat down on a metal stool, rested her elbows on the kitchen island, and stared at the marble countertop in a daze.

Maggie put the kettle on the stove, turned on the burner, and took out a cup, saucer, sugar, and milk for the tea. "Are you going to tell me what happened?" Her voice was gentle and soft.

Lara nodded groggily. "I was in Foggy Bottom, paying Fiddler's daughter another visit." She glanced over at Sanchez. "By the way, it *was* her car at the warehouse. I tracked her today in a silver Honda. Here's the plate number." She showed the detective the photo on her smartphone.

The detective sat down on the stool next to her. "Did you get any more information from her?"

"No, she appears to have left town... indefinitely."

"Well, now that's suspicious behavior," Maggie said.

"I'll call it in right now and put out a BOLO on her car," Sanchez said, pulling out his phone.

Lara grimaced. "I'm not sure she's involved in any of this... but yes, I can see how her skipping town makes her look guilty of something."

Detective Sanchez nodded. "Her presence at the warehouse and connection to her father makes her a person of interest in the case."

Sighing, Lara continued. "Anyway, she left me a library book. And I found my baseball glove at her practice. I thought it burned up in the fire, but turns out someone stole it."

"What? Where is it?" Detective Sanchez asked.

"In my seat compartment with the library book—"

"Do you think Anita took it?" Maggie asked.

"Uh... I don't know how or why she would. It would mean she was at my house after the fire and that doesn't feel right to me."

Sanchez rubbed his chin. "We'll get it tested for prints and

DNA. Maybe the glove will tell us something about how it got there. What's the deal with the library book?"

"It's a travel guide on Australia that Fiddler checked out ten years ago from the Takoma Park Neighborhood Library. I think Anita is trying to help us find out where her father is hiding out."

"Sure, she's helping us…" the detective grunted. "If Fiddler had a library card, then he gave them a real address… from ten years ago." He rubbed his forehead. "We might actually find him." Sarcasm laced his tone.

The kettle started to whistle. Maggie took it off the stove, poured the hot water into the tea cup, and set the mug and a saucer full of cookies down on the counter in front of Lara. "You should wait for it to steep for a few minutes."

Lara nodded, pulling the mug in close to her and stuffing a cookie into her mouth. The warmth of the mug on her hands comforted her.

"I was heading over to the library to check it out, but then a swarm of those awful genetically modified Christmas beetles attacked me. They crashed into me all at once and started biting… it was hard to breathe."

"Oh sweetie. I'm so sorry." Maggie came over, put her arms around her, and then hugged her tightly.

Lara pulled away. "They bit me several times… what if?" Lara showed Maggie one of the wounds on her arm. Her friend's eyes grew large. She grabbed Lara's arms and lightly brushed the spot with her finger, which made Lara wince.

"That hurts?" Maggie asked.

"Yes, they are all inflamed, itchy, and painful," Lara said.

Maggie inspected the bites on her body. "Hmmm. The beetles must have injected saliva into your skin, and you're having an allergic reaction."

"Do you think I have the plague?" Lara asked, biting her lip. "If it helps, I did manage to catch one of them… it's in my…"

"You brought one with you?" Maggie asked, her eyes lighting up.

"It's outside… in the compartment underneath the seat of my motorcycle. I can't touch it again. I'm too—"

"That's okay, mate. I'll go get it." Maggie went into her kitchen, grabbed a plastic container, and then disappeared into her bathroom. She came out with gloves and tweezers, grinning from ear to ear. "I'll be right back."

"Bring the baseball glove and the book with you while you're at it," Sanchez commanded a bit too gruffly. Maggie glared at him as she walked out the door.

Lara and the detective sat in awkward silence at the kitchen island. Lara sipped her tea. "So, you and Maggie, huh?"

"Yeah." Sanchez avoided her gaze.

"How did *that* happen?" Lara's mouth curved into a smile.

The detective shrugged his shoulders. "We met when I picked you up in her lab… and uh, I called with some follow-up questions."

"Follow-up questions, eh?" Lara raised her eyebrow, smirking at him.

"She's a great girl," Sanchez said.

Lara's face became serious. "I know she is. So, don't mess it up."

He nodded, but his lips formed a deep frown. He probably hated that she knew his personal business, which gave Lara an edge. She was okay with that.

Maggie walked back into the apartment, her eyes lit up with excitement, and held up the plastic container. "It's a good thing I keep basic assay materials in the apartment. I'll test the beetle now to see if it's carrying the plague. Then we'll know what to do with you."

Maggie pulled out a black medical bag from her closet. Inside were all sorts of plastic gadgets and gizmos that looked like they came from a laboratory. After a few minutes of searching, she took out a dipstick. "This rapid immunoassay test is capable of detecting *Yersinia pestis*, the bacteria that causes the plague. I just need a sample of the saliva from the beetle…"

Maggie opened the container and grabbed the beetle with her fingers. Lara shivered and turned away.

Maggie smirked. "Don't worry. I already removed the microelectronics package outside. We don't need anyone overhearing this conversation. And we certainly don't want this Fiddler character knowing we're onto him."

The beetle struggled to get free while Maggie inserted a needle into its mouthpart to extract saliva. When she finished, she put the beetle back into the container, closed the lid tightly, and put it in the freezer. "That beetle won't bite anyone else."

Lara breathed a huge sigh of relief.

Maggie put droplets of the beetle saliva onto the dipstick and laid it on the counter.

"How long do we have to wait?" Lara asked.

"A few minutes. It's like a pregnancy test. If it changes color, the sample is positive for the bacteria."

They stared at the dipstick in silence.

TWENTY-EIGHT

Biological Attack

LARA THOUGHT she could see a tinge of blue appear and began biting the ends of her nails. After about five minutes, the blue color saturated the dipstick, making the finding undeniable. The blood drained from her face. The diagnosis brought attention to her wounds, and they throbbed and stung even worse than before.

Maggie frowned. "The bad news is you're probably infected with the plague. The good news is that it is treatable, and I happen to have an emergency stash of streptomycin on hand. Let's get you started on that right away."

Maggie walked into her bathroom and a few seconds later came out with a prescription bottle. "Here, take one of these every day for the next seven days. If you show any symptoms, we'll get you to the hospital right away. But I doubt it will come to that."

"Thanks, Maggie. I don't know what I'd do without you." Lara threw her head back and swallowed the first dose.

Detective Sanchez pointed to his smartphone. "Maggie, we should probably get Special Agent Martin out here and brief him on what's happened. I believe we've got a credible threat on our hands, and the Feds need to be involved. Is that okay?"

She nodded.

Sanchez and Rob sure are becoming a first-rate team.

Sinking into a leather chair in Maggie's living room, Lara sipped the last drop of her tea. She felt completely normal about seeing Rob again and smiled, pleased at the realization.

At least something good has come of all of this.

In the kitchen, Detective Sanchez pulled out his work tablet. Maggie disappeared into her bedroom to get dressed into something proper. On the bookshelf in the far corner, the framed photo of Maggie with the Christmas beetle caught Lara's attention again.

"Maggie, how come you never told me you had a picture of yourself with a Christmas beetle?" Lara projected her voice toward the bedroom.

Maggie stepped out of her bedroom as she wound her auburn hair up into a bun. Lara raised her eyebrows and gestured at the picture. Maggie walked over to the bookshelf and shrugged.

"What do you mean?" Maggie asked as she slipped a sweater over her camisole. "I'm an Australian bug scientist… it would be *weird* if I didn't have a picture of one. They are quite common. As a child, I loved seeing these beetles and considered it to be good luck if I spotted one." She paused, and then took a step backward, one hand to her chest as her eyes widened. "Surely, you don't think I had anything to do with this?"

"I'm not sure what to think anymore." Lara felt so grim, so unsure about everything.

"Hey now." Maggie frowned. "What do you mean? You know me, Lara."

Lara avoided her gaze and pulled her keys out of her pocket. She held up Sully's Yoda figurine keychain. "I found this in your kitchen drawer a few days ago."

Maggie's face screwed up in confusion. "What is it?"

"It's a key. What does it look like? It belonged to Sully. Don't you recognize it?"

Maggie shook her head. "I've never seen it before. You found it in my kitchen drawer?"

"Yeah. Any idea how it got there?"

Maggie thought for a few minutes, staring at the ceiling with her hands on her hips. Then realization came to her eyes. "Sully must have put it there when he spent the night," she whispered. Her face flushed a rosy pink, and she glanced nervously at Sanchez.

"So, Sully was here... but when?" Lara whispered so as not to alert Sanchez to the conversation. Maggie wasn't one to limit herself in romantic exploration, but she also wasn't tacky enough to talk about it in front of someone she was sleeping with.

"It was the night of the party, late. He called and then came over to... apologize for leaving so abruptly," Maggie said, her voice low as her eyes darted from Lara to Sanchez.

Lara handed the keychain to Maggie. "And you're sure you don't recognize this key or know what it might go to?"

Maggie shook her head.

Why did you hide it here, Sully? Did you know I would find it?

She wished he was still here to answer her questions. Mention of the party at Wicked Bloom brought bittersweet memories. Not wanting to dwell on them, she leaned toward Maggie with a smirk on her face.

"So, you and Sanchez?" Lara whispered, pointing to the detective in the kitchen and smiling.

Maggie rolled her eyes.

"Um... I can hear you from over here, Ms. Kingsley." Detective Sanchez looked up from the table and glowered at Lara. Maggie's face went pale, and she made a did-he-hear-me face.

Lara shook her head subtly and walked into the kitchen.

"Now that I've seen you half-dressed, I think you can call me Lara." She grinned at him from ear to ear and picked up the kettle to pour another cup of tea.

"Not if I can help it, Ms. Kingsley."

The doorbell rang, and Lara set the kettle back down.

"That must be Rob... I'll get it." Lara said as she walked over and opened the door.

Rob, dressed in his favorite ripped jeans and plaid shirt, stepped in, looking handsome as ever. "Hey Lara, I hear you got yourself poisoned with some beetle juice." His light brown eyes twinkled at her.

He's having too much fun with this.

Lara glared at him and left him standing in the open door.

Rob reached out and grabbed her arm, pulling her close to him. She could smell his cologne, and her heart fluttered. "Seriously, though, are you okay? When Sanchez said plague... well I..."

Rob made eye contact, his gaze one of concern and care. It sent a pleasant shiver down her spine but stung at the same time.

Maybe I'm not quite over him after all.

She stepped away, pulling her arm free of his gentle grasp. "I'm fine. The beetle tested positive for the plague. Maggie gave me a round of antibiotics." She shrugged it off as if it were no big deal.

"Good." He paused, his eyes lingering on her face. "Hey Sanchez, thanks for giving me a call." He walked over and took a seat next to the detective at the island in the kitchen.

"It's really your case at this point," Sanchez said stiffly. "But I thought we should put our heads together before things get out of hand."

Rob slapped the detective's back lightly and nodded. "It's great timing. I wanted to fill you in on what the FBI evidence response team uncovered at Beautific Creations, besides the video footage."

"What else did they find?" Lara asked, hopeful that she was about to get some answers.

"By the time we arrived to talk to Linda, the warehouse had been mostly cleaned out. Files were shredded, and all the indoor surveillance videos were destroyed. They even wiped down the whole place to remove print evidence. Linda and her accomplice were obviously trying to make a clean getaway when we arrived. The money laundering unit is taking a look at the case. They think the Beautific Creations operation was cleaning money from illegal activities. But…"

"But?" Lara asked, sitting on the edge of her seat.

"Butt," Rob said, smirking. The detective nodded at him as if he were in on the joke.

"But what?" Lara asked.

"She left a cigarette butt behind." Rob grinned and then smacked his leg while laughing.

Lara rolled her eyes. "Nice. Not funny. At all."

Rob grimaced. "Anyway, the forensics scientist matched the DNA profile from the warehouse to Martje Hussny."

"The woman who messed with my bike?" Lara asked.

"So… Martje Hussny must be Linda Maxwell's alias," Sanchez concluded. "At least we know who she is now."

Rob nodded. "That's not all. We also matched some prints and DNA trace evidence to Anita Fiddler. Her data was in the system from the NSA investigation several months ago."

"Anita?" Lara gaped. "But—"

"See, told ya," Sanchez said, not hiding his triumph. "We'll pick her up and have a nice long chat."

Lara glowered at the detective.

"Sanchez told me you've had quite the day," Rob said, turning to Lara. "Are you going to fill me in?"

Lara remained silent for a moment, bothered by the finding and the detective's arrogant attitude. Then she walked over to the stove and poured herself another cup of tea. Rob followed her into the kitchen and waited for her to speak. Lara told him everything that had happened earlier that day with the stakeout, the visit to Anita's practice, and the beetle swarm. He was particularly perplexed about the discovery of her baseball glove.

"It seems we do have a credible threat here." Rob rubbed his forehead. "Fiddler appears to be planning a biological attack. The problem is we don't have a lot of information to go on—at least not enough to alert the public health authorities and organize an effective response."

"Do you think Fiddler is acting alone?" Lara asked, leaning against the kitchen sink and holding the warm mug in her hands.

"Well, I don't know. I'm not sure how much Ashton was in on it," Rob said. "We didn't have enough evidence to charge him, so the kid is back on the street now."

"Dammit Rob, I told you to let me keep talking with him," Lara said. "He didn't say anything else after I left?"

Rob shook his head. "I tried to get the District Attorney to offer him a deal in exchange for information that could help us, but she doesn't want to budge from possible murder charges at this point."

"Even though you can't make any charges stick?" Lara asked.

Rob nodded. "I planned to put a tail on him, but then he disappeared."

"Fiddler's daughter, Anita, has also fled," Sanchez said. "Coincidence? I'd say not. Maybe they're both in on it with Linda."

Lara lifted an eyebrow. "I don't think Anita is involved in this. Her father must have told her to get out of town for some reason."

"How can you be so sure?" Sanchez creased his forehead.

Lara shrugged. "I don't know… it's a gut feeling."

"Well, I prefer to build my cases on fact." The detective placed a fist on the counter and nodded his head once. "If you want to keep doing detective work, you really need to avoid blind spots for certain suspects. As far as I'm concerned, Anita is still in play."

"You could put out an APB and at least get a search started," Rob suggested.

"My thoughts exactly. Already on it." Sanchez pointed at his tablet and gave Lara a teasing smirk.

Gah, he is so annoying.

"Good, if we can find her… maybe she can answer some

questions for us." Rob began pacing the room. "What do we know about Fiddler's plan?"

Lara put her hands on her hips. "Well, he's developed the ultimate delivery system for spreading the plague." Her thoughts drifted to the Bible verse from the Basilica. "The beetles are quite beautiful... I mean if you like bugs."

"And most people are not afraid of them because beetles are not known to bite or carry disease," Maggie said.

"And he's already testing swarming techniques," Sanchez added, pointing at Lara.

"These metallic golden beetles would catch people off guard. They could swarm and bite a number of times before people could take cover or shoo them away," Lara said. She balled her fists as she resisted the urge to scratch.

"Untreated plague can lead to serious casualties," Maggie said. "If the infection gets into the lungs, the disease becomes contagious and can spread on its own from person to person."

"Any idea on possible targets?" Rob asked.

"Well, we found the two maps at the violin shop," Lara said. "Fiddler appears to be targeting two government installations: USAMRIID at Fort Detrick, where he worked, and Fort Meade, home to the NSA."

Sanchez grunted. "I don't understand why the guy would change his name to Fiddler and then go work for the organization responsible for his mother's death," the detective said. "It makes no sense."

"Another mystery." Rob frowned.

"What about his motive for targeting the NSA?" Sanchez asked.

"His son-in-law worked at the NSA before his untimely death." Lara said. "Fiddler thinks CyberShop works there. And we know he suspects CyberShop of killing his son-in-law Frank and his grandson. He's also probably furious with the NSA for framing Frank—and later Anita—for the leak. I think that's a pretty good motive."

"Hmmm…" Rob sighed heavily. "We need more information."

Lara crossed her arms and turned to Rob. "I think Ashton knows a lot more than he is letting on. You should press the District Attorney for a deal. Maybe he'll come out of the woodwork if he thinks he's safe."

"We need a location on Fiddler." Rob let out an impatient huff. "Has Vik figured anything out yet?"

Lara shook her head. She hadn't heard from Vik all day.

"We should pay that library a visit," Sanchez said, looking at his watch.

"It's already closed," Lara said, pressing her lips together.

"Did you ever look into how Fiddler got his hands on an Australian Christmas beetle?" Maggie asked. "He must have traveled to Oz. If he has a passport, he would have provided an address on the application form."

"Good thinking. Let me make a call to my friend at the State Department." Rob took his phone out of his pocket and walked over to the other side of the room.

Her pocket buzzed. She pulled out her smartphone. The text from an unknown caller read:

DON'T INTERFERE WITH MY PLANS AGAIN
IF YOU DO, SOMEONE YOU CARE ABOUT WILL DIE

Trembling, Lara accidentally dropped the phone to the floor.

"Are ya okay?" Maggie asked.

"Fiddler knows."

"What does he know?"

"He knows we're all here… he knows we're trying to stop him."

"How?" Maggie whipped her head back and forth, scanning her apartment.

Out of the corner of her eye, Lara glimpsed something glimmer from above. "Up there… on your curtain." She pointed to the curtain around the sliding door. A golden beetle perched on the curtain rod and watched them.

"It's transmitting a recording of our conversation to Fiddler, isn't it?" Sanchez said, his voice low. "He's outside somewhere, controlling it."

Maggie grabbed a fly swatter and ran over to the curtain. With one strong swat, the beetle fell to the floor. She stepped on it with her foot, making sure to crush its body underneath her weight. When she lifted her foot, the beetle was dead. Maggie picked it up with her fingers, walked to the kitchen, put the beetle in a plastic bag, and tossed it in her freezer.

"I can't believe you just did that." Lara's mouth hung open.

"What?" Maggie exclaimed.

"You love bugs."

"Not bugs that spy on us and try to kill my mates."

TWENTY-NINE

The Remote

November 6, 2027

WHILE ROB and the detective searched high and low for signs of Ashton and Anita around D.C., Lara had spent the past two days lazing around her apartment, weak and suffering from bouts of fever and chills. Maggie said the flu-like symptoms were normal and to be expected given the large number of beetle bites. Even so, her friend called every few hours to check on her.

Not wanting all of her leads to run cold, Lara decided it was time to search Sully's townhouse for the remote box, even if she felt like death warmed over. Her body ached as she drove across town on her bike, but the crisp fall air refreshed her. After a thirty minute ride, she pulled her motorcycle into the alley behind Sully's townhouse and parked next to the gate.

She'd been so consumed with figuring out what Fiddler was up to with the beetles that she completely dropped the ball on solving Sully's murder.

I need to find that box.

During the interrogation, Ashton mentioned that Sully had purchased a remote from CyberShop over the Dark Web, and the package was delivered by mail to the townhouse. Maybe the box had a return address, or better yet, a clue to CyberShop's identity.

Lara desperately needed to solve the case. She couldn't afford to keep working it for free. Since her arrest, Sanchez tolerated her collaboration, but had not offered to pay the usual consulting fee. She worried Vik might quit if she couldn't pay him soon. So far, every lead on Fiddler's location had come to a dead end. The same went for Sully's killer.

Rob's call to the State Department about the passport revealed that Fiddler held two passports, one under his own name and another under Henrik Speelman, his father's name, with Fiddler's picture, of course. Both were associated with the address of his old house. And neither passport contained a stamp for Australia.

How did he get the beetle? Does he have a third passport?

Rob had stopped by Takoma Park Neighborhood Library with a warrant to check if Fiddler still had an active library card. Unfortunately, Fiddler's account was linked to the same address he'd used for everything. The same one kept coming up over and over. Another dead end. Rob would have to establish probable cause for a full top-to-bottom search of the commercial complex, and thus far, they had come up with nada.

Shivering, she pulled her leather jacket tightly around her to keep warm. She entered the back door, her nose wrinkling at the stench from the garbage still strewn all over the place.

Sully's next-of-kin had not yet tended to his townhouse. Perhaps no living relatives had been identified, or his property had gotten tied up in probate. She bit her lip as she surveyed the mess. She'd always connected with Sully over their shared orphan status, but right now, it felt sadder than before.

Is this what will happen to my stuff when I'm gone? It'll all rot away or be taken by a bank or something?

Lara sighed and began sifting through the trash and recycling remnants, looking for any evidence of a cardboard box belonging to the remote. After inspecting every box and mailer on the ground, she was convinced Sully had not put the package in the trash.

No, that would be too easy.

Wiping her hands with a partially used paper towel, she marched toward the townhouse. This time, the back door to Sully's townhouse was locked.

I should never have given the keys to Detective Sanchez.

She thought about calling him, but wasn't in the mood for any of his usual hassles. If they found nothing, the detective would grumble at her for wasting his time. If she struck gold, he'd be angry it wasn't his idea. It was lose-lose.

She tried the key attached to the Yoda keychain, but it didn't fit. She examined the windows, but they were all secured from the inside.

Damn.

Fortunately, she'd picked locks on occasion. It was a natural talent. Lara took out a lock pick from her coat pocket and began fiddling with the lock. The lock disengaged within a few minutes, and she opened the door.

She stepped into Sully's kitchen, which remained in complete disarray. The smell of rotting food had grown more putrid since her last visit. At the dirty sink, Lara washed the grime off her hands and considered possible hiding places for the box.

Sully, where would you put something you wanted to keep hidden?

The logical place for unpacking the remote would have been Sully's safe room, but he had emptied it before he died. After searching through his dining room, the library, and the living room, Lara finally went upstairs to check out his third-floor bedroom.

It felt weird to go through his personal belongings. The top shelf in Sully's closet was stacked with old shoeboxes. Lara began opening them one by one, looking inside and throwing the empty boxes in a pile on the floor. She found nothing interesting except that her dead friend had a penchant for expensive footwear. Frustrated, Lara sat down on his bed. The floor creaked underneath the added weight.

Floorboards, Sully? You were old-school.

As she stood up, the hardwood floor squeaked underneath her feet. Lara got on her hands and knees and rolled back the huge Persian rug. Knocking on each floorboard, she listened for a hollow sound. Toward the center of the room, Lara found a floorboard smaller than the rest. When she pressed down on one end, the other end lifted up.

Just like that.

Lara removed the floorboard; something was hidden in the hole. Adrenaline surged through her veins and her heart started to race. Reaching under the floorboard into the hole, she felt a cardboard box and pulled it out.

Perfect-size box for the remote.

Sully's home address was on the outside of the box. The return address was a post office box.

Maybe the P.O. box is associated with CyberShop's physical address…

Of course the post office wouldn't just give Lara that information, but Justyne already proved she could pull some strings by flashing her government badge. Lara opened the flaps. Inside, she found pictures of a familiar black BMW convertible with Maryland license plates parked in front of the neighborhood post office.

190 24K

The plate doesn't match Linda's. Could it be the plate for Stepanov's car? Lara flipped through the other pictures. Several were of Linda Maxwell entering and leaving the post office. *Was Linda driving Stepanov's car to visit her P.O. box?*

On the back of one of the pictures, Sully had scribbled the BMW plate number with an address:

LAUREL LAKES APARTMENT COMPLEX, APARTMENT 302
248 MARYMONT DRIVE, LAUREL, MARYLAND 20707

Sully had already done much of the legwork. It looked as though he had gotten a physical address for an item purchased through secret online channels.

Vik is right. The Dark Web is overrated.

Like everyone else, black market dealers depended on postal systems or couriers to send their physical wares to their customers. Physical items could be tracked as they moved from sender to recipient. Law enforcement authorities could conduct surveillance, seize packages, and investigate who they were being sent to or where they were coming from.

Lara shoved the picture in her back pocket. *This might be what the intruder was looking for on the night of Sully's murder.*

Something else caught her eye. Reaching into the hole in the floor, she pulled out Sully's passport, a thick wad of $100 bills, and a business card for SpaceSaver Self-Storage. She turned the card over in her hand to find a three-digit number written on the back.

Unit 506? Is this where you moved your files? Would the Yoda key open the storage unit?

Lara smiled to herself. Finally, she had some decent leads. She took out her phone and called Rob for backup to check out the apartment at the address. The call went to voicemail, so she hung up. If he wasn't available, she could visit the storage space on her own instead. After all, Sully meant her to find the Yoda keychain.

Stashing the cash in her pocket, Lara put the box back into the hiding place, replaced the floorboard, and rolled the carpet back into place.

Back on the main floor, she paused for a moment in the library and stared at the shelves that hid the entrance to Sully's safe room.

It wouldn't hurt to look one more time. Would it? Just in case I missed something?

Lara lifted the book, pressed the button underneath, and waited as the shelves creaked and moved slowly outward, revealing the secret door and electronic keypad. She entered the code from memory and stepped back, expecting the door lock to release. Instead, a loud beeping sound pierced the air. Startled, Lara stepped back, wringing her hands.

Someone must have deactivated the code! The security company will be alerted. Oh my God. I have to get out of here.

The safe room door squealed open. Terrified, Lara froze in place. Inside, a familiar curly brown hair and a cocky grin waited just beyond it. Lara let out a breath she'd held in.

"Rob, what the hell are you doing here?" The blood drained from her face as a thought crossed her mind.

Did he see me search the place?

"I'd ask the same of you, Lara. I guess this is payback." Rob looked handsome in his brown leather jacket and ripped blue jeans.

"Ha!" Lara smiled uneasily. "Did you trigger the alarm to scare me?"

Rob nodded. "And I just disabled it. Don't want the security company showing up and finding us here. That could be... awkward with Sanchez, if you know what I mean."

Yes, I do. Lara grimaced. "You're on the clock?"

Rob shook his head. "My boss wanted me to check out the townhouse one more time, and I was in the neighborhood on a personal errand. It looks like you found something interesting." He pointed to the box in her hand.

"How did you know I was here?" Lara peeked into the safe room.

The room was completely empty. Even the computer and the video screens were gone. Lara breathed a sigh of relief. She'd forgotten the D.C. police had been there and removed any remaining evidence. So, Rob hadn't seen her take the cash after all.

"I saw you pick the back-door lock and hid myself in the safe room." He smirked at her.

"Oh," Lara said. "Are you going to arrest me for breaking in?"

"I might." His eyes twinkled. "So, what's in the box?"

Lara opened the box and handed him the pictures. "An apartment address, pictures of Linda at the post office, a post office box address, and a picture of a black BMW convertible with a Maryland license plate. And it doesn't appear to be Linda's."

"Wow, you really won the lottery." Rob stared at the picture and then turned it over in his hands to inspect the address. "We'll run the license plate through our databases, but it looks familiar. If I recall correctly, this one belongs to Stepanov. Detective Sanchez looked it up a while back."

"Of course… I might have also found the place where Sully hid his case files. He left a business card for a storage company and the key to his unit."

"Well, that's convenient." Rob stood grinning in the doorway, blocking her entry.

"Let me in, please," Lara demanded. "I want to get another look in the safe room."

He waved a hand at her. "The safe room is clean, Lara. I've searched it from top to bottom. But please, be my guest… if you think you can do better."

Lara shrugged her shoulders. "I don't doubt you've searched everywhere, but I would feel better if I checked it out one more time."

"Go for it." Rob shot her a fake irritated look, moved aside, bowing at the waist and motioning for her to enter.

Lara rolled her eyes as she walked past him into the storage room with the bunk beds. She got down on her hands and knees. Lying on the floor, she squeezed herself under the bottom bunk bed, feeling under the mattress and along the back wall.

"How's it going down there?" Rob asked. "Finding anything? Are you stuck?"

She pulled herself back out and got to her feet, making sure to give Rob a proper glare.

Rob grinned. "I already told you, there's nothing here. No need to get yourself covered in dust."

She moved back into the office. Rob followed closely on her

heels like a stray dog. Turning around, she shot an exasperated glance at him. "Do you mind?"

Grinning, he stepped back to give her some space.

Lara opened the drawers of the filing cabinet and scanned each one again.

Empty.

Checking one more time, she slid her hands under the bottom of each drawer. "Ha!"

Rob loitered behind her, trying to see over her arm. "What ha?"

Under the bottom of the top drawer, she felt a large envelope. *How did I miss this last time?* She stood on her toes. "There's something here, but I can't get to it."

Rob reached over her shoulder and slid the envelope from underneath the drawer. Lara could smell his cologne wafting under her nose and feel the heat of his body close to hers. Her skin flushed and tingled, and her heartbeat throbbed in her ears.

The sound of a loud thump and squeal pulled her out of her temporary distraction. Startled, they both turned to see the safe room door close with a heavy thud.

"Um, did you accidentally close the safe room door?" Lara asked.

"No..." Rob ran over to the electronic panel and entered his code to open the door.

On the other side of the door, Lara thought she heard something shatter, followed by heavy footsteps. She looked over at the blank wall where the screens once hung and wished she could see what was happening.

"The code isn't working," Rob said, punching in numbers.

"You're punching it in wrong! Hurry before we're locked in!"

Rob tried two more times but failed, each time the panel beeping at him angrily.

Several seconds later, a series of heavy snaps and clicks sounded as the lock engaged. Then the bookshelves began screeching as they hid the safe room door.

"Holy shit, we're locked in here." Her eyes were wide. "What the hell happened?"

* * *

SITTING ON THE CEMENT FLOOR, they waited for Rob's team of FBI agents outside the safe room to break them out and restore air flow. Someone had smashed the electronic keypad and cut the wires, complicating the effort to open the door.

"I should call Vik." Lara took out her phone.

"No, my guys have this." Rob stared at his phone, impatient for an update on their progress.

Lara sighed heavily. "They've been at this for several hours, and the temperature is rising fast."

Both Rob and Lara had shed their leather jackets and were sweating through their clothes. Whoever had locked them in also disabled the safe room air intake system. Sully had installed a pressurized ventilation system as protection against a biological attack. The irony was not lost on Lara.

The contents of the large manila envelope from the filing cabinet lay on the floor between them. It contained a police file on the car accident on the Chesapeake Bay Bridge that killed Anita's husband Frank Moore and their son, Jayden Moore. Lara flipped through the pages in the thin file, reading the document summaries.

"The police didn't think it was an accident," Lara said to Rob. "The detective on the case claimed it was a homicide made to look like an accident."

"Based on what evidence?" Rob asked, fiddling with his phone.

"The speed and angle of the car. Plus, Anita claims a car driving on the wrong side of the bridge forced Frank to hit the railing. She thought it was a dark-colored BMW, but only saw it a few seconds before her car went over the side of the bridge."

"But they never identified the driver?" Rob asked.

"No, the accident took place on a dark, rainy night. That part of the bridge was covered by surveillance cameras, but when the cops checked the videotapes, they only found footage of Frank's car driving across the bridge. The tapes were static at the time of impact, the same for those pointed in the opposite direction."

"In other words, the camera either wasn't working properly or someone tampered with the footage."

Lara nodded. "And of course, Anita couldn't recall the plate number of the oncoming vehicle. The case finally closed a few months ago, determined to be an accident."

Rob crinkled his forehead. "Hmmm... I'm thinking Sully wouldn't have kept that file well-hidden if he agreed with that finding."

"Sully definitely kept it secret for a reason," Lara said.

"What if CyberShop was in the other car, trying to kill Frank?" Rob ran his fingers through his hair. "Didn't Fiddler's son-in-law work at the NSA at the time of his death?"

Lara nodded.

"So, Fiddler assumes CyberShop is a double agent, working for the government and selling Top Secret encryption technology over the Dark Web. Maybe Frank found out about it, and CyberShop killed him to keep him silent?"

"Sounds like a plausible theory to me."

"But who is this CyberShop character?" Rob asked. "Any information in the file?"

Shaking her head, she stuck her hand in the manila envelope to check that they'd found everything and pulled out a few papers stuck to the bottom.

"What is that?" Rob asked.

Lara scanned the documents quickly. "Holy shit. This might change everything."

"What?" Rob gaped at her expectantly.

"Anita and Frank's bank records for the past two years, showing a regular influx of some major cash. Way more than they'd earn monthly between the two of them."

"Can you tell where the transfers are from?"

Lara shook her head. "There's also an internal brief from the

NSA, listing the suspected sales of advanced defense technology over the Dark Web."

"So, now do you think Anita is guilty?" Rob asked.

A growing sense of unease made Lara squirm. "I'm just not as convinced of Frank's innocence. Maybe Stepanov was his accomplice, and Linda laundered the money for them. That could explain the transfers before and after Frank's death."

"Sounds plausible, but don't you think Anita would know about it? The money is in their shared account."

Is Detective Sanchez right? Do I have a blind spot where Anita is concerned?

She was silent for several minutes and wiped the sweat from her brow. "Can you have one of your guys run the plates for the BMW from the picture while we're stuck in here?"

"Good idea." Rob called one of his team members on his cell and switched the audio to speaker. "Hey, you guys close to getting us out of here?"

"This is Agent Carter. We're trying our best, boss. The wiring is restored, but the system's encryption is rather sophisticated." Rob rolled his eyes at Lara.

Lara glared at him. "What? I'm good at my job. And Vik is a kickass programmer." She was proud of the foolproof system she'd installed for Sully.

"It might take some time yet, boss. Best to sit tight for now."

Rob grimaced. "I've got a license plate and an address I'd like to run through the databases. Do you mind?"

"Sure, boss… give it to me."

Rob gave Agent Carter the license plate and address.

"Got it. I'll let you know if we get any hits."

Lara's stomach growled loudly.

"Was that you?" Rob grinned at her.

"Yep, I didn't plan on spending all day here… so I didn't eat breakfast." Lara looked at her watch. They'd been locked in the safe room for three hours now.

"So, what should we do while we're waiting in here?" Rob's eyes twinkled playfully.

"Um... don't you have a girlfriend?" Lara looked at him sternly.

"You don't think I meant—"

"Don't play coy with me. You know what you meant." Lara glowered at him. She didn't like being toyed with.

Rob opened his mouth to say something and then hesitated. He sat silent after several attempts. "Maybe I made a mistake..."

"What mistake?" Lara stared down at the file on the floor, shuffling through the papers, wondering what Rob thought he'd missed. "No, I think we've covered everything here."

"I'm not talking about the case. I meant with Alexa," Rob muttered.

Lara gave him an incredulous stare. "You *think* you made a mistake?" She enunciated every word, unable to believe what she was hearing. "You're calling what you did to me a mistake? You cheated on me! You betrayed our trust. You broke my heart and practically ruined my life." Lara picked herself up from the floor and paced in a tight circle, her fists clenched. "A mistake?" Tears formed in her eyes. She turned her face so Rob couldn't see. He didn't deserve to see the pain he'd caused her.

"Lara, please..." When she turned, Rob looked up at her with pleading eyes. "I was a complete idiot... I—"

Her eyes blazed with rage. "An idiot?"

"Okay, okay, a pig-headed, stupid, cheating, bastard asshole! Is that what you want to hear?"

She threw her hands up in the air. "I didn't ask for this."

"For what?"

Lara's heart pounded so hard that it felt like it would come up through her throat. She turned to glare at him. "For any of it. Don't you get it? I never wanted to see you again, let alone work with you on a case. And I certainly didn't want you to bring up your cheating while we're here, locked in this fucking safe room. You haven't changed a bit, have you? Always thinking about yourself first. Do you think this has been *easy* for me? Do you actually think I want to talk about this right now?"

"Lara… I'm sorry… I'm…" Rob rubbed the back of his neck and looked down and away.

"You know what? I'm finished with this conversation. I don't want to hear any more about your fucking mistakes."

Lara leaned against the wall, sliding down the cool cement and sinking into the corner and onto the floor.

They sat together in silence for another hour before Lara stood up and shook her head in frustration. "Your guys are never getting us out of here. I'm calling Vik."

THIRTY

Memex

A LOUD SQUEAL of delight came from outside the safe room. "I did it! I did it!"

She imagined Vik jumping up and down, his face lit up with glee. The excitement was music to Lara's ears. She shuddered at the notion of being cooped up for another minute with her ex-boyfriend. After his clumsy attempt at an apology, the atmosphere between them had grown uncomfortably chilly. The warm, stuffy air further heightened her discomfort and made it nearly impossible to breathe.

The safe room door lock made a loud noise when it disengaged. *Free at last.*

As the door creaked open, a cool draft of air rushed in toward them. Lara inhaled the fresh air eagerly. Even though he deserved it, she refrained from giving Rob a look that said "I told you so."

Relieved, she wiped the sweat from her forehead. Rob picked up their leather jackets from the floor and handed the black one to Lara, his eyes cast downward and sullen. Glaring at him, Lara seized her jacket and strode toward Vik, smiling with pride.

Outside the room, the FBI team cowered in the corner, probably waiting for Rob's angry reprimand for their failure.

The agents breathed a bit easier when he walked by them, not saying a single word.

Vik beamed at her. "Someone destroyed the keypad and cut the wires. I had to reprogram the system from scratch. Luckily, I kept a copy of my administrator code on my smartphone, so I was able to reset everything to work as it did before. As easy as a lollipop."

"You mean piece of cake?" Lara asked, smirking.

"It's how we say it in cricket." Vik grinned.

"Boss, I got a hit on that plate number you gave me," Agent Carter said from across the room to Rob.

Lara's ears perked up.

"The black BMW is registered to Anton Stepanov, and the apartment address belongs to Linda Maxwell. Both suspects are already on the big board in your office. You think they're working together?"

Rob nodded, deep in thought.

Lara forgot her anger for a moment. "What? Anton Stepanov from DARPA and Linda Maxwell from Beautific Creations are working together?" She'd sooner guess Vik was Sully's killer before thinking those two were partners.

Is one of them CyberShop?

"Well, it tracks with CyberShop's connections to the Russians. You know what this means," Rob said, turning to Lara.

She nodded. "Both Linda and Stepanov drive the same kind of car."

Or is it the same car with different plates?

"Great work, Agent Carter," Rob said. "Let's round up the team for a *Die-Hard*-style takedown."

Agent Carter nodded. Rob took out his phone and sent off a text. A minute later, his phone buzzed. "Guys, never mind, we're standing down."

Lara raised her eyebrow. *Rob standing down?*

Rob sighed. "Justyne thinks CyberShop will see us coming from miles away if we go in hot, and we'll lose our shot. She's gonna meet us out there, and we're gonna try a lower key approach."

Lara tilted her head and raised her eyebrows at him.

Rob returned a defensive glance. "What? She's been keeping out of the limelight for her cover at DARPA. I promised to call her when we made a break in the case on CyberShop. Do you want to go check to see if our friend Linda is at home or not?"

Lara nodded. Truthfully, she didn't want to spend any more time with Rob at the moment, but she refused to miss out on a major break in the case. She'd follow his lead. At least for now.

"Do I get to come, too? Please, please?" Vik asked, his hands folded together under his chin.

At first, Rob appeared uncertain, but then he nodded reluctantly. "Okay, you earned this one, kid. But things could get hairy, so you're going to stay in the car if I say so. Do we have a deal?"

Vik nodded excitedly and grinned like a dog with a fresh bone.

* * *

AFTER A THIRTY-MINUTE DRIVE IN SILENCE, the FBI cruiser arrived at the Laurel Lakes Apartment Complex, a set of newly built three-story condominiums constructed with high-end materials and surrounded by pristine, lush landscaping. Their website showed that each luxury building housed about twelve apartments. They were each decorated with a tan and red veneer brick pattern and light green siding. The pictures on Lara's phone gave her a good idea of the layout of the complex.

Rob drove into the parking lot and traveled around the perimeter of the complex in search of the black BMW convertible. He'd almost driven the entire length of the parking lot before Lara spotted it parked in a corner, just a few feet away from the address Sully had written on the back of the picture.

The memory of nearly being killed on the street flashed through her mind. *That's the car.* As Rob parked his cruiser, he pulled alongside the BMW. Lara glanced at the plates and crinkled her forehead.

"Huh, that's strange," Rob exclaimed, climbing out of the cruiser and motioning for Vik to stay put. "The plate number is 190 24K. This one's registered to Anton Stepanov."

"I was thinking they drive the same car but switch out the plates," Lara said, nodding in agreement.

Rob walked around the car, inspecting both the front and back plates and then peered through the windshield to write down the car's VIN.

"Do you think the plates are fake?" Lara asked while scanning the inside of the vehicle. The BMW was clean and in mint condition, inside and out. There was nothing inside the car except the USB cable for a cellphone and a coffee cup in the cup holder.

"We'll know for sure once I look up this VIN." Rob placed his hand on the hood of the car. "It's warm." They locked eyes.

Just then, Lara heard a car drive up from behind. She turned to find a white Honda with Maryland plates pulling into the spot next to Rob's cruiser. Justyne stepped out of the vehicle, sending a cloud of tropical flower perfume wafting toward Lara. Her stomach already nauseous from being sick, she held back a gag.

"Lara, good to see you." Her tone was cool.

"Sure, you too." Lara bit her lip. Her stomach gurgled angrily as uncertainty swept over her. She knew Rob and Justyne were investigating CyberShop as part of an FBI-NSA collaboration. But by now, Lara thought *she* was Rob's partner on the case.

Am I jealous?

"Isn't that Stepanov's car?" Justyne asked.

Rob nodded. "Think so."

"Interesting. Shall we?" Justyne said, motioning for them to follow her.

Rob followed Justyne toward the front door of the apartment complex. Lara lumbered after them, clenching her fists. As they approached the building, Rob drew his gun and instructed Justyne and Lara to get behind him. Lara did as she was told, her hand positioned on her holster. Unarmed, Justyne hung back slightly.

Linda's apartment was situated on the third floor of the building closest to the BMW's parking spot. Lara raced up three flights of stairs after Rob, reaching the top stair with ease. Behind her, she could hear Justyne huffing and puffing from the physical exertion.

I may not be put together all the time, but at least I'm in decent shape.

Leaning his body against the wall, Rob banged hard on the door of apartment 302.

"Open up, this is the FBI," Rob shouted. "Linda Maxwell, open the door."

No one responded; not even a rustle sounded on the other side of the door.

"Linda, this is the FBI. Open up—FBI, open the door, or I will force entry." Rob gave his last warning. Seconds later, he kicked the door with all of his might, but it wouldn't budge. He winced and hopped on one foot for a second. He grunted and shook it out. "Stand back," he said, pointing his gun at the lock.

"You're not seriously going to shoot the lock with that pistol, are you?" Lara asked. "Someone could get hurt."

Rob shot Lara an angry glare. "And what would you have me do? We need to gain entry. Now."

Shrugging her shoulders, Lara motioned for him to press on and took cover with Justyne around the corner, both of them putting their hands over their ears. Rob unloaded several rounds into the lock, and it busted open. They followed Rob into the apartment. To their surprise, the space was completely empty. Not even a single piece of paper left on the floor.

Rob ran from room to room, shouting "clear."

Lara pursed her lips with disappointment. "Linda knew we were on to her and moved out, but Stepanov's car is outside. That's odd, don't you think?" She bit her lower lip, thinking through the possibilities. As she did, her eyes swept the room for anything she might have missed. The sliding door caught her attention; it was cracked open.

Without hesitation, Lara was at the door in just a few strides. She pushed it open the rest of the way and stepped outside. A long, makeshift rope of sheets tied together dangled from the railing. "Rob," Lara said over her shoulder. "Come look…"

Rob came out onto the balcony and gaped at the sheets. "Well, that's definitely old-school, but it works."

Lara's smartphone buzzed. She pulled it out of her pocket; the screen displayed a text from Vik:

> LINDA IS GETTING AWAY!
> SHE TOOK OFF IN THE BMW RIGHT IN FRONT OF MY EYES
> I COULDN'T DO ANYTHING TO STOP HER

"Shit." Lara showed the text to Rob, and his face went slack. They'd missed her by only a few minutes.

"Let's get out of here," Rob said, holstering his gun and heading out the door. "I'm going to get an FBI evidence response team over here to search the place from top to bottom. Maybe we've missed something."

Justyne hesitated, lingering in the apartment. "I'm going to stay behind, wait for the evidence team, and see if they find any leads."

Rob nodded. "Okay, let us know if they find something."

Back at the car, Vik was in a frantic state with his hands on his head. "Here, I took some photos before she got away." He handed his cellphone to Lara. The photos showed the woman with auburn hair from Beautific Creations in a tan trench coat getting in her car and then racing away.

Lara scratched her head. *She's driving Stepanov's car. I must be right. They share it.*

Rob got on his cellphone, called Agent Carter, and asked him to send an evidence team to the apartment complex and put out an APB on Dr. Anton Stepanov. On his second phone call, Rob requested an arrest warrant from a judge.

"I can't believe we lost yet another lead." Lara leaned against the car and stared sullenly at the ground. "I feel like all we do is take steps backward on this case. It's driving me mad."

"Patience, Lara. We're almost there now. Linda won't get very far," Rob said, hanging up the phone. "The entire police force in the National Capital Region is already on the lookout for her."

She knew Rob was trying to make her feel better, but it didn't work. The case was going round and round and getting nowhere. And she needed to earn some money again. Rob motioned for them to get in the car. Lara climbed into the passenger side of the FBI cruiser while Rob started the engine.

As Vik situated himself in the back seat, he put a hand on Lara's shoulder. "Don't worry, boss. Everything is not completely lost."

"Oh really. Do you know something I don't know?" Lara didn't usually snap at Vik, but she wasn't in the mood for any snark. Rob began driving out of the lot, and she watched the buildings go by.

Vik didn't lose a beat. "Well, you know how I have been constantly wearing my DigiSpecs and typing on my virtual keyboard like a crazy person?"

"You *have* been buried in that screen thing a lot lately. What did you find?" Lara's mood lifted at the prospect of a clue.

"I've been using a tool called Memex to search the entire World Wide Web. Memex helps me access the websites on the Dark Web that are not indexed by standard search engines."

Lara furrowed her brow and scrunched her face. "What does that mean?"

Without warning, Rob took a corner at high speed, jerking her forward. She grabbed the door handle to steady herself and shot an irritated look at Rob.

What's his problem?

"Remember we talked about Tor?" Vik asked, his head bobbing up and down, clearly enjoying the bumpy ride.

"Oh yeah, sorry."

"I created a machine-learning algorithm to build a log of all of KillerBot's activities on the Dark Web, and I think I'm getting closer to figuring out Fiddler's location."

"A machine-learning algorithm?"

Vik nodded. "It's a program that pulls certain types of information using Memex from the Internet and the Dark Web. Using big data analytics, a computer can identify correlations of interest more quickly than humans."

"Okay, so what's Memex again?" Lara asked.

"DARPA invented Memex to search the entire network of websites, including the Internet, the Deep Web, and the Dark Web."

"I don't get it. If the Dark Web is hidden except through Tor, how can DARPA search it?"

Lara didn't like it when there were technical things beyond her understanding, and cyberspace had a tendency to baffle her. She couldn't fathom who came up with the idea of setting up an ungoverned and easily accessible network of computers, vulnerable to all sorts of malicious behavior.

Vik smirked. "Because DARPA developed Tor and the Dark Web in the first place. The U.S. Navy created the original onion routing technology in the 1990s to protect U.S. Intelligence communications. The U.S. Naval Research Laboratory later released the code for Tor under a free license. Since then, DARPA developed a search engine for the Deep Web called Memex, which combines the word 'memory' with 'index' to—"

Lara frowned. "Wait, so criminals use technology created by the U.S. Government to hide their illegal activities? That doesn't seem like the smartest idea."

Vik pretended to shoot himself in the head with his finger. "Well, it's not that smart. How many times have I told you the Dark Web is overrated?"

"I'm going to drop you and Vik off at your office," Rob interrupted. "I've got to head back to the FBI Washington Field Office and make sure we get that warrant to search the commercial development that keeps coming up for Fiddler."

"But what about my bike?" Lara now regretted letting Rob drive her.

"Can't you just get it later?" Rob asked.

Lara glared at him, her cheeks flushing pink. Despite her anger, Rob still held sway over her. She sat silent for a few minutes, trying to refocus on the issues at hand. She turned back to Vik. "How does Memex help us find Fiddler?"

"Lara, I was trying to explain it to you so that you understand. Memex is designed to pull from a larger pool of data sources, searching unindexed information on the Internet and the Dark Web."

"So, you have better tools, but Tor hides locations and identities. How do you get past that?"

"Okay, we already know Fiddler uses the pseudonym KillerBot, so he no longer enjoys anonymity from us. The challenge becomes discovering his current physical location. And for that, we can exploit the vulnerabilities of onion routing. Even though the layers of encryption hide locations and identities, there are records of connections between nodes, the time they occurred, and the amount of data transferred. I'm using a technique called traffic analysis to search the records of connections between a website or forum, trying to match the timing and data transfer amounts to recipients. Then by exploiting compromised nodes in the network, I can rebuild the data chain and determine if there are any patterns of communication. If the compromised nodes are the final nodes in the chain, I can actually get some useful raw data."

"Vik, you lost me. Plain English please."

"Basically, my algorithm analyzes specific traffic over the Dark Web pertaining to KillerBot and CyberShop. By digging through this information and exploiting vulnerabilities, I can ascertain personal information such as passwords, private messages, bank account numbers—"

Rob slammed on his brakes and honked angrily at the car in front of him, even though the offending driver had no control over his self-driving vehicle. Lara eyed him, but he didn't notice.

Turning back to Vik, she asked, "So, did you find something or not?" Lara tapped her fingers against her thigh, impatient for a response.

Vik shook his head. "Not yet, but I'm close. Traffic analysis is tedious and time-consuming work. So far, I've inferred from past communications that some type of event may be imminent."

"Vik, keep at this. At this point, you might actually solve this case for us."

Lara's smartphone buzzed. Hitting the accept call button, she said, "Lara Kingsley."

"Ms. Kingsley, Detective Sanchez here."

Great. I'm not in the mood for a lecture.

The detective cleared his throat. "I'd like you to come down to the station. We're about to go over our list of suspects and thought we could use an extra set of eyes. Are you free?"

Well, this is a surprise. The detective wanted her help for a change. Lara glanced over at Rob, who remained focused on the road and pretended he wasn't listening. "Sure… I can be there in fifteen minutes."

"Good, see you soon."

The line disconnected.

"Uh, Rob?"

"What?" Rob sniped at her.

Sheesh. Lara didn't know what had angered him more: his team failing to get them out of the safe room, losing Linda, or her angry response to his idiotic attempt at an apology. She didn't really care.

"No need to snap at me," Lara retorted. "I'm gonna need you to make two stops. Detective Sanchez wants me to swing by the station, and Vik needs to get back to the townhouse to head over to his class."

Rob sighed audibly and looked at his watch. "Fine."

For the next twenty minutes, they drove in complete silence. Rob jerked the cruiser around like he was taking out his frustration on the vehicle.

"Here we are," Rob said, pulling up to the First District police station in southeast D.C.

Lara breathed a huge sigh of relief.

"Sorry to leave you stranded without your bike," Rob said.

Lara motioned with her hands, brushing off his attempt at an apology. "Yeah, okay. You'll let us know about the warrant?"

Rob nodded, but didn't look at her. Lara waved goodbye to Vik as the cruiser sped away, the tires squealing.

THIRTY-ONE

For Hire

CLIMBING the steps to her townhouse, Lara's stomach growled angrily and her body ached. Every bone in her body screamed for her to lie down. She felt as if she hadn't eaten or slept in days. The antibiotics were doing their job, but the symptoms of the plague still lingered.

She'd spent the afternoon at the police station going over the list of suspects and evidence with Sanchez. While she and the detective both agreed that Stepanov and Linda were the most likely suspects for Sully's murder, they disagreed vehemently on Anita's involvement in Fiddler's beetle plot. For some reason, the detective remained stuck on the notion that Anita was no good, convinced she was behind the leak at the NSA.

Lara glanced at the stack of mail on the floor of the hallway. There were several new past due notices. She sighed heavily, tucking them under her arm as she climbed the stairs to the second floor. When she reached her apartment door, an envelope taped near the keyhole made her cringe, but the sticky note from Vik made her stomach drop.

RECEIVED THIS FROM JAKE WHILE YOU WERE OUT
WE NEED TO TALK

Crap. It was a letter from Jake Crawford, her landlord. *That can't be good news.*

This was not how she'd wanted Vik to find out the truth about their living situation. It wouldn't be easy for him to forgive her dishonesty. They'd grown close when Rob had left her; Vik had been such a good friend. Lara couldn't justify keeping such a big secret from him—personally or professionally. But there never seemed to be a good time to come clean.

She walked into her apartment, her hands shaking, and ripped open the envelope. At the top of the official letter, in bold red ink, were the words "writ of eviction." She skimmed the notice, her heart pounding in her ears.

Lara had failed to pay the past due rent within the thirty-day timeframe and missed the court hearing that took place when she was in the hospital. For this reason, the judge had issued Jake a writ of eviction, giving him the right to call the U.S. Marshal's office to remove her from the premises. The envelope also contained a handwritten note from Jake saying he would give her one more week to pay the outstanding rent, fees, and court costs in cash or by certified check.

Lara stuffed the letter in her pocket, put the rest of the mail on the console in the hallway, and hung her leather jacket on a hook next to the door. From the moment she turned around and surveyed the apartment, she knew something was amiss. Her instincts fired on all cylinders.

The living room remained almost exactly how she left it. Almost, but not quite. A chair was moved ever so slightly toward the couch, and someone had shuffled through the magazines on the end table. The November issue of *Wired* lay on top of the pile, and she'd remembered having it at the hospital. When she packed everything up to come home, she couldn't find it anywhere.

How did this get here? Did Vik bring it back?

She opened the magazine and eagerly flipped through the pages, looking for her case notes, but they were missing. She checked the floor to see if the notes fell out. Instead, she spotted a small piece of paper peeking out from under the chair. She bent down and pulled it out of its hiding spot. The handwriting was familiar. It was the note from Sully's lawyer. She remembered sticking the paper, along with her notes, in the magazine. Lara turned the paper over in her hands, studying it for a moment, before a soft thump in another room startled her.

Stuffing the paper in her pocket and drawing her gun, she walked the hall toward her bedroom only to find no one. Lara went from room to room, sure she had heard someone, but nothing was out of place. The apartment was empty. There weren't any obvious signs of theft. Just small things here and there caught her attention as being a little off.

Who was here and what did they want?

She inspected each of the windows to make sure they were secure.

Whoever it was didn't want me to notice they'd been here.

In the kitchen, a draft of cold air from a crack in the window made her shiver. The light of the early evening sun poured into the room, counterbalancing the creepy feeling in her gut.

Am I imagining things?

Glancing at the floor, Lara spotted a pen. She looked back at the window.

Was this the sound I heard? A pen rolling onto the floor?

She strode over to the window above the kitchen sink, which overlooked a fire escape that ran down the back of the building.

Did someone climb in the apartment through the window again?

She saw no evidence of an intruder in the alley.

Maybe I'm being paranoid.

Lara looked back at the pen and shook her head. As she closed the window and locked it, her arm brushed against a strange-looking potted plant sitting beside the sink. It had been hidden behind her dish detergent, out of the way, small enough to escape notice.

Now that doesn't belong here.

Lara picked up the small and intricate plant and examined it carefully. Given its delicate shape and its bark footing, she knew it must be some type of bonsai tree. It was an odd thing for an intruder to leave behind.

A welcome home gift? Someone broke into my apartment to leave me a potted tree?

She set the small tree on the kitchen table, put her gun in the back of her pants, snapped a picture of the tree, and spoke into her smartphone. "Watson, could you identify this tree for me?"

The screen lit up with a familiar face. "Of course, Ms. Kingsley, I'd be delighted to do so," Watson said.

She was pretty sure the culprit was Fiddler. Lara stared at the tree, searching for answers.

But why? What clue is he tantalizing me with?

The tree was planted in a blue, hand-thrown, flat-based ceramic pot. The varied color of the bark and the thin pointy leaves reminded her of the time she had spent in Northern California on a military assignment. Leaning closer to it, she detected a funny smell like a cough drop.

Watson sprang to life on her phone. "I've identified the tree as a bonsai Eucalyptus tree, which is native to Australia and grown locally. I've found an exact match to your picture on this bonsai website."

A Eucalyptus tree? She read through the online profile. *Okay, this is definitely Fiddler. What is he trying to tell me?*

Rob had been unable to find definitive evidence of Fiddler's trip to Australia. Was Fiddler trying to make her doubt Maggie?

I won't make that mistake again.

On closer inspection, Lara spotted a tiny crack between the foot and the body of the pot that didn't seem to be intentional on the part of the potter. She got up from the table and found a knife in the kitchen drawer. Lara stuck the blade into the crack and pressed downwards. The gap widened, and the foot broke off. Inside the foot, she found a high-tech surveillance bug.

At least he didn't send me another beetle.

She paused for a moment, wondering if Fiddler was there, listening on the other end. Ever since she'd spoken to Ashton posing as Fiddler at the Basilica, she couldn't get his offer of $100K out of her mind. Given her dire financial situation, the money would be a godsend.

But at what price? Her conscience gnawed at her.

Lara didn't believe Fiddler killed Sully. She was also convinced that getting close to Fiddler would get her closer to discovering CyberShop's true identity. But she worried about what Fiddler was really up to, what his endgame was, and of course, his mental state.

For most of her life, Lara had always tried to do the right thing. This sentiment had driven her to join the military and serve her country in the first place. But for what? When push came to shove, even the U.S. Government didn't have her back.

Even in a democracy built on equal rights for all, the world consisted of two groups of people: rule-makers and rule-followers. Rule-makers did whatever they damn well pleased and were rarely held accountable for their actions. Rule-followers didn't question things, for the most part. They were content as long as peace reigned on their home turf.

Reaching out to Fiddler was risky, but at this point, she'd run out of good ideas. She needed to learn the details of his plans for the beetles. Fiddler also knew something about Sully's killer. At the church, impersonating Fiddler, Ashton claimed to have met CyberShop.

Could Fiddler identify CyberShop from a lineup?

Lara leaned in toward the bug and whispered. "Is your offer still on the table?"

She waited for a few minutes, but nothing happened. Lara laid the flat end of a knife against the bug, ready to crunch it into pieces, when a high-pitched noise erupted from the small device.

"Yes, it is," a cold, smooth voice responded.

A two-way transmitter?

Lara nearly fell off her chair from shock. "Am I finally speaking with John Fiddler?"

A moment of silence followed, long enough to make Lara wonder if she'd imagined the words.

"Yes," the voice hissed.

"How do I know it's really you this time?"

"You thought I didn't see you outside the café…" The voice paused. "But I did. You were wearing the glasses I gave to your assistant."

Lara froze, a chill travelling through her core, making her hair stand on end.

Fiddler knew I was there. He's tracking my every move. She closed her eyes, wishing she'd asked Vik to get rid of the DigiSpecs. *Did he hack into the glasses after Vik debugged them?*

"Did you like my little beetle swarm?" The voice hissed again. "I warned you not to involve my daughter. It was only fair to punish you for your disobedience. You don't like following instructions, do you?"

She ignored his nasty quip. "Your daughter is involved whether you like it or not. The authorities are closing in on her as Stepanov's and Linda's accomplice. They think they have evidence of her complicity, and her leaving town has put a huge target on her back. Help me prove them wrong."

The silence on the other end of the transmitter was deafening. After a few seconds, a click was followed by heavy breathing.

"Why did you pay the drone deposit and then renege on the deal?" Lara asked. "It was to offer the NSA evidence of Anita's innocence, wasn't it?"

"Come work for me and find out," Fiddler hissed.

Lara said nothing for a few seconds as a slight tremor passed through her body. "I know what you're planning with those beetles."

"Oh, do you now?" Fiddler's voice sounded pleased. "And you've already helped me so much with that plan. After I sent the swarm to attack you, I was able to calibrate the software for my next attack. And now, you're interested in helping me with the next steps? That tickles me to no end, Lara. It makes me so happy."

Lara's pulse raced, the sound of her heartbeat thrashing in

her ears. Her clammy hands were a stark contrast to the sweat beading on her forehead.

Who am I fooling? This is a bad idea.

Without hesitation, she grabbed the knife and crushed the transmitter. With one last squeak, it was disabled. Lara gazed with uncertainty at the smashed metal on the table.

He won't tell me who CyberShop is now...

But the thought of meeting him in person made her hair stand on end. Her instincts had screamed at her to disconnect. Fiddler might be able to help her with information, but it wasn't worth the cost.

That's a definite no-go.

She exhaled a breath of relief. She'd solve Sully's murder on her own. After sitting in silence for an hour, Lara realized she'd forgotten to pick up her motorcycle from Sully's townhouse. As she got ready to leave, she found the business card for SpaceSaver Self-Storage and the key in the pocket of her leather jacket. In all the excitement of chasing Linda Maxwell, she'd forgotten to check out the storage company that might hold all of Sully's files.

Better late than never.

Before leaving the apartment, Lara checked all the windows again to make sure they were secure and then locked the front door. On the steps outside her townhouse, she called a GoGo driverless cab and waited on the sidewalk next to the empty spot where her bike usually stood. A large, unmarked white van sat across the street.

Are the contractors still working?

Straining her ears, she could hear the thump of hammers on the first floor through one of the new windows. The contractors had repainted the brick facade an ugly, dull brown. The prospect of moving to a new place brought a sigh to Lara's lips. But, with the break-ins and the arson, part of her wondered if it would be for the best.

THIRTY-TWO

The Files

THE GIANT SPACESAVER facility consisted of rows and rows of ground-level self-storage units, each with a bright orange garage door. At the front gate, a large green neon sign illuminated the darkness and directed customers to the front office.

Lara parked her bike out front and entered through the glass door to find the attendant sound asleep with his head resting on the reception desk. The air reeked of something sweet and putrid, much like the dark alley behind her old high school where the potheads smoked at recess.

"Excuse me, sir?" Lara whispered, not wanting to startle him. She held her nose to prevent the strong odor from overwhelming her. "Hellooo?"

The twenty-something attendant with long, messy dreads sat up straight, rubbing his bloodshot brown eyes. "What? Who?" He wore a scruffy plaid shirt, old jeans, and a name tag with the company logo. When the kid finally focused his sights on Lara, he squinted at her and snorted. "What do *you* want?"

"I'm looking for unit 506," Lara said. "Can you tell me where it's located?"

"Ma'am, can't you read that sign?"

"What sign?" Lara gave him a confused look.

"It. Says. Self. Storage." He enunciated each word slowly. "That means, you can go find your unit yourself."

Lara stood there and continued to stare at him, waiting for his assistance.

He rolled his eyes and yawned. "Unit 506 is located in aisle three. Turn right when you exit and proceed to the third row of units. The signs indicate the unit numbers. You know how to look up numbers posted on doors, right?"

Lara threw him a nasty glare. "Thank you. That wasn't so hard, was it?" *Kids these days.* She turned on her heels and exited the office.

A fresh, cool breeze greeted her outside, and she eagerly took a deep breath. The full moon shone from a clear sky, casting eerie shadows on the cement in the parking lot.

When she reached the third row of units, she turned the corner and stopped dead in her tracks. A shiny black BMW convertible with the Maryland plate 190 24K was parked about midway down the row. Her pulse spiked, sending adrenaline through her body.

She wasn't sure who it would be—Linda or Dr. Stepanov. Either way, she had walked into a party she wasn't invited to. And the hosts weren't going to be friendly. Loud noises came from an open unit located across from the car.

Someone is searching Sully's unit.

Drawing her gun, Lara stalked toward the unit, keeping her body as close to the wall as possible. When she reached the edge of the open unit, she listened carefully. Against the background of crickets and distant traffic, the rustling noises indicated the presence of only one person. Lara looked up and down the empty row of units. No one else in sight.

Here goes nothing.

Swinging around the corner, Lara pointed her gun into the unit and shouted at a large man dressed in a suit. "Freeze! Put your hands where I can see them, or I'll shoot."

With his back to her, the pudgy man with white hair froze in place, dropped the file he was holding, and raised his hands slowly. Several loose papers floated to the cement floor below. Lara surveyed the unit. A dim lightbulb threw some light on the clutter in the small space. Several filing cabinet drawers hung open, papers strewn about everywhere. He'd clearly not found whatever he was looking for.

"Please don't shoot," he cried out.

The accent was faint, but she recognized it. "Turn around slowly. Keep your hands in the air," Lara demanded.

He turned toward her. She was right. The old man wearing thick-rimmed glasses and a bowtie was Dr. Stepanov. A look of recognition flashed across his face when he saw her.

"Where's Linda?" Lara asked.

"Linda who?"

"Don't play dumb with me. I saw the same BMW at Beautific Creations." Lara pointed at the car.

Stepanov's face became pale. "I... I don't know what you're talking about."

"I'm talking about your relationship with Linda Maxwell."

"I don't know her," Stepanov kept his hands raised.

"Then why were you at her apartment yesterday?" Lara pressed.

Stepanov's eyes widened. "I wasn't. I was at work the entire day."

"How do you explain your car then?"

"What about my car? I took the metro to work, so it was at home in my garage."

"Interesting coincidence. I saw an identical black BMW convertible with the same plates at Linda's apartment yesterday. In fact, she took off with it, escaping pursuit by the FBI."

Stepanov's mouth fell open. "I don't know anything about that..."

"And you're sure you want to stick with that story?"

Stepanov nodded his head vehemently.

"How do you explain the identical plates?" Lara asked, her eyes narrowing.

"I don't have a clue. Maybe the plates are fake? You'd need to check the VIN number to make sure the car belongs to the plates."

Dammit Rob, you never called me with that info. Lara put one hand on her hip as she held the gun in place with the other. "You expect me to believe you?"

Stepanov shrugged his shoulders helplessly. "I don't know what else to tell you."

"How about you tell me what the hell you're doing in Sully's storage unit?"

His lips moved, but no sound came out.

"If you don't answer all of my questions satisfactorily, I'm ready to use this." Lara motioned with her gun.

"Please don't hurt me. Sully gave me the key, I swear." A panicked look spread across his ashen face. It was not the look of a cold-blooded killer. Still, Lara found his presence odd and unsettling.

Lara lowered her gun slightly. "I'm good friends with Sully, and I had no idea you two knew each other. Tell me the truth. What are you doing here?"

Stepanov's lower lip trembled. "He told me he feared for his life. Sully said if he died, he wanted me to help find his killer."

"What?" Lara's mouth fell open. She swallowed hard, a painful tightness constricting her throat.

Sully confided in Stepanov and not me?

She shook her head. "I don't believe you…"

Surrounded by stacks of case files, Stepanov panted, out of breath, and tried to steady himself, but the stack next to him fell over, sending papers flying in all directions.

"Look, Sully gave me a key to his storage unit and told me to find the file that would prove who killed him." Stepanov held out the Star Wars R2D2 keychain, the last in the set Lara had given Sully. "I've been coming here every night for several weeks, combing through his files in search of evidence. I've found nothing." His voice had a trace of desperation. "Honestly, I have no idea what I'm looking for. Sully promised to leave me clues in his journal in a lockbox at DARPA, but when I looked for it, it was gone. So, I'm literally searching in the dark here."

"I found his journal," Lara said flatly. *And it burned up in the fire before I could read all the entries.*

"You did?" Stepanov looked relieved. "Thank God, I thought this CyberShop character might have gotten to it first."

Lara nodded. "It was in a lockbox, just as you said. Sully put the entries on a burner cellphone. Tell me how he had access to DARPA?"

Stepanov nodded. "I made him an ID card. I wanted to make sure he'd have access to the lockboxes and could do the drop when he got the chance."

Lara rubbed her chin. *He did help Sully.* She had so many questions that she didn't know where to start. "When did you first meet Sully?"

"It's a bit of a long story." Perspiration shone on his wide brow.

"I've got time," Lara said, relaxing her stance. "And I'd like to hear everything from the beginning."

Stepanov gave her an uncertain look. "Okay... We believed someone within NSA or DARPA used the pseudonym CyberShop to sell classified technology. I think the real culprit misdirected Sully, who followed the evidence until it led him to me."

Lara's eyes grew large. "You think someone is setting you up?"

Stepanov nodded. "At first, Sully thought I was involved in the scheme. He monitored my local post office and took pictures of my car parked outside. Sully looked up my license plate and paid me a visit at my house, thinking I was the leak. He accused me of renting a P.O. box at the post office."

"And did you?" Lara asked.

"Well, yes, I did... but not for the reasons Sully thought. I rented a P.O. box to protect my identity online, but Sully thought I was using it to send and receive mail from illicit activities on the Dark Web. He had a postal address from a package sent by CyberShop. I showed him my records to prove it was not mine."

"Did Sully believe you?" Lara asked.

"I think so. I mean, I'm here, aren't I? When Sully confronted me, I explained to him that I worked for the NSA and that we were on the same team. Several weeks ago, Sully contacted me and told me he was worried someone might kill him. He had a working theory about CyberShop's identity but was not yet ready to go to the authorities. That's when Sully gave me the key to his storage unit."

"And did he share his theory with you?" Lara raised her eyebrow. Her thoughts were spinning in all directions. Stepanov's story sounded plausible, but something didn't feel right.

Why would Sully trust him?

"No," he answered. "He never explained in detail. He said it would be in his journal entries."

Another thing bothered her. "Then why didn't you help me when I came to you?"

Stepanov stared at his feet. "I didn't trust you. Sully didn't mention you. For all I knew, *you* were CyberShop."

"Did you know about Justyne's investigation?" Lara asked.

"My colleague, Justyne? Of course I know about it." He waved his hand dismissively. "She was obsessed with a senior analyst at NSA named Frank Moore. You see, I was Frank's supervisor. I suspected they were having an affair, well, at least until he died in that terrible car crash. Then Frank came under suspicion for selling Top Secret technology to the Russians and anyone who would pay the steep price. For a long time, the NSA and FBI suspected Frank's wife Anita to be his accomplice. Then Justyne had the audacity to accuse me of having something to do with Frank's death or at minimum with CyberShop's illegal activities. She caused me all sorts of trouble at work. To escape the toxic environment, I went on detail assignment to DARPA. And then Justyne followed me there. You might now understand why we don't get along too well?"

Lara furrowed her brow. She wasn't sure if she bought Stepanov's story. It made sense, but so did an alternate version of the facts. If Stepanov was CyberShop, he could know all the same information and be trying to squeeze himself out of a sticky situation. Stepanov could have misled Sully about the purpose of his P.O. box, stolen Sully's storage unit key, seen Sully hide the burner in the lockbox on video footage, and lied about knowing Linda. It all came down to the license plates. *Were they real or fake?*

Dammit, Rob.

"Do you think Frank committed treason and sold the technology to the Russians?"

Stepanov shrugged. "The evidence the NSA had against Frank and Anita was pretty strong, but there was no smoking gun. Either they're guilty and destroyed the incriminating evidence, or they were set up by a brilliant mastermind."

"How do I know you're not the mastermind?" Lara asked.

Without warning, the lights went off, pitching her into complete darkness. Before her eyes could adjust, a blunt object walloped her in the back of the head, knocking her to the ground. Hearing the sound of slamming doors and squealing tires, her vision blurred with stars and then went black.

* * *

WHEN SHE PULLED herself up from the pavement, Lara had no idea how long she'd been out. She dug her smartphone out to look at the time. At least an hour had passed. As she braced herself on the side of the unit, her head throbbed mercilessly. The black BMW convertible had disappeared.

Did I just let Sully's killer escape? Is the answer here, among these endless piles of paper?

It would take hours—if not days—to search through everything carefully. Exhausted and unable to think straight, Lara closed the garage door of the unit, locked it, and staggered toward her motorcycle, trying to quiet the drumming in her head.

I'll come back tomorrow.

Lara pulled her smartphone from her pocket and started dialing Detective Sanchez. As she threw her leg over her bike, the loud rumble of an engine startled her. A gust of wind whipped passed her as a white van pulled up, screeching as it put on the brakes.

Before she had time to think, someone wearing a mask jumped out, grabbed her from behind, put a hood over her head, and pulled her into the van. In the struggle, her smartphone slipped from her hand and shattered on the cement beneath her.

Lara struggled and kicked, but her assailant was too strong. He shoved her to the floor of the van and kicked her in the stomach, causing her to cry out in pain. A sharp ache in her stomach made her nauseous. Her attacker yanked both of her arms behind her back and tightened plastic ties around her wrists. Then he did the same to her ankles.

She heard the side door of the van slam shut. The passenger door opened and closed. Seconds later, the engine took off at high speed, the tires squealing. At the front of the van, Lara could hear the muffled voices of two men arguing. One sounded older than the other. She thought she recognized the younger voice, but she couldn't make out the substance of the conversation.

Putting her ear to the floor of the van, Lara focused on the sounds of the city in an attempt to decipher where they were going. She didn't think they had driven over any bridges, so chances were, they were still in Washington D.C. or nearby Maryland.

After about thirty minutes, the van screeched to a halt. Both front doors clicked open and slammed shut. The men refrained from speaking to each other. The side door of the van opened, and cold air rushed in. A strong hand grabbed her arm, and she detected a sweet scent that smelled like jasmine.

The last time I smelled that...

"Ashton?" Lara asked.

"Sit up," a gruff voice said, ignoring her question.

Lara tried to sit up, but the black bag over her head disoriented her. Between the pain of getting kicked in the stomach and her restraints, she could only prop herself up on one elbow. "I can't…"

The man shoved his arms underneath her armpits and tugged on her as hard as he could. Her feet dragged across the floor of the van. As he pulled her out of the vehicle, Lara's hip hit the side of the sliding door, sending a sharp pain down her leg.

The man dropped her onto the cold cement. Her feet landed with a thud on the ground, and she toppled over sideways. He cut the ankle ties, yanked Lara to her feet, and pushed her forward. Still wearing the hood, Lara couldn't see where to step on the rough pavement, and she stumbled a few times over the bumps and grooves.

A heavy steel door opened in front of her.

"Watch your step," the gruff voice said. "Two stairs."

The man steadied her as she climbed the stairs and entered the building. Inside, Lara smelled a mix of industrial odors. There was a dinging and the sound of steel scraping against concrete. The man shoved her, and she stumbled several steps until she hit a railing. Her hands could feel an iron grated wall. The floor jerked and a high-pitched squeal sounded as the space moved upward.

An industrial elevator… maybe this is a warehouse of some kind?

A breeze drifted through the grated walls, and she guessed the elevator was large enough to carry freight. The elevator moved slowly and rattled when it reached the right floor. When the door opened, the man shoved her forward down a hallway and into a small space that felt like a closet. The humid air smelled of lemon-scented cleaning supplies. She fell to the floor, the thud of the door closing behind her and sealing her fate.

THIRTY-THREE

The Beetle Farm

SEVERAL HOURS PASSED before footsteps approached and the door banged open. A strong set of hands grabbed her arms, pulled her up off the floor, and steered her roughly into a hard, wooden chair.

The man yanked the hood off her head, the rough fabric scratching her nose. The static electricity made her hair stand on end. Lara shielded her eyes with her bound wrists as the bright light shone directly on her. She squinted until her eyes adjusted.

The small room was empty except for a broom, some cleaning supplies, and a few folding chairs. From the exposed piping and air vents above, Lara guessed she was being held in an industrial facility. Behind her, she could hear her captor rustling around.

When he stepped into view, he gripped a Taser, pointing it right at her.

"Ashton?"

The dark circles under his bloodshot eyes made him look even more ragged than he'd appeared during the interrogation at the FBI. There were also multiple beetle bites on his arms and face.

I guess Fiddler tested the swarm more than once.

"Yeah, what's it to you?" He snarled.

"What are you going to do with that?" Lara gaped at him, horrified at the sight of the Taser. Instinctively, she pulled back. "Why are you doing this to me?"

"Well, why not? Fiddler asked me to pick you up and paid me well to do it. You know I've been working for him. And it's too late for me anyhow. I might as well make some more money before I go to prison."

Fiddler had me kidnapped? Lara raised an eyebrow. "I don't understand. How is it too late for you? You haven't been charged with anything."

Ashton gritted his teeth. "Don't be stupid. It's only a matter of time before the police arrest me, Lara."

"Why? What did you do?" Lara stared at him, wide-eyed.

"Well, for one, I made it possible for Fiddler to control the beetle swarm. I'm the one who developed the microelectronics package that enables autonomous navigation. And now, he is going to kill hundreds of people with it. I'll be charged as an accomplice or something."

"But you didn't know what he wanted to do with the beetles," Lara said, attempting to reassure him.

Ashton shook his head. "No, I didn't… but if I'm honest with myself, it wouldn't have mattered. I needed the money."

Lara shook her head. "Ashton, you're not responsible for how Fiddler uses those beetles. It's not too late to do the right thing."

Ashton paused, contemplating her words. "Maybe… but—"

"But what?"

"I killed Sully." Ashton wiped sweat from his brow.

"What? That's not possib—" Lara blurted and then stopped herself. They'd found Ashton snooping at the Botox supply facility. And Ashton went behind Sully's back to work with Fiddler. He had motive and opportunity. Maybe he was telling the truth.

"Yes, it is." Ashton nodded vigorously. His eyes bulged as if they might pop out of his head.

Lara's mouth hung open, and she blinked several times, trying to process what Ashton had said. "If you killed Sully, then how did you do it?"

"I—I stole one of Fiddler's beetles, you know the type he modified to carry the plague. I planted it in Sully's townhouse. Remember, you found it there. That beetle bit him, and he got sick with the plague. That's how he died at the ballpark."

Recognition dawned on her face. This whole time, Ashton thought he'd been the one who killed Sully. No wonder the kid was desperate. "Actually, that's not how he died. You didn't kill him, Ashton."

"What?" Ashton grabbed the chair across from her to steady himself. "But… then… how did he…?"

"Someone poisoned Sully with botulinum toxin. You were right… and wrong. He was infected with the plague and showing symptoms, but the disease didn't kill him. Before he died, Sully was taking antibiotics, so he would have survived the plague."

Ashton collapsed into a chair. His face turned ghost white. "You mean… I didn't kill Sully?"

"No, you didn't. The FBI is homing in on a few suspects, and you're not one of them. You see, so it's not over for you. It's not too late to make things right and to get out of this."

Ashton shook his head and covered his face with his hands. "But even though I didn't kill Sully, I'm still guilty of attempted murder. No matter how I look at it, I'm going to jail."

Lara saw her opportunity. "Look, I'm friends with FBI Special Agent Martin. I can get you a deal. It's not too late for you."

"You'd help me?" Ashton asked, his voice uncertain.

Lara nodded. "I'll do whatever I can to help you. I promise."

A pensive look came across Ashton's face.

Lara held out her hands. "Could you please untie me now?"

Ashton paused for a moment. Then he nodded, got up, and walked toward her. Lara heard a soft click behind them, like the sound of a door opening gently. As Ashton reached to untie her wrists, he froze and his face turned ashen white.

Ashton backed away from Lara. His posture became rigid, and he tripped over a board, falling backwards to the floor. In the corner, he cowered next to the broom and whimpered for mercy. "Noooo... not the tank again, please, boss."

The air shifted, charged with Ashton's terror. Lara's heart beat wildly. Her stomach dropped, and the feeling of being watched returned tenfold. Lara craned her neck to see a man with a swarm of beetles hovering above his head. Her throat tightened. When the gaunt man wearing a white lab coat came into full view, he showed vivid signs of old age—the white hair, wrinkled skin, and menacing, sunken gray eyes. He looked much older than when she'd seen him in the coffee shop.

Fiddler.

Ashton cringed, wrapping his arms tightly around his stomach. "Please, boss... I didn't mean it. I was just playing along with her. I didn't mean any of it." His wrapped his arms tightly around his knees and began rocking back and forth on the floor.

"You expect me to believe you didn't mean to help Lara?" Fiddler hissed.

Ashton nodded vigorously. "Yes, boss. She made me do it."

"Do you mean she also made you leave behind a vast array of clues at the violin shop? The maps of my targets? Internet articles about the accident? Directions to the warehouse?" Fiddler's voice grew sharper with each item. "How many *other* times did you assist Lara?"

Ashton shook his head fiercely. "No, I didn't help her... I swear. I don't know how she found all of that."

"Do you think I would let you work in the violin shop without adult supervision?" Fiddler's eyes narrowed.

Ashton's face became a shade paler.

"I bugged my old violin bow and hid it in my violin case under some plastic. I know all about how you betrayed me. Shall we show Lara what happens to bad boys and girls?"

That explains the abandoned violin bow. Another listening device.

Lara shuddered when she thought about Fiddler overhearing her private conversations.

"Please, boss… please don't…" Ashton begged.

Fiddler's eyes gleamed. "Attack," he commanded. With one word, the beetles swarmed around Ashton, flying in tight circles around his body, and then closing in on him.

Seconds later, Lara watched in horror as the swarm began biting him all over his body, devouring his flesh. Ashton struggled and cried out as the beetles overwhelmed him. Drops of his blood spattered the floor. Within minutes, Ashton lay in a pool of his own blood, not moving. The beetles continued to gnaw angrily at his skin.

I've got to get out of here! Lara gasped for air, but her chest was too tight for anything but shallow breaths.

Turning, Fiddler gazed at her. His hollow eyes bored into her. When she looked away, Fiddler pulled the hood tightly over her head, grabbed her roughly by the arm, and dragged her out of the closet into what Lara guessed was a long hallway. Their footsteps echoed as they walked.

Fiddler opened a creaky door and shoved her into another room. The moist air smelled of soil and plant life. Her heart pounded like it might burst. He pulled the hood from her head. At first, she could barely see in the dimly lit space. When her eyes adjusted to the darkness, floor-to-ceiling glass terrariums formed out of the shadows, lining the perimeter of the spacious room. A special sprinkler system hung from the ceiling, presumably to water the trees and terrariums. Judging by the puddles of water around the drain at the center of the room, the space had been recently watered.

Hundreds of metallic golden, green-flecked beetles outfitted with tiny backpacks were swarming around a dozen miniature Eucalyptus trees planted in large pots. The trees had each grown about eight to nine feet tall. Lara froze in place, unable to move.

"Welcome to my beetle farm," Fiddler said with distinct pride in his voice.

He shoved her forward, and she stumbled toward the trees.

Lara shuddered at the sight of all the golden beetles flying around the tree tops.

"Are they?"

"Carrying the plague?" Fiddler anticipated her question. "No, not these. Not yet. That would be too dangerous, don't you think? To let them fly around so freely?" He slipped her a curious glance. "Lara, I'm disappointed that you would think me capable of such wanton destruction." Irony saturated his words.

She didn't doubt his capability, but she did question his intentions. Lara turned away from the frightening scene and tried to focus her attention on the floor.

There aren't any beetles on the floor.

Every bone in her body wanted to flee from the room, but Fiddler pulled her closer to one of the terrariums and grabbed her face, forcing her to look into it.

Soil and wood chips halfway filled the terrarium. Underneath the soil, Lara could see the eggs and white larvae of immature Christmas beetles. Grass and other vegetation sprung up from the soil. Above the surface, the adult golden beetles moved about, feeding on the plant life.

Fiddler pointed to the glass terrarium in front of them. "The larvae feed on grass roots and decay in the soil. Eventually, they will move close to the surface to pupate. Several weeks later, they will emerge as adults like the ones you see above." He waved his hand toward the beetles flying around the room.

"My friend Maggie said you managed to genetically modify the beetles?" Lara feigned interest in an attempt to distract him. It was probably best to keep Fiddler in good spirits.

"Ah yes, Maggie is your rather intelligent entomologist friend. I do like her." Fiddler clapped his hands together, his eyes crazed with excitement. "She's quite right. I used CRISPR to edit the DNA sequence for the mouthpart of the beetle to make it capable of biting humans. Then I used a gene drive to alter the genome of new generations of the beetles. Several years ago, I removed all beetles from the population that did not carry the new mouthpart gene, and now all of these beetles in this room are capable of biting humans and reproducing the same. More recently, I modified my beetles to respond to light pulses and allow me to leverage the steering neurons in the beetle's brain for better flight control."

"You've been doing this for years?" Lara was honestly surprised by the complexity of his operation.

Fiddler seemed pleased with her question. "Well, it started out as an experiment in the lab at work until—"

"You mean at USAMRIID?"

"Lara, I see you've been researching me. I'm so flattered." Fiddler caressed her cheek, his smile making Lara cringe inside. "Many years ago, my leadership tasked my team with exploring the potential of synthetic biology for causing harm to Americans. Our agency was charged with ensuring effective bio-defense for the nation. With the discovery of CRISPR gene editing in 2012, I began to worry about the possibility of terrorists developing novel vectors for transmitting disease."

"Novel vectors?" Lara asked.

Fiddler clasped his hands behind his back and rocked from heel to toe, his smile growing wider. "A vector is an organism, typically an insect, that transmits a disease to a new host. At the time, we considered the possibility of a biological attack by terrorists as imminent. I wanted to show my leadership how easy it would be to transform different insects into vectors for disease." He gestured toward the terrarium. "You see, flying insects are the perfect delivery system. They are small, hidden from sight, can reach any location by flight, and tend not to raise alarm bells. Most people are not afraid of insects."

Fiddler glanced at Lara's trembling hands. "Well, you're not most people, are you? You know, fear is a funny thing. I've been looking you up too, Lara. Explain to me how you can deploy to Afghanistan, get shot at by insurgents, watch your friends get their legs blown off by IEDs, and still be afraid of these beautiful creatures?" Fiddler caught one of the beetles with his hand and stroked it gently with a finger.

Lara shrugged. She couldn't explain it. Fear wasn't rational.

Her deployment to Afghanistan had left her with many more irrational fears she didn't understand. These days, a sudden loud noise, a bright flash of light, or even the sight of a drone could still send her into a panic attack. She'd seen a military therapist for PTSD for a year after returning from active duty and had made little progress.

Changing the subject, she asked, "You were saying before, you were afraid terrorists might use gene editing tools to make insects capable of killing people by infecting them with disease?"

"Oh yes, I was…" He paused for a moment, and then picked at the air, shuddering as though he were pulling something delightful out of storage. He raised a finger like a professor in the middle of a lecture. "I wanted to see if it was possible to alter the genes of a species of insects to carry a pathogen and then multiply the insects. But my boss said no. He argued that the project lacked sufficient merit for U.S. bio-defense planning."

"What do you mean?" Lara asked.

Fiddler threw up his hands in frustration. "My boss claimed the project amounted to biological 'space exploration'— whatever that means. He said I was creating a problem in search of a solution. When I took my proposal a level above him, my organization's leadership argued that there wasn't any credible information about our adversaries developing novel vectors. They told me there were no known countries interested in conducting entomological warfare. Without a real threat, there was no prophylactic need to develop them. I disagreed. So, I did the research anyway in my own lab at home. When my boss finally found out, he got me fired for conducting an unauthorized gene editing experiment." Fiddler stared gloomily at one of his terrariums. "I got fired for wanting to protect our nation from terrorists…"

"I'm curious, why would you work for USAMRIID in the first place when they were responsible for your mother's death?" Lara pressed.

"How did you find out about that?" Fiddler's eyes widened,

suddenly full of distrust. He frowned and began fidgeting with his lab coat.

Lara feared she might have said the wrong thing. "Sully left behind some newspaper clippings with your real name, Jan Speelman."

"Ahhh, good ol' Sully. I didn't realize he'd figured that one out." Fiddler's expression dulled. He was lost in thought for a few seconds. "Many years passed before I learned the truth about my mother's death. The U.S. Army had masterfully covered up what it had done. When I finally lost my lawsuit against the government, I was beside myself with rage. I couldn't even play the violin anymore. I needed to do something, to take some action. My anger fueled me to study molecular biology at the University of Maryland. Back then, I had a grand vision of taking my revenge on the government."

Fiddler rubbed sweat from his forehead. "But when I delved into the field, I realized how much malicious potential existed, and I began to understand the rationale for the tests undertaken by the U.S. Army. They were exploring the possibility of dispersal to save millions of lives. The only way to test the effects of a biological attack was to run the experiment on an actual U.S. city. I understand that now. And I've made my own mistakes, too." A wistful look crossed his face.

"What sort of mistakes?" Lara asked.

Fiddler hesitated and began pacing the room. "At some point, after I got over my mother's death and gave up on my plot for revenge, I actually believed I could affect positive change from within the Army." He shook his head. "I *actually* believed that. And I was willing to make major sacrifices to bring about that change. I spent every waking minute in the lab to secure our nation from biological threats… and I've given so much of myself to the government. But I didn't mean for the accident to happen." Fiddler's mouth twitched slightly.

"Mean for what accident to happen?" Lara asked. She wasn't sure if she wanted to know the answer. Still, understanding Fiddler's regrets might help her decipher his motivations.

"Several years ago, as part of my research, I ran a gene editing experiment in my lab at home. It was supposed to be a harmless test of CRISPR's capacity for adding in a new set of genes to a bacterium. I didn't realize part of the gene sequence I added to harmless bacteria would make it infectious. When my wife cleaned the lab for me, she exposed herself to the bacteria and became severely ill within a few days. The doctors prescribed a powerful antibiotic, but it didn't have any effect. She died a week later. I'll never forgive myself for what happened to her, for forcing Anita to live without her mother, just like I did."

"I'm so sorry for your loss," Lara said.

"When I took my experiment results to my boss at USAMRIID, my superiors reprimanded me for conducting a dangerous experiment in an unauthorized lab and put me on probation. They took all of my data and classified it as Top Secret/Special Compartmentalized Information and then restricted my clearance to keep me out of the loop. As far as I know, nothing more came of my work, and my wife died in vain. Rather than engaging in the forward thinking for which the Army laboratory was designed, USAMRIID has proven itself to be a soulless, slow-moving, rule-oriented bureaucracy that will never be capable of defeating our enemies." Fiddler slammed his fist against a Eucalyptus tree.

Lara needed to calm him down. "So, why did you want to hire me?" she asked, changing the subject.

"I think Ashton told you, didn't he? I needed you to replace Sully. You're an orphan too, like Sully, aren't you?" Fiddler asked pensively.

The random question surprised Lara. She nodded. "Sully and I were family, at least the only family we ever really knew. That's why I need to know who CyberShop is. I need to get justice for Sully." Lara paused, hoping her timing was right. "Ashton told me you've met CyberShop?"

Nodding, Fiddler began ranting to her about his son-in-law,

how Frank knew the identity of CyberShop, and how he was about to file a report to expose the traitor right before he died.

"Is CyberShop male or female? What does CyberShop look like?"

Fiddler ignored her questions and continued with his tirade. "I began my own investigation into CyberShop's activities. I even brought it to the attention of the NSA. Those bastards gave me the runaround and even framed my own daughter in an attempt to cover it up. They were afraid U.S. Congress might get wind of it and shut them down entirely. Then they reported me to the FBI for suspicious behavior. The NSA set me up and even produced fake evidence. Next thing I know, the FBI is trying to run a sting operation against me. So, I flipped the script on them and had them orchestrate the drone show to prove Anita's innocence, for once and for all. When I learned I was compromised, I hired Sully to carry on with the investigation. And now he's dead, too."

In that moment, Lara understood Fiddler. Like her, Fiddler had been unfairly treated by the system. At least in one way, they responded the same to the injustice they'd suffered. Both continued to work for the system that had betrayed them and sought to make the world a better place. But something went wrong for Fiddler along the way. Perhaps his wife's death or his grandson's had pushed Fiddler over the edge of sanity, and he wasn't coming back.

He has to be stopped.

Fiddler began to pace around the room, shaking his fists at the air. "That filth destroyed my family." The fury in his eyes sent chills down Lara's spine. Fiddler's nostrils flared and his mouth curled. "I will bring a plague upon them. They will be sorry they ever crossed me."

Lara shivered, wondering what fate Fiddler might bring upon her. She watched him as he stood in silence for a few minutes.

Then, like someone had flipped a switch, Fiddler turned to

her and smiled. "I hear it was botulinum toxin that did Sully in?" Fiddler asked. "Brilliant choice... just brilliant."

How did he know the results of the autopsy?

Lara looked away, avoiding eye contact. She had no idea how she was going to get out of this one.

THIRTY-FOUR

The Lab

FIDDLER GRIPPED Lara's wrist so tightly that the plastic ties cut deep into her skin. She winced as he pushed her past the terrariums, through a heavy steel door, and into a smaller adjoining room.

After one final shove, she stumbled forward a few steps on the slippery, white ceramic tiled floor. A musty stench assaulted her nose. Her eyes darted from the brown liquid in the test tubes on the counter to the high-tech lab machine, a large stainless-steel refrigerator, and to the white lab coats hanging from hooks next to it. Fluorescent bulbs cast a yellow light over all of it.

Fiddler's laboratory.

Fiddler shut the door behind him. Both hands on her shoulders, he sat her on a stool in front of a stainless-steel workbench at the center of the room. He took a seat on the other side of the bench, in front of a computer monitor. Lara absorbed her surroundings out of the corner of her eye.

There were pipettes on a tray at the end of the workbench. Test tubes, petri dishes, and flasks were set up next to growth media on the counter underneath the cabinets. On the wall next to the cabinets, a large dry-erase board took up the majority of the space. Formulas were written all over it, though their placements revealed no rhyme or reason.

He must use this room for his biological experiments…

Despite her discomfort, Lara breathed an audible sigh of relief, thankful to be away from the beetles. Her stomach growled angrily. She couldn't remember the last time she ate something, and she was parched.

I guess things could be worse—much worse.

Images of Ashton being devoured by the beetle swarm flashed through her head. Shuddering, Lara wondered what Fiddler had in mind for her.

"This is where I do my research," Fiddler declared with pride.

Lara nodded.

He turned his attention back to the computer screen. For a few minutes, he tapped away on the keyboard as though she weren't there. While Fiddler seemed distracted, Lara casually studied the lab in more detail.

On the wall behind him, the clock showed 9 p.m. By now, Vik would be wondering about her whereabouts, but unable to reach her on the broken smartphone. She hoped Rob or Detective Sanchez might be looking for her and track her smartphone signal to the storage company. But would they even know she was missing?

I didn't tell anyone I went to check out Sully's files. What was I thinking?

Lara had done it again. Vik would be livid.

Why don't I ever think to ask for help?

She'd risked her life more than once on the battlefield as she'd gone behind enemy lines, gathering information to thwart insurgent plans. It had been worth it.

This will be worth it, too… if I can figure out an exit plan.

Lara focused on lowering her pulse, inhaling deeply through her nose, and exhaling through her mouth.

There has to be a way. Just think.

It was time to get some answers from Fiddler. If she broke

free somehow, the information she'd gathered on this mission would be key to stopping him. Her risk would be rewarded.

The counter against the wall with the glass equipment drew her attention. There were a few fancy-looking machines like the ones Lara had seen in Maggie's lab. Fiddler had clearly spared no expense in setting up his own workspace.

Lara craned her neck to see behind her. A black violin case leaned against the wall in a far corner. It appeared to be the same one she'd found at the violin shop. She furrowed her brow.

How often does Fiddler find time to play his instrument? Does he even play at all anymore?

Somehow, she couldn't quite picture a mad scientist playing soothing tunes from Vivaldi or Mozart. Something hanging on the wall behind her caught her attention. There were two large maps taped there—the same ones of Fort Detrick and Fort Meade she'd found in the violin shop. Both had red marker scribbled all over them, presumably indicating entry points and targets.

I was right. He's planning an attack on the two bases.

Next to the maps hung several giant images of Christmas beetles. And beside them, a massive photograph of a golden frog.

Now, that's curious. What kind of frog is that?

When she turned back around, Fiddler was staring right at her with his cold, gray eyes. Her heart nearly stopped, and a flush crept over her face.

"Admiring my handiwork?" Fiddler said.

"Your handiwork?" Lara asked, her brow furrowed.

He pointed at the maps. "I still can't get over the beauty of my plan, and I haven't had the opportunity to share it with anyone. Maybe you'll indulge me?"

"Sure." Lara shrugged, not wanting to appear too eager. "Indulge away."

"I remember when the idea first came to me to use *real* bugs to bring about a plague on two of the biggest 'bug' agencies in the U.S. Government. To bring about a *plague* with the plague. The irony!" He chuckled to himself.

"Ha," Lara said. "I get it."

It *was* a good pun. Scientists at USAMRIID handled live viruses and bacteria, aka living bugs, and the NSA used surveillance bugs to monitor communications. If it weren't for the whole "bringing the plague" thing, Lara might have laughed for real.

The plan is definitely ironic. I'll give him that.

Lara cleared her throat and pasted a friendly smile on her face, like they were two buddies sharing secrets. "You're a clever man, Fiddler. I can't wait to hear the details."

Fiddler started to talk again, but then he shot her a suspicious look. "I see what you're doing. You think you can cajole me into sharing my plans… and then you think you and your FBI friends can stop me. I'm the *only* Fiddler around here. No one plays me for a fool."

Lara gulped. *Okay, getting information won't be so easy.*

A few seconds later, his dark mood dissipated, and he smiled warmly again. "On the other hand, I *have* been dying to tell someone." Fiddler clasped his hands together. "Besides, I have special plans for you. There's no way you'll have the chance to tell *anyone* anything."

What the hell? Lara's flesh prickled, her hair standing on end.

Fiddler pointed to the maps on the wall. His grin spread wide. "In two days, I'll deliver swarms of beetles to the parking lots at Fort Detrick and Fort Meade. The beetles will fly into the trees, unnoticed, and sleep peacefully during the day. Since they are nocturnal creatures, I won't even have to wake them. The beetles will come to life when the sun goes down and take flight right as unsuspecting employees head home to spend the evening with their families. I've programmed the beetles to disperse and attack individual targets. When they bite, people won't think much of it. After all, it's only a bug bite, right?"

Lara shrank back at his unbridled enthusiasm for killing people. Fiddler was more unstable than she'd ever imagined.

One second he seemed happy, almost gleeful. Other times he seemed contemplative or excited about scientific data. In those moments, she thought she glimpsed the man Fiddler once was—before he suffered the terrible loss of his family. Without warning, however, his mood would also turn dark and ominous.

Like Dr. Jekyll and Mr. Hyde.

Will I make it out of here? Repressing the thought, Lara lifted her chin and looked directly at the mad scientist. *Confidence is the best strategy.*

When their eyes connected, Fiddler gestured toward the wall of maps and photos. "A few days after the attack, people will begin experiencing symptoms... fever, chills, nausea, vomiting, and diarrhea. Some people will visit the doctor. Others won't. Even if the doctors prescribe antibiotics, they won't know what they're treating. And since the typical antibiotics are not likely to work, infected people won't recover. Some people will develop plague in the lungs. That's when the disease becomes contagious, and they'll spread it to their loved ones. Without proper treatment, almost everyone infected with the plague will *die*. It will take weeks before doctors realize they are dealing with a plague epidemic. And months before they figure out the source."

Lara shivered, thinking of her own symptoms. Even on antibiotics, the disease knocked her off her feet for two days. The bite wounds on her arm itched angrily, but she couldn't reach them since her hands were tied behind her back. "But you're going to kill innocent people who had nothing to do with what happened to you."

Fiddler's upper lip curled. "Wasn't my mother innocent? And what about my grandson and son-in-law? What did they have to do with anything? No, these people are filthy bureaucrats—all of them. They belong to the system that sold me out, betrayed unsuspecting innocents, and killed my family. To do the real work of protecting our nation, they forced me to experiment in my own lab. So, my wife's death is on them, too. And now, in return, I will kill them all."

Lara's blood ran cold. She could tell Fiddler meant it, he was fully committed to his plan, and believed nothing could stop him. "I don't understand. Isn't your grievance with CyberShop? Do you really need to kill all of those innocent people? Think about your daughter, Anita."

Lara didn't think she could talk him out of it, but she could at least try.

Fiddler gave a bitter laugh. "Don't you get it, Lara? CyberShop merely represents the corruption of these agencies. Killing one man would not be enough, not after everything they've done to me."

"But don't you want me to investigate CyberShop's identity?" Lara asked. "Isn't that why I'm here?" As soon as she uttered the words, she realized how ridiculous they sounded. After all, she'd destroyed the bug, rejecting his offer, and he'd resorted to kidnapping her.

Fiddler choked back laughter. "Surely you didn't think I'd let you waltz out of here and run back to your FBI boyfriend with the details of my plan? This is my masterpiece! No, my concerto! No, my serenade! My serenade for America. When it is finished, those agencies will have learned the most difficult of lessons, and the people of this country will finally be safe from their incompetence."

His expression made her flesh crawl. Fiddler walked over to her, his eyes wild. He grabbed her by the arm, dragging her from the stool.

"You're hurting me," Lara said.

"You know nothing of pain." Fiddler tightened his grip around her arm. "Do you really take me for such a fool? You know far too much about me—about my plans—and you're too smart for your own good. I brought you here to tie up a loose end. I've been working on something special, something I made specifically for you. I've tested it a few times on Ashton. He also needed punishment on occasion."

Lara swallowed hard. She couldn't control her heartbeat

anymore, and it raced inside her chest, thumping against her ribs. Her stomach turned as her body chilled.

"You see, I've been watching you for the past few weeks, and I know how much you *dread* my precious beetles."

Fiddler yanked her into a dark room next to the laboratory. A small, yellow bulb hung from the ceiling, flickering as it swung from its cord. When her eyes adjusted to the inconsistent light, she gasped in horror and stepped backwards, crashing into Fiddler. He shoved her forward with all his might, and she nearly fell headlong into the glass wall of a six-foot tall tank full of golden beetles. With her hands tied behind her back, Lara bent her knees and pressed them against the tank wall to brace herself. Fiddler put one hand in the middle of her back and the other on the side of her head, pressing her face hard into the glass.

"To learn your lesson, you'll spend some quality time with my precious creatures." His cruel voice reminded her of the hissing over the transmitter.

She bit her lip so hard, she tasted blood. A knot formed in the pit of her stomach.

Fiddler pointed to the cameras hanging in the corners. "And I'll capture it live on camera and send the video to your pathetic boyfriend."

"You're sick," Lara said. As much as she tried to maintain a tough posture, intense fear swirled in her gut.

Now or never.

She put all her weight on her left leg and slowly bent her right knee, bringing it up to her chest. With all her might, she jabbed the back of her foot into Fiddler's groin. For a moment, he moaned in surprise and released his grip. Her right foot planted back on the ground, Lara turned to face her captor and blanched at the barrel of the handgun in Fiddler's hands.

Fiddler set his jaw and narrowed his eyes at Lara, the gun pointed straight at her. Lara kept her distance, her hands still tied behind her back. Fiddler reached for the glass door of the tank and opened it. He motioned for her to enter.

"No way," Lara said, shaking her head, keeping her eye on the gun.

Fiddler lunged toward her, gun in hand. He pressed the barrel of the gun to her temple. "Move," he said.

Lara's body froze. It was either the gun or the beetles, both of which were deadly. Going out like Ashton... that wasn't an option. Fiddler pushed her toward the door, but Lara braced her arm against the edge of the tank and dug in her heels. She desperately searched her mind for a third option.

"I'm not going in there!" Lara grunted as sweat dripped down her face.

Fiddler backed up slightly, and Lara cowered, thinking he was going to hit her in the head with the butt of the gun. But instead, a loud crack filled the room as Fiddler fired the gun, and Lara's instincts made her dive to the floor... right into the tank. As she dove, the side of the tank scraped her arm, ripping her shirt and removing a layer of skin.

Lara had closed her eyes, the sound of the gun filling her with fear. Now, she opened them to find that Fiddler had shot the ceiling, and she lay inside the tank. With a wicked grin, he closed and secured the door with a heavy padlock. Her energy was spent, and she couldn't fight anymore.

"No, please!" Lara screamed, squeezing her eyes shut. "Please, don't!"

Fiddler turned off the light, closed the door, and the room became pitch black.

"You can't leave me in here!" Lara screamed at the top of her lungs.

Horrified, Lara curled up into the fetal position. When the first beetle landed on her bare arm, exposed by the tear in her shirt, she cringed. Her instinct screamed at her to writhe and flail, to get them all off her. But then she froze.

If I remain still, maybe they'll ignore me.

The six small feet of a beetle pricked at the fresh scrape on her arm. She fought to overcome the urge to shake it off her. Without warning, a sharp pinch caused her to yelp in pain. The beetle had bitten her, near the wound on her arm. Blood bubbled up and dripped onto the glass floor. The buzz of the swarm overhead grew louder.

My blood is attracting them.

She looked up to see the beetles descend upon her. They landed and crawled all over her, nipping angrily at her flesh. A wave of nausea hit her, and she tasted bile.

THIRTY-FIVE

The Tank

November 7, 2027

LARA TUCKED herself into the fetal position, her arms still tied behind her back, trying to remain as still as possible. In the darkness, time passed slowly. She had no idea how much of it had passed by as she lay there helpless.

Her chest rose and fell with rapid, short breaths. As long as she didn't move much, the beetles refrained from biting her—for the most part. On occasion, tiny claws tickled her skin, as a beetle crawled from one part of her body to another. The sensation made her want to scream out loud, but she bit her tongue.

Lara closed her eyes tightly to forget her surroundings. In her head, each second lasted for an eternity. Her mind raced through the events leading to her capture and torment.

This is not happening to me. How did I end up here? What did I do wrong?

And then it hit her.

Going it alone. That's how I got here.

Vik's voice echoed in her memory: "Lara, why must you always act before thinking things through?"

Oh Vik, you're right. I'm too headstrong for my own good.

She'd always assumed Fiddler meant her no harm, but clearly, she'd miscalculated. What had she done to convince Fiddler she deserved this terrible fate? He'd called her a loose end? Why, because he feared she might stop him? Why not just shoot her dead?

We'll see about loose ends.

Fiddler had made a crucial mistake leaving her alive. She'd see to that.

Her eyes fluttered open for a moment, and she caught a glimpse of a beetle on the glass by her nose. Then she remembered her prison, the beetle tank from hell, with no promise of an escape. A lump formed in her throat. Every beat of her heart felt like a bomb going off inside her chest, the pounding in her ears driving her insane. Anger surged in her gut, and her nostrils flared. She released a guttural roar and then shouted with all she had.

"Fiddler! Let me out of here!"

Nothing. No response.

"Fiddler, get me out of here now!"

Silence.

Can he even hear me?

Lara kicked the side of the tank with her feet. Her action rustled the beetles from their slumber. They began buzzing angrily around her head. Lara froze, cringing as the beetles flew closer and closer to her face. She shut her eyes to protect herself from her reality.

This is not happening. Not happening.

She stayed like that, holding her breath, until she passed out from exhaustion. But restless sleep offered her no relief from the physical, mental, and emotional exhaustion crushing her chest like a bowling ball. Fear plagued her even in her dreams.

When she woke, reality punched her in the stomach. Tears came to her eyes.

Is this it? Is this how it ends?

Everything she wanted for her life flashed through her mind, tormenting her with dreams that would die with her.

I want to fall in love… for real this time. Own a home. Find a place to belong. Maybe have a family. Probably not kids, but a couple of dogs would be nice.

A tear rolled down her cheek as she thought of Rob.

Where are you when I need you?

Her breathing slowed as she thought about him. The memory of him when they were together and happy calmed her.

Do I want another chance with him? I should've forgiven him, at least. Will I ever get the chance to find out?

Over the past few weeks, the dynamic between them had been different. She didn't know if Rob had been kind to her because her life had been a wreck, or if he was actually sorry. She knew her independence had made things hard on Rob when they were together; he was the kind of guy that liked to play the knight in shining armor every once in a while.

Why couldn't he just love me as I am? Am I really so bad that Bimbo Barbie looked like a good idea?

As the hours passed, Lara ran out of thoughts. She ran out of questions. She had no more wishes, no more hope. Finally, Lara surrendered to her fate.

It's over.

Her limbs were heavy and numb. The dry, sour taste in her mouth reminded her of how long she'd gone without any water. Her body quaked each time a beetle ran across her skin, her nerve endings on high alert. She wanted to scream each time, but she knew it would be of no use. No one would hear her. Ashton was dead, and she was alone, in her worst nightmare.

Metal clinked against metal. Lara didn't move; she was so exhausted, she figured she was hearing things. But then, the door opened. A stream of light poured in from the crack in the door.

"Lara?" A soft voice called out.

"Who's there?" She gasped, holding her breath as if that would help her hear better.

"Are you in here? It's me… Justyne."

Lara jerked her head up.

Justyne?

Her movement attracted a beetle. It landed on her cheek, and she went rigid.

The light flicked on, illuminating the room. The beetle on her cheek took flight in pursuit of the incandescent bulb above. The rest of the beetles agitated excitedly toward the top of the tank while Lara's stomach fluttered at the prospect of escape.

Squinting through her lashes, she saw Justyne standing in the doorway, dressed in a black trench coat and heels, staring down at her with a grim look on her face. Justyne moved from the light switch toward the tank and back to the door. She messed with the padlock connected to a chain.

"Hold on for a minute. I'm going to get you out of there," Justyne said as she went into the laboratory.

The next few minutes felt like an eternity. In the next room, Justyne fumbled around, opening drawers, searching for something. She returned to the room, armed with a bolt cutter and a fly swatter. After snapping the padlock, she opened the glass door and used the fly swatter to ward off any stray beetles.

"Crawl slowly toward me." Justyne reached out her hand.

Lara did as she was told. When she got close enough to the door, Justyne reached in behind her back to cut the plastic ties. With her hands free, she wriggled out of the tank quickly and brushed herself off.

"Do I have any of them on me?" Lara unfolded her legs slowly, shaking off her arms and legs.

Justyne shook her head. "No, you're good. They're too busy dancing in the light." She pointed up toward the top of the tank.

"How many bites did I get?" Lara asked.

Justyne turned Lara's body around, inspecting every inch of her bare skin. "Looks like about twenty. Not bad for hanging out with that swarm."

Lara shuddered. "Good thing I'm already on antibiotics. I don't know if those beetles were infected with the plague or not." She stopped suddenly and stared bewildered at Justyne. "How in the world did you *find* me here?"

"Remember Fiddler's address, the one I got from the post office?"

Lara nodded. "But—"

"Well, we're at that address. 3300 White Oak Drive, Silver Spring."

"What?" Lara stood still for a moment, as if paralyzed. Something didn't compute. They'd found that address over and over again. Rob and Detective Sanchez had checked it out twice and found nothing, at least not on the surface. "We thought it was a dead end."

Justyne nodded. "Me too. When I first checked it out, I was fooled by the list of occupants—a bunch of tech startups. After tracking past communications between CyberShop and KillerBot, I found recurring evidence of this location and came to search for the second time. I began poking around, paying each of the companies a visit and asking lots of questions. That's when I realized one of the companies was not what it seemed to be."

Stunned, Lara opened her mouth to say something, but nothing came out.

Justyne continued. "Fiddler used a front company to hide his laboratory and beetle farm. To uphold the facade of being a real tech company, the door to the lobby was open for visitors. I entered the lobby and looked around, but no one was here. Not a soul. When I did some further research, I discovered the business owner was listed as Frank Moore."

Lara gaped at her.

"Fiddler used my Frank's name as an alias. That's how I realized his laboratory was here after all."

Lara shook her head in disbelief. "It was in front of us the entire time."

"Well, if you didn't know you were looking for a tech

company owned by Frank Moore, you wouldn't find it. And thank God I did, and got to you in the nick of time. How long have you been in there?"

Lara shrugged. "I'm not sure. At least several hours. What time is it?"

Justyne glanced at her watch. "It's 7:15 a.m."

"I don't think I've ever been this glad to see anyone," Lara said. Slowly, she felt the color return to her face, but a moment later it drained again as she recalled everything Fiddler had said. "We have to get out of here. I don't want Fiddler coming back and finding us."

"Oh, he's long gone. I saw him take off in a white van, in quite a hurry. Any idea where he might be going?"

"He must be getting things ready for tomorrow. He is planning to let swarms of beetles loose on Fort Detrick and Fort Meade."

"Fort Meade?" Justyne raised her eyebrows.

Lara nodded. "He wants revenge for the deaths of his son-in-law and grandson."

"Hmmm…" Justyne was silent for a few seconds and then began leading Lara through the laboratory and out another door into a spacious lobby surrounded by glass walls.

Lara gaped at the sight of the modern reception desk and posh waiting area, complete with contemporary lounge chairs, a glass coffee table, and a wide array of subscription magazines. Soft music played in the background. A giant metallic logo hung on the wall behind the desk.

TECHNOVATION INDUSTRIES, LLC

No wonder Rob and Sanchez couldn't find it. The operation looks legit.

"Did you find Ashton?" Lara asked, afraid of the answer.

"Do you mean that poor kid in the other room who got bitten by the killer beetles?" Justyne asked.

Lara winced and nodded. "Please take me to him."

Justyne frowned. "There's not much left of him, I'm afraid. You didn't know him, did you?" She motioned for Lara to follow her back through the lab and the beetle farm, and down another hallway to the last door.

"Kind of. He was Sully's assistant, and he worked for Fiddler. But that didn't turn out very well for him."

"No, it didn't."

When they entered the storage room where she'd been held the previous day, Ashton lay on the floor, motionless. The beetles were gone. Lara ran over to him, bending down to touch his shoulder.

"Ashton, can you hear me?" Lara asked. She shook him gently and felt for a pulse. When she detected a weak thump of blood pumping from his heart, she breathed a sigh of relief. "Justyne, he's alive. Call an ambulance now!"

"Oh, no," Justyne said as she shook her head. "I thought he was dead. I was going to just leave him here." She began dialing 911 on her phone.

Ashton's eyes fluttered open. "Lara?" His voice was weak.

Lara gave him a half-smile. "Yes, it's me. You're going to be okay… listen, this is really important."

"Lara?" Ashton rasped.

"Ashton, listen to me. I need you to tell me something. Do you know where Fiddler went? Do you know what he's planning?"

Ashton lifted his head slightly and nodded. "He… snakes."

"What do you mean? We need to know where Fiddler went. We need to stop him from killing innocent people."

"Lara…" Ashton trembled.

"Yes, I'm here," Lara said.

"He said—Fiddler said he… cut heads off snakes."

"You're not making any sense."

"Lara, listen to me." Ashton reached up to grab her shirt. His eyes grew large. "He'll cut… heads off of the snakes."

"Yeah, I got that, but I don't know what it means."

Ashton's eyes bulged, he let go of her shirt, gasped violently for breath, and then fell silent.

"Ashton, Ashton, stay with me!" Lara shook him, trying to get him to open his eyes again. She slapped his cheeks a few times and then began CPR.

"Lara, it's no good," Justyne said.

"No, I have to help him." Lara kept going for several minutes, but there was no response.

Justyne put a hand on her shoulder. "Lara, he's dead. He was barely alive when I got here."

Lara stopped, realizing the truth. She reached over and closed his eyes. After a few minutes had passed, she got to her feet.

"What was he saying about snakes?" Justyne asked.

Lara shook her head. "I have no idea… something Fiddler said to him."

Justyne took a deep breath. "We need to get moving. There's nothing we can do for him now. The ambulance will take him to the morgue."

Though Lara didn't want to leave Ashton's body, Justyne was right. There was too much at stake for them to stay immobile. She reluctantly followed Justyne back toward the elevator.

Lara rubbed at the back of her neck. "I need to call Special Agent Martin. The FBI needs to scrub this place from top to bottom for evidence." Lara reached in her pocket but remembered her smartphone was smashed into pieces on the pavement at the storage company. "Can I use your phone?"

Justyne nodded and handed Lara her phone. Lara stared at the keypad and slowly entered Rob's cell number. She still had it memorized even though the days of endless chatting were long over. The phone rang, and she hoped the number was right.

"Special Agent Martin," Rob answered.

"Rob, this is Lara. I'm calling from Justyne's phone. Listen, we don't have much time. Fiddler kidnapped me and locked me up in his secret laboratory."

"Holy shit, Lara! Are you okay? Where are you?"

Lara sighed. "I'm fine. We're still at the building now. The address was the one we kept finding, the commercial complex on White Oak Drive. Fiddler owned a front company called Technovation Industries under the alias of Frank Moore, his son-in-law. You should send an evidence team out here right away. Maybe there's something here that will help us confirm Fiddler's plans."

"I can't believe I was there and didn't notice it." Rob sounded disappointed.

He hates being wrong. But then again, so do I.

Lara tried to sugarcoat it a little. "Fiddler hid it well. How could you know? None of us figured it out."

"Well, Justyne found it, didn't she?" Rob returned in a defensive tone.

"She said herself she was lucky to have found me."

Lara told Rob about Sully's storage unit, finding Stepanov rooting around the night of her abduction, and his escape after the power outage.

"I'm coming out there to get you," Rob said.

"No, I'm heading back to D.C. with Justyne. Just send a team over here to collect the evidence. Maybe there's more information about Fiddler's next moves. He told me he plans to orchestrate a biological attack against Fort Detrick and Fort Meade tomorrow. So, we don't have much time. Oh and... Ashton is dead."

"What?"

"He helped Fiddler kidnap me. Then he got a conscience, and Fiddler killed him for it. The maniac attacked Ashton with a swarm of beetles. There wasn't much left of him. He died a few minutes ago. I tried to see if he knew what Fiddler was up to, but I didn't get much."

"Uh... that's terrible."

Lara knew Rob had seen his fair share of gruesome deaths, but it wasn't every day that someone got viciously devoured by beetles.

"Where should Justyne and I meet up with you?" Lara asked.

"Come down to the FBI Washington Field Office. I'm going to put together an interagency meeting to discuss the Fiddler situation and plan the response."

"Got it. See you in a few. Just gotta stop somewhere and get a new phone." She felt naked without it and figured she'd need access to information while they tried to stop Fiddler.

Justyne sat down in the driver's seat of her white Honda and unlocked the door. Climbing in the car, Lara inhaled deeply, thankful to breathe fresh air again.

THIRTY-SIX

The Targets

LARA RECOILED at her reflection in the glass door of the FBI Washington Field Office as she pulled it open. Justyne had helped her smooth her greasy hair into a tight bun, and she'd busted out an arsenal of mascara, powders, and eye pencils stored in the trunk of her Honda. Still, Lara looked like death warmed over. Her eyes were baggy, her forehead scratched up, little beetle bites everywhere, and her hair clearly still a ball of grease.

So much for make-up… I wonder how bad I looked before Justyne's help.

Compared to the top-heavy, dreary FBI headquarters where Rob worked when they were dating, the new construction of this building surprised Lara. The modern interior was outfitted with state-of-the-art technology and furnished with contemporary furniture, a refreshing change from the typical drab environment of federal government buildings.

The only stench in the building came from her clothes. Lara gave herself a whiff and pulled up her nose. She'd been wearing the same clothes without a shower for several days.

Ugh, not again. Rob had not seen her in the best shape lately.

Rob met her and Justyne in the lobby and stared anxiously at the bandages covering Lara's bites. Her heart fluttered unexpectedly.

Am I happy to be alive or happy to see him?

He stepped toward her and gestured awkwardly with his arm, like he was going in for a side-hug, but then he pulled back. "I'm glad you're okay," Rob said, giving her a half-smile.

"Me too," Lara said, her cheeks burning hot. She avoided looking straight at him; pity was the last thing she needed.

"Justyne, you have my eternal thanks for saving Lara's life. I don't know what I—we would have done if we lost her."

Lara's cheeks flushed hotter.

Justyne shrugged. "I was in the right place at the right time."

Rob nodded and smiled. "Do you mind if I speak to Lara for a few minutes privately?"

Justyne raised an eyebrow at Lara and then nodded. Lara shrugged to Justyne as Rob pulled her arm gently toward the corner of the lobby and stared at her for a moment. Then his eyes drifted toward the wearable smartphone on her wrist.

"Hey, is that new?" he asked.

"Yeah," she muttered. "My other phone bit the dust, and this one might be more shatterproof."

"I never thought I'd see the day..." Rob's face broke into a goofy grin.

When they were dating, Lara had ranted against the notion of wearables. A sharp pang flared in her stomach. The last time they'd argued about her resistance to certain new technologies was the day he'd dumped her. *For Bimbo Barbie.*

Rob seemed to notice the grim look on her face and stopped smiling. He stared at his feet and shifted his weight around. "Um, I know it's not the best timing, but I wanted to talk about what happened between us in the safe room."

Facing death had enabled Lara to let go of Rob's insensitive comments. It also confirmed something she'd been bouncing back and forth since she first met Rob at the coffee shop.

I'm not over him. And that fact was hard to accept.

"What about it?" Her tone was sharper than she'd intended.

Rob took a deep breath and made eye contact. "I wanted to tell you how truly sorry I am for what I did, for how I hurt you. When we spoke last time, it came out all wrong... what I meant to say then is that..." He hesitated, as if waiting to see her response. "I've never forgotten about us... how you made me feel. Working with you over the past few weeks... and then you nearly getting killed... made me realize that—" He paused again, looking uncertain and taking her hands in his. "Lara, I'm still in love with you. And I don't know if it's possible, but I want to be with *you.*"

The words came crashing down on her like a meteor from outer space. She'd sensed something from Rob over the past few weeks, but she didn't expect a declaration of his love. Not now, not here. Lara focused on suppressing tears and keeping her face slack.

She pulled her hands away. "Then why did you do it? Why did you cheat on me?"

Rob's face twitched, his annoyingly adorable brown eyes brimming with tears. He rubbed his hands together and stared at the floor as if he didn't know what to say. "Because I'm a complete idiot."

"Well, that's an understatement, but I'm gonna need more than that."

"Um, it took me a while to realize this... you're so smart, talented, and independent. After a while, I got tired of feeling insignificant and useless. I didn't get the sense you *needed* me... for anything. I worried you'd dump me one day, no questions asked."

Because I'm so awesome, you cheated on me?

Lara's eyes widened and her chest pounded. She wanted to shout at him for being so stupid, but she remained silent to let him finish.

Rob's lips quivered. "So, I betrayed you out of fear. I thought I'd feel more significant if I dated a girl like Alexa. At first, I did. But then I felt suffocated by her neediness and became bored with her superficiality. I'm so sorry, Lara. If I could, I'd take it all back."

Lara held up her hand, motioning for him to stop. She sighed heavily. "Why didn't you just tell me you were feeling this way when we were together?"

"I dunno, Lara. I keep asking myself the same thing. If I had another chance, I'd do things differently."

Several minutes of awkward silence passed between them. Lara fought to hold her tears at bay. *Do I want another chance with Rob?* Her feelings were too muddled to answer the question, and her body ached with exhaustion. She needed to think about it.

"Thanks for telling me all of this." Lara took a long breath. A rhythmic clicking drew her attention to Justyne, who tapped her foot impatiently across the lobby. Rob seemed to notice as well. "But, I really don't know how to respond right now. I need time."

Rob breathed a sigh of relief. "That's okay. I'll take it. I mean, thank you for thinking it over. We should probably get to the meeting. We can talk more later?"

Lara nodded.

They rejoined Justyne in the center of the lobby. Rob apologized for making her wait and then escorted them through security and took the elevator up to the seventh-floor conference room.

After placing their phones in lockboxes outside the SCIF, they entered the large conference room and took seats at the long oak table. Unfamiliar faces greeted her, but as Lara scanned the room she recognized a few. Sanchez smiled at her from across the table. Maggie sat right next to him, a wide grin on her face. Lara shook her head and smiled as her best friend winked at her.

"Okay, let's get started. Thanks to everyone for coming in on a Sunday." Rob seated himself at the head of the table. "As the WMD Coordinator for the FBI's Washington Field Office, I've organized this meeting to discuss what Dr. John Fiddler, our suspected bioterrorist, may be planning and to assess the credibility of the threat. If we agree the threat meets minimum criteria, we will begin coordinating the response across the federal government. You all have the investigation file in front of you. I hope you've had a chance to read it."

Rob cleared his throat. "Before we begin, a few introductions." He introduced Lara and Justyne to the group. Gesturing across the table, he said, "Detective Mario Sanchez is here representing the D.C. Metropolitan Police as the lead for the investigation into Phil Sullivan's murder. We believe Fiddler is somehow connected to Sully's death. Always great to be cooperating with local law enforcement."

The detective smiled warmly.

Rob went on to introduce Maggie and explain her specialized expertise on insects and gene editing. "Dr. Brown doesn't have a security clearance, but her knowledge of the beetles is indispensable. I've received special permission for her to sit in on this meeting to ensure an effective response."

Rob continued to introduce the others. "To my left is Deputy Assistant Secretary Maria Santos from the Federal Emergency Management Agency of the Department of Homeland Security. Her agency will support the response effort in coordination with the FBI. Next to her is Mr. Harold Johnson from the Office of the Assistant Secretary of Preparedness and Response at the Department of Health and Human Services. His team will handle the public health aspects. And finally, Dr. Peter Styvens from the Department of Agriculture who will help us figure out how to neutralize the beetles. On the phone, we have representatives from the U.S. Army at USAMRIID, NSA headquarters, and the FBI's Critical Incident Response Group (CIRG) in Quantico."

Rob clapped his hands together. "Okay folks, we don't have any time to spare. Fiddler plans to attack his targets sometime tomorrow. Before we leave this room today, we need to assess the threat and activate our response plan. First, let's review what we know about the threat. Lara, could you tell us everything you learned while you were being held hostage?"

"Sure," Lara said, looking around the room at the

apprehensive faces. She relayed the long-term planning and the extent of Fiddler's operation. "Fiddler has raised hundreds if not thousands of adult Christmas beetles in his lab, all of which are outfitted with microelectronics backpacks and have genetic modifications allowing the beetles to bite people and transmit the plague. Based on what he told me, he started the research as an effort to demonstrate critical vulnerabilities to emerging threats and was fired for it."

"That sounds like a decent motive for his planned attack against Fort Detrick," Sanchez noted, rubbing his chin. "That and his mother's death many years ago."

Lara shook her head. "He seems to have gotten over his mother's death... I think his motivation has become more complex than a simple revenge plot."

Rob shot her a confused look.

Lara continued. "In his time at Fort Detrick, Fiddler became a true believer in the bio-defense efforts undertaken by the U.S. Government. His belief in the precedence of bio-defense became so zealous that he could not accept any deviation from the goal of protecting America from bio-threats. For example, Fiddler didn't understand why the U.S. Army was willing to conduct the bioweapons tests in the 1960s on American citizens, but unwilling to explore our increasing vulnerabilities to bio-attacks arising from gene editing tools."

"So, the Army's hypocrisy pissed him off, and he experimented at home?" Sanchez asked.

Lara nodded. "His wife ended up dying as a result of one of his home experiments. He seemed quite broken up over it and blames the Army for forcing his hand."

"His wife's death must have caused him to snap somehow," Rob said. "Did he move his lab to its current location after her death?"

Lara shrugged. She didn't know.

Justyne leaned forward, resting her elbows on the table. "Based on my research, Fiddler set up the front company several years ago under the alias of Frank Moore and moved his laboratory into the space before his wife's death. I'm not sure why he was still running experiments at his home."

"Lara, do you have anything more to share?" Rob asked.

She told the group about CyberShop's alleged role in the deaths of Fiddler's son-in-law and grandson, Fiddler's suspicion that CyberShop worked at NSA, and his anger about the NSA's attempt to frame his daughter.

"Are we absolutely certain these are the two targets?" Rob looked directly at Lara.

She sighed. "Well, Fiddler had maps of both sites on his wall… with markings indicating a plan of approach for the release of the beetles. They were the same maps we found at the violin shop. What other sites could he possibly be targeting?"

"I just want to be certain." Rob frowned. "You don't think Fiddler misled you in any way? Maybe trying to throw us off the scent?"

Lara shook her head in exasperation. "He told me his plans in excruciating detail, and he expected that beetle tank would be the end of me. He left me there to die, so why go through the trouble of misleading me?"

Rob nodded apologetically. "Okay, okay. We need to be absolutely sure of the targets before we decide to move around limited resources in response to the threat. What else can you tell us about his plans?"

"Fiddler plans to release the beetles during the day tomorrow. He mentioned that the beetles are nocturnal and will cluster in the trees until dusk. He expects the beetles to become active when employees leave work and head out to the parking lots to go home."

"Become active? I thought he controlled the beetles with the microelectronics packages," Maggie interjected.

Lara shrugged her shoulders. "Maybe they're easiest to control at certain times of the day?"

No one had any answers.

"That timeline means he would be moving the beetles into place today." Rob turned his face toward the teleconferencing phone in the middle of the table. "Let's station some additional security forces at the perimeters of Fort Meade and Fort Detrick to keep an eye out for anything suspicious. Representatives from NSA and U.S. Army, can you support that?"

"Copy that. We've already called in an extra unit for Fort Detrick," the Army Representative said, the gruff voice blaring over the teleconference speaker.

"Same here," the NSA representative confirmed.

"Did he say if someone else was working with him?" Rob asked, turning back to Lara.

She shook her head.

Rob creased his brow. "If he has to control the beetles, even in swarms, he can't attack both sites by himself. Ashton is dead, and we don't know of anyone else working with Fiddler."

"Maybe Fiddler doesn't need to be at both sites at the same time?" Maggie asked. "Perhaps he can release the beetles and control them from afar."

"That would require an impressive signal range for controlling both swarms," Rob said. "The two sites are more than fifty miles apart."

"He didn't say how he would do it," Lara added. "Remember Ashton talking about the upgrade he engineered to allow for autonomous navigation?"

"Maybe the swarms are pre-programmed?" Maggie offered.

Lara nodded.

"I suppose that's possible," Rob said, frowning skeptically.

The detective cleared his throat. "I don't think Fiddler is acting alone. Anita must somehow be involved in the attack. She has as much motive as her father. And now she's…" he used air quotes, "'left town'? Sounds guilty to me."

"Based on what evidence?" Lara asked. "I thought you didn't build cases on your gut alone."

Sanchez scowled at her. "There's plenty of circumstantial evidence to support her involvement—NSA's suspicions about her being Frank's accomplice, the cash infusions to her bank account, her prints and DNA we found at the Beautific Creations warehouse, matching the prints on your baseball glove, trace DNA evidence at your townhouse, the list goes on and on." He raised his voice a bit with every example. "When we searched her office at the practice, we also found an old computer with Tor installed. That's where Anita must have logged on to the Dark Web message board as CyberShop."

Anita used Tor? The cops found her DNA? She didn't know where to start or what revelation surprised her more. In the hours she'd been held hostage, she had missed out on a great deal.

Lara's eyes widened. "Anita left DNA at my townhouse?"

Sanchez nodded. "We found trace evidence matching Anita's DNA profile in your apartment. We also tested your baseball glove, the one you found at her office, and found several sets of prints, including Anita's."

"Whose prints did you find?" Lara asked.

"We also found yours, Justyne's, and Stepanov's prints."

"Both Stepanov's and Anita's prints?" Lara's jaw dropped. She glanced over at Justyne, who nodded.

Lara couldn't believe what she was hearing. When she visited Anita at her practice, Lara remembered raising her eyebrow at the ancient and bulky computer, but that could be explained away by Fiddler's paranoia. Her father probably insisted on communicating over the Dark Web. Plus, the DNA could have been planted.

The detective dipped his head. "That's not all. A bystander recently responded to our call and submitted video footage of the attempt to run you down... we got a plate number, and it matches Stepanov's car. With his access to advanced defense technology, the black BMW convertible, the matching license plate, and his prints, Stepanov is at the top of my suspect list for Sully's murder and for attempting to burn down your townhouse. And I think he was working with both Anita and Linda."

Justyne nodded. "That matches all of my evidence as well. I believe Anita ran the operation from the outside as CyberShop.

Stepanov worked as her accomplice inside the NSA. And they used Linda's company to launder the money and gain access to the murder weapon."

Lara shook her head vigorously. "I don't see how all of that makes Anita an accomplice. I just don't see her being involved with the attack."

Rob massaged his temples and closed his eyes for a second. "We're getting off track here. Deciding who killed Sully or leaked the classified information from NSA doesn't matter for planning purposes. We can't afford to waste more time speculating on unknowns. Let's focus on what we know about the attack."

The group around the table nodded. No one else was interested in a trip down the rabbit hole of Sully's murder.

Rob opened the file in front of him. "Okay, based on what we know, we need to protect two targets Fiddler plans to hit with biological weapons, to be delivered by beetles sometime tomorrow." Rob paused for affirmation by the group. "I think we have sufficient evidence to deem the threat credible and significant." Again, head nods all around the room. "I'd like to avoid causing a public panic if possible, and I think the situation is containable if we act now to prevent illness." He turned to the representative from the Department of Health and Human Services. "Harold, can we activate the National Strategic Stockpile and distribute medical supplies in advance?"

Harold cleared his throat. "Yes, we can. We have a good chance of containing the plague outbreak as long as we can start all personnel at both sites on antibiotics as soon as possible. To minimize casualties, antibiotics need to be started within twenty-four hours of the first symptoms. The incubation period for the plague is anywhere from two to six days after exposure. Do you know how many people we are talking about?"

"This is Colonel Jenkins from the Army," a voice squawked over the teleconference phone. "Fort Detrick has about eight thousand personnel on base during any given weekday."

"And NSA has about forty thousand personnel operating out

of Fort Meade on a daily basis," the voice from NSA chimed in over the phone.

Harold rubbed his forehead. "Okay, good. Supply won't be an issue. The stockpile contains ten-day antibiotic packages for over three hundred thousand people. If we can distribute the packages by tomorrow, we should have plenty of time to stave off any infections and contain an outbreak of the plague. Our quickest option would be to send out two twelve-hour Push Packages from the stockpile. We can request the Centers for Disease Control and Prevention get those out immediately, and they should be there by midday tomorrow." Harold looked at his watch to check the time.

"What does one of these push packages contain?" Rob asked.

"About fifty tons of prepackaged emergency medical supplies, including antibiotics. We could instruct the leadership at both sites to keep everyone inside the building until the antibiotics have been distributed."

"And what if we're wrong about the agent?" Rob asked.

"Fiddler is going to use the plague," Lara said impatiently. "He didn't mention anything else."

"I'm just asking the 'what if' for contingency planning purposes," Rob said, glaring at her.

Harold nodded. "If we need a specific treatment or antidote, assuming one exists, the CDC can deploy additional supplies within twenty-four to thirty-six hours."

Sanchez piped up. "How do we make sure the push packages arrive safely at Fort Detrick and Fort Meade? I don't want to risk interception or any delays. Do you need assistance from the Maryland or D.C. police?"

Harold shook his head. "The supplies will be delivered in unmarked trucks and securely escorted by U.S. Marshals."

Rob nodded and pointed at the man. "Harold, make the call now. I don't want to lose any more time on this."

Harold nodded, got up, and left the SCIF to call the CDC.

"Okay, what are we going to do about the beetles?" Rob asked the group. "We have to prevent them from leaving the sites and flying into residential areas, infecting unsuspecting people and children. Can we spray them with pesticide?"

Peter shook his head. "The Department of Agriculture has approved several pesticides for controlling beetles, but it's not that simple. If we spray them with pesticide, the swarm will disperse and flee into unaffected areas. That would lead to exactly the opposite of what you're hoping to achieve."

"Yeah, that doesn't sound good. We need to figure out how to contain them," Rob said.

"You could try jamming the radiofrequency signals," Sanchez suggested.

"That might not work," Lara said. "What if Fiddler acquired sophisticated encryption technology from CyberShop to protect radiofrequency and GPS signals against jamming?"

"Plus, if the beetles are operating autonomously, there will be no signals to jam," Justyne added.

"Both good points," Rob said, his face falling. He looked back up, surveying his team. "Any other bright ideas?"

"I might have one," Maggie said, wringing her hands. "Christmas beetles are clumsy little buggers and terrible at flying. What if we sprayed them out of the air with high-pressure fire hoses? They would drop to the ground and be unable to fly for a bit. Once they're stuck on the ground, we could douse them with pesticide and gather them up so they can't escape the area."

Rob's eyes lit up. "Peter, do you think that would work?"

Peter nodded, raising his eyebrow and smiling at Maggie. "Yes, I think it could."

"But what if it's already dark when the swarms are put in play?" Rob asked.

Maggie wrinkled her forehead as she contemplated her answer. "Beetles are attracted to light. We could shut down all the lights except for one bright spotlight and attract the swarm to it. We should still be able to get them out of the air with jets of water, but the darkness would make it difficult to make sure we got every last one of them."

"What about infrared light? Would that work to track the beetles in the dark?" Lara asked.

Maggie nodded.

"Okay, we'll make sure we have night vision goggles on hand. I think this is our best plan, day or night, for capturing the beetles," Rob said. Turning to Maria, "Can you have FEMA organize fire brigades at both sites to hose down the beetles? I want as many units as we can round up."

"Absolutely," Maria said.

"Okay, we'll send CIRG units to both sites, fully equipped and ready to provide extra help in handling the situation."

"Copy that," a voice from CIRG said over the phone.

The door opened, and Harold returned to the room with a panicked look on his face. "Um, Fiddler appears to be texting whoever owns the wearable smartphone. Multiple texts popped up on the home screen in the last few minutes, and he appears to be demanding an answer now."

The blood drained from Lara's face. That was her phone.

How did he get my new number?

"Did you read them?" she asked, getting up to leave the room and check her phone.

Harold's face turned ashen. "Something about Vik being safe and sound in his custody, but only as long as you agree to cooperate."

Lara's blood ran cold.

Fiddler has Vik.

THIRTY-SEVEN

The Plague

_____

November 8, 2027

SITTING in the front seat of the FBI cruiser, Lara clenched her wearable smartphone with her sweaty hands, still uncomfortable wearing it on her wrist. She kept glancing at the screen, hoping to get more information about Vik.

Since Fiddler's ominous text, she hadn't received any further communication. Lara wondered what the mad scientist would ask of her in exchange for Vik's safe return. She'd never forgive herself if something happened to him.

Throughout the night, Lara and Rob had done everything they could to figure out Fiddler's and Vik's whereabouts, but they had turned up nothing. Rob traced Fiddler's text to a burner phone that had been disposed of near the scientist's laboratory in Silver Spring.

Lara presumed Fiddler had returned to his lab, discovered her escape, and took his revenge by snatching Vik as insurance. They checked his lab again, but it was empty. In a last-ditch effort, Lara and Rob even stopped by Sully's townhouse again to see if Fiddler was hiding out there.

Where are you, Fiddler?

Lara closed her eyes. She recounted in her mind a checklist of what they knew. In the middle of the night, the FBI evidence team delivered a report on their search of Fiddler's laboratory. They turned up a few things of interest. For one, the beetle farm was empty. Fiddler must have rounded up all of his beetles for the attack after he'd put Lara in the tank. They also found a mysterious stockpile of lancets used for diabetes blood tests and tiny pen needles used for insulin injection.

Perhaps Fiddler is a diabetic?

In Fiddler's office next to the laboratory, the evidence team found a fish tank with two small golden frogs hopping around inside. Lara suspected they were the same kind of frog she'd seen in the large picture hanging on the wall in Fiddler's lab. The agents were not able to identify the species and sent the frogs to the FBI Laboratory for identification.

Are the frogs related to the pending attack?

By now, Lara realized Fiddler was a strange and unpredictable man, deeply fascinated by living creatures that could cause death. The simplest explanation was usually the best one. Maybe the frogs were his pets.

The FBI cruiser raced toward Fort Meade at high speed with its flashers on and sirens wailing. Inside the vehicle, the silence was deafening. While Rob focused intently on the road, Justyne sat in the backseat preoccupied with her tablet, the periodic clicking of her nails on the Bluetooth keyboard pricking at Lara's patience.

Rob had sent Maggie to Atlanta to be their point person at the CDC. Detective Sanchez was sent to Fort Detrick to coordinate with FBI agents and first responders who were preparing for the attack. The 12-hour push packages of medical supplies had arrived at both military bases. They were ready for whatever Fiddler threw at them. As ready as they could be.

Her thoughts turned to Ashton, and she shivered at the memory of the beetle swarm devouring his body.

Please don't do that to Vik.

She couldn't get the image of Ashton's death or his last words out of her head. Ashton said Fiddler was going to cut the heads off the snakes.

What did that mean? Lara sat up straighter as an idea popped into her head. *Maybe Fiddler was planning to target the leadership of the two organizations?*

Lara peeked around her seat. "Hey Justyne, you don't think Fiddler is going to target the USAMRIID Commander and the NSA Director, do you?"

Justyne looked up from her tablet. "Why do you ask?"

"Remember what Ashton kept saying before he died?"

Justyne gave her a blank look.

"Ashton told us Fiddler planned to cut the heads off the snakes. Not the head of the snake. He said more than one... the heads of the snakes. Since Fiddler is targeting two different sites, I thought he might be going after the leadership of both organizations. Maybe we should warn them?"

"I guess it's a possibility. Let me call the NSA and find out if the Director is at Fort Meade today." Justyne dialed a number on her phone.

"Yes, hi Cindy, this is Justyne Marsh calling. We're heading over to Fort Meade now... yes, the FBI has already secured the perimeter... The first responders are onsite and they have the medical supplies ready. Listen, Cindy, I have a quick question. Do you know what the NSA Director has on his schedule for today?" A few seconds went by. "Oh really? And what is he doing over there?"

Lara sat on the edge of her seat while she eavesdropped on Justyne's call. For several minutes, Justyne listened in silence. When she got off the phone, her face paled.

"What?" Lara asked.

"The NSA Director is not at Fort Meade today," Justyne said.

"Where is he?" Lara asked as her pulse sped up.

"At the Pentagon for a ribbon-cutting ceremony. The Secretary of Defense plans to unveil the new BioScan system designed to defend the country against any biological attacks."

Lara's stomach dropped.

"Several defense leaders will be present at the ceremony, including the USAMRIID Commander, NSA Director, the Secretary of the Army, and the Chairman of the Joint Chiefs of Staff. They're planning on demonstrating the new bio-detection technology, which is capable of detecting threats delivered through the air in real-time."

He wants to cut the heads off of all the snakes.

"Oh fuck," Lara said.

"What?" Rob asked.

"Fiddler isn't attacking Fort Meade and Fort Detrick today. He played us... I mean me. He's going after the Pentagon. He wants to take out defense leadership at the highest level while they're demonstrating the new system for preventing bio-attacks to the public. That would prove the ineffectiveness of their new system for preventing the full spectrum of bio-attacks. With those maps and his big speeches, he knew we'd send all of our resources out to Fort Detrick and Fort Meade, leaving the Pentagon exposed."

Rob slammed on the brakes, pulled over to the side of the highway, and made direct eye contact. "Lara, are you sure about this?"

She panicked for a moment. Knots formed in the pit of her stomach. Her instincts told her she was right, but she didn't have much information to go on. Except for Ashton's last words. Her chest tightened so she could barely breathe. Everything was riding on her gut instinct.

"Yes," Lara said, trying to sound certain. Her heart pounded in her ears.

In an instant, Rob pressed his foot down on the gas, the tires squealing. As the FBI cruiser careened toward the next highway exit, the smell of burnt rubber crept into the car, making Lara even more nauseous.

"Text Sanchez. Tell him your latest theory and ask him to stay at Fort Detrick just in case we're wrong. Tell him to relay the new information to all FBI agents and first responders at both sites. I want to keep all response forces in place for now, but if Fiddler's at the Pentagon, we're going to need some backup over there. Have Sanchez call my boss to send in a CIRG team and coordinate with the Pentagon Force Protection Agency."

Lara texted the information to the detective and received an immediate affirmative response.

Looking up from her screen, Lara asked, "What about the medical supplies? Shouldn't we redirect them to the Pentagon?"

Rob frowned. "Are you even sure Fiddler will be using the plague?"

Lara shook her head. *Not anymore.*

She blanched at the thought of another miscalculation. Fiddler had manipulated her, and she'd bought his story hook, line, and sinker.

But how did he know Justyne would find her and set her free?

Lara smacked herself in the forehead. "Come to think of it, Fiddler told me when he gave me the grand tour of his laboratory that the beetles were not carrying the plague. Fiddler explained it would be too dangerous, but I didn't believe him. I'm sorry I didn't realize this sooner."

"What do you think he'd use instead?" Justyne asked.

Lara racked her brain, running through all the information she'd gathered on the case. "Well, Sully was killed by botulinum toxin... Fiddler was quite impressed by the idea. You don't think he borrowed the idea of using a toxin from that, do you?"

"It's plausible," Rob said. "The plague is not the best microbe for killing people. It takes several days before an infection occurs, and it can be easily treated by antibiotics. Maybe he wanted something more effective... more dramatic. A toxin would do the trick."

"More effective at killing lots of people?" Lara asked in disbelief.

Rob nodded.

"What about those frogs the FBI evidence team found in Fiddler's office? Are they poisonous?" Justyne asked. "You said they were golden... did the frog picture look like this one here?"

She handed Lara her phone, which showed an image and profile of a golden frog from Colombia.

"That's identical to the picture hanging in his laboratory." At that moment, Lara recalled something they may have missed. "Rob, do you remember if either of Fiddler's passports had any stamps in it?"

"Uh, yeah. The passport under his real name had a stamp from Colombia. He made a recent short trip there."

Lara's jaw dropped. "How recent? Before or after Sully's death?"

Rob furrowed his brow. "After Sully's death. I didn't think anything of it at the time."

Lara threw up her hands. "I can't believe you never mentioned this. The clue was sitting in front of us the entire time."

Rob shrugged his shoulders. "We were so focused on finding his physical address and the Australian beetles that we didn't think anything of it. What do we know about this golden frog, anyway?"

Lara read the profile from Justyne's phone. "It's called a golden dart frog, and it's considered the most poisonous animal on the planet. American Indians used to dip their darts in the poison secreted from their skin. The poison is called batrachotoxin, which is a neurotoxin that affects the nervous system and is highly toxic to the heart. Death usually occurs by cardiac arrest. A lethal dose is only about 140 micrograms for an average-sized person. There's no antidote for the toxin."

"About how much is 140 micrograms?" Rob asked.

"About twice the width of a human hair... smaller than a pinprick," Lara said.

Pinprick?

The tiny needles and lancets the FBI evidence team found came to mind. "He's going to use the beetles to deliver the toxin and inject people using the tiny needles he had in his lab. He must have figured out a way to affix them to the beetles."

"But how much of this toxin do you think he collected?" Rob asked. "He had only a couple frogs in the lab…"

Lara scrolled through the profile. "It says here the amount of toxin in a single frog is enough to kill about thirteen people."

"That's it?" Rob asked. "Do you think he found a way to get more of the toxin? Or is he only targeting defense leadership?"

Lara scrolled further and continued to share. "Scientists were able to synthesize the toxin several years ago. They published their results online."

Rob rolled his eyes. "Oh, that's fantastic. Very convenient for criminals and terrorists around the world. In other words, Fiddler could have produced the toxin synthetically in mass quantities by now."

"It would appear so," Lara said grimly. "Who knows how many people he could kill."

THIRTY-EIGHT

The Building

From the 14th Street Bridge on Highway 395, Lara looked out across the Potomac River. Several sailboats were traversing the Pentagon Lagoon Yacht Basin, a small body of water leading to the main river.

Lara never understood why authorities allowed a private marina to be located so close to the headquarters of the Department of Defense. With a boat, it was possible to come within a thousand feet of the front entrance to the Pentagon.

It's almost as if they're asking for trouble.

Rob took the Pentagon South Parking exit off the highway, arriving at South Rotary Road inside the Pentagon reservation. As the FBI cruiser sped around the tightly curved road, Lara could see a crowd gathering in the parking lot. The assembly stood below a huge stairwell that led to the raised entryway to corridor 3 of the Pentagon. Up above, she could see a podium and a bright red ribbon tied between two pillars.

Several people in suits and military uniforms scurried about, busy making last minute preparations for the ribbon cutting. Lara scanned the Pentagon reservation; the Pentagon Force Protection Agency was out in spades. Pairs of armed security guards were positioned at various points, likely to protect the ceremony and the VIPs in attendance.

"They didn't heed our warning and cancel the event," Lara said, rubbing her sweaty hands on her pants.

Rob's forehead wrinkled. "When I called the Secretary of Defense's office, his military assistant said they'd take our security concerns into consideration. He warned me, however, that the SECDEF was keen on proceeding with the ribbon cutting ceremony. To cancel this event due to a threat of bio-attack would severely harm the credibility of the new BioScan system."

"Indeed, it would. Fiddler was probably counting on that," Lara said. "The BioScan system is designed to warn against pathogens and toxins in the air, not those delivered and injected by a swarm of insects. Fiddler wants to demonstrate how vulnerable we are to novel vectors. That was the whole point of the experiment that got him fired."

As Rob turned left onto the Pentagon access road, Justyne placed a hand on the shoulder of his seat. "Let me out here. Fiddler won't attack until the ceremony starts. I'll take a look around to see if I can find anything suspicious and keep an eye on ceremony preparations. I'll let you know when the SECDEF takes the podium."

"Good idea," Rob said. He pulled up to the curb to let her out and then sped away.

"Let's take a drive around the Pentagon on Boundary Channel Drive," Lara proposed. "With heightened security, Fiddler won't be able to park nearby without attracting attention. He must have found a hidden location to run his operation."

Rob nodded and drove along South Rotary Road. "What are we looking for?"

"I don't know... I'm pretty sure Fiddler took me hostage using an unmarked white van."

She glanced at the parking lot and counted at least ten

unmarked vans, none of them white. On the right, the Columbia Island Marina came into full view.

It's the perfect vantage point.

"What about the marina?" Lara asked. "Maybe Fiddler plans to control his beetles from a boat with a good view of the Pentagon."

Rob shook his head. "Nah… we don't have any evidence that Fiddler even owns a boat. I think we should drive around the Pentagon a few times and see if we can find the unmarked white van. If I were Fiddler, I'd want to get closer to the ceremony and have a full line of sight."

Lara crossed her arms. "You can drive around in circles if you want, but we're running out of time. I want to go check out the marina now." She put her hand on the door handle, threatening to exit while in transit.

Shaking his head, Rob pulled over the SUV and slammed on the brakes. "Fine, I'll let you out here, if you want to go so badly. You check it out. Probably best for us to *split up,* anyway."

Lara glared at him as she exited the vehicle. She watched as Rob raced off in the FBI cruiser on a mission.

He never did take my ideas seriously.

Turning toward the marina, her shoulders sagged at the long stretch between her and the docks. She almost wished she'd asked Rob to drop her off closer. But then she shook her head and quickened her pace as his last words rang in her ears. She set her jaw.

I don't need him, anyway.

* * *

THE COLUMBIA ISLAND MARINA was located on a long strip of land in the middle of the Potomac River. Breaking into a run, Lara crossed the footbridge and made her way through the lush Lyndon B. Johnson Memorial Grove.

Her wearable phone buzzed from her pocket, and Lara's heart nearly stopped.

Could that be Fiddler?

Instead of an unknown caller, however, a D.C. number showed up on the screen, one she didn't recognize.

"Hello?" Lara answered tentatively.

"Lara?" a woman's voice asked.

"Yes, this is Lara."

"I'm so glad I finally found you." The woman was out of breath. "This is Anita Fiddler."

Lara slowed her pace to a stop. "Anita? I thought you'd left town."

"Yes, I did, but I came back... I needed to—"

"How did you get my new number?" Lara asked suspiciously.

"I tried the number you provided my assistant, but it kept going to voicemail. Fortunately, you also gave Lindsay contact information for Detective Sanchez. So, I called him. And boy, did I get an earful. He gave me the runaround for nearly twenty minutes before finally coughing up your new number. I tried to convince him I have nothing to do with my father's plot and came back to town to help stop him."

Yeah, that sounds like Sanchez.

"Did he tell you about the APB he put out on you?" Lara asked.

"Yes. He also confronted me about your baseball glove, the money, and my DNA. I explained to him I have no idea how the baseball glove made it into my practice or how my DNA ended up at the warehouse or your townhouse. I suggested someone might be trying to frame me. He seemed satisfied with my alibi for the fire. I was at a medical conference in California and couldn't have set the fire or snatched your glove from the scene immediately afterwards."

"What about the money?" Lara asked.

"My father sent me and Frank money to pay for Jayden's chemotherapy." Anita sniffed and became choked up at the mention of her son.

"Chemotherapy?" Lara asked.

"Jayden was diagnosed with acute lymphocytic leukemia and was undergoing treatments when he died. The insurance would only cover so much, and my father didn't want us to worry about the expense. Once the detective called the hospital to verify my story, he seemed convinced I was telling the truth. At least enough to give me your number."

"I see." Lara breathed a sigh of relief. At least her instincts had not failed her on one account. "But why are you calling me now?"

Anita took a deep breath. "When I met my father for coffee earlier this week, he was talking gibberish about an imminent bio-attack in the D.C. area. He detailed some sort of conspiracy theory about a new bio-detection system to be unveiled by the Defense Department. He told me the ribbon cutting ceremony was a complete farce to cover up a series of tests being conducted on unsuspecting civilians by the Army. He reminded me of how my grandmother died and told me it wasn't safe for me to be in D.C. He begged me to leave town immediately, said if something happened to me, he would not be able to live with himself. So, I left town."

"Where did you go?" Lara asked as she started jogging briskly.

"To my mother-in-law's house on the Chesapeake Bay for a few days. But then I started to wonder and did some digging. You see, my father snapped after my husband and son died—in a way I didn't expect. He'd been frail of mind since my mom died, but lately, I barely recognize him. For example, he's been obsessed with finding the driver of the car who ran me and Frank off the bridge. He even dragged me to some warehouse against my will to prove CyberShop's existence."

"Do you know who CyberShop is?" Lara asked, her heart pounding.

"My father was convinced a woman named Linda Maxwell was working in collusion with Frank's former supervisor, Anton Stepanov. I'm not so sure anymore."

"So, why did you come back?"

"I called my father's old boss at USAMRIID to find out the real reason he was fired. My father sold me some story about his colleagues devising a conspiracy against him, but I was too wrapped up in my own grief and scandal to ask the right questions. I also knew my father liked to tinker with beetles, microelectronics, and surveillance at some lab he set up for himself. It was a strange project, but I thought it was mostly harmless. At the time, I hadn't realized my father was fired for experimenting with genetic modifications related to the plague. When his boss told me about his meltdown and his theft of *Yersinia pestis* strains from the Army lab, I became worried my father might be involved in a revenge plot against the government."

"Do you know where your father is?" Lara asked, hoping to get a tip on Vik's whereabouts.

"No. I tried reaching him on his cell, but he wouldn't pick up the phone. When I came home yesterday, I was shocked to learn from my assistant that the D.C. police had searched my practice and home for evidence. Is there anything I can do to help stop my father?"

"I'm glad you called. We need all the help we can get," Lara said breathlessly as the marina dockmaster's office came into view. "Do you know if your father owns a boat, by chance?"

"Not since mom died. I don't know what he did with his yacht. He probably sold it."

Lara would still check the marina, but more importantly, Anita had just given her an idea about how to stop Fiddler. "Okay, listen carefully. Your father plans to launch his bio-attack against the Pentagon, most likely from a boat. I need you there right now for the ribbon cutting ceremony. If your father sees you in the crowd, I don't think he will launch his attack. We can save hundreds of innocent people from being killed. Would you do that for us?"

"Of course, I'll do whatever I can to stop him. I'm in Foggy Bottom at my practice. I can be there in thirty minutes."

"Anita, please hurry. We don't have much time."

"I'll be there soon."

Lara jogged up the stairs to the marina dockmaster's office. As she walked up to the door, a scruffy man with a red face and white beard greeted her with a frown.

"Sir, I need to find the boat owned by John Fiddler," Lara said, breathing heavily.

"And who may I ask wants to know?" the man answered gruffly.

"I'm Lara Kingsley, a private investigator." She flashed her badge. "It's extremely important that I find Mr. Fiddler."

"Well, there's no one by that name at this marina."

Lara gave him a confused look. Maybe Fiddler used a different name. "Jan Speelman?"

"Nope, that name don't ring a bell either. Missy, I think you've got the wrong marina." He turned to leave.

Then Lara remembered Fiddler had used his son-in-law's name as an alias. "What about Frank Moore?"

"You're looking for Frank?"

Lara nodded eagerly.

The dockmaster scowled at her. "Even if I knew someone named Frank, I'm not letting you bother our patrons. Unless you plan on purchasing a year's membership and renting a slip, I'm gonna need you to leave, missy." He turned his back, sat down at the desk, and began typing at his computer.

Lara stared at him for a minute, her eyes darting to the gate leading to the dock. From her position, she could see it was unlocked. Her smartphone buzzed. The text from Justyne read:

THE CEREMONY HAS STARTED
SECDEF IS NOW MAKING HIS OPENING REMARKS

Without thinking, Lara dashed toward the gate as fast as she could.

Behind her, Lara could hear the dockmaster yelling. "Hey missy, stop! You can't go in there. It's private property."

She threw open the gate and ran through it, racing down

toward the dock marked with an "A." When she reached the entrance, she sprinted around the corner and began inspecting each of the boats moored at the slips. She reached the end of the dock without finding anything suspicious.

Not this one.

As she spun around, loud footsteps pounded down the main dock toward her. When she turned the corner, she came face to face with the white-bearded dockmaster, huffing and puffing, his face even redder than before.

Lara's face went slack at the double-barrel shotgun in his hands. She froze in place and watched him closely. Her eyes darted to the right and then to the left. She was trapped. The only way out of the marina or toward the other docks was to run past the dockmaster, and she didn't think he'd let her get by without a struggle. Time was of the essence. She needed to find Fiddler before it was too late.

He wouldn't actually shoot me, would he?

The dockmaster shook his gun at her. "I told you no trespassing! The cops are on their way. Now get out of here, or I'll have to use this."

"The cops are on their way? Good! I'll need the backup."

The dockmaster's face contorted, showing a mixture of confusion and anger at her snark.

Lara scanned her position for any way out. There was only one way… and she didn't like it one bit. Not wanting to lose any more time, she turned on her heels, raced back to the end of the dock, and dove head first into the river.

The shock of the cold water pierced her skin and knocked the wind out of her. It took a few moments to recover. She looked back for just a moment. The furious dockmaster stood wide-eyed at the end of dock A, waving his shotgun angrily in the air.

Lara turned to face the rows of docks and focused on the task at hand. She needed to find Fiddler's boat quickly. In the icy water, there wasn't much time before symptoms of hypothermia would set in. Her wet clothes clung to her body, making it difficult to swim.

A loud bang was followed by the sound of a bullet whizzing by her head.

He shot at me.

Another bang and whiz. Wasting no time, Lara threw her energy into the breaststroke, pulling her body through the water as fast as she could.

THIRTY-NINE

Poison Darts

AFTER A FEW MINUTES, Lara lifted her head to see how far she'd gotten. She'd almost cleared the entire marina. The dockmaster was gone from sight. Fifty feet away, she glimpsed a sign at the end of the last dock, marked with the letter "H."

Need… to make it… to the dock.

Her limbs numbed and grew heavy in the freezing water. With each stroke, her breathing slowed, becoming labored. A wave of exhaustion came over her. A sudden collision sent pain throughout her aching body. Startled, she looked up to find the pylon of dock H right in front of her.

Heaving her upper body onto the dock, she lay there facedown for a few minutes, her feet still dangling in the water. Rolling herself over to catch her breath, she stared up into the white fiberglass hull of a 72-foot motor yacht moored at slip 2 on the end of the dock. Her eyes wandered to the name on its side. *The Speelman.*

Lara launched herself to her feet, wringing out her clothes and shaking her head at her dumb luck. Without trying, she'd found Fiddler's boat. From the outside, the boat appeared to be empty, floating peacefully on the water. Without making a sound, Lara drew her gun, crossed the boarding ramp, and slipped onto the main deck at the stern. Once on the boat, dripping sounds followed her every move, forming small puddles wherever she stepped. Peering inside the window of the saloon, Lara found no sign of Fiddler or his beetles.

If he's here, Fiddler must be down below.

Pointing her gun forward, Lara walked through the door, into the saloon, and toward the galley kitchen, checking every nook and cranny. The teak wooden interior of the yacht was spotless, like it hadn't been lived in but was cleaned frequently. Even the coffeepot in the kitchen was unused. Peeking into the pilothouse at the bow of the yacht, she found no evidence of activity at the helm. The yacht appeared to be abandoned.

Lara climbed deftly down to the lower deck. The small landing at the bottom of the stairs led to five identical doors. She'd been on a yacht only once in her life, when she was a little girl. If this yacht had any resemblance to the one she remembered, each of the doors would open to a luxury stateroom.

As she reached for the doorknob to the middle room, it swung open and slammed against the wall. Vik came tumbling out, falling to his knees, gagged and with his hands tied behind his back. His black hair was disheveled and greasy. His pale, gaunt face made his dark eyes appear oversized and the look of terror on his face more pronounced. Fiddler came out of the room right behind him with a wicked grimace on his face. He jammed a gun into Vik's back, causing him to whimper through his gag.

"Lara, I had a feeling you might be joining us," Fiddler said, his upper lip curling. "Looks like you had a run-in with the old dockmaster, eh?" He eyed her drenched clothes up and down. "I do pay him generously to keep his mouth shut and any unwanted visitors out of my hair. How *did* you find me?"

"Your daughter told me," Lara said defiantly, pointing her gun back at him. Her hand trembled slightly.

"You're lying," Fiddler roared, waving his gun about and

sending Lara back a few steps. "Drop the gun now, or I'll end your friend's life right here."

Lara kept her gun trained on Fiddler.

He poked the gun into the side of Vik's head. "Do it. Now!"

Vik's eyes bulged out of their sockets.

"Okay! It's going to be okay, Vik." Slowly, Lara bent over and put her gun on the floor.

"Now, kick it to me!" Fiddler demanded.

Lara kicked the gun halfheartedly toward Fiddler, forcing him to step forward and pick it up. "If you try anything funny, your friend will die." Fiddler ripped the gag off Vik's mouth, causing him to wince in pain.

Vik looked at her with apologetic eyes. "I'm so sorry, Lara. I tracked Fiddler to the boat using traffic analysis and the DigiSpecs. Turns out he knew I was coming and intercepted me before I—"

"Vik, don't worry about it. You did good." Lara gave him a reassuring look.

Now is not the time to get emotional.

"Yes, Vik, you did good," Fiddler hissed. "You used the glasses I sent to you as a gift and brought her to me. Honestly, I didn't expect my decoy hack would make you miss the nearly untraceable remote access program I installed to track your usage. But it worked! And now, thanks to you, I get to force Lara to witness the deaths of hundreds of people, and then she'll watch me *kill you.*"

Vik shuddered.

Lara raised an eyebrow. *I knew using those glasses was a bad idea.*

Fiddler pointed the gun at Lara. "Move." He motioned for her to open the next door.

"Why are you doing this?" Lara asked, opening the door. "I don't understand—"

"You lied to me. You've been lying to me all this time, to get information on my plans. I know why you pretended to be interested in working for me. You thought you could play me, to stop me somehow. I'm trying to bring about justice for my mother, my son-in-law, and for my grandson. And you interfered. You will *pay* for your betrayal."

Fiddler kicked Vik in the back, his eyes narrowing. "Get up!"

With his hands tied behind his back, Vik struggled to get up. Lara rushed over to help him. Fiddler motioned for her to stop and pressed the gun into Vik's back, shoving him forward.

"Move!" He pushed Vik toward the next door, which opened into a high-tech command center lined with video screens, displaying feeds from the beetle cameras. Fiddler waved his gun, motioning for Lara to follow him.

Once inside, Fiddler closed and locked the door behind them. The shades were drawn, and the room was pitch black except for the light coming from the video screens.

"Where are your precious beetles?" Lara asked.

"Oh yes, my babies." Fiddler's eyes grew bright. "The beetle swarm is resting quietly in the trees at the Pentagon, near the ribbon-cutting ceremony that has just started. They await my attack command. Once I give it, they will descend upon the crowd like a plague, taking revenge for my family and teaching the U.S. Government an important lesson."

"But your beetles aren't carrying the plague, are they?" Lara asked.

Fiddler clasped his hands together and said with glee, "Oh my dear, you've exceeded my wildest expectations. Tell me, how did you figure it out?"

Lara shrugged. "It wasn't hard. You told me yourself the beetles weren't carrying the plague before you put me in that tank. And there was that picture of the golden frog on your wall in your laboratory. The FBI found two golden dart frogs in your office. But what sealed the deal for me was the stamp in your passport showing that you traveled to Colombia recently. That was no coincidence." She stretched her neck. "I'm curious, why did you change your mind about using the plague?"

"Smart girl. I was truly inspired by CyberShop's choice of weapon—botulinum toxin. It made me realize the plague was a clumsy option. It would take days before people would get sick, and then they might be saved with antibiotics."

"So, you decided to go with a toxin instead," Lara added.

"Yes. After some thought, I decided a toxin would be a much more effective weapon. So, I did some research and found batrachotoxin to be the ideal choice. Can you believe those idiot scientists published the synthetic formula for a dangerous toxin in open literature? All in the name of science? No thought given to what might happen if the wrong madman got a hold of such a deadly formula. The hard work was already done for me. All I had to do was produce a sufficient quantity of the toxin. Of course, I collected a few live specimens in Colombia to get one hundred percent confirmation I had the correct formula. Plus, the frogs make delightful pets, don't you think?"

"But how are you going to deliver it?" Lara asked. "The beetles can't transfer the toxin through their saliva."

"Oh, it's quite ingenious, actually. You see, I've constructed microdarts made from tiny needles used to inject diabetics with insulin. I filled these tiny needles with small amounts of the toxin and attached them to the beetles' backpacks. When a beetle bites a victim, the cap on the needle slides backward, activating a small spring mechanism, causing the needle to puncture their skin. The spring pushes the plunger forward and delivers a tiny amount of the toxin. Just enough to send them into cardiac arrest within a few minutes. You want to see one?"

Lara nodded. The toxin would kill people instantly, and there was no antidote. Fiddler posed a much greater threat than she'd anticipated. And as a result, many people would die.

It's all my fault. He fooled me.

Fiddler opened a desk drawer, pulled out a tiny dart, less than half an inch long, and gave it to her. Holding it between her thumb and index finger and squinting her eyes, she could see the coil spring was pressurized, and a small cap covered the needle. Suddenly, the cap moved backward and a tiny needle pricked her thumb.

Feeling the blood drain from her face, Lara recoiled and

dropped the microdart on the floor. A drop of blood appeared on her thumb where the needle had pierced her skin.

I'm poisoned!

Fiddler laughed, clearly enjoying himself. "Don't worry, that one doesn't have any toxin in it. That would be dangerous to give you a weapon, don't you think? I'm not crazy, you know." He paused for a moment, watching her recover from her horror. "Did you know poison dart frogs become toxic because of the beetles in their diet? The poison came from beetles!" He threw his head back, laughing heartily. "It all comes full circle. And now, the toxin will be delivered by beetles. There's nothing better than a good irony." Fiddler paused and gazed at her fondly. "You know, it's such a shame…"

"What?" Lara asked.

"With that head of yours, I bet you'd figure out CyberShop's identity in short order. It seems I placed my bet on the wrong horse. Sully was good at his job, no doubt, but *you*. You, my dear, are brilliant. Sadly, it's too late for regrets… or second thoughts." Fiddler turned his attention toward the video screens.

The screen directly in front of her appeared to be focused on up-close greenery, perhaps the leaves on a tree. Among the leaves, she glimpsed the metallic beetles and shivered.

"Can you see my beauties hiding in the leaves, waiting to descend on their victims?" Fiddler asked, smiling at her.

He began typing commands into his computer to communicate with his beetle swarm. Lara could see the leaves quiver and the swarm move about the trees in response.

"Ashton developed a fully autonomous navigation system for me, but I prefer to have a bit more control. These beetles respond to wireless signals sent from my computer. I've pre-programmed a range of commands on the microchip in their backpacks."

Fiddler activated a single beetle and directed the camera toward the Secretary of Defense, who still spoke from behind the podium. Over the audio, Lara could hear the crowd in the parking lot clap enthusiastically in response to his remarks. A few feet away from the Defense Secretary, she caught sight of the NSA Director and USAMRIID Commander.

His main targets are in view.

"Lara, if you wouldn't mind, I'd like you to do the honors."

"What honors?" Lara asked, her lips trembling.

Fiddler gave her a wicked look. "I want you to press the activate button, which will send my beetle swarm to inject the unsuspecting victims with the deadly toxin."

"No, I won't do it." Lara shook her head vigorously.

"If you want your friend to live, you don't have a choice." Fiddler pressed his gun against Vik's forehead. "Press the enter key."

Lara shook her head.

"Press enter NOW!" Fiddler hissed, his finger hovering over the trigger.

Her hand shaking, Lara pressed the enter key. The swarm responded immediately, flew straight up into the air, and then descended slowly in a circular motion, hovering for a few minutes above the crowd. She felt her pocket buzz, but didn't dare look down.

I should have worn the damn thing for once.

Fiddler stared intently at the video screens, giving her a brief window of opportunity. Slowly, she reached her hand into her jacket pocket. Tilting the screen toward her, she saw a text from Anita.

I'M IN THE CROWD
NEAR THE FRONT

"Fiddler, call off the attack now, or Anita will die," Lara shouted. "She's in the audience at the Pentagon. You don't want her to die, do you?"

Fiddler shoved her aside and began rapidly typing new commands into the computer. The beetle swarm froze in the air, hovering, then flying in a circle above the crowd.

With the joystick, Fiddler controlled a single beetle again, directing it to fly down toward the crowd. The camera on its back zoomed in to get a closer look at the people standing below.

Over the video screen, Lara spotted the tall and striking blonde woman standing at the front of the crowd. Anita seemed to spot the beetle with the camera and waved. Fiddler threw the joystick across the room and began pacing. Lara eyed the gun he'd set down on the desk.

"How did this happen?" he roared, his rage exploding as he kicked the wall and swept his hand across a table, flinging a notebook and a cup of pens across the floor. Turning to Lara, he pointed a finger at her chest. "You… you did this. You told Anita to come here and ruin my plans." Fiddler paced back and forth, wringing his hands.

Lara inched closer to the desk. *Just a few more feet.*

Fiddler stopped and stared at his daughter on the video screen. His expression dulled, and the light in his eyes disappeared.

"No. This doesn't change anything. I will have my revenge. Anita has already lost everything and can't bear to live without her family, anyway. You're the one who has put her in danger."

While Fiddler picked up the joystick from the floor, Lara dove for the gun. As Fiddler pressed the attack button and the beetle swarm dove into the crowd, Lara pointed the gun at Fiddler. "Call it off now, or I'll shoot."

The video screen revealed beetles swarming their victims below, and people began running in all directions, screaming. "I said now!"

Fiddler shook his head.

Pointing the gun, Lara fired a round into his chest. Fiddler convulsed and sank against the wall, the joystick falling from his hand onto the floor. Lara lunged for the joystick and began fiddling with the buttons, trying to make the beetles stop their attack. She looked at the video screen, horrified as the swarm became more energized.

Dammit. I just made things worse.

"Lara, let me try," Vik shouted, holding up his hands restrained by plastic ties.

Her head spinning, she yanked open the drawer of the table where the notebook and pens had been, found a letter opener, and sawed off the plastic ties. After shaking his arms out, Vik went to work on the joystick. The beetles responded immediately to his commands.

With a loud crack, the door burst open, startling Lara. Rob barreled through the door, his gun drawn, Justyne close behind him. They both appeared to be shocked to find Fiddler crumpled on the floor and bleeding from his upper chest, near the shoulder.

"Are you okay?" Rob asked.

Lara nodded, her eyes glued to the video screen as Vik guided the beetle swarm away from the crowd. He typed additional commands into the computer, and the beetle swarm flew back into the trees.

"How did you do that?" Lara asked.

"It's rather simple, Lara." Vik gave her a toothy grin.

Of course it was. Lara smiled, glad to have him back.

She turned to Rob. "How did you find us?"

"We heard about the shooting at the marina over the radio, but it was Justyne who located you," Rob said.

Justyne nodded. "Of course, it helped that Rob knew you were already over here. For the life of me, I don't know why he doesn't follow your nose for these things. The beetle transmitters operate on a frequency. Once we figured out which one Fiddler was using to communicate with them, we used radio source triangulation to track the signal back to the boat."

"But I thought the signals were encrypted," Lara said.

"Fiddler was using an encrypted frequency, but with advanced decryption technology, we were able to pick up the signals," Justyne said.

Lara looked back at the screens and bit her lower lip. "How many casualties are there?"

"I'm not sure," Rob said, looking confused. "People seem shaken up, but I haven't heard about any injuries or deaths."

"That's strange." Lara tapped her chin with one finger. "No heart attacks?"

Rob shook his head.

"What about the beetles?" Lara asked.

"First priority is getting folks medical attention if needed," he said. "And then we'll take care of the beetles as we planned."

"If I ever see another metallic beetle again, it will be one day too soon," Lara said.

"Yeah, you and me both, sweetheart," Rob smirked.

FORTY

CyberShop

November 9, 2027

A FLUORESCENT LIGHT flickered and buzzed intermittently above the small interrogation room at the FBI Washington Field Office. Lara opened the top buttons of her shirt to get some relief from the lack of ventilation.

Why are these rooms always so damn stuffy?

Her leather jacket hung on the back of her hard metal chair. She thought about balling it up and using it as a cushion for her rear end. She understood uncomfortable chairs for criminals, but they could roll in something nicer for the interrogator.

Lara sat across from Fiddler, her elbows resting on the steel table between them. Rob was watching the interrogation from the other side of the one-way mirror. Rob had tried questioning Fiddler several times and gotten nowhere. With permission from his boss, he finally agreed to give Lara a chance. Maybe her experience interacting with the mad scientist would loosen his tongue.

The District Attorney refused to offer any leniency on the long list of charges facing Fiddler in exchange for information on a homicide case. So, he had no reason to talk, unless of course it was in his interest to do so. Lara needed answers to catch Sully's killer, and she knew Fiddler wanted to bring justice to CyberShop as badly as she did. She was counting on it.

Relaxing her shoulders, she took a deep breath. She hadn't interrogated anyone since her time in Afghanistan and felt a bit out of practice. Usually, she had a partner to share the duties of good cop and bad cop. It was far more difficult to play both roles simultaneously.

Fiddler stared at her with his expressionless gray eyes. Having received treatment for a bullet wound to his shoulder, he wore his left arm in a sling. His good arm was chained to the table. Gray stubble was beginning to appear on the old man's cheeks and chin, and there were dark circles under his eyes.

"How are you feeling?" Lara asked, trying to seem sympathetic. She despised the man in front of her for everything he'd done: the stalking, the attempts on her life, the attack on innocent people, and most of all, for hurting Vik. Still, Lara somehow felt bad for shooting the old man.

Fiddler shrugged. "Good thing you're such a bad shot. The bullet went straight through so no permanent damage. The doctors said I'm lucky. Still, in my estimation, I feel quite unlucky, and you've had a great deal to do with that, haven't you?"

Lara shifted uncomfortably in her seat. "Yes, I have." She paused for a moment, wondering how to play it. Taking a deep breath, she continued. "In the end, I think I saved you from yourself. You started this crazy plot against the government to get revenge against CyberShop and to find justice for your family. I believe you lost sight of your true goal. Your mother was innocent, but so were those people in the crowd. Hundreds of people could have died from your stupid beetle stunt. And I don't think you ever planned to kill innocent people, starting the whole cycle again."

"But no one died, did they?" Fiddler grimaced.

Lara shook her head. After the first responders administered first aid and antibiotics, shot the beetles out of the trees with firehoses, and cleared the scene, public health officials and scientists swarmed the site of the attack to collect the beetles for transport to the CDC. Working through the night in Atlanta, Maggie confirmed that the genetically modified beetles were infected with the plague and could transmit the disease to humans. There was no evidence of any toxin or microdarts.

Lara furrowed her brow. "I don't get it. Why lie to me about the frogs and the microdarts?"

Fiddler shrugged. "For the hell of it. It made you sweat, didn't it?" He looked as if he'd enjoyed her terror. "I did think about changing my plans to use the toxin, but Ashton refused to help me put together the microdarts. And I couldn't do it myself in such a short timeframe. In the end, I realized the toxin would have taken attention away from my real purpose—to conduct a test of a novel vector and demonstrate the ineffective planning of the U.S. government."

Lara shook her head in disgust. "You attempted to hurt innocent people just to prove your damn point."

"The BioScan system is a scam, and I exposed the truth to the American people." Fiddler slammed his left hand on the table, wincing from the vibrations to his injured shoulder. "It can't protect against the vulnerabilities our country faces. I wasn't going to let the Secretary of Defense lie about it and make the public feel falsely at ease."

Lara glowered at him. "You're no better than the Army officers who authorized the tests on American cities decades ago and ended up killing your mother."

"Bullshit!" Fiddler screamed. "I am better than them. I showed the government how easy it is to leverage insects for spreading disease, and they refused to listen. So I needed a demonstration to prove my point. I did it to save my country from bad actors. I sacrificed everything for the good of my country."

Lara glared at him. "At the moment, you're the only bad actor we need to protect our country from. All you've proven is there are crazy people who want to harm the government and the citizens of this country. Crazy people like *you*."

"Noooo!" Fiddler kicked and screamed from his seat across the table, trying to shove it against her body, but it wouldn't budge.

"We found your penthouse," Lara said, hoping to rattle him.

Fiddler sat up straight in his chair, eyes wide. Then he relaxed a bit, scoffing at her. "Took you long enough."

"Admittedly, we failed to find your lab, and it sat under our noses even after several attempts to investigate. Once we discovered your front company, Technovation Industries, and figured out your fondness for aliases, a quick search led us to the penthouse apartment across the street that was under Frank Moore's name."

"What's your point?" Fiddler scowled.

Lara crossed her arms. "We've now established a definitive link to your former identity, Jan Speelman. We also found your personal journals, which not only reveal the true cause of your wife's death, they clearly lay out your plans for revenge. With that evidence, the District Attorney plans to add second degree murder charges to the growing list. We also found your file that proves Frank and Anita's innocence in the leak at NSA. What we didn't find is any evidence against CyberShop... so we need your help."

Fiddler turned his face away and stared blankly at the wall.

Lara got up from her seat, moved into his line of sight, and looked down at him. "Do you want to see your daughter again? Because I have the power to make it happen." She paused to see if his expression changed. Fiddler continued to stare unmoved at the wall in front of him.

"You're about to be sent to a high-security federal prison far away from here. This may be your last chance to see her for a very long time. I know Anita wants to see you... despite everything you've done."

Fiddler scowled at Lara.

I'm finally getting to him.

"If you want to start making this right, you'll help me find Sully's killer," Lara said. "That's what you want, right? To put CyberShop behind bars? To get justice for Frank and Jayden? Isn't this the real reason for everything you've done? And isn't CyberShop responsible for your family's recent suffering? If you help me, I'll make sure you get to see your daughter Anita, and I'll bring justice to CyberShop."

Lara looked Fiddler directly in the eyes. He stared back at her coldly, not blinking.

"So, will you help me?" Lara asked.

After a few minutes of silence, Fiddler muttered, "Yes."

Lara sat back down in her chair and rested her elbows on the table once more.

"Okay, tell me how you met CyberShop," Lara said.

Fiddler hesitated and turned his gaze to meet hers. "We met on the Dark Web, on the TechNow message board. We met together with Droneman, who I quickly figured out was the FBI undercover. CyberShop claimed to be an expert in encryption and offered access to advanced drone technology. This peaked my interest."

"Why were you on the Dark Web?" Lara asked.

"I was interested in high-tech drones, military-grade, capable of long-range surveillance missions. But I figured out Droneman and CyberShop were not who they seemed. I knew the FBI was watching me after my interactions with the NSA over my son-in-law's death and their attempt to frame him, and later Anita, for the leak. I began to suspect CyberShop to be the real culprit behind the sale of classified technology and Frank's death, but they wouldn't listen to me. For fun, I convinced Droneman to put on a drone show. The FBI called it a sting operation. Ha! The sting was on them, not me."

"You intended the drone show as a trap for CyberShop?" Lara asked.

Fiddler laughed, enjoying the memory. "Yes, to prove Anita's innocence. I wanted to steal a drone at the demonstration as the final proof, so I bought a high-end jammer and drone interceptor from CyberShop, which was supposed to be capable of spoofing the signals and taking control of a drone. That was the remote Sully had on him when he died. I don't think it worked, but Sully didn't get the chance... CyberShop duped us both and then killed him."

Fiddler averted his gaze, as if Sully's death bothered him. *Does he feel guilty about it?*

"Did you ever meet CyberShop?" Lara asked.

"Once... before I hired Sully. She wanted to meet me, so I indulged her. She was tall and had reddish hair... maybe auburn, but it could have been a wig. And brown eyes."

Lara pulled out a picture of Linda Maxwell from a manila folder and put it in front of Fiddler. "Is that her?"

Fiddler leaned forward and studied the picture, his forehead wrinkling. "No, that's not the woman I met."

"Are you sure?"

He looked closer. "Wait, there is... some resemblance. Yes, in the eyes, that could be her. But not her face, unless she's had some work done and gained some weight."

"Why did she want to meet you in person?" Lara asked.

"I'm not sure. Because she killed my family? Of course, I didn't know that at the time. I suppose she wanted to size me up to see if I was a threat. I became suspicious and hired Sully to figure out her true identity."

"What else do you know about her?" Lara asked.

"At one time, she worked at the NSA as a specialist in encryption. That's how she knew my son-in-law. Frank discovered she was selling Top Secret encryption technology, told her about his suspicions, and was going to inform his leadership. When she became irate, Frank decided to get his family to safety first and drive them out to his mother's place in Ocean City. That's why my family was driving across the Chesapeake Bay Bridge that night."

Tears welled up in Fiddler's eyes as he slumped against the back of his chair. Unable to wipe his face, a tear rolled down his cheek. For a moment, he didn't seem like the mad scientist anymore. He looked like a sad old man who had lost everything that mattered to him.

"Is she your primary suspect?" Fiddler asked, pointing to the picture.

Lara nodded. "Her name is Linda Maxwell. We first met her during our investigation of a company called Beautific Creations, a beauty product supplier that was the source of the botulinum toxin that killed Sully."

"So, I was right," Fiddler said grimly.

"You were there that day, weren't you? I saw Anita waiting in her car, but you and Ashton were hiding in the warehouse. What was your plan?"

"Well, before you and your miscreant FBI boyfriend showed up, I was planning to take her out. But it seems you were always meddling in my plans."

"The FBI has done a thorough investigation on Linda. We can't find any evidence she worked at the NSA in the past. Instead, we suspect she must have had an accomplice with ties to the NSA and Russia by the name of Anton Stepanov. Does that name ring a bell?"

"Oh?" Fiddler's eyes brightened slightly. He looked as if he was pondering this new information carefully and trying to match it up with his recollections. "Ah yes, Stepanov was Frank's supervisor. Do you think he was the inside man at the NSA, working with CyberShop?"

Lara nodded. "We haven't had much time to conduct an investigation into his background. I've been on the run ever since we connected him to Sully's death. Navigating multiple attempts against my life and your plot to attack the government kept me busy."

"What evidence did you find against them?" Fiddler asked.

"We've connected Linda to the remote in Sully's possession and to the black BMW convertible. We think it's the same car that drove your family off that bridge."

The door behind Fiddler opened. Rob walked into the room, stomped over to her, and handed her a file.

"Droneman, we meet again," Fiddler snarled at Rob.

"Lara, we found a body," Rob said, ignoring the bait.

"What?"

"I sent an FBI evidence team over to Beautific Creations for another sweep. They found Anton Stepanov's body in the warehouse. He took two bullets at short range, one to the chest and one to the head. His BMW was parked outside. The plates match the VIN this time. Linda drives an identical car."

Lara's jaw dropped.

"That's not all. We found the ingredients for napalm in the trunk of his car."

"You mean Stepanov attempted to burn down my townhouse?" Lara asked.

Rob nodded. "If Stepanov and Linda were working together, they must have had a disagreement. Or Linda merely used him to carry out her plans. Anyway, she has fled the country. My colleagues at the FBI are trying to track her down overseas. Justyne has returned to her post back at the NSA and offered to help the FBI by providing SIGINT on any calls between Linda and her foreign associates. That's all I have at the moment."

"Linda must have known I tried to recruit you as my private investigator," Fiddler said, a knowing smirk on his face.

"What? *He* tried to recruit *you?*" Rob pointed at Fiddler and then gave Lara an incredulous look. "You *never* told me that."

Fiddler laughed and smiled as though he'd found a pot of gold. "She didn't tell you I offered her one hundred thousand dollars to work for me?"

Lara shot Fiddler a furious look.

Rob crossed his arms. "No, she failed to mention that."

"Did she tell you she almost accepted my offer?" Fiddler grinned broadly at Lara.

He is enjoying this way too much.

Lara cleared her throat. "I declined your offer when I crushed that bug. I believe I paid dearly for my mistake when you shoved me in your tank full of beetles." She turned to Rob. "And as for you, I don't want to hear any more about this. You've kept secrets from the beginning on this case. Is there something else you needed to tell me?"

Rob shrank back at her harsh words. A sinking feeling settled in her gut. She hadn't meant to lash out at him. Without looking at her, Rob left the room. The door slammed behind him.

"He loves you," Fiddler murmured. "And you love him."

Lara raised her eyebrows.

"Anyone can see that," Fiddler said.

Lara shook her head. "He left me for another woman."

"That doesn't change what I just saw."

Lara ignored the comment. She didn't want to delve into her terrible love life with the mad scientist who had tried to kill her on more than one occasion. Even if, for a moment, she felt sorry for him.

Lara got up from her seat. "I'd say thank you for your help, but this is barely more than I already had."

His eyes widened. "What about my—"

"I'll make sure you get to see Anita one last time. But I'm doing it for her, not you."

"Thank you," Fiddler gave her a weak smile, and Lara left him there, content to never see him again.

FORTY-ONE

The Anagram

November 16, 2027

A WEEK PASSED QUICKLY after the beetle attack on the Pentagon. Lara had grown weary of the case. She wanted things to return to normal and to put the pieces of her life back together. But first, she had to bring Sully's killer to justice.

After combing through Sully's files in the storage unit, the FBI found sufficient evidence of Linda's involvement and the existence of an accomplice, but nothing helpful for tracking her whereabouts, her activities as CyberShop, or the identity of her accomplice. Interpol launched a Europe-wide search for her and her known aliases, but there was still no sign of her.

Now, Lara followed Justyne down the endless winding hallways of the NSA at Fort Meade. This time, Justyne donned an indigo blue Dolce & Gabbana suit ensemble, a Hermes scarf, and gaudy jewelry. Her matching high heels clicked loudly on the tile floors. Lara felt rather underdressed in her black leggings, gray T-shirt, and leather jacket. The rubber soles of her worn out running shoes squeaked as she tried to keep up with Justyne's pace.

"Thanks for coming all the way out here. I know it's a long trek from D.C., especially on the weekend." Justyne's shiny black hair swooshed back and forth to match her gait. Her perfume wafted past Lara's nose. It was always the same tropical, floral scent.

"Not a problem," Lara said. "The Baltimore-Washington Parkway is rather beautiful this time of year."

"I'm sure the fall colors were a great relief after all you've been through on this case," Justyne said, shaking her head in disbelief. "The beetle attacks, nearly getting hit by a car, Fiddler taking you hostage, and even arson in your own townhouse. I'm not sure I could have survived all of that."

Lara checked her wrist for her wearable smartphone, and her stomach lurched. Then she remembered it was safely locked up at the visitor control center. She felt vulnerable without it.

"Yeah, it's been quite the ordeal," Lara said, trying to pay attention to her surroundings. She wanted to memorize the route through the building, but couldn't keep track of where Justyne was leading her. Every hallway looked identical, barren, and lined with stark white walls. The occasional unmarked doorways didn't help, either.

"And I owe you my life at least once," Lara added.

"Now, now… anyone would have done the same thing in my place," Justyne said, turning the corner. "And don't forget, you rescued me from that beetle swarm."

All the doors were made of steel and marked with room numbers. Lara let her imagination go wild as they navigated the halls, picturing what might be hidden behind them. Many of the rooms were SCIFs to allow for Top Secret classified work and could only be entered through a combination key code and with proper clearance.

"This is where I live when I'm not on detail," Justyne said cheerfully, shielding the keypad as she punched in her code. When the lock released, she opened the door and motioned for Lara to enter.

Inside the SCIF, the office suite was much larger than Lara

had imagined from the hallway. Six blandly decorated cubicles occupied the center of the suite. They were surrounded by offices with doors on either side. The computers and lights were off, and there was no sign of any activity.

"It's really quiet in here," Lara said, fidgeting with her jacket zipper.

"No one works on weekends, except when there's a crisis of some sort," Justyne said, walking into a windowless office and turning on the light. "Thankfully, things have been pretty quiet the past few days."

Justyne motioned for Lara to sit in the leather chair across from her desk while she booted up her computer and entered her password. Lara draped her leather jacket around the back of the chair and took a seat.

Opening a desk drawer, Justyne pulled out a pack of cigarettes. "Do you mind?"

Lara lied and shook her head, but immediately felt uneasy. "You smoke?"

"Once in a while," she said, lighting up a cig and taking a long draw, blowing the smoke above her in Lara's direction, "to relax after a stressful week."

Not once had she detected the smell of cigarettes on Justyne. Of course, the woman always lathered herself with strong perfume.

Is that why? To cover up the smell of smoke?

Lara shifted uncomfortably in her seat as a hint of smoke assaulted her. The whole thing reminded her of the conversation with Linda in the warehouse.

Something feels familiar.

But Lara couldn't put her finger on it.

"I heard from Agent Martin that the FBI found Stepanov's body in the warehouse at Beautific Creations. So tragic." Justyne frowned. "It seems that Linda had no further need for her accomplice."

Lara nodded, suddenly wanting to cut to the chase. "Rob said you had SIGINT that might help us determine where Linda Maxwell may be hiding out."

Justyne nodded. "Yes, we caught several conversations coming over the wire. Our SIGINT analysts are examining the transcripts for possible leads. It seems Linda is well connected with known international criminal networks across Europe."

"Oh really?" Lara raised her eyebrows. During her short time at Beautific Creations, she didn't get the sense Linda was shrewd enough to be engaged in international crime.

"Okay, here we go," Justyne announced, opening up some files on her computer. "Just pull up a chair, and you can read over my shoulder."

"Would it be possible to get a hard copy? Reading on computer screens makes my eyes go buggy," Lara said. It was a simple ruse to give her a moment to look around and collect her thoughts. *Something was off.*

"Sure. I'll go print two copies on the classified printer, and we can review them together and see if we can find any information on Linda's whereabouts."

Justyne walked out into the office suite, leaving Lara alone for a few minutes to peruse her office. Even without windows, the office was comfortable, spacious, and well-furnished, reflecting Justyne's apparent seniority in her department. Lara wondered why Justyne moved over to DARPA for a temporary assignment.

Was it really for the internal investigation?

Behind the oak desk, a large bookshelf ran along the back wall. It was filled to the brim with books on encryption, cryptology, espionage, and coding. Lara got up out of her seat to get a closer look at Justyne's vast collection.

A book on drone technology on the top shelf caught Lara's attention. Then the book underneath it sent chills down her spine—*A History of Napalm.*

Standing on her tiptoes, Lara grabbed the two books down from the shelf. As they slid down into her hands, a large black object sitting on top came crashing down with it and landed on the floor next to her with a loud thud.

She looked down to see what had fallen, and the blood drained from her face.

Sully's remote?

Lara picked up the black gadget with thick antennae and examined it carefully. It was the same remote she'd seen on the cement floor next to Sully's dead body.

Why does Justyne have it?

Justyne's heels clicked on the tile floor of the hall as she approached her office, and Lara shoved the napalm book onto a lower shelf and froze, holding the remote.

"What are you doing?" Justyne asked, her tone stiff.

Lara's heart raced. "Uh... I was um... intrigued by your book on drone technology. When I pulled the book from the shelf, this gadget fell onto the floor. I hope I didn't break it; it looks expensive."

"It's fine," Justyne said, waving it off. Her lips were pressed into a thin line as she eyed the remote.

Lara paused for a moment, contemplating her next words carefully. "This looks like Sully's remote, actually."

Justyne grabbed the remote from Lara and put it on her desk. "Well, it's not. I had a replica made as part of my investigation into CyberShop."

Lara furrowed her brow. "But how did you know what it looked like and what technology was used? This is an exact copy."

"I studied Linda's communications over the Dark Web with Fiddler and reverse-engineered it." Justyne avoided eye contact. "Now, let's take a look at these transcripts. I thought we could each read through on our own, and then exchange ideas on anything that stands out."

Lara stared at the paper and tried to read, but her thoughts lingered on the remote. Her mind raced as she analyzed everything she'd learned over the past several weeks. Her review suggested two possibilities. Either Justyne was telling the truth about replicating the remote, *or* Justyne had taken it from the townhouse after setting the fire. Lara looked up, scrunching her face at the woman sitting across from her.

Justyne's piercing blue eyes narrowed at her. "Are you done reading yet?"

"Uh… no, sorry. My mind wandered off for a minute," Lara said. She bit her lower lip and looked back at the paper.

"If you wouldn't mind focusing on the task at hand, I do have other things to take care of, you know." Justyne's voice was terse.

"I know… I'm sorry. I've been a bit distracted by everything that's been going on. Actually, now I'm wondering about something."

"And what might that be?" Justyne crossed her arms and raised an eyebrow.

"Why are you no longer on detail assignment over at DARPA?"

Justyne waved off her question. "Oh, that? It ended a week ago when I returned to my office here. I told you my assignment was related to the internal investigation into CyberShop. And we found sufficient evidence on Stepanov."

Like a bolt out of the blue, the answers came flooding to Lara. There was only one thing that made sense.

Justyne is CyberShop.

All the evidence fit; well, at least most of it did. Justyne was there when her fuel line was cut. Justyne stole Sully's remote from her townhouse and set the fire. She returned to the scene of the crime to steal the baseball glove and left it at Anita's practice. She must also have stolen samples of Anita's DNA to plant in the warehouse and at her townhouse. Justyne was the other female voice on the intercom and the BMW getaway driver at Beautific Creations.

This also explained Fiddler's confusion about the picture of Linda… because he'd actually met… Justyne.

They do look alike.

The biggest problem was all the DNA and fingerprint

evidence matched Linda—the DNA from her bike, the hair from her townhouse, and the saliva on the cigarette butt from the warehouse.

No, the evidence matched Martje Hussny.

Lara sat up straight in her chair as a revelation entered her mind.

Martje Hussny is an anagram for Justyne Marsh.

Suddenly, it all became clear. It was never Linda's alias after all. Justyne must be deaf in one ear. *That's why she stands so close to me all the time.*

"You're the one who cut my fuel line, aren't you?" Lara said, her heart racing.

Justyne's eyes grew large. "No, that was Linda. Come, let's focus on finding out where she ran off to."

"The jig is up, Justyne." Lara's heart beat wildly. She knew CyberShop to be ruthless, knew she was taking a risk, but the words were out before she could really think about it. "I know Linda didn't do it. You were the only other person there that day."

"The cops found Linda's DNA on your bike, not mine," Justyne snapped.

"That black BMW convertible is *your* car, isn't it? It's the same one that ran Frank and Anita off the bridge. The same one that tried to run me down with fake plates." Lara shook her head. "I should have known a woman like you would never drive a white Honda."

And all the makeup in Justyne's trunk must have been from Beautific Creations.

"You're the one who doctored the video feed from the beetle, aren't you?" Lara asked, recalling the grainy video and missing footage.

"Lara, I don't know what you're talking about. Stop this nonsense now." Her eyes narrowed.

"It was you—all along." Lara gasped. "It was right in front of my eyes, but I didn't want to believe it. Linda is your identical twin sister, isn't she? I mean, you two are so different in demeanor, even a little off in weight. But, you look enough alike to be sisters. That's why the DNA evidence pointed to her. Your DNA is identical."

Justyne glared at Lara, pinching her lips closed. For a few minutes, an awkward silence hovered between them.

Then a mirthless smile fell across Justyne's face. "Yes, Linda is my twin sister. After all her plastic surgery, she doesn't look identical to me anymore. And the brown contact lenses keep people fooled. And yes, I hacked the wireless transmission of the beetle and corrupted the file. I couldn't have you see me and my sister toss Sully's townhouse, now could I? Of course, I left some footage of my sister and Ashton to send you in the wrong direction."

Lara's jaw dropped. Only now could she see the close resemblance and imagine Justyne's face under all of Linda's plastic surgery. She was ashamed she'd not realized it sooner. "What were you looking for at Sully's townhouse?"

Justyne grimaced. "I knew Sully moved his case files to some secret location, but I was convinced he still had the cardboard box from the remote I sent him. That box could have led authorities to the apartment out in Laurel. I needed to get it back."

"Why did you kill Sully?" Lara asked.

Justyne began pacing her office. "He was relentless in his investigation into CyberShop's identity and discovered our fall guy Stepanov was innocent. When he caught on to my sister's activities, I had no choice but to get rid of him."

"Did you kill Frank Moore and his son, too?" Lara asked.

"That nag Frank wouldn't leave me alone. He watched me like a hawk. One day, he found some real evidence against me and asked me about it. What a naïve man…" Justyne shook her head. "He actually came to me with the evidence and told me he wanted to give me a chance to explain myself before reporting me. What choice did I have?"

"But his whole family?"

Justyne shrugged her shoulders. "It looked like he was

running away. I worried he would disappear, report me, and return only when I was behind bars. It was them or me. I made a choice."

"You were at Beautific Creations that day, weren't you? It was your voice over the intercom when we came to meet Linda. You've been setting up your sister to take the fall for you."

Justyne nodded. "Yes and no. Linda always managed to get into trouble with the law, even as a teenager, so she had a record. She owed me for bailing her out and was glad to help me out of my tight spot. We used her name to register the BMW and sign my apartment lease. We created fake plates that matched Stepanov's to throw you off. I left my DNA on the fuel line of your bike, knowing the profile was in the system as Martje Hussny. I knew if we got caught, suspicion would be directed toward Linda instead of me."

"But why did you help me so many times?" Lara asked, confused. Justyne had set up the appointment with Dr. Grayson, backed her up several times, and even saved her life.

"As soon as you showed up at DARPA, I knew you had taken over Sully's investigation of CyberShop. I tried to push you off the scent, but you're as persistent as a dog after a bone."

"Actually, I was investigating Sully's murder, not CyberShop," Lara snapped. "I didn't know who killed Sully at that time. I simply followed all the clues, and they led me here."

"When you called me to come out to the Cryptologic Museum, I decided to pretend to work with you. Maybe you could lead me to Fiddler. He was my final loose end and was getting too close to Linda. I couldn't relax until he was eliminated. I tracked your movements with a surveillance drone."

So, I wasn't crazy. I was being watched.

"That's how I knew you visited Anita," Justyne said. "So, I planted your precious baseball glove at her office to confuse you. Of course, I brought it to the office at DARPA first and put it on Stepanov's office chair to trick him into touching it. I also locked you and Rob in the safe room and destroyed the keypad to keep you in there. I had an inkling you'd discovered my apartment and needed time to pack up everything and help my sister escape."

"But we got there before she'd left," Lara said. "And you knew I was kidnapped by Fiddler at the storage company. Because you tracked my location using your drone."

"Yes." Justyne grimaced. "Actually, the drone surveillance allowed us to kill two birds with one stone. When we saw Stepanov was there as well, Linda and I cut the power at the storage company. She snatched up Stepanov and got rid of him —for good. And I walloped you over the head, stole the file Sully put together about me, and then kept my eye on you until you were kidnapped. It's a good thing I did, don't you agree?"

"Why didn't you just kill me then, when I was unconscious?" Lara asked.

"Because I needed you to lead me to Fiddler. When he kidnapped you and brought you to his lab, that's when I figured out we had Fiddler's address all along."

"Why did you do it?" Lara asked, sneaking glances around the office to plan her escape. She knew Justyne would not have confessed everything if she intended to let her live.

"Do what?"

"Why did you betray your country to sell Top Secret technology? Why did you kill innocent people to protect your secret?" Out of the corner of her eye, Lara glanced at the door.

"Do you think I can afford such nice things on a government salary?" Justyne pointed to her designer watch and jewelry. "I wanted the good life like everyone else. I wasn't going to get that being a public servant. I didn't think I was hurting anyone. Frank stuck his nose where it didn't belong. That's when things got out of hand."

"You sold your soul for trinkets?" Lara shook her head in disgust.

"I think we've talked long enough." She opened her desk drawer and took out a syringe. Lara didn't have to guess what was in it.

Botulinum toxin.

"I hoped it wouldn't come to this." Justyne sighed and stepped toward Lara. "But you never stop."

Lara's eyes darted toward the exit, and she jumped up from her chair. She bolted toward the steel door, opened it, and burst into the office suite. She ran down the aisle through the cubicles and grabbed the handle of the steel SCIF door, but it wouldn't budge.

Justyne's heels snapped quickly on the floor behind her. Panicking, she looked for a button to engage the lock. She pressed it, but the door remained locked. On the wall next to the button was an electronic keypad. Lara's heart sank. She would need Justyne's key code to get out.

She turned around, and Justyne lunged toward her with the syringe, trying to stab her in the arm. Lara dodged the swipe and ran back toward the cubicles, rolling office chairs into her path to block the way.

"You're trapped!" Justyne yelled. "There's no way out."

As Lara ran around the cubicles, something wrapped around her left foot and she tripped, the weight of her body thrusting her forward. As she fell to the floor, she glimpsed the thick cable that had caught her foot.

Seconds later, Justyne pressed her knee into Lara's back and put her arm around Lara's throat, bringing the pointy end of the syringe to her eyes.

"Don't worry, it'll be over fast." She pulled the needle away from Lara's face.

Lara closed her eyes and waited for the needle prick.

FORTY-TWO

My Hero

A LOUD BANG sounded from the direction of the SCIF door. Startled, Justyne let go of Lara's head. Sensing her opportunity, Lara jabbed her elbow behind her, hitting Justyne squarely in the ribs. Stunned by the blow, Justyne fell backward for a moment, releasing Lara from the full weight of her body. Lara crawled forward, struggling to get free. But before she could get up off the floor, Justyne grabbed her by the ponytail, pulling Lara back toward her.

As the syringe needle grazed her neck, a gunshot rang out. The bullet zinged past Justyne's body and entered the wall next to them. When Justyne ducked and turned to look for the shooter, Lara went on the attack.

Placing her weight on her left leg, she thrust her right leg backwards into Justyne's stomach. The blow caught Justyne by surprise. She tumbled backwards, dropping the syringe. Lara jumped to the floor and kicked the syringe across the room. She looked up to see Rob standing in the open doorway. An embarrassed federal agent stood next to him, holding the smoking gun.

"Rob!" Lara said. His face was pale, but he smiled at her. The federal agent raced over to Justyne, his gun drawn. Justyne put her hands in the air in surrender. Rob jogged toward Lara, and she threw her arms around his neck, resting in his strong embrace.

"Are you hurt?" Rob asked. "Or maybe I should ask Justyne if she's hurt. You pretty much had that situation under control."

Lara smirked, watching as the federal agent cuffed Justyne. "Not sure I would have gotten the upper hand without the distraction. So, thanks for that." Lara paused, touching her neck where the syringe needle grazed her skin. "Did she get me?"

"There's a small mark," Rob said. "We should probably have you checked out by the medical team. They're already en route."

"How did you know?" Lara asked.

"Honestly, I had no idea Justyne was CyberShop until Ashton's autopsy report came in this morning. He died of botulinum toxin poisoning."

"What?" Lara shrieked in surprise. "But I thought—"

"When I learned the true cause of death, I remembered it was Justyne who rescued you from Fiddler's lab. She was the only one who had the opportunity to inject him with the toxin. She must have finished him off with one of her syringes."

"Why did the autopsy take so long?"

Rob glanced awkwardly down at his feet. "Um, Agent Carter pissed off the medical examiner again, and there was a bit of a delay in getting the results."

Lara shuddered, realizing her fate had hung in the balance of Carter's love life. Had they burst into the SCIF one second later, she might have shared the same fate as Sully and Ashton.

Rob continued. "Then I realized you were coming out here to go over SIGINT reports involving Linda's communications, and I knew you were in grave danger."

"Well, that's an understatement. The door was locked with a key code. I couldn't get out. If you hadn't come for me, I'd be…"

"Let's not talk about that, okay?" Rob paused for a few minutes. Their gazes connected, and neither looked away. "Lara, I… I…"

Lara knew what was coming, and she pressed her finger to

his lips. Ever since he'd confessed his feelings for her, she'd tried to decipher her own heart. Deep down, Lara still loved Rob. The question had been whether he deserved another chance.

But things finally clicked for her when he didn't listen to her theory about Fiddler and the marina. He'd never really trusted her instincts. Either he didn't want to, or he couldn't get past his own insecurities. As long as he felt inferior to her, he'd never fully appreciate her.

I deserve more than that.

"Rob, I care about you, too. But it took me a long time to get over what you did to me. And I've moved on." She'd practiced that response over and over. It wasn't a lie, but it also wasn't the whole truth. Lara didn't know if Rob could become the right man for her, but she wasn't going to wait to find out. She knew better than that.

A blush crept up his neck, and Rob stared down at his feet. "Can we at least try to be friends?"

Lara smirked and lightly punched his arm. "After saving my life, I think I can manage that."

* * *

AFTER THE EXCITEMENT at the NSA and nearly getting injected with deadly toxin, Lara spent most of the day at the FBI in debriefing sessions with Rob, Detective Sanchez, and officials from the NSA. Interpol apprehended Linda about the same time Lara had been tussling with Justyne. The case against Justyne and her sister was airtight. Stepanov was cleared of any involvement.

Lara stood on the stairs leading up to her townhouse. The railing felt cool under her hands, and she leaned against it. Her body was heavy, aching all over as if she'd been hit by a semi-truck. Sleep had eluded her for weeks, and she couldn't remember ever feeling so exhausted. Looking up, she watched as delivery drones buzzed overhead and obediently dropped off their packages to nearby customers.

I did it! I actually found Sully's killer and brought her to justice.

A tear dropped down her cheek, followed by another and another. She sat down on the stairs and put her face in her hands. Soon, the tears flowed like a waterfall. She cried for Sully, the premature end of his life, and the pain of his loss. She cried for letting Vik down, for the failure of her business, and her uncertain future. And she cried for the loss of her home and for her lack of options.

Eventually, the tears stopped. For over a month, she'd held almost everything inside, postponing her emotions until she had time for them. Until it was safe to express them. Sometimes, she marveled at her ability to compartmentalize her emotions. When she couldn't hold it in anymore, everything would come tumbling out of her at the same time—either in rage or anguish.

That's when she wished she didn't tuck everything away all the time. But that tendency acted as the key to her strength, determination, and survival through many tragic experiences— her parents' death, the loss of her unit in Afghanistan, nearly dying in a fire, and her ability to catch Sully's killer. None of it would have been possible if she'd handled her emotions differently.

She laughed softly at herself as she touched her puffy eyes with her fingertips.

I must look like a crazy drunk.

She dabbed her face dry with her sleeve. She pulled herself up and brushed off her pants. Lara walked into her townhouse and closed the door behind her.

Home sweet home.

At least for a few more days. Her landlord, Jake, would call the U.S. Marshal if he had to, and she wasn't about to wait for his next move. Vik had texted her earlier that day, saying he'd already packed up most of the office into moving boxes while Maggie had made significant headway in packing up her apartment.

Lara was not yet sure where she would end up. Since she didn't have the money to find a new place, she'd rented a storage unit to hold her belongings and would stay with Maggie until she could figure things out for Kingsley Investigations.

After a long debate and many tears, Vik had given her his resignation. He had no choice but to look for a new job to be able to afford rent on a new place. In the meantime, Rob planned to let him sleep on his couch.

She could smell food cooking from the hallway. Her stomach growled angrily. It had been several days since she'd eaten a real meal, and Vik offered to cook an impromptu dinner to celebrate the end of the case and Justyne's capture.

When she walked into the office, Vik ran toward her, throwing his arms around her, squeezing her so hard she couldn't breathe.

"Uh… Vik."

"Lara, I'm so glad you're in one piece." When he pulled away, he grinned from ear to ear.

"Me too, Vik. Me too."

"Rob told me everything. I knew that woman was no good from the beginning. You must promise to never go off on your missions by yourself again," Vik said, shaking a finger at her and setting his jaw. "I must insist. Time after time, you get into so much trouble without… me." His face fell.

"I promise I will always have backup from now on," Lara said, knowing she would not be able to keep her word. She was pretty sure she wouldn't find a more reliable and loyal sidekick than Vik. "It smells like a feast in here. What are you cooking?"

"Your favorite curry recipe," Vik said, brightening up. "And I even made you a mango lassi to help with the spice. I do not understand why you like to torture your stomach." He pointed to the glass of yogurt blended with water and fresh mango sitting on the counter next to her.

Curry was one of her all-time favorites. As a child, her mother's idea of spices for cooking had stopped at pepper and salt. Lara had not tried Indian curry until her late twenties. A few minutes after taking her first bite, Lara's face had flushed red and sweat had beaded on her forehead. She fell in love, immediately a fan of Indian food.

Vik said he would rather eat beef than consume another pot of curry for the rest of his life. The fact that he would only cook it for her was one of the reasons they were good friends.

"Thanks, Vik." She smiled. "That was sweet of you. I'm starving."

"Perhaps we should wait for the others to arrive?"

"Others?" Lara asked, desperately searching for a reflective surface to get a view of her face.

"Yes, I invited Rob, Detective Sanchez, and the bug lad—I mean Maggie."

Lara sighed in disappointment as she glanced at the simmering pot. Her stomach growled.

"Don't worry. They told me I should feed you first to avoid another hangry episode." He smirked. "They'll get here when they can."

Lara's face broke into a broad smile as Vik scooped her a healthy portion of curry onto a plate and pushed it toward her. Then he filled his own plate and pulled up a stool to the shiny, new granite island.

"You're eating curry, too?" Lara smiled, stuffing a large spoonful in her mouth. "But I thought—"

"It reminds me of home." Vik grinned at her.

She knew exactly what he meant. Lara took in the nearly restored townhouse for the last time. The boxes containing all that was left of Kingsley Investigations stood in the corner.

"Vik, you know you're my hero, right?"

Vik grimaced. "But wasn't it Rob who saved you?"

"Hardly. I shot Fiddler myself. You handled the beetles. Rob burst through the door in the nick of time. But you're the one who unraveled most of the case. And you got this place back into shape at the same time. I don't know what I'm going to do without you."

"With this new hero status, do I get a raise?" Vik tilted his head and raised his eyebrows.

"Uh… I thought you quit. And besides, haven't you heard? Kingsley Investigations is broke."

Vik squinted at her. "Um, Lara, have you checked the account lately?"

"Which account?" Lara asked.

"The one for shared expenses… because I checked it this morning and the balance shows one hundred thousand dollars."

"One hundred K?" The blood drained from Lara's face.

Vik nodded.

"That can't be right. Show me," Lara demanded.

Vik woke up his tablet next to him, logged in to the bank account, and turned the screen around to face Lara.

There it was. Lara couldn't believe her eyes. There was one hundred thousand dollars sitting in her bank account. She knew who put it there. "I have to return it."

"To whom?" Vik asked, his eyes growing large.

"This money is from Fiddler for solving the case… for finding CyberShop."

"Would it be the first time you accepted money from an unsavory character?" Vik asked.

"No," Lara said, feeling ashamed when she thought about some of her past clients.

"Then, why is this any different? You got paid to solve a murder. Okay, so our client also happens to be the mad scientist who wreaked terror on innocent people, but focus on the transaction."

"I don't know…" Lara wrung her hands.

"Boss, we've been working for weeks on this case, unpaid. We earned this money."

Lara's wearable smartphone buzzed. When she looked at the screen on her wrist, she didn't recognize the number. Before picking up, she pulled the phone off her wrist, placed it on the counter between them, and switched to speaker mode. "This is Lara."

"This is Wyatt Turner, the executor of Phil Sullivan's estate. I've been trying to get a hold of you for weeks and finally stumbled across your new number. I just wanted to call to make sure you received the deposit?"

Vik's eyes nearly popped out of his head as his jaw dropped open.

Lara raised her eyebrows. "Do you mean the one hundred K that mysteriously appeared in my account?"

"Yes. Upon his death, Mr. Sullivan instructed me to immediately transfer you one hundred thousand dollars as my first action in closing his estate. In his will, he named you as the sole beneficiary and bequeathed all of his assets and his townhouse to you."

"What?" Lara gaped at Vik as they both tried to absorb the information.

The lawyer continued. "Mr. Sullivan kept detailed records of all of his assets and had almost zero debt. Even so, it may take a bit longer for you to assume possession of the townhouse and receive the remainder of his money. I'm still waiting to hear from a few potential claims."

"He what?" Lara sank back onto her stool and stared blankly at the screen. "Sully left everything to me? How much?"

"Yes, ma'am. When he died, Mr. Sullivan was worth over two million dollars, including the townhouse. He doesn't have any living family members and was very clear in his instructions to me. He said in a letter that he entrusted you with the proper use of his earthly possessions in order to carry out his mission to bring the bad guys to justice."

Lara couldn't help a few tears from welling up. "Uh... thank you. This is... unbelievable news."

"Anyway, I'm glad I finally found you because he left me a few other strange instructions. Mr. Sullivan restored all the key codes and passwords to the ones you used to install his systems. He thought that would be helpful in catching his killer in the event he didn't make it. He also wanted you to find a number of things he left hidden for you."

Sully knew he was going to die?

Lara and Vik exchanged glances.

"He left keys for you to find in the filing cabinet and toilet tank in his safe room. If you look—"

"Uh, thanks, but we already found both of those."

"What about the key in the kitchen drawer at Maggie's apartment?"

"Found that one, too."

"And the newspaper clippings in the gun case, his burner phone at DARPA, and the box under his floorboards?"

"Yep, yep, and yep," Lara said, sighing audibly. Vik rolled his eyes.

This information would have been very helpful early on.

"Is that all?"

"Yes, I'm afraid so. Anyway, I'll let you know when the deed to the townhouse is transferred to you."

"Thank you, Mr....?"

"Turner. Just doing my job," he said. "I'll be in touch."

Lara pressed the red button on her wearable smartphone and slid it back on her wrist.

"Well, I guess that resolves your money issues," Vik said, grinning at her.

"I guess so. Should I go rip up your resignation letter?"

Vik nodded, but he looked like he wanted to say something else.

"What?" Lara asked.

"I thought you said you'd never get one of those," Vik said, pointing to the wearable smartphone.

Lara smirked, remembering her little soapbox speech to Vik. "Well, I'm probably not going to shatter this one, so I guess wearables do have some perks after all."

Vik sat silently for a few minutes. "So... what do you think our next case will be?" His eyes gleamed with excitement. "What about a bionic spider?"

"Are you crazy? I sure hope not." Lara leveled her eyes at Vik. "Please don't jinx us."

"I was kidding," Vik said, cringing a little. "Too soon?"

Lara smirked. "Yeah, Vik. Too soon."

Epilogue

PULLING her puffy down coat snugly around her body, Lara traversed the curved pathway and landscaped terraces of Oak Hill Cemetery. The historic garden cemetery was located in the heart of Georgetown, along the border of Rock Creek Park and only a few blocks from her old townhouse. In her coat pocket, Lara's gloved hand clasped Sully's keychain.

The bitter wind blew hard against her face, causing involuntary tears to form in her eyes and her cheeks to sting. Even for late November, the temperatures in the region had fallen unusually low. Despite the inclement weather, the time was long overdue to pay respects to the only family she'd known since her childhood.

Better late than never. Right?

Even though she had a legitimate excuse, Lara hadn't been able to forgive herself for missing Sully's funeral. She'd heard from Maggie it was quite the elaborate ceremony, attended by the D.C. mayor herself, the FBI Director, the D.C. Police Commissioner, and several other famous Washingtonians. Sully couldn't have cared less about these things. And she knew none of it would make up for her absence. Especially not after what he'd done for her.

He saved my bacon.

Thanks to Sully's generosity, she finally had a place of her own to call home—her first since her parents died when she was a child. And of course, Kingsley Investigations would survive to see another day of installing surveillance systems, maybe even several more years if she managed her newfound wealth wisely. Since inheriting all of Sully's hard-won assets, Lara resolved to do better in the finance department.

Ever since Sully's lawyer called, she couldn't shake the last words in his letter. They haunted her. When he first persuaded her to become a PI, Sully had wanted the two of them to be partners against crime. But Lara preferred straightforward surveillance jobs to facing the dark underworld of humanity. Now Sully had entrusted her with carrying out his lifelong mission to bring the bad guys to justice. Outside of catching Sully's killer and stopping Fiddler's plot, she had no real experience solving crimes and dealing with hardened criminals. And yet, Lara felt she owed him at the very least to give it a try.

Bring the bad guys to justice? What were you thinking, Sully?

A gust of wind nearly blew her knitted cap off her head as she trudged up the hill. She tried to shield her face from the frigid air. Her watery gaze drifted up toward the peaceful chapel perched on the highest ridge of the cemetery.

Designed by the famous architect James Renwick in 1850, the quaint one-story chapel stood on a steep hill nestled amongst old maple trees and thick shrubs. She admired its exquisite Gothic-styled structure—its high-pitched rooftop, the black granite stones accentuated by light-colored mortar, the red sandstone trim, and the ornate circular and arched windows carved from limestone.

Oh Sully, if you only could see this place, you'd love it. Who knows, maybe you can see it.

When she gazed into the gray sky above, several snowflakes landed on her face. For a brief moment, she smiled at the notion of Sully looking down on her from the heavens. Then she shuddered at the thought of him watching her every move. The warm feeling vanished, leaving a dull and bottomless ache. She still couldn't wrap her head around the gaping hole he'd left behind. She preferred not to think about it.

Treading over snow-dusted leaves, Lara turned a sharp right on the narrow, red brick road leading to the chapel. She glanced at the names on some gravestones. In recognition of Sully's many heroics in service of the nation's capital, D.C.'s mayor had pulled some strings to snag him a coveted gravesite along Chapel Avenue, next to many of Washington's notables.

When she finally reached Lot 921, sheltered by a large oak tree, Lara spotted Sully's shiny, black granite gravestone in the far corner and strode toward it. A thin layer of snow lined the top of Sully's grave. As it came into full view, she read the words carved in the stone:

HERE LIES

PHILLIP J. SULLIVAN

BORN IN BALTIMORE, MARYLAND

12 JANUARY 1993

DIED

19 OCTOBER 2027

"I'M FOR TRUTH, NO MATTER WHO TELLS IT.

I'M FOR JUSTICE, NO MATTER WHO IT'S FOR OR AGAINST."

—MALCOLM X

When she finished reading the words of the epitaph, the deep tone of his voice rang in her head. It was Sully's favorite quote. She could remember the first time he'd shared it with her. Sully valued truth and justice above all else and pursued both relentlessly.

If he were still alive, he'd use the famous quote to explain to Lara why he'd worked for a man like Fiddler, spent his final days on earth seeking justice for the mad scientist and clearing Anita's name, and why he'd expect Lara to do the same.

In that moment, the reality of Sully's death came crashing down on Lara. A solitary tear rolled down her cheek as she stooped to lay the Star Wars storm trooper keychain at the foot of Sully's grave. Her thoughts turned to how he'd guided her after his death, putting the clues in her path.

Oh Sully, why didn't you tell me you were in trouble? Why didn't you let me help you?

She really didn't need to ask the question. Lara knew why he'd kept her at a safe distance—to protect her from harm. She and Sully behaved the same way. Growing up as orphans, they'd learned to be self-sufficient and rarely asked for help from others. And definitely not if it would put a loved one in any danger. Her eyes flooded with tears.

Would things have gone differently if I'd agreed to be his partner? Could I have saved him from his terrible fate?

As feelings of guilt washed over her, she shook her head in disagreement. *No, if I'd gotten in the way, Justyne would have killed me, too. She almost did.*

The bone-chilling wind howled and blasted her without mercy as it passed through the branches of the tall trees. A flurry of snowflakes danced around her. With her finger, she traced the letters in the word "died," wiping off the ice crystals. The finality of it all pierced through her heart like a knife. When she thought of Sully's body resting beneath her feet, gone from her life forever, she took in too much air and nearly choked on her own breath. Lara sank to her knees, the wet snow soaking through her pants.

He died. Sully is gone.

A painful knot formed in her stomach, and her chest tightened. Warm tears began rolling down her cheeks and mixing with melting snowflakes. The moisture pricked her skin in the wintry air. She braced her body against the cold, hard gravestone, buried her head in her hands, and wept.

Want More From Lara and Her Friends?

Acknowledgments

This novel began on a whim. I came up with the idea of crowdsourcing a novel as a way to build up my audience. At the time, I was enthralled with created a political thriller trilogy and probably shouldn't have distracted myself with yet another writing project. But I was desperate to connect with readers and didn't want to wait until I finally published.

I chose mystery as my genre, the year 2027 in Washington D.C. as my setting, and a strong female protagonist as my amateur detective. The journey to publishing *Bionic Bug* ultimately began scene by scene: I wrote a scene, uploaded it to my website, offered my readers three options for the next scene, and gave them a week to vote. Then, I wrote the scene receiving the most votes. I am indebted to my first readers for their enthusiasm about the story and receiving one draft scene at a time—Marina Abrams, Jennifer Batts, Reneé DeVries, Min Kim, Katie McCurdy, Steve Mechels, Laura Marsh, and Cheryl Tolley. Without them, I wouldn't have begun this crazy endeavor in the first place or completed a first draft.

I owe the relative ease of my first editing experience to the genius work that is *Story Grid*. Shawn Coyne created a revolutionary editing concept over twenty-five years of helping bestselling authors to make their stories work. I was selected to participate in the first-ever Story Grid workshop co-led by Shawn Coyne and Tim Grahl in New York City in February 2017. It was at this workshop where I met my first writer friends and learned the five commandments of story—inciting incident, complications, crisis, climax, and resolution. Using Shawn's unique approach to editing, I outlined the global story spine and built a detailed spreadsheet analyzing each scene, to see if they were "working" and if not, to diagnose the problems. The Story Grid approach was my GPS, and without it, I would have lost my way.

With my edited first draft in hand, I was fortunate to have several beta readers provide feedback. I am grateful for helpful and insightful comments from Kimberly Kromwell, Cheryl Tolley, Janyre Tromp, Jerri Williams, and Annette Whitney. Even after many revisions, your suggestions and encouragement have left behind a positive and lasting imprint.

This novel benefited from the insights and skill of two amazing editors. I can't remember the author I was before working with my story editor, Clark Chamberlain, for the first time. Before working with him, I often floundered during my editing process, unsure of my strengths and even more of my weaknesses. By showing me what worked and what didn't, Clark brought forth the gust of wind that enabled me to fly as a writer and self-editor. I am eternally grateful to him for his passion for storytelling, his authenticity, and his dedication. I would also like to thank Brianna Boes for taking every line of *Bionic Bug* to the next level. When I first received her edited sample, I realized how far I'd yet to go as a writer and knew she'd make me a better writer. I feel lucky that she left her mark on my first novel. Also, thank you to Christie Hartman who helped catch any loose errors and typos. Any remaining errors are my own.

I was fortunate to benefit and learn from the successes and failures of a vibrant and generous community of fellow Indie authors. I am grateful to Joanna Penn for sharing her knowledge about starting a publishing business and becoming an author-entrepreneur on her weekly Creative Penn podcast. Listening to her insights, I not only realized my dream of becoming an Indie author, but I also felt empowered to do so. For their wisdom, support and encouragement, I owe a great deal to Sean Platt and Johnny B. Truant of Sterling and Stone and the many amazing writers and creators at the Stone Table. Finally, I'd like to thank Mark Leslie Lefebvre who generously gave of his time and helped me make tough decisions about my path as an Indie. He nudged me to pursue this series and my crowdsourcing idea.

Special thanks to my National Defense University colleagues Dr. W. Seth Carus, Dr. Margaret Sloane, and Mr. Yong-Bee Lim for reading my book and providing their expert insights on biological weapons and gene editing. Any inaccuracy in the novel is my own and should not reflect on them. Moreover, the views expressed in this novel are those of the author and do not reflect the official policy or position of the National Defense University, the Department of Defense, or the U.S. Government.

Many thanks to Karen at Magic Design Co. for perfectly capturing the mood and essence of Bionic Bug on the cover.

I am grateful to my parents, John and Maria Bajema who always encouraged me to pursue my creativity through art and writing stories, but wisely counseled me against the life of a starving artist. Without my day job, I would not have my muse or the financial freedom to invest in a writing career.

And finally, I turn to my dear friends Reneé and Cheryl to whom this book is dedicated. They not only read every word of every draft I've ever written, but they also eagerly urged me onwards to write more. Because of their persistence and my determination to deliver, I am now a published author. Thanks for stoking the fire under my butt.

About the Author

NATASHA BAJEMA lives in Rockport, Texas with her two dogs, Malachi and Charlie, and works as an independent consultant on national security. She has been an expert on national security issues for over 20 years, specializing in weapons of mass destruction (WMD), nuclear proliferation, terrorism, and emerging technologies. For ten years, Natasha worked for the National Defense University where she taught an elective course to senior military officers on WMD and film and led a research project on the impact of emerging technologies on national security. Natasha holds a Ph.D. in international relations from the Fletcher School of Law and Diplomacy at Tufts University.

For more information:
www.natashabajema.com

Printed in Great Britain
by Amazon